In honor of the

MILLENNIUM CHRISTMAS

2000

BOOK DESIGNED & PRINTED BY:

C. JOHN COOMBES

EBOOK ISBN 9780982221334   0982221339
PRINT ISBN 9780982221372   0982221371

CLAUS

A CHRISTMAS INCARNATION

A novel by
C. JOHN COOMBES

Escape to a time
When life was an adventure.

Our nation was young,
And so were her people.
A time of struggle and setback,
Of pain and perseverance.

A time also of freedom, joy,
And the birth of new traditions.
The future was fearful and uncertain,
But no more so than for the children.

For them, let us say,
Fate brought forth a man.
He was wealthy and influential,
He was good-hearted and generous.
A man of conjecture and mystery.
He was there for them, a savior,
A second chance, a hope.

Only one person may have known him.
A person who struggled to understand him
Through the eyes of a child,
Through the heart of a woman.

A disciple named Elizabeth.

ILLUSTRATIONS BY:

C. JOHN COOMBES

THE M HART EDITION

THIS EDITION REPRESENTS THE SECOND EDIT
OF VOLUME TWO UNDERTAKEN SPECIFICALLY FOR A
6X9 PAPERBACK PRINTING

It would be preposterous
To assert that
Fact is born of myth.

Conversely...
It has been proven
Myth is a child of truth.

BOOK TWO

The woman

PART TWO

THE M HART EDITION

FORTY-ONE

For all the misery that winter might bestow, it also had good points often overlooked. During that time of year, there were uncelebrated benefits and advantages to be had by those who chose not to suffer cabin fever or fret over the disappearance of another season's fruits and flowers.

Winter was the work of cutting, moving and milling trees. The business flourished in the forests and backwoods of the north when snow quieted all else. It was a time of needed wages, when fields lie fallow and frozen beneath traces of autumn's harvest past.

The industry as a whole waited impatiently for snowfall and frigid temperatures because it was impossible to move anything like the weight of logs through the mud of springtime roads. And after a summer sun baked the knee-deep sludge into dusty rock-hard trails that would support such burdens, most wagon wheels would not.

Weight was moved on runners, and that is why for every wagon in a farmer's field, there were bound to be two or three sleds. They were simple in construction and well suited for the business of hauling. To look along a snow covered trail and see a twenty-foot high stack of logs moving slowly atop an ox drawn sledge was to see money in the making.

In a perfect world, the dead weight of a log began its journey to the mill by rolling murderously down a riverbank and plunging into a stream turned turbulent under a vertical wall of up flung water. Unfortunately, most of the world's timber was beyond the slope of a riverbank, and out there, felled trees went nowhere with ease. Timber that needed to reach the river was best moved on sleds across flat frozen ground covered thick with hard and slippery ice.

As the cold season drove birds south, it brought north a migration of giants that overran all of upper New York, especially towns like Tonawanda and Buffalo. Everywhere there were to be seen creatures of a transformed breed, creatures born to replace the disappearing ranks of rivermen that poled endlessly upstream exercising arms the size of spiles. Mankind's giants were now lumberjacks who gripped axes and sported arms equal to the girth of timber they dropped to earth. Like the rivermen before them, they were a rowdy and unruly lot, and should gainful employment escape them, there was always plenty of boasting and brawling to be had.

Contrary to European thought, winter was also an excellent time to travel providing one kept warm and dry. To begin with, the devil's plague of mosquitoes, black flies, hornets, wasps, gnats, no-see-ums and whatever else Hell might produce was put to sleep, or better yet, killed outright by a typical northern freeze. The same could be said for snakes, spiders, and all manner of pests bent on making death preferable to life on the trail.

Traveling in the still and humid air of a hot summer's night was generally miserable beyond measure as one crossed battlefields thick with blue smoke and scenes of men fighting bugs with mounds of burning stumps and smudge pot fires. Even cabins had soot and smoke wafting out from windows and doors.

In contrast, beneath crisp clear winter air, frozen streams were easily forded by sleds that sped down trails free of the bone jarring, backbreaking ride of a wheeled vehicle. Sleds slipped effortlessly along paths once easily lost within dark secluded forests, but which now stretched openly beneath clear skies free of summer's suffocating foliage. Whereas, people tolerated the summer wagon, they touted the winter sleigh ride.

Some folks preferred to remain hidden within the thick underbrush while traveling so as to move unseen, but I much preferred the prairies and oak clearings with their open views. They were often far reaching and not only served to alleviate the feelings of claustrophobia, but also prevented us from being waylaid in surprise by, wild animals, or worse, renegade Indians.

Having flaunted so many of winter's benefits, to be fair, it should also be said that November and December were definitely not the months to be caught foolishly upon the waves of the Great Lakes. There were hundreds of sunken ships and many more lost sailors whose spirits would attest to the brutality of winter gales upon these waters. The lakes were notorious for coming up suddenly to catch one unaware. Ships shortened their journeys, lightened their loads, and stayed within sight of shore as captains worked their way closer to home during these final unpredictable days when wind, waves, and fog could quickly seal one's fate.

We set sail before an offshore breeze that kept the east end of Lake Erie settled, and belied what I was warned would certainly lie ahead. Wisps of snow overtook us, moving across our stern to swirl about the mast and rigging overhead before blending into the pallid sky beyond our bows.

I watched white flecks collect on the backs of men who clung to the cabin handholds as they worked the lines in a testy breeze. I suffered to see the blue-white and blotchy red color of cold skin upon their faces and hands. I watched as they slapped their fingers hard against their legs in order to keep the blood flowing and ward off the stiffness that might cause them to lose their grip and suffer the consequence.

A plunge into the cold waters would most certainly bring death. Unlike the dark opacity of some seas, these waters were clear as glass and greenish-blue by nature, green like jealous eyes, blue like a fine aquamarine—blue like *liquid ice*. A chill sliced through me as I shivered in sympathy for the men on deck.

If a woman wished winter more miserable, she merely boarded a lake packet. No amount of wool or warmth would repel the invasive damp found below in a ship's cabin. Seas were always rough and flooding across exposed decks to work their way down through every unseen crack and crevice. The incessant drip of icy water always managed to be above the one place you chose to eat or sleep. Realities such as these drove my traveling companions to complain openly of their regret in allowing me to drag them aboard a sloop for any reason.

At least we were blessed with the best that could be expected upon casting off. We made good our start by that easterly wind and a gentle following sea. It saved us the misery of hammering waves head-on and drinking the freezing spray.

Our sloop hugged Erie's south shore. It stayed beyond the surf, but always close enough to hear the call of a wild animal or the holler of some stranger among a throng of folks barely discernable upon the flat beach. And indeed, flat was the only word to describe the shoreline of this lake. It was nothing like the towering cliffs of the Palisades or the steep hills bordering the Hudson. This coast was dead flat in comparison to the coasts of Boston or any coast I ever could recall.

These shores appeared little more than thin ribbons of forest rooted in the water they bordered. They stretched eternally horizontal from sunrise to sunset, broken only by the occasional collection of wooden structures crowded about white steepled churches. And speaking of flat, the word wholly failed to describe what lay off our starboard bow, for unlike the swells of the sea, this view offered nothing but a dead level expanse of irritated, agitated, liquid hell from hull to horizon.

Days grew short and often difficult to separate from night. Thick clouds were standard fare in these northern lake territories and served to make the setting worse. The sea was often indistinguishable from a sky stitched to it by impenetrable strands of ghostly mist, or worse, a wall of fog as well defined as any white cliff of Dover.

At least our captain was good natured and sensible, and after leaving New York far behind and finding ourselves deep into Pennsylvania; he sailed into Presqu'lle so we might spend our night in port and enjoy our rest in safe harbor and peace of mind.

I learned from the old salt that a canal not unlike the Erie would soon pass through Presqu'lle, essentially opening an uninterrupted flow of business from the Ohio River to New York. Thus goods could travel from ships entering the Gulf of Mexico, move up the Mississippi, then east and north along the Ohio and its tributaries until meeting the proposed canal, which would direct boats to Buffalo, Albany, and eventually the merchant shelves of New York. It was a distance nearly incomprehensible. In my mind, I saw our country pulling itself up by the bootstraps, drawing up its boundaries to better define itself and its strengths.

The following morning found us seabound with a fresh coating of ice that glazed the rigging and lines. Long rows of miniature icicles hung in perfect lines off the varnished boom and hardened edges about our vessel. Winds had shifted to the northwest and life became at once miserable with snow and sleet being driven upon us by a cold blow come hard. It whipped the waters into unending rows of frightful froth-covered ridges that rolled into us with a cruel and unsettling indifference to our fate. The captain was forced to reduce his sail as towering crests foamed and spit across our bulwarks with stinging force that kept us huddled below in cramped quarters.

The captain paid close attention to the unending attack of these waves. They came in sets of six or seven and each wave had to be reckoned with as if it were the only one that mattered. His experience was evident as he gauged their size and speed before steering the rudder to best advantage in hopes of keeping our boom and sail off the water. I voiced my admiration time and again for he struggled at the helm many hours through this heavy sea.

The three deckhands rotated turns coming below to warm themselves. I wondered how with bare hands, they could stand to hold so firmly the ice coated lines or how they could work in the freezing spray with only wet clothes to protect them. It made my one and only verbal complaint of dripping water in our cabin pathetically trite and most embarrassing.

Crest by crest we plunged our way toward Detroit. We said good-bye to passing Pennsylvania and made our way along a hundred or more miles of Ohio shoreline until catching a glimpse of Sandusky Bay. We then we moved away from shore and entered into a labyrinth of islands positioned to surround a body of water known as Put-in-Bay. It was here that Commodore Perry won his celebrated naval battle over the English.

At least this grouping of islands seemed to settle the sea and wind as well, enough so that our sloop next veered to starboard and away from the security of land's edge. In a northwesterly direction we worked our way through the maze of earthy spatterings. The captain pointed across my left shoulder and introduced me to the distant and barely visible settlement of Port Lawrence at the mouth of the Maumee. The river was a well-known course for many traveling between Lake Erie and the Ohio River.

As the hours progressed, the seas subsided and I convinced my troupe to go above for fresh air. They did as I bid, and in spite of the cold air, through tightly wrapped shawls and scarves we observed the spectacular glow of a sun set low in the western sky. Its well-defined beams directed our eyes toward two of the three Sister Islands now off both bows, one in shadow, the other aglow. Beneath that sun, the settlement of Monroe stood at the mouth of the River Raisin on Lake Erie's western shore.

The sea was now off our port bow, coming from the west. It was more settled, not having the time nor distance to build its treachery, but instead pitching our mast and deck back and forth slowly, steeply, side to side. The cloud-covered sky was wiped clean by an air so cold in short time it drove us back down to the cabin. I remained in the company of Rachel, Caleb and Taa to raise spirits, for they were all very nauseous and still apprehensive of waves previously intent on sweeping them overboard.

Our captain paid frequent visits as well, in order to offer assurances and ascertain our state of mind. He apologized for nature's inconsideration, and acknowledged the season was surely drawing to an end by stating that he might be forced to winter over in Detroit once arrived should he fail to depart immediately.

It wasn't long thereafter that the Canadian coast sprouted its features and directed us to the mouth of the River of Detroit. In time, we coursed against her current until I spied upon an eastern shore the British Fort Malden along with the many structures that surrounded it, for their shapes unfolded to the very edge of the river. The scene came as a welcome sight after battling nature for days with only six or seven souls standing by my side.

As I strained to focus upon the picturesque setting, there came another sight, this one most unwelcome as it sped toward us from the western shore. My attention was drawn to five birch bark canoes manned by Indians that were yelping and howling like banshees. Soon after coming into earshot, I could see black, blue and red designs spread across their bodies, arms, and faces. In total, they were a most frightful looking bunch, and seeing them paddle directly for our small sloop unsettled me to no end. So uncivilized was their manner, that I swallowed hard in fear of their motives.

The captain took notice of my reaction and moved to reassure me.

"Don't be concerned, Miss Claussen."

"Easier said than done, sir. I should think they would scare the wits out of any sane person." I replied. "Are we equipped to protect ourselves?"

"True enough, they are a rough looking lot, but you have nothing to fear. They are in search of hard drink and only that. The furriers ruined these people by stealing their pride and soul. The English and Americans have bought their pelts, their wives, and whatever will they once possessed with jars of cheap watered down whiskey.

"There's a certain justice in how Detroit and Fort Malden now pay dearly for those unconscionable actions of past. Today, this area is trapped out and the beaver all but gone. Yet, there remains for certain, a forest full of drunk oafish Indians who's only purpose is to openly stagger down the orderly streets of the settlements. It's a problem of no small proportion that they have brought upon themselves, and I might add; it has been well-earned. You are fortunate that it is late in the season and many of the Indians have gone south for the winter months. These are but a few stragglers."

I watched the Indians circle around us, hugging our hull and studying our decks with great interest until I assumed they determined we possessed nothing to their liking. At that point, they darted off silently across the water's surface as quickly as might the fish beneath their feet. They collected to cast nets near a bank just north of the fort.

As did their island kin, the British who populated the place still held feelings of resentment toward the up-start Americans that populated our young nation. Even so, my mother and Lady Rebecca were both English, and I was caused to possess a private but natural affinity for anything associated with England or this side of the river.

We stopped briefly at Fort Malden to make a delivery and pick up passengers before casting off for the river's north shore where lay Detroit, *'the city of the straits'*. I noted that upon these shores there were yet a number of ships moored even in this late season. Snow was falling thick as milk, settling silently upon the now calming water. The anchored ships in the distance were turning white and left one shivering but for the sight of them. The captain stated positively that not unlike himself, they would all be headed south within days.

FORTY-TWO

In spite of my being told Detroit had nearly three thousand inhabitants, my first impression was of it being much larger than I would have envisioned a city upon the outer banks of civilization's northern boundary. I was disappointed to have missed

530

the great fort that stood here until just a few years ago. The stronghold was deemed unneeded and its dismantling was a notable sign of how tame were now the times.

And so it seemed, as I spied the many people milling about the wharf awaiting our arrival. Our great sail had been lowered and no sooner were the dock lines tossed than there came back the sound of my name. To say we four were surprised would be to say the least.

From our huddle on deck, I spied the souls braving the discomforting cold and blinding snow while in wait of our sloop. In particular there was a couple, a middle aged man escorting a woman who seemed to be watching me with certain excitement. I was looking directly at her when she called out once again.

"Elizabeth Claussen?"

"I am Elizabeth Claussen," I replied. My announcement caused the woman's face to beam with delight.

"Elizabeth! I can't believe it! I just can't believe it! I'm Julia, Julia Tonazzo! You made it!"

"Julia! My word! What are you doing here?"

"Well, what do you think?" She laughed. "I've been waiting! We've been waiting all day!"

As we hollered our disbelief back and forth, the plank was dropped and the six of us met on shore. Julia and I embraced cordially.

"Let me look at you," she said. "My god, you grew up to be absolutely gorgeous. Tony, she was such an adorable creature as a child." She confided to her companion and then looked back at me. "I am embarrassed you should see me, I haven't fared nearly as well."

"You are embarrassed! Pray, say nothing more, look at my face. You've made me red as a beet."

"Elizabeth, this is my husband, Antonio."

"Please, call me Tony."

"It's my pleasure, Tony. Your darling wife is much too modest. I should hope to look so handsome after fighting the wilds of Michigan day in and day out."

"Si, yah, I agree."

"If I may, this is my friend, Rachel Cook—, her husband, Caleb—,and Taa'sooma'hane, which means Shadow Hunter; you can call him Taa. I am blessed with their company." Tony and Julia listened to my introduction, at first visibly unsure of my relationship with the Negroes and an Indian, but quickly accepting them as my friends and moved forward to embrace all and extend their welcome. I prayed Taa'sooma'hane acted civil or something of the sort, for according to Julia's letters, Antonio was Italian and true to his breed. He gushed with affection even toward the standoffish Indian.

Julia was equally affectionate and took me by the arm at once. She was about to lead our group up the street when she looked back just long enough to witness the expressions of Caleb and Taa'sooma'hane. They were clearly stressed, standing awkward and red-faced with veins popping out on their necks.

"What on earth are they carrying?"

I looked back at them. "My trunk. It's full of books. Books for you, just as I promised."

"Oh, for the love of god. I said *a* book, *one* book, not a library. Bless you, bless you, Elizabeth." Julia stepped over to Caleb. "Mercy me, set that down before you break your backs. Tony, we need a wagon. This trunk is too unwieldy for a horse. Is it just the one?"

"One trunk and our bags," I answered. Caleb, Rachel and Taa'sooma'hane had no belongings to speak of. They used their bags more for carrying food than articles.

"Aspeto un momento, Julia. I don' wanta fight no roada wit' a wagon," said Antonio. "I fetch a coupla horses anda carta from ta livery." Antonio and Julia had only expected me, and so arrived at river's edge on horseback with one extra animal in tow. Julia frowned.

"Elizabeth, I had assumed that you were traveling alone and would stay with us, but I suppose that was short-sighted and rude of me. I forget; ours is not a life you are accustomed to. Did you prefer to put up in one of the local inns with your company? There is plenty of comfort to be had here in Detroit, and a number of inns noted for their service and fare."

"Ahhh—."

"I mean, Tony and I would love to have you, but we have just moved and our present cabin is small. I can promise it would be cozy and there is plenty of fresh food and blankets. But it is a simple place where we pretty much fend for ourselves. You are welcome to see it for yourself, and we could return tomorrow if you decide you would prefer to stay here in Detroit. Otherwise we will set about at once to find you accommodations here in the city."

"How far is your place?"

"About two hours west of here, in Washtenaw County. It's about a mile north of a place called Tecumseh"

"You mean, Tecumseh, like the Indian?"

"Like the Indian, yes."

Anything connected with Indians made me subconsciously wary. I studied the wide streets of the city, the many inviting shops, and the commotion still evident at this late hour. I had no desire whatsovever to face another two hours of travel this late in the day, in the cold, and on horseback. I looked up into a dark sky to see a flurry of snowflakes forming and falling without mercy. The ground was now fully covered in white. However, contrary to what I might have felt, it only required one glance toward my companions to understand they preferred nothing other than the seclusion of the cabin. Crowds were especially worrisome for all three. I sensed their apprehension and hopes for my decision to press on.

"I think we can still manage another two hours of travel."

"Wonderful! We can manage the storm. Better cold and dry than cool and wet. We should manage fine, I think."

Julia broke into a broad smile. She was happy, as were Rachel and Caleb. My decision being made, Antonio then encouraged Caleb and Taa'sooma'hane to mount up on the other horses and accompany him to the stables in order to bring back four more animals and a cart. We women awaited their return.

"How did you know to be here when we arrived?" I asked.

"Well, Tony and I have been watching for you quite some time, essentially since the day I received your post from Boston. We made light of the fact you might come this way and asked all our friends to keep a ear clear an' an open eye for your arrival.

"I was so excited at hearing first rumor of you traveling the canal. It came hand in hand with great ado about a boat for schooling children. I just couldn't believe it. I couldn't believe it. I thought to myself, now that is Elizabeth, is it not? Always helping someone else. Oh, lord, to think how excited I was.

"I pressed on Tony to find out everything possible about the boat and your intentions. We must have had fifty people keeping watch and finally word came that you had arrived in Buffalo and might well make it to Michigan. At that point, I began to note all planned arrivals. They are rare this late in the season unlike during the summer when we get seven or eight arrivals daily. Anyway, here I am, and here you are."

"Tell me, for the sake of curiosity, who told you I was thinking of going to Michigan?" I asked.

"Specifically?"

"Yes."

"A man named Victor Barker."

"Victor Barker." I thought hard on the name.

"He's a buyer. He and Tony do business together on occasion and Tony knew that Mr. Barker bought timber for mills in Buffalo and Tonawanda. So Tony asked him to keep out an eye for you. Mr. Barker deals with Mr. Woodburn, who's the administrator of Darby Lumber Mill in Buffalo. Do you remember speaking with a man by the name of Randolph Woodburn?"

"Oh, sure. I wouldn't have remembered his last name, but I have only spoken with one Randolph in recent times."

"Well, that's how we found out. Mr. Woodburn mentioned to Mr. Barker that he advised you to take the Sauk Indian Trail to Fort Dearborn, and that advice made me all too nervous. So, I wanted to make sure I found you."

Obviously, there was a warning in the wind, and I immediately confronted Julia. "Is there something I should know about that trail?" She urged me onward with a friendly tug.

"Most definitely yes," she smiled. "The Indians in these parts are restless, and presently, one would be well advised to travel to Chicago with prudence."

"How restless?"

"Very."

"Oh, joy."

"Don't misunderstand me, people still travel the trail; but you would want to take care and not do anything foolish."

Darkness encroached stealthily as we loaded the trunk and belongings into the cart. We were brushing snow off of everything until at last we brushed off the saddles and mounted up. We took care to wrap ourselves warmly in our preparation to face the cold of a Michigan winter night. Once satisfied, we headed out along Woodward Avenue with our cart in tow until reaching a large square at which point we turned left onto the Chicago Road.

535

FORTY-THREE

After an initial rush of conversation about Detroit and the shops bordering the streets we traveled, our troupe entered the quiet of the wood and fell back into private thoughts as if shushed by the seclusion of falling snow. The silence was abrupt and interrupted only now and then by a passing remark from Julia to Antonio or between Rachel and Caleb, and on occasion by the unsettling *howl of a wolf*—the first of many such cries that set my hair on end.

"Glory be! Tell me that's not what I fear." My eyes were at once wide open and looking about the woods. Rachel and Caleb were doing the same.

"It is," replied Julia.

"Should we be worried?" I asked with justifiable concern.

"Mmm, I don't think so. We should be fine."

"Julia! For the love of god, you don't sound very convincing."

"No, don't worry. The settlers in this area have driven most of the wolves away. They don't much care to be around people, but they do like chickens and such. Besides, that was a lone wolf. Should you hear them howling as a pack, then you best start paying attention."

"Een all my 'ears walkin' ta landa I only 'ava few close calls, anda tat was way up nort'. Ta wolves t'ere arra very big anda not so friendly," said Antonio. "Down 'era, you no worry."

In my opinion, the discussion ended with weak consolation, and I found myself crowding Antonio and Julia rather than falling behind to become dinner for some unseen salivating animal lurking alongside the road.

The stillness of the forest returned us to our private thoughts, yet there was no objection. The lack of conversation may even

536

have been wanted due to our weariness. It certainly didn't matter to Taa'sooma'hane. He never uttered a sound; he was born to be silent. As for Rachel and Caleb, no words were necessary to convey their feelings; the eyes said it all.

We made a number of stops at homes along the way in order to warm hands and give our backs a break. They were short visits, being little more than an introduction to Julia's friends and neighbors over a gulp of hot tea. I learned at our first stop that Julia had dropped in on these folks and asked if they might keep a kettle hot for our return trip. They were unexpected blessings. For our sake, the visits were kept just long enough to put the heat of life back into us, but short enough to speed our way home.

Whilst inside paying our last call, the snow outside finally came to a halt. When we again set out upon the trail, the sky was clear and the moon shown bright overhead. The air was still, and this was no small blessing for the temperature seemed to continue its downward spiral. We endured mile after mile of this unforgiving cold, often stopping to rearrange our blankets and wraps.

We endured mile after mile of cold. We wrapped ourselves tight in blankets. Beneath my coat, I had placed my old ship's blanket across my chest. I tried to think of anything but the cold. I reflected on Dorrie and the SCHOOLBOAT. I wondered what she was doing with the orphans this night. I imagined them sitting about the big black-bellied stove to have their hair combed out while laughing over childish things.

I thought of Christopher and tried to imagine his whereabouts and what would be my plans; would I dare to try for Chicago or give up and go home. For the first time, I felt a pang of home-sickness. I thought of Mary, Allen and the boys, and tried to make real the warmth of their cottage. I tried to focus on Mary's kitchen, the heat of her stove and the aroma of cinnamon and Amelia Simmons' applesauce pie, but it was near impossible. There was no escaping this pervasive cold and no blanket, wrap, or coat made could ever offer enough protection for the likes of me.

I pulled a timepiece from my inner pocket and using hands both cold and stiff; I attempted to open the cover. In the light of a bright moon, I clearly noted twenty after the hour of ten. My act made Julia uncomfortable.

"Was it inconsiderate for me to have brought you into the wood," she asked. "It was, wasn't it? You were tired, and I should have encouraged you to stay in Detroit. I wish I could have gotten word to you in Buffalo. I would have had you land in Monroe. As the crow flies, it is so much closer to our place. It's more of a backwoods route, but it travels easy in the winter and you could have been spared much time."

The thought of anything *more* backwoods while wolves howled in the distance was simply out of the question. "No, Julia, you did f-fine. We much prefer the comfort of your cabin to an inn. Don't trouble yourself with worry; this road is no problem. But, I must say f-frankly; I'll be glad when we arrive. I am *f-f-f-freezing*."

"Ch-change o' ch-chains! I thought it was j-j-jus' me! I fear I am about-t-t-to fall out of this here saddle for the way I sh-sh-shake. I c-can't feel my legs anymore." Rachel sputtered out word fragments with a voice that vibrated.

"Keep ta fait', my ladies. We arra only 'alf a mile from ta cabin," said Antonio.

"Oh, th-th-th-thank the L-L-L-ord," whispered Rachel.

True to his word, it was but a few moments more and we turned off the road and onto a path leading toward Julia's homestead. In the blue world of moonlight, I could see that the cabin was only a short distance, which turned out to be very convenient for me. Not only did I not go out of my way to visit Julia, but also it was a place I might find again on my own.

The sight of the cabin seemed to emphasize how frosty was the night air. Its form was routinely obscured by the mist of my breath. The night was cold, as was I, very cold indeed. The storm we endured upon the lake passed over to be followed by clear skies, which now saved us stumbling in the blind. The moon and stars were in full show and passing their light through leafless trees to brighten the road and surroundings.

Unfortunately, the clear skies also exposed us to the dead cold of the universe. Julia seemed unbothered by the temperatures, but I am certain Rachel and I both shivered fearfully for all of the last two hours. I don't believe either of us ever warmed up after leaving Buffalo. The damp of the lake drove to the heart of the bone.

When Antonio and Julia threw open their door, we were quick to enter. We huddled shoulder-to-shoulder in the shadows and trembled before a stone-cold hearth. A mantle lamp was lit. Darkness fell away at once to reveal dimensions and features of the room within which we waited impatiently for a feeble glow to be strengthened by the light and warmth of a roaring fire.

We leaned over Antonio, who was on his knees carefully pumping a bellows and encouraging a deeply embedded coal to sprout a fresh flame. It blossomed not a moment too soon and in short time beckoned us to open our clothes and spread palms before the welcome rays of a surrogate sun.

There was a plentiful stew left earlier in the day to cook in the coals, and now only in need of a warming. All six of us sat huddled upon the carpet before the comfort of the fire and ate until fully satisfied.

"Oh, Julia! I can' tell you how good was that stew. I feel so much better havin' been warmed from inside out," said Rachel.

"I'm glad you enjoyed it."

"I did. Honestly, I did. It was excellent. However, I must say, I am so tired I can no longer keep my eyes open. I fear any second now, I shall rudely drop off in your company. I am embarrassed, I must lay down." Rachel's eyes were heavy as she dropped her head onto Caleb's shoulder.

"Embarrasseda naw'teeeen." Antonio stressed. "You *shoulda* be tireda after a long day o' travel, especially 'avin' been on ta lake. T'em waves coulda make ta Blesseda Virgin weak. Tey'll suffer one's nerves till you arra plum wore out. You getta some sleep; take ta extra bedda, Rachel. Elizabet, you go wit' Julia een ours. I sleep by ta fire wit' Caleb anda Taa."

"But—." I was about to object on taking Antonio's place next to Julia.

"Shhh, shhh. I no wanta 'ear it. Per favore, cara mia, you arra my guesta an' I insista."

"As you wish." I relented lacking the energy to disagree.

In such crowded conditions, nobody was eager to face the embarrassment of using the chamber pot, so going outside to relieve our selves was to be the last misery of the day. Thankfully, it was cut short by another howling wolf and a race back into the warm cabin. Without hesitation, Julia, Rachel and I jumped into soft beds and burrowed deep beneath piles of thick feathered covers. My eyes closed at once, and as I drifted into the hallucinations of sleep, I heard a final whisper rise from the floor.

"Buona notte, bella."

"Night-night, honey. Sleep tight."

Such were the sleeping arrangements, and judging by how I slept; it was a perfect arrangement indeed.

FORTY-FOUR

As if to respect each other's morning peace, little was said while we six arose to meet the day. Having no desire to break the silence, I sat at the table sipping hot coffee and studied Julia and Antonio. She had dropped to the floor and slipped beneath his blanket to ward off a chill. Antonio put his arm around her as naturally as taking his next breath. He drew her close to his chest without thought. They lay together lovingly before the rekindled fire. Next to them in similar embrace lay Caleb and Rachel. I tried not to stare, but my insides sank with envy as I watched such comforting closeness.

To ease my longing, I dismissed the thought for another; one that had to do with a notable peculiarity about people like Antonio and Julia. I noticed it during our neighborly visits the night before while en route and wondered if I would find it true to all settlers in these parts.

The inhabitants of this territory lived in the severest of manner. That is to say, they had basic shelter and sustenance, but little else. Their cabins were of nothing more than a construction of trees fallen, collected, notched, and stacked. They had fire. They had a bucket for water. All of their family possessions might fit within the space of a single trunk or upon a single shelf. Luxury was a handmade rough-hewn table with two or three stool-like chairs and a good bed. And yet, to my amazement, upon that coveted table one might find a fresh copy of Detroit's news journal, or even a daily from New York, or a collection of books including volumes on etiquette, history, and geography. And always there would be a bible.

These were not a migration of uneducated pioneers from the isolated hollers of Kentucky or Tennessee. The Tonazzos and their neighbors were city folk from Syracuse and Albany, from New York and Boston, and all along the East Coast. Everything about their nature seemed wholly out of place and unfitted for what they faced.

In Europe, people who dwelled in such basic environments possessed no more learning than the barnyard animals that often shared their space indoors. The miserable lot existed in a world of insurmountable ignorance. Yet, here in this paltry hut were two of the many intelligent well-read individuals who appeared to possess all the refinements of city folk who might dress this evening to attend an opera. Like so many others, they had transplanted themselves into the middle of a perfectly unimaginable wilderness with all manners and graces miraculously intact. They were fully prepared to discuss any issue; be it a simple comment on the weather, or a debate about our nation, our president, our present situation or the situation of any country in Europe. These settlers were surprisingly worldly within their wilderness.

Social gatherings, if not inspirational affairs, were at least intellectual and host to conversations worth merit. There were roads to build, railroads to survey, land to clear, bridges to construct, barns to raise, Indians to fight, in essence there was both the foundation and future of a nation to consider. It was a nation of the people and everyone had an opinion. Settler's were not the castaways or banished tribes one might expect, but well-informed and often well-heeled gentlemen and ladies who followed dreams of something greater in life that could be found just a few miles farther west along the trail.

FORTY-FIVE

The cabin proved to be as small and simple as Julia foretold. Yet, I found everything about it and its inhabitants endearing and so determined to remain for a spell. The following days were ones of pleasant discoveries. It was a time for me to learn everything about this woman with whom I had corresponded with since childhood.

Our letters, like most of my correspondence with the orphans was generally little more than notices of births, deaths, weather, hopes and health, and disbelief about the number of years having passed us by. Now, I was able to fill in the thousands of gaps and work to build a personal relationship that would surely last for years to come.

Antonio listened to our conversations with half heart until I mentioned my belief that Christopher had been surveying land in the Michigan territories.

"You say 'eez name ees Clowsen?"

"Claussen. Yes. Christopher Claussen."

"Clowsen. Hmmph.," He shook his head. "I 'era Julia talk ov t'ees man, butta I don' t'eenk I know 'eem. I doubta eez been arounda 'ere, because I know mosta all ta cruisers een ta lower terreetory."

"Cruisers?"

"Si, teembercruisers, landlookers; whatever you weesh to call 'em. Tat ees me. T'at ees whata I do."

"What *do* you do?" I asked, laughing.

"He plays in the woods." Julia said with a taunt.

"Yah, I play een ta woodas. Julia, she wantas me to farm een ta worsta ways. I clear landa forra farm, das all right, butta nawt'een' more. I no wanta be a farmer. Eet's notta me. I hunta forra food. I trap forra skins, anda while I'm doin' tat, I scouta ta woodas forra gooda standas o' pine anda farmin' landa."

"It isn't so much that I want him to be a farmer; it's more that I don't want him to be a timbercruiser. He's getting older now, and I don't like him being gone all the time. I didn't like it when we were young, and I like it less now, especially with the Indians being so restless.

"I might feel different if I knew there was absolutely no other way to make a living, but he can make good money clearing land all around this area, and the work isn't any harder than logging. There's a lot of settler's coming over from New York with plenty of money for land, but little time and maybe less ambition to get it cleared for planting before winter sets in.

"I much prefer that Tony find himself a good oak clearing. There's still plenty of them around that can be made into good farms. We can buy the land cheap, maybe a dollar and a half an acre. We can go right in and girdle whatever trees we want cleared for plow land or for marking the boundaries of the claim. Following year, everything girdled is dead and we fell trees. Year after that, we buy a young team of oxen, train them to pull stumps and do our burnin'. When the land is ready for a plow; we sell the team, which is now trained to work and worth far more than we paid. We buy more cheap land and start over again.

"There's a growing demand for cleared land, and it just gets better all the time. The longer you are willing to hold on to your acreage, the more you get for it. I just think it's easier and a lot more sensible than the timber business."

"She notso dumba, yah?" Tony laughed.

"I learned something of the timber business from Christopher. His involvement in forestry is profound, legendary in fact". I added.

"E vero? Yah? Well, mine ees notta. I scouta forra a small meel above Detroita, naw'ting much, butta eet putas a few dollars een my pocketa—*Julia's pocketa*, I should say. My lovely Julia, mi' bella donna." Antonio blew Julia a kiss.

"Don't let him fool you. He does better than he lets on. He's earned enough to buy his own stands, and he's given me a much better life than this little cabin implies. I say he plays, but he plays hard." Julia smiled his way before continuing. "My youngest daughter, Victoria, was married last year, and he gave her our last cabin along with all the furniture as soon as he heard she was with child. He's done that for all three of our children. His heart is too big for his britches, but it eases their concerns

544

and gives Tony a reason to put up a new cabin. That way we live wherever he clears trees and I know he is always close by. This is our sixth cabin."

"How far would you travel as a timbercruiser?" I asked Antonio.

"Oh, eet dependas. I look forra pine, anda pine forestas starta nort' o' ta Kekalamazoo River orra up arounda ta eendian camp atta Granda Rapeedas, abouta meedways up ta terreetory. Tat's ware startas ta besta teember to be founda. T'os trees getta duo cento, eh—two hundreda o' feeta tall. A lot o' eet ees whatta we call cork pine cuz eet's a gooda wooda wit'outta knotas o' any kine, an' eet ees so lighta tat eet pract'cly floatas on top o' ta water—justa like cork. Tare's some mighty nice standas up tat away. You getta t'ree anda twenty as often as notta, anda—."

"Tree and twenty?" I repeated. Antonio looked at me and correctly determined I knew less about the timber business than he believed.

"Si, t'ree anda ten, t'ree anda twenty. When we survey forra ta mills, tey no wanta senda team wit'outta knowin 'ow many t'ousandas of boarda feeta tey can getta outta ta standa. So we look atta trees anda we say 'ow many to make a t'ousanda boarda feeta. You can do eet wit' t'ree trees if t'ey arra 'uge, ta really tall ones, si? Usually, eet's morra like fife. If we say fife anda twenty, tat means fife trees arra neededa anda twenty per cento of ta tree ees free of branches orra knotas anda can be made eento logs."

"Oh, three and twenty, I understand."

"Down 'ere, from Kekalamazoo to la Eendiana-Ohio border, ta woodas arra meexed wit' oak, beech, birch, 'emlock, elm, maple—you know, mostly burnin' wooda. Tare arra some gooda patches o' pine arounda 'ere, butta you really 'ava to pay attention to finda eet. You can walk righta pasta gooda standa o' pine, missing eet by less t'an twenty orra t'irty rodas."

"How do you know where to look?" Antonio thought about it for a minute.

"Een winter eet's abouta all tat's green. I guess—you justa look up. Pine arra tall, very tall. If you finda a bluff anda look outta over ta foresta, you can see pine easy. Sometimes you justa climb a tree anda look abouta. If you arra eento ta thick o' ta woodas anda you know youra bizasness, t'en maybe you justa lees'en."

"Listen?"

"Mmm. Pine grows way above ta resta of ta foresta, anda when ta winda blows—." Antonio made a motion with his arm to indicate a tree vibrating in the breeze. "T'ey don'ta 'ava leaves anda so t'ey make a wooshing sounda. Crusisers call t'em whisperin' pines. You standa steel anda you lees'en. T'ey call to you. Een time, you know ta sounda ta tree."

"That is hilarious. Wait till I tell my friends that I know this man Antonio, who walks about the woods listening for a tree to cut down." I laughed.

"Yah, it's true." Antonio smiled and then changed the subject. "You know, next week I go to Detroita forra you, anda maybe down to Monroe anda see if I can finda a recorda of Mr. Clowsen's claims. Mosta o' ta landa down 'ere ees well surveyeda so settlers can make aclaims wit'outta confusion. Eet weel take asome time, butta I do some askin' eef you wanta."

"Tony, I fear for the amount of travel and time you will incur. I would rather propose a business deal, if you'll take no offense."

"Say whatta you weesh. I don' bite, no."

"I will pay your wages and all expenses for whatever time you deem necessary to exhaust every avenue. I will then base my decision on what next to do upon your report. We all know that Mr. Woodburn suspected Christopher would be very interested in Chicago. I ask you. Is that the place for me to go next?"

"It weel be a coupla o' weeks forra certain."

"Whatever."

FORTY-SIX

Having made preparations, Antonio mounted up and departed with food, blessings, prayers for a safe journey and something unexpected—*Taa*. There was an immediate bond between Antonio and Taa'sooma'hane. Julia and I laughed, saying it was due to the fact that neither of them could pronounce my name.

It was apparent that Taa'sooma'hane understood Antonio's way of life, traveling the woods alone, hunting, trapping, and understanding its mysteries with a confident intimacy. As with Caleb, in Antonio's company, Taa'sooma'hane felt comfortable; Taa talked. Taa's priority was to find his people and this was an opportunity to go out and seek information. And so it was to the two of them, we bid farewell.

We expected their return in a fortnight and were left to our own business. During their absence, Rachel and I helped Julia in whatever manner possible. For the most part, Rachel and I sat with Julia at the fire knitting and stitching clothes for the hopeful birth of a grandchild.

Nobody would hear of Caleb leaving Rachel under any circumstance, so Caleb was left behind to chop firewood pretty much sun-up to sunset, which I add without any desire to diminish his hard work, was a rather short day. The sky was always overcast and daylight was from little more than ten to four in the woods.

Caleb came in for a drink of water, and Rachel looked up from her embroidery to stare at him.

"I dare say, Caleb, if you looked like that on the auction block, you'd a fetched a good hundred dollars more."

I nearly choked. I wasn't sure if it was proper for me to laugh about such a horrible thing or not, but Caleb broke into a wide grin that put aside my worry.

"Rachel isn't kidding." I said to Julia. "When Caleb turned up at our boat in Buffalo, he looked little more than a drowned cat, sopping wet, cold, and half starved—no bigger around than a twig."

"Jus' like on the block," said Rachel. "All them broad-chested black boys an' then comes my wisp of a man, Caleb. If I wasn' cryin' so hard, I'd a laughed myself to death. He definitely was not a field hand."

"If you have any doubt about Rachel's cooking, there's the pudding." I pointed at Caleb.

"All I gotta say is it's right easy to lose weight when you're thinkin' 'bout what kind of bug to eat for dinner." He looked down. "Right now, I wish onliest to move the puddin' from here to here." Caleb moved his hand from his stomach to his shoulders. We all laughed.

"You jus' keep choppin' that wood, honey. You're lookin' a might good to me," teased Rachel.

"Ooooooo." Julia rolled her eyes. "Remember that tonight, Caleb."

Caleb and I were both suddenly very self-consciousness. I looked away at once so Julia and Rachel wouldn't invite further comment from me, and Caleb stumbled on his words before stepping back out into the cold, for the safety of the woodpile.

"You—you—lordy, you two are nothin' but naughty. Naughty!" The door closed behind him. Julia and Rachel were bent over laughing as I looked on with my pretend *'knowing smile'*.

* * *

There was plenty of worry to go around by the time Antonio and Taa returned to the cabin. A fortnight passed a week prior, and to see the concerns that Julia attempted to conceal was reminder enough that this was yet a land of sudden death and tragedy. The worry worsened with each passing day until at last they were spotted coming up from the road.

It was a day of relief. Joy, yes. Thankfulness? Of course, but relief more than anything else. Julia wasted no time in stepping out onto the porch for assurances that her man was unhurt. Her eyes were glued to his frame. She studied his every move and manner as they rode up the path. At last she ran out into the yard to touch him, to be sure. Satisfied that the two men suffered nothing more severe than growling appetites, she was all smiles. Strapped across the hind quarters of Taa's horse was a freshly slain deer and so dinner was set into motion with Rachel in full command.

The men were well fed and in good shape. After dinner, the men having no need of sleep, Antonio chose to acknowledge the patience I exhibited. I was seated at the table with Julia when he addressed me.

"You arra kinda to let me seata anda eata wit' my Julia wit' outta asking one seengle question. So now, I tell you whatta I 'ava deescovareda abouta Mr. Clowsen. Yes?"

"It can wait until tomorrow," I replied.

"No, no, fa niente. T'is now ees a gooda time."

"Very well, thank-you."

"I am heerra to say, I founda many claims made by Mr. Clowsen. Een facta, so many claims, I founda myself trying to make sense o' whatta 'ee deed. Uno momento, eet seemed 'e was een search of teember, t'en eet seemed eez eenterest lie only een gooda farmlanda, butta mosta confusing, was eez purchase of t'ousands of acres of wort'less scruba, orra so I t'oughta. Don' getta me wrong, 'e boughta all eez landa atta govarenmenta prices anda can sell t'em off forra t'ousands of times whatta 'e paida. Santa Lucia! Eez 'oldings arra wort' a fortune now.

"E boughta so much landa t'at I began to lay outta eez claims on a map so I coulda tell which away 'e 'eaded, anda een doing so I deescovareda t'are were two clear pat's t'at ran parallel easta to westa. One pat' go along da Cheecago roada; ta ot'er followeda a trail along ta Kekalamazoo River Valley anda towarda Granda Rapeedas.

"All eez claims forra gooda teember orra farmlanda were connecteda to t'ese two pat's of sortas, lying eit'er nort' orra sout' o' ta routes. Eet took awhile forra me to see ta obvious. You know w'at ta man ees doin', Elizabet?"

"What?" I shook my head having not a clue.

"Eez laying grounda forra railroadas orra purchasing landa in ta mosta reg'lar places t'ey mighta get builta. Eez teember woulda be wit'in easy reach o' ta rails anda queeck to move to Detroita orra Cheecago. I tell you—to see a man wit' such wealt' putting somet'ing like t'is toget'er ees wonderful. E does eet alone, anda I dare say 'ardly a soul woulda know deeferenta.

"I t'ink forra you Elizabet, is this. Mr. Clowsen has notta purchaseda anyt'ing in tis terreetory forra last tree years as besta I can tell. Ta last recorda I coulda finda was dateda eighteen tventy-nine. Taa' sooma'hane anda I even po-keda arounda between Eendiana anda Ohio, butta I finda nawt'ing to show 'e made a claim anywhere near ta border."

"So you believe he went from Detroit to Chicago, just as Mr. Woodburn suggested?"

"Si, si. I do. Yah. Forta Dearborn. We go t'are. I take you."

FORTY-SEVEN

Although my ambition was to depart Buffalo for a warmer climate, by the end of December I was undeniably stalled in what some might have called the white wastelands of Michigan territory. I had made good on my intention to escape the notorious snowfalls of Buffalo only to be pinned down by three feet of white powder surrounding our small cabin.

In my heart, I knew what might have been worse. It was true that we six were cramped within our quarters, but our situation caused us to become all the closer. It was for this reason that on December sixteenth, the party for my birthday was all the more special. I had friends close about me with whom to share the first day of my thirty-fourth year.

"I want you to know how much I've enjoyed this day because of you."

"You're *supposed* to enjoy this day. It's your birthday," said Julia.

"It's truly your day. Nobody can take it from you. Now, blow out the candle and cut the cake. I want a piece," said Rachel.

"I wanta piece too," said Antonio

"We all want a piece," said Caleb.

I looked at Taa'sooma'hane. "Do you want a piece of my birthday cake, Taa?" He nodded yes.

I stared into the light of the candle. How unlike this, was my birthday last, when I sat upon a comfortable bed in a spacious apartment overlooking the gray snow of Boston only to feel utterly miserable and depressed. How unlike this, was my wish for someone besides Mary to knock on my door and wish me a happy birthday. How opposite this, were my tears a year ago.

I remembered the wish I made in desperation as I blew out the candle before Mary and Allen on that birthday. How I had wished with every fiber in my body that my life might change. I was so full of frustration and disappointment on that day. The fact that my wish was fulfilled did not escape me now.

"Ara you going to blow out ta candle orra no? We'ra getting' hungry."

"Shush, Tony! She's making a wish."

"'Ow long does eet take to t'ink I wish to eat a piece o' cake?"

I wish I would find Christopher soon—soon, soon, soon.

I blew out the flame. "Who wants theirs first?"

"Me!" cried Antonio. "T'at Rachel knows 'ow to bake a cake!"

Julia frowned at her husband, as we laughed. Unfortunately, there was no denying the truth of it.

FORTY-EIGHT

Any sane individual would readily appreciate that even the best of characters would eventually show signs of strain when cooped up in close quarters for weeks on end. We were no different. We had met Julia's children and grandchildren. We had met her neighbors. We had played pop-goes-the-weasel, turkey in the straw, money musk, and every other conceivable parlor game that came to mind. We sang a few songs, but that wasn't really fair to Taa'sooma'hane. He did sing an Indian song for us and we were left spellbound by the eeriness of the melody. We had discussed all the world's problems, past, present, and future until mentally spent.

We were wearing thin. Nobody was ever rude, but all dreamed of privacy and time away from the scrutiny of other eyes. Day walks through the snow were no longer sufficient.

Even a shivering trip to the outhouse was a welcome moment away from the others. It was time to make the break, and so it was with certain relief that I demanded we set firm plans for our departure.

Julia and Antonio expressed bittersweet acceptance, but insisted we stay for the duration of the Holy Days. Antonio convinced me it best I travel during January, which he claimed was cold, but a much better month to be on the road. In Michigan, blue skies and sunshine were more the norm during that month.

In the meantime, Antonio would take us to Detroit for a few days and break the hold of cabin fever. We would shop for Christmas gifts and dinner treats. All relished this plan, but none more than me. It would be impractical to buy much for Rachel, Caleb or Taa as we needed to travel light, but as for Julia, I had every intention of spoiling her rotten for putting up with so much.

The neighbors not only offered us the use of their horses, but it seemed half of them decided to join us for the trip. In total there were about twenty-five who made the journey. I was unsettled to overhear conversations about the Indian concerns and the relief expressed about traveling in a party greater than the usual six or seven as was customary for safety. I much preferred to hear our large group was collected to enjoy the fun guaranteed to be had in Detroit.

As soon as our troupe arrived in the town, we took up rooms in the inns that were for the most part empty this time of year, for the River of Detroit had frozen over and all shipping and traffic had stopped shortly after our arrival. The inns were mostly story-and-a-half structures, often converted homes with steep roofs and dormers.

The ground floors were divided into either four or six sections with a large fireplace situated in the center of the dwelling to radiate heat. Collections of pots and pans were crowded about the hearths. The windows were shuttered on both inside and outside. The fact that they could also be barred made me wonder if the boards were protection against winter or marauding Indians.

The upper floor of our inn was one large room. It could be sectioned off with a portable blind for a woman's privacy when needed. There were a number of bunks and the floor was covered with three wore out bear rugs. The chimney was the only source of heat and so blankets were plentiful.

In contrast to assumptions made in a warmer climate, Detroit was a place of gaiety and abundant activity during the hard months of winter. The lakes were slowly disappearing beneath a thick crust of ice and snow, something the River of Detroit had done weeks earlier. It was now one large expanse of ice. The town was no longer teeming with strangers and transients. It was forcibly closed to the outside world.

Indoors, were the gatherings of townsfolk fighting off cabin fever with fine foods, neighborly conversation, the tunes of fiddlers, and the stomp of dancing feet. The roar of laughter along with the aromas of stews and skewered meats were swept up by blustery winds and carried down streets where families and friends walked to shop and play.

Outside, there were hundreds of people attending skating parties up and down the river. There were pony races, sled races and sleigh rides upon the ice. There were snowball fights the likes of nothing ever seen.

Winter in Detroit was a time of relaxation, a time to take a break from the murderous pace of summer's business and the ever growing stream of settlers that overran the city from first sign of spring and the opening of the Erie, to the last falling leaf and the draining of the canal. Winter in Detroit was a private affair attended only by its inhabitants and the few outsiders lucky enough to get there in time.

I so enjoyed the break from our cramped quarters at the cabin that I willingly paid three nights stay for all. I would have stayed a full week to be sure, but many in our company were concerned about leaving their cabins unattended. The issue was again one of Indians. Comments were kept secretive out of respect for Taa'sooma'hane, but I was told that there was a very real threat of Indian atrocities in the area.

All that was rumor and hearsay back east about the Indian chief Black Hawk was here a living fact. According to the locals, he was working hard to stir up unrest among the Potawatomi who lived in the woodlands beyond the borders of the city. There had been numerous reports of cabins being torched along with killings and scalping. One was of a mother whose husband and sons were killed and whose baby girl survived being scalped and having her neck slit.

There was a story about the keelboat OLIVER that had been attacked by Black Hawk and his warriors. Four men had been slaughtered and the boat suffered seven hundred bullet holes. There were numerous reports of travelers on their way to Chicago that had been terrorized and fired upon by unknown bands of Indians.

In view of the facts that the Potawatomi had plenty of blood on their hands from years past and more recently by one of their chiefs, Big Foot, who hated settlers with a passion, and that there no longer was a fort in Detroit, many of the women in our group were filled with dread when hearing anything of Indians. They often refused to even discuss the matter.

I respected the apprehensions that surrounded me and was not one to stand in the way of our return to the cabins. At least we had filled our sacks with goods for a fine Christmas dinner, and the day could not have been better for travel. The sun was bright and blessed our cheeks with its warmth.

The feast was not had at Julia and Antonio's cabin. Instead, we ate at the cabin of their oldest daughter. It was the largest of the cabins that Antonio had built, and it also had a small barn. Ironically, the house was even more cramped than Julia's place due to the increased number of people at dinner. We were crowded to the point of hilarity; but because we fully expected this beforehand, we planned accordingly and all went well.

A sizable table was constructed specifically for the occasion. It seated the adults, whereas the children were left to eat where they may. We enjoyed a meal of plenty, it being a mix of wild game, venison, turkey, and fowl of all kind. There was a wonderful rabbit stew, a sizable roast beef and salted fish. We enjoyed baked potatoes smothered in butter and all assortments of dessert. In fact, the availability of coffees, teas, and liqueurs to enjoy with our desserts was a testimony to how civilized was this faraway city of Detroit. I found its stores stocked as well as any to be found back east in Boston.

For a moment at least, nobody was left wanting. Of course it was only for a moment because under the pressure of impatience, the dinner table was cleared to make a place for opening gifts. Children young and old were beside themselves with excitement, for I had been generous in quality and quantity. It was the least I could do to repay the hospitality given me and my companions.

I sat before a mural of smiling faces. It was a blur of joyfully unrestrained spirit that pulsed with laughter and random shouts of glee as it resonated within the walls of this frontier cabin. So much so, that it became something of a drone within which I found myself fading from their presence. I found myself being pulled away from this happiness, pulled back to Boston and the embrace of Mary and Allen, but at the same time being madly driven to go to Christopher in all haste.

The day was at an end, and as I stared at the toys spread out about the floor, my thoughts were now only of Christopher. These were fine gifts and they reminded me of those gifts he had given to me during my life, especially the ones at Christmas. Of course, I had to acknowledge he had given many gifts to many people, rich and poor at Christmas. He was a generous man, that was the long and short of it.

"Christopher, Christopher, Christopher", my thoughts were whispered aloud. Why was he such an obsession? What was it that so compelled me to find him? I shook my head in wonder. I had no answer, nothing rational, but the feeling to find him was intense, and I knew at this moment it was time for me to leave.

FORTY-NINE

Antonio continued to press Julia into changing her mind. He was gentle, whereas I was not. And so on the day of our departure only five of the six horses were saddled for riders. The sixth was saddled with my trunk and supplies for the journey to Chicago. Julia was to remain home. She was visibly disappointed and remained noticeably quiet.

"I know how you wish to join me, Julia, but it isn't worth the risk. It's the dead of winter and there need be only one small, unexpected misfortune, one unforeseen event and then what? It doesn't have to be a rogue band of Indians. Maybe only a falling limb or a stumbling horse."

"I know."

"Oh, Julia. I have so enjoyed my stay and the time I've had to make you more than words on paper. After all these years of writing, we have truly become friends in the flesh. You will forever be in my heart, a close friend, and it would do me wonders to know that you are safe here at home with your kin. I beg you read the books I have brought, enjoy them and think of me. That is what I want the most. That would make me happiest."

"I know."

"Give me a hug."

Julia and I embraced. I mounted the horse and looked down upon her. At last she smiled.

"The reason I so dearly wish to go is I know I will never see you again."

"You can't say that."

"I know it, Elizabeth. I know it in my heart." Julia studied my face. "You are so special to me. Your letters helped me hold on to so many memories of my youth, memories of England, times aboard the REBECCA, times long gone. Who else would know of my past. Only another orphan would understand. Your letters steadied me as I was carried off to the frontier with a family of complete strangers, people I didn't know. I will never be able to express my gratitude. I always felt that you and Lady Rebecca were there for me as a child and I feel that way yet to this day."

"And you should, for I still am. I always will be. I will write. I promise."

"Pray take care. I worry for your safety."

As if given an unspoken instruction, I reached into my bag and retrieved my amulet. I slipped it over my neck.

"There, I am told this possesses great power and protects me. Now rest assured, I will be fine." I smiled with confidence.

Julia looked at me as though she had mentally missed a step, yet chose not to question my action.

"May God be with you, Elizabeth."

"And you, Julia."

I turned away to look at my waiting party. Of the four faces that paid me mind, one in particular beamed with pride. Taa'sooma'hane was visibly elated to see the amulet upon my breast. It may have been the greatest show yet of the silent emotion he expressed.

FIFTY

The five of us started our journey west along the Chicago Road. The silence that befell us on our day of arrival was again with us as we trod along the trail. The only disruption to the quietude of nature was the distant sound of an axe or the more frequent howl of wolves. The wilderness impressed one to meditate. Often, I would snuggle up in my coat and meditate so deeply that I would nearly nod off and then awake with a jolt seconds before falling completely out of the saddle.

Here was a time when a coach would have meant the world. I might have laid my head back and slept away the miles without fear of falling off an animal. I might have hovered over a foot warmer and been protected from the winds of winter. I might have sat across from Rachel engaged in conversation while completely oblivious to what wolves passed by outside the cabin door. Unfortunately, no driver was about to risk getting stuck in shoulder deep snowdrifts and having to walk twenty or thirty miles to safe haven. So, it would forever be a dream.

At least the indecision of November and December skies was behind us. By January, winter was set in its ways, cold and stable under a cloudless canopy of flawless blue and a bright low-slung sun. The weather was now more predictable just as Antonio promised.

Unfortunately, we saw little of the brilliant January sunshine because Antonio and Taa'sooma'hane determined it best for us to travel at night. The main reason for this was the need to keep warm during the coldest hours of the night and also because of the wolves. They did not like the idea of sleeping at night when the wolves were on the prowl. In order to protect us it would be necessary to keep a sizable fire going, which provided much wanted warmth, but also much unwanted attention during a time when Indians were provocative.

In spite of nights being long, we started out riding only six hours, and then seven, and eight. We increased the hours on horseback until we rode as close to ten hours as possible, none of it in daylight. It was mostly a matter of how much abuse Rachel's and my body would tolerate. Between battered backs, bruised buttocks, and inner thighs covered with a creeping rash of skin rubbed raw, it was clearly hard on a person who was not conditioned to ride for such long duration. I was living proof.

If an inn was available, we would make use of it. Otherwise, at the first sign of dawn, we would leave the road and work our way up an unfrozen creek if possible then ride into a thicket or to ground beyond a rise in search of a safe place unseen from the trail. There we would follow Taa'sooma'hane's lead and search out a stand of saplings, which he would tie together and then drape with a large oilcloth to form a small temporary tipi.

Inside we would trample down the snow and cover the packed surface with anything dry, preferably tall grass or oak twigs, which often retained many of their crisp bronze leaves. In the center of the tipi Taa'sooma'hane would scrape a shallow bowl out of the frozen ground with his knife. He would pile the dislodged earth around it's perimeter.

Outside, Caleb would scour the area for firewood and set it to blaze. By dawn's approach, having rode the whole of the night, we most wanted to sleep long and warm on a full belly, and so Rachel would make best of Caleb's fire by speedily setting out a spread of leftover meat, biscuits, beans and molasses. It was quick fixin's and in light of our hunger, as tasty as any-thing prepared on a stove back home. I heated snow into hot water and rinsed our cups, pans, and utensils.

After eating, Taa would scoop up the coals and carry them into the tipi. There, he would drop them into the crater he had carved out of the frozen ground, and then cover them with the dislodged earth. By the time we collected our belongings and stowed them away, the mound of dirt was giving off a comforting heat. It was an inviting warmth that persuaded us to gather around curled up in our blankets and succumb to our weariness. We would always fight the cold, which was ever pervasive, but at least we slept secure knowing we were reasonably sheltered from the wolves and winter winds. We relied on the horses to warn us of bears.

By and large, all awoke at three or four in the afternoon with time enough to make use of the remaining hours of daylight. Caleb dismantled the tipi, folded up the oilcloth, and set about collecting wood sufficient for a dinner fire. The wood was piled upon the coals, now unearthed, and was soon freshly ablaze.

Antonio and Taa'sooma'hane took advantage of the fading light to hunt. Antonio carried a gun, but it was Taa'sooma'hane who felled the game. Everyone preferred the silence of his arrows. There was never a shortage of appetite or food taken, and so at night we were certain to dine on roasted meat or fowl.

We were quick to establish routines and responsibilities that saved time and benefited all. On occasion, we dined in the company of others whom we met in passing. We remained on our guard each time we encountered a stranger, but every instance proved to be one of good company and conversation.

Our journey went well in every respect until struck head on by a blizzard of unusual severity. We rode into a burst of snowfall that snuffed out any hint of moon or starlight leaving us in complete blackness and blind to the trail but for the amount of snow that piled up upon our heads and horses. It came upon us with such ferocity that within minutes of its onset, we were left no choice about what next would be done, and so we immediately went searching for a place to camp. We talked to each other so as not to lose anybody. It was a fearful situation as we spread out to find saplings sufficient to support our tipi.

Over the next two days and nights, a fresh three feet of snow accumulated on the flats. Our tipi and tree trunks alike had snow drifted four and five feet high on their weather side. The side of trees facing west was encased in snow for as far up into the branches as one could see. There was nothing for us to do but wait, wait, and wait.

While I did so, I began to chuckle and question how I ever ended up sleeping on the ground in a freezing blizzard when I had the all the resources needed to sleep in a warm overstuffed bed at the best of hotels. What astonished me most was the realization that the question hadn't been my initial thought and in fact far from it. It had only come slowly after a good deal of daydreaming. Was I changing?

I also realized for the first time that Rachel, Caleb and Taa'sooma'hane were addressing me as one of their own. I sensed myself being folded into the passages of their lives as much as they were into mine. The difference in our backgrounds was beginning to blur. It seemed to be less a matter of haves and have-nots and more one of common needs and companionship. I guess while never having given it a thought, I had been paying my dues.

We struggled against the storm that kept us pinned inside the tipi and huddled together to cherish the heat of exhaled breath which we often blew beneath our blankets. It was impossible to find firewood beneath so much snow and nobody wanted to open the flap to forfeit whatever heat was inside.

If not for the misery of going outside to relieve ourselves nobody would have moved a finger, for any trip outside caused one to return caked in snow that only served to melt and leave a person sopping wet and chilled. The men merely stood outside the opening of the tipi and peed to one side, but for Rachel and I, modestly dictated we seek out privacy at whatever the frigid cost.

The morning of the third day brought an overcast sky, but no wind or snow. Our schedule of sleep had been disrupted and on that morning, I lay awake in the early hours as dawn filtered through the woods. I had parted the flap of the tent enough to peek outside. No words can describe the perfect serenity of that moment when I stared from beneath my blanket into the cold air beyond.

For that short space of time, *nothing* moved, not a single snow-covered branch, not one animal large or small—nothing. There was no sound of any sort, and that alone had to be impossible in such a vast country. I was utterly transfixed by the silent beauty before me. I was lost in a scene void of color. It was an unspoiled, unsoiled world of white where every detail seemed to be formed from heaven's clouds. Virgin white, an indescribable white that was nothing short of that magic realm, where dwelled the mysterious Mistress of Winter.

Of course such perfection couldn't last and my eyes were drawn up into the treetops by a spread of black across this all white world. It was up high on a branch that I observed a very large turkey. It spread its enormous wings and leaned over as if about to leap, then retracted them and sat back having a second thought. It did this a second time, and a third, and a fourth, all the while succeeding in capturing my fullest attention.

It was a rather comical scene, appearing as though it possessed a fear of flying. Then to my astonishment, it leaned forward and instead of spreading its wings to fly, it merely jumped into space and came crashing down through a web of branches, all snapping and splintering within an avalanche of snow until it disappeared with a great thud into a drift at the base of the tree.

It was such an outrageous sight, I laughed softly under my breath, only to have a hand grasp my shoulder from behind. I turned around to see Taa'sooma'hane place his finger to his lips and motion me to remain quiet. He had witnessed the scene over my shoulder and nodded his amusement. He gestured that the animal was brainless. I watched him rise to his knees after there came a second and third crashing through the trees to end any further stillness of the morn.

Taa'sooma'hane reached for his bow and quietly strung it. He selected an arrow with which he poked the tipi flap and ever so slowly opened if further. He then selected a second arrow and positioned it to the string. I lay quietly beneath him and turned back to watch outside as a large tom moved toward a hen in a windswept clearing. The hen being distracted by the tom made a move in our direction.

I heard the soft rustle of movement as Taa'sooma'hane drew back the bowstring. In the blink of an eye, the hen dropped to the ground even as the soft swoosh of a feathered arrow was still upon my ear. I watched the dumbfounded look upon the remaining tom as it bobbed up and down and looked around in confusion.

The bird looked at the dead hen then around the woods, and again at the dead hen and around the woods. After a time or two of this, it suddenly mounted the dead hen as if about to repopulate the forest single handedly. My jaw dropped. And to think there were those fools who believed the turkey should be the national bird! Never, in all my life, had I witnessed such stupidity in an animal. I for one would croak before seconding such representation for my country! Thankfully, Taa'sooma'hane did Mother Nature a favor and disposed of the oversexed bird as well.

FIFTY-ONE

Having endured the cramps and stiffness of being cooped up in the tipi for three days, we were out walking about at this first break in the weather. It was good to get back on our feet. The horses were well rested but hungry as were we all. A sizable fire was put to good use drying out our clothes and putting life back into cold feet and limbs. Both turkeys were roasted then picked clean off their bones and washed down with steaming hot coffee. We dismantled camp the moment breakfast was finished. We folded up the oilcloth, finished packing the horses, mounted up, and headed out beneath a cloudy sky coming apart amid a web of bright blue fractures. For once, it was nice to travel during the day.

Whether it was a matter of luck, the time of the year, or the unexpected blizzard that stopped everything in its tracks for days, fact was we encountered no trouble to speak of along the road to Chicago. The trail did become noticeably less pronounced the farther west we went, but even so, small settlements had taken root the whole of its length.

We were presently at one of these settlements, where we had spent two nights at an inn for the sake of warmth. Rachel and I simply could no longer handle the cold. We were unlike the men. We needed to thaw out and rest before we became sick. The inn was called the 'Crossroads' for good reason.

"Well, my friendas…I am sorry, butta I musta now go back. Eef you stay on t'is trail, you weel go up arounda ta farra side of ta lake anda finda Cheecago een four orra fife days. Eef you take t'is pat' to ta lefta, you weel 'eada towarda ta Kankakee River anda tat weel take you to ta Eelinois River. Eef you go to Cheecago, you weel t'en follow ta Des Plains River to ta Eelinois. Eit'er way, ta Eelinois weel take you to ta Meeseeseepee. You go sout' on ta Meeseeseepee anda you weel come to St. Loueese on ta west shore."

I could not escape the fact that each departure of a friend became ever harder. I supposed it made sense, for each friend left me with prayers and wishes of good luck, but always farther into the unknown wilderness and the dangers it possessed.

As we bade Antonio farewell, I was overcome with apprehension, for I knew the difficulty of returning to Detroit without his guidance. The sense I had passed a point of no return was most unbearable as it churned up my insides. I did my best to hide this inner torture for the sake of Rachel, who visibly displayed the apprehensions I dared not. I knew she was watching my every reaction to our situation and for me to show a sign of weakness would have been devastating for her.

I wasn't sure about how Caleb felt, but I was supremely grateful I had no clue to what Taa'sooma'hane thought about anything. He was my salvation. He never faltered. He remained stoic and unmoved by whatever event came our way. My only relief was in looking at the Indian and blindly accepting a belief that the farther from civilization we traveled, the more he was in his own element. Mentally, I leaned on him.

As much as I wished otherwise, even Taa'sooma'hane left one decision to me—which way would we precede? Nobody could offer an opinion because the whole point of my being at the Crossroads was to find Christopher, and leaving any stone unturned would be my decision, my decision alone—a decision I would suffer to make.

On the surface, Chicago had been my destination and often advised, but underneath, I sensed St. Louis and the Stony Mountains was where I must go. Whatever force was pulling me toward Christopher was pulling me toward St. Louis. It was becoming evident that whether I chose to accept this truth or not, I was in fact taking one small step after another in that direction.

Fate seemed agreeable in allowing me whatever time needed to consider each consecutive step until I found it to be surmountable and only logical I should inch myself that much farther west. The Divine Powers waited patiently for me to conclude that any thought of retuning to Boston empty handed was ridiculous and most certainly out of the question after having traveled so far.

And so, subsequent to great mental deliberation, I decided we would stay on the trail bound for Chicago. It was by far the longer of the two routes to St. Louis, but to bypass the settlement after being advised by so many to head there seemed unwise. I would bypass the Kankakee and instead make due course along the Des Plaines trail that headed west out of Chicago once arrived.

Besides, there was a great deal of comfort in knowing that during this time of Indian discontent, but for Black Hawk being on the prowl, Chicago remained the largest settlement and enjoyed the protection of Fort Dearborn.

All being said, it was with heavy hearts that Rachel, Caleb, and I started out in the absence of Antonio. Taa'sooma'hane seemed unmoved in spite of the fact I knew they had become good friends. As if to deepen our dismay, the weather became noticeably more violent. In reality, it was about the same as always, but the terrain was changing.

FIFTY-TWO

Our journey began in the heavily wooded forests of eastern Michigan that served as an effective windbreak. The wind might howl overhead as it rushed through the upper branches, but all that reached the ground was a cloud of snow sifted so fine, it was little more than a descending swirl mist. As we progressed farther west, there was a thinning of the wood and more frequent encounters with ever-larger oak clearings and prairies.

Often when traversing these treeless spaces, which were nothing more than matted grasslands with snow piled on top, the depths could easily reach five feet. As a rule, it never exceeded three feet; but even so, it was sufficient to slow the progress of our horses and dampen our spirits. It was becoming ever more certain that we would hold up in Chicago for a few weeks once arrived.

What frightened me most was the combination of unrestricted wind and the blinding swirl of blowing snow across the feature-less fields. It could turn one around as easy as being lost in a cave beneath ground without the slightest ray of light. Like the cave it was a suffocating blindness made thick with dark and snow. If not for Taa'sooma'hane, we would have been hope-lessly lost within minutes of our departure. The shifting snow quickly erased any hint of a trail, and yet, Taa'sooma'hane always managed to pick up the path as soon as we came upon another stand of wood.

Whenever we crossed a clearing, Taa'sooma'hane rode with us. In the seclusion of the woods, Taa'sooma'hane left our party and rode out ahead of us as a scout. He explained it was best to know beforehand what lay in our path, and so he was not with us when we heard a horse galloping our way at great speed. Naturally, we assumed it was Taa'sooma'hane returning for some reason.

And we were correct, although confused by the commotion, for he returned in haste and the stillness of the night was lost to the snorting of Taa'sooma'hane's panting horse. It was obvious he had been driving the animal hard for some time and that something was wrong. Rachel, Caleb and I were quickly becoming apprehensive and afraid of what Taa'sooma'hane had come to say. Certainly, there was trouble ahead.

"Come! We ride fast. Much trouble. Indians! Much trouble. Come now!"

To my surprise, Taa'sooma'hane struck out at a full gallop, but instead of running away, he turned back in the direction from whence he came. There was no time to question his decision, and so, we struck out at once riding foolishly fast in the darkness of night, but too fearful to consider anything less.

When we caught up to Taa'sooma'hane, he was waiting at a streambed ribboned with a dark shadow that snaked along between the banks and proved to be a flow of water in this frozen land. It was obviously a spring fed creek as was Mary and Allen's. While his horse quenched its thirst, he explained what next we must do.

"We ride up stream. No touch banks. In water. No touch banks! Come, now!"

With that, Taa'sooma'hane was off in a gallop, splashing his way up the watercourse. Something was surely wrong to warrant soaking ourselves in the dead of winter. That alone could kill off any one of us in short time.

"Change o' chains, hwat is the matter?" cried Rachel.

"I have no idea, but obviously there's no time to explain. I heard what you heard, something about Indians. Must be there is a band coming our way. Let's go; we'll find out soon enough." The thought of Indians completely unnerved Rachel and me, but we buried our fears behind the worry of stumbling in the creek as we did our best to keep up with Taa'sooma'hane. About a quarter mile upstream, we halted the animals before a tree that had fallen into the creek bed. He instructed us to step our horses over the trunk and then climb up the bank as close to the tree as possible.

"You stay by tree. Come, now!"

The tree trunk hid our tracks from view of anyone who might have been following. Taa'sooma'hane led us about two hundred yards away from the stream where he dismounted in a thicket. There, he tied off his horse. We three remained in the saddle unsure of what next to do.

"Come!" He whispered loudly.

The fact Taa'sooma'hane had whispered at all, probably served to scare me as much as anything. I dismounted at once, and with Rachel and Caleb following my every move, we tied off our horses.

Taa'sooma'hane grabbed his oilcloth, a blanket, and his bag of food, which he held before us and shook as if to instruct us to grab likewise. He then led us back to the vicinity of the fallen tree that crossed the creek. Nearby, he spread the oilcloth across the ground behind another fallen tree. Without a word spoken, he took each of us by the arm and led us to stand on the oilcloth.

"Sit!" We did.

Taa'sooma'hane then grabbed the back edge of the oilcloth and pulled it up over our heads. He gathered up some of the limbs that where scattered about the dead tree and formed an upside down vee against the fallen trunk that served to prop up the cloth. This provided an opening that faced toward the creek bed. He then pinned the oilcloth to the tree trunk with additional limbs and branches that also served to better conceal our shelter.

Taa'sooma'hane then moved away. We waited inside and listened to his footsteps wander off.

"Hwere's he going?" asked Rachel under her breath. Nobody responded.

"Hwere's he going?" she asked again.

"I don't know." I answered.

"Shushhhhhh." Caleb hushed us gently. "Shushhhh, listen."

We remained stock still, and in short time the sound of footsteps could be heard coming back our way. My first thought was *whose*. Nobody moved. Then the back of our oilcloth was raised slightly. With the incoming rush of cool air across our legs came a bow and quiver followed by Taa'sooma'hane. He crept to the center of the shelter and sat cross-legged so as to face the open vee. He slid his bow outside and laid it across the fallen tree trunk. It had been strung. He pulled his blanket around his neck and shoulders and settled himself before the opening. His eyes never left the creek bed, but in a low voice he answered our questions.

"What happened, Taa?" I asked while suffering appalling anxiety.

"Indians. Burn two cabins. I see them, but they see me. I come back. They follow. Very bad," he whispered. "You rest. Keep warm. I watch."

That proved to be impossible. Rachel, Caleb and I propped up little areas of the oilcloth so that we all could peer outside across the fallen log and spy any movement that might come our way. We were terrified. I thought about the looks upon the faces of those women in Detroit every time a word was whispered about murdering Indians. *God! I hated Indians.* No, I couldn't really say that. Taa'sooma'hane was an Indian. I didn't hate Indians. I was just scared to death of them. *God! I was scared of Indians.*

"Shushhhhhhhhhhhhhh. Don't move."

Long and low, Taa'sooma'hane quieted us with a warning. The sky was overcast and the moon weak, and so it was with great difficulty that we could make any sense of the form that moved cautiously into our midst. Taa'sooma'hane had made known the stranger's approach long before I heard his horse or saw the shadow of his form.

I could feel another deplorable attack of anxiety about to grip me as I watched the shadowy figure stop in the creek a few feet short of the fallen tree. He studied the tree and then the bank. I was certain he had seen our tracks. The Indian pulled a gun from his saddle. I heard the click of its hammer being cocked. I swallowed hard. I watched as he slipped off his horse and stepped onto the fallen tree, scaling it to the top of the bank. This time there was no doubt as he looked down to where our tracks would have been in the snow. He knew we were here somewhere. Leaving his horse behind, he stepped cautiously, moving silently through the woods off to our right. Taa'sooma'hane eased the blanket off his body and slipped the quiver over his head and shoulder.

My insides twisted about until knotted up tight. I could scarcely breathe for the panic that welled up within my chest. I was fixed with fear, wondering whatever would we do. I trembled as the Indian studied the shadows in the woods then swung his gaze back and forth past us again and again. At last he focused on our thicket and my breathing stopped dead. It seemed he was yet only curious about our tangle of tree limbs, but enough so that he began to step cautiously in our direction. He stopped. He stared. He listened. He stepped forward. Then slowly he raised his gun in our direction and began to crouch lower as if he knew.

At the same time the stranger moved, Taa'sooma'hane remained stock still, staring into the dimly lit distance. Very slowly he adjusted himself from a cross-legged position to a kneeling posture shifting his weight onto one foot. Slowly, he reached for an arrow and fit it to his bow, which was now halfway out of the opening.

The stranger had moved beyond my line of sight as he walked further around to the side of our place of hiding. I could only guess at where the stranger stood by studying Taa'sooma'hane's eyes. All I wanted to do was run. All I could do was pray and stay put. In dread of what might next happen, I secretly reached over to Rachel, who took my hand into hers.

Without forewarning, Taa'sooma'hane suddenly exploded upward, springing to his feet and scaring the very life out of everyone as he whipped the oilcloth free of his frame.

TWANGswooooosh.

Instinctively, I swept the oilcloth past my head as I looked outward with all the frantic attention of a cornered animal. The shock of what was happening came to me with the swoosh of an arrow, not unlike the death of the idiot turkey. This time there came the thud of impact.

I looked in that direction and watched with horror as the Indian leveled his gun straight at us. Limbs nearby exploded stinging my face with splinters of wood. I cowered, raising my hands far too late to do any good. Rachel screamed aloud as Caleb fought to free himself of the oilcloth. Out of the corner of my eye, I sensed Taa'sooma'hane's movements, but all my senses were focused on the floating cloud of spent gunpowder that concealed the Indian.

TWANGswooooosh.

TWANGswooooosh.

THE KILLING

There came a second thud afterwhich the stranger staggered out from the fog to tumble forward face down into the snow.

Everything went at once silent except for my heart which most certainly pounded like a drum to be heard beyond my ribs—except for my breath which roared in my ears like the wind—except for whimpers coming from Rachel. Everything went still except for my stomach, which was suddenly moved into my mouth—except for the chattering of my teeth and the shaking inside and out of every muscle, especially my hands, one of which was being crushed by the painful grip of Rachel.

I covered my face with my free hand as if to prevent the world from reaching me. I was not about to accept the fact I had just witnessed the execution of a man, but reality was indifferent to my wishes and the truth of it clobbered me hard enough to cause me to tremble as uncontrolled as the world about me. How could I possibly have become part of this calamity? What had happened? It wasn't but twenty minutes ago, I was riding along the trail trying to keep warm and minding my own business, and now, my god, cold was the only thing I didn't feel.

Taa'sooma'hane turned to look at me and interrupted my thoughts.

"Bad Indian. He kill you. *Slowly.* He take your hair. Good color."

The thought of a slow death and scalping did something to ease my remorse, but I hardly felt cleansed. I stared at Taa'sooma'hane as he stepped across the oilcloth and walked off. I watched as he sped quietly down to the creek and reached for the dead man's horse. He led the animal away.

My feelings for Taa'sooma'hane had instantly changed. He was suddenly a stranger as well. He was incomprehensible. He was now Night-Shadow-Killer-Hunter just as he said. In whatever manner I may have begun to accept him as one of us, it ended that moment. He now was very Indian. He was primal. He was also driving me crazy with an overwhelming exhilaration in knowing that this man would most likely commit the ultimate sin in order to protect me. God forgive me. I drew the oilcloth back over my head and curled up in my blanket alongside Rachel.

A few minutes later Taa'sooma'hane returned and lifted the corpse across his shoulder. He disappeared from sight with the body. The only way I could impress upon one how severe was our state of shock, would be by saying that during those minutes in which Taa'sooma'hane was absent nobody uttered a word, not Rachel, not Caleb, not me. We three lay beneath the oilcloth stunned and struggling with our thoughts. There was to be no further travel that night.

Taa'sooma'hane did leave our shelter the following morning to determine if anyone else was about. He believed that he had been seen by two Indians before the killing. However, he returned to say that the Indians had left the area, no doubt because of the number of whites that had collected about the burned out cabins. For fear of death, Taa'sooma'hane did not want to be discovered meandering about by the whites, and so returned to our shelter for the remainder of the day. It wasn't until well after dark that we packed up our belongings and returned to the Chicago Road.

FIFTY-THREE

"Stop! Don't move! Freeze!"

From every direction came commands that badly startled us. In the darkness was heard a flurry of movement and then came a lantern's light within which appeared three heavily armed men.

"Don't move a muscle if ya care anythin' fer yer life!". The threat came from within the woods.

The younger of the three visible men, whom I judged to be in his twenties, stepped forward and raised the lantern.

Taa'sooma'hane and Caleb were in the lead and Rachel was halted between the man and myself. The man yelled back over his shoulder.

"We got us a couple of niggers an' a Injun!" A murmur moved through the shadows.

"I beg your pardon, sir!" I spoke up with all the authority I could muster. The man fell silent at once. He moved the lantern in my direction.

"Glory be. Forgive me, my manners, ma'am." He then yelled out again. "We have us a white woman in this troupe." The man focused his attention on me. "I'd be Samuel Parson at your service, ma'am. Is everything in order?"

"Just barely, sir. It has been a rough journey and none the better for this scare which you have put upon us."

"I beg your pardon, ma'am, but are ya aware o' the danger in these parts? We've just suffered the burning o' two cabins an' the slaughter of four settlers. The neighbors are in a frightful mood an' are fully apt t'shoot first an' ask questions later. I trust ya would understand that t'travel after dark is most assuredly unwise."

"I take your comment to heart, sir. Allow me to say we do so only to protect ourselves from being attacked by wolves as we sleep. I would also say that we too were attacked by one of the scoundrels, and he was summarily put to death by my scout Taa'sooma'hane this night past. The pony in tow belonged to the ruffian." The muttering and mumbling arose anew in the darkness.

The man shone his light upon the riderless animal and spied the saddle with its unmanned gun. He returned to look at me again. "D'ya have papers for the Negroes, ma'am?"

"No sir, I do not. They were washed overboard with most of my luggage during a storm while crossing Lake Erie. However, I assure you I am a Claussen; it is a reputable name, and they would be my property. If you are unfamiliar with the name, you may convey me to Fort Dearborn, where I am confident it will be proven true."

"May I ask o' what be your business in these parts?"

"Most certainly. I am originally departed from Boston, and more recently Albany, Buffalo, and Detroit, where I stayed with friends for the Holy Days. I am now in route to Chicago for the purpose of locating one Christopher Claussen, a member of my family."

The man gave thought to my words. "I must speak with my commander. In the meantime, take hold o' this light an' keep it upon yourselves if ya wish no trouble. I will return momentarily."

We sat within the lantern's glow and waited in silence until another man emerged from the shadows. It was with an authoritative voice that this person delivered the plans now made for us.

"Good evening, Mrs. Claussen."

"Good evening, sir."

"I will have you and your troupe escorted to Fort Dearborn. This is for your safety and an act of no small sacrifice, for I can scarcely afford to lose a man. I would emphasize, you cannot imagine the danger you bring upon yourself by traveling at night. I assure you it is not wolves, but wary settlers that will cause you harm. You are lucky not to have been shot as it is. Take my advice and make good use of the men who accompany you."

"Thank you, sir. I will see to their prompt return."

"That would be appreciated. Good evening, Mrs. Claussen."

It was apparent that the man in charge was in no mood for conversation and so we parted in haste. Our group was now six instead of four. We only traveled an hour at best before putting up at a nearby inn. It was made clear to us that we would not be traveling at night. In spite of this direct order, our two escorts proved both agreeable and accommodating. They knew well the area, and so ended the practice of sleeping out of doors. We enjoyed their good nature as much as their protection all the way to Chicago.

FIFTY-FOUR

Journeying during daylight proved a welcomed change, for I would have spent too much time wrestling with my thoughts and rethinking the death of the Indian at the hand of Taa. Daylight distracted me not only from the darkness of night, but also a darkness of conscience.

Taa was riding ahead with the escorts and out of earshot on the one and only occasion I sought to resolve my feelings about his killing of the Indian. I began by expressing aloud my misgivings to Rachel and Caleb. To my shocking surprise, they appeared not at all affected by the grizzly event as I might have presumed. After discussing the issue, I came to understand that my lack of *brutal* experiences left me unprepared, whereas Rachel and Caleb simply accepted the death as just that. To them, the incident was nothing more than another of the many unwanted experiences life had forced upon them.

This lesson was mine to bear, mine to be learned, and until done, it would be difficult to turn a page and freely face life's next chapter. My collection of written thoughts while attempting to resolve this matter of conscience easily made my diary's next chapter.

We journeyed to the edge of Lake Michigan where I spied miles of sand hills that now rose to our right. These hills formed in part the southern shoreline of the lake and opened on occasion to offer glimpses of the frozen waters beyond. As soon as possible, we passed through the hills to ride upon the flat open beaches free of the tall grasses and wood.

With astonishment and dismay, I discovered that Chicago loomed much larger in name than facility. Fort Dearborn with its two bastions and palisades was a sight for sore eyes; everything else was simply a sore sight. I found no objection to the term 'settlement', for there was one framed house and a couple of solid looking structures. What annoyed me was how loosely the adjective *'largest'* was applied, as if to indicate this place might somehow possess a hint of Detroit's prominence.

According to our escorts, there were about one hundred and twenty-five people that called this place home. I had little choice but to accept the claim at face value, for there was an unrelenting horizontal blow of snow that whited out any feature beyond a stone's throw before us. The winds persisted to howl, and it was no wonder, for there was scarcely a tree to be found that might thwart its attack.

The forests of the territories appeared to split wide open at Chicago leaving nothing but an open unending vista to the west that funneled in winter and reflected something of the white stilled seas of Lake Michigan. It was the frozen flatness of land and water that formed both boundary and shore to the settlement. We too were whited out by winter's assault; sporting aprons of snow, we appeared kin to snowmen come to life when passing by the fort's sentry.

Little can be said of our stay in Chicago. Unlike Detroit, there was none of the festive activity surrounding wintertime. Day to day life was a battle against death. We were held hostage, confined to the safety of the fort by winds so inhospitable that neighbors rarely ventured out to socialize unless scrounging for food or attending the services of Rev. Beggs, a Methodist who arrived a few months before.

At Chicago, the winds of winter immobilized the world. The fearsome weather sucked heat and life out of existence, leaving only colorless collections of form, statues of every shape and size sharing a common frozen curse. It was said to be the worst winter in memory. Except for Sunday services, the only signs of life were the occasional stirrings of fear when word of another suspected Indian atrocity surfaced, or the twice a week delivery of mail from Niles, Michigan.

January 29, 1832

The coldest sight I should ever see is that of Lake Michigan with its jagged spires of ice, its frozen explosions of water, its every wave suspended in place and time. Each arches over the next and waits silently for spring to unleash their power and set them free to crash down upon the shore.

For weeks, I have listened to the grinding and grumbling complaint of shifting ice. I stand in awe of the frozen expanse and stare at unseen forces sounding out like gunshots with each fresh fracture that cracks across untold miles of brutal beauty.

I miss you so. I think Allen may finally be right. He said I would pray to sit in my armchair amid a stack of books before the warmth of a friendly fire. You can't imagine how wildly impossible would be that wish. You can't imagine how wild is this area even before the death-like grip of winter sets in. Oh, how I long for applesauce pie....

I had witnessed many of the ice-covered beaches that led us around the southern shoreline toward Chicago, and I couldn't imagine any arctic landscape to be more hostile to the eyes. Those memories and the unrelenting storms turned me inward to give thanks for the comfort of the fort. It was within that thankful shelter that I put together what little I could of Christopher's activities in the village.

I was depressed to discover that he had spent time in this area back in eighteen twenty-nine when the settlement was

581

scarcely a camp, but in that year the fort was an Indian agency and for the most part occupied by different personnel. Nevertheless, Christopher was said to have surveyed a good deal of land along the shores of the lake and the River Calumet. This I learned from one Lt. Davison, who was at the fort in that year and by the grace of God was now the commanding officer of its garrison. He had been paid by Christopher to witness surveys.

"He is an ambitious man, I'll give you that. He seems bright enough, but to hear him talk of what he imagined would come of this place was enough to cause one to reconsider. I'm sure he was in his right mind, but speaking frankly I have heard less preposterous babble from drunken Indians and lunatics—but the pay was good so I listened and let him ramble on."

"With all due respect, sir, everything Mr. Claussen touches turns to profit. I have seen this the whole of my life. I am confident there is something of worth about your fort."

"The promise of Eden. Easterners all think alike. I ask you to look for yourself; what is there of value around here? Ice? I think not. Fish? There's plenty of fish to be sure. Yet, if I were a fisherman, I'd keep to the boat before stepping upon this shore. You're not so bound to get scalped. This place is too far from humanity, Mrs. Claussen, too far to make good of fish or anything else.

When I paid visit in twenty-nine there may have been fifteen people camped out here and nothing more. Today there is upwards of a hundred inhabitants and still I question the expense of reoccupying this fort. It is a remnant of the war. And if not for the Indian trails and the movements of Fox and Sauk through this area it would certainly be abandoned.

Only because of red skins does Chicago have a fort. I would hardly consider that an encouraging omen or reason to settle this shore. An easterner will see these materials collected for the construction of a lighthouse and write home of explosive

582

growth and potential, but anyone who lives here knows we lack the simplest port. I hear talk of canals and dock building, but for now ships are forced to put down anchor half a mile out. The havoc wreaked by shallows and sandbars is a far cry from welcoming boats leaving Buffalo and the Erie Canal. As for St. Louis, we have but a trickle of business from that great city and there is where lies our future.

In Chicago, one risks drowning on these waters, slaughter in these woods, or freezing every winter. If Mr. Claussen and I had been standing down south on the shores of the Ohio, I'd speak differently for that is a place of potential. But there was no arguing with Mr. Claussen. He said the proposed Illinois-Michigan canal and the one in New York would change every-thing once opened. Well, it's been two long years and nothin's changed yet except for an upsurge in Indian attacks."

I wasn't about to contradict my host, but Lt. Davison came to Chicago from the south, up through Kentucky as did many of these pioneers, and he was accustomed to a settled country far more hospitable than this frigid northern shore. Yet, if he had come by way of New York and the Erie Canal, and been witness to the mounting wave of migration about to overrun these parts, no doubt his perspective would have been markedly different.

Nobody else in Chicago or at Fort Dearborn knew anything about Christopher except that his surveys of certain stretches of shoreline would cause Lt. Davison to remind speculators and residents alike that Christopher had been walking off those areas—much to their annoyance.

...I must tell you, Mary, in all honesty, I really had expected more, a good deal more. Such scant information did little to soothe Rachel or Caleb, especially in light of the fact that Lt. Davison had seriously questioned Christopher's good sense.

I know they now question mine, for we are a long way from civilization and sanity.

In their eyes, it would seem plausible that I was duped by a mysterious man, that I might have been misled or blinded by emotion. I had been so vocal about my certainty in finding much of Christopher in Chicago that I fear this setback has reduced my stature substantially although nothing is said aloud.

I was forthright and first to admit that there was hardly anything to Chicago, let alone Christopher. I made no attempt to hide the fact that I had failed myself as much as my companions....

However disappointing the facts, I could honestly say the following weeks of forced relaxation only served to strengthen my resolve. I regained my fortitude and determined more than ever to forge ahead. I may have lacked the courage to make any mention of my plans to Mary and Allen for fear of upsetting them, but my sights were now set squarely on St. Louis.

Those travelers arriving from the west brought with them certainties of how terrible was this winter with reports of snow in excess of six feet on the prairies and drifts double that depth. Suffering was prevalent. Settlers unable to move beyond their cabins were turning fences and clapboards into firewood for heat.

Animals of every sort, especially deer were everywhere frozen on hoof still standing in their tracks. Food was plentiful only for the amount of starved birds and animals lying dead and littering the snow cover that kept them from reaching the grasses and grains buried beyond reach.

The prospects of resuming our journey to face this especially brutal season made Lt. Davison's invitation to winter a while longer at Fort Dearborn most welcome. And so we stayed put. Taa stayed to himself but dared not venture off for fear of being killed by a settler. I spent most days writing in my journal and mending clothes. I spent most evenings about the warmth of a fire in passing conversation with Lt. Davison.

"The fort was originally constructed in eighteen and three," said he. "Of course, it was then merely a collection of wooden shelters and a stockade. It was raised by forty US troops under the command of Captain John Whistler. He named the fort after Henry Dearborn, the Secretary of War, who was instrumental in planning the removal of red skins from lands east of the Mississippi.

"For the next decade, life about the fort was peaceful—then the War of 1812 broke out. The British were sorely adept at inflaming Indians already incensed over the loss of their lands to the Americans. Matters turned for the worse when the British succeeded in capturing the American garrison at Mackinac. Their victory greatly encouraged the red skins and seriously elevated the danger of those in and about Fort Dearborn. Due to the severity of this threat, the Commander of US forces, General Hull, ordered this place to be abandoned.

"At that time, the commanding officer was one Captain Nathan Heald, a man who procrastinated until some five hundred red skins were camped outside his walls. Eager to amend his foolishness, he faulted further by making a hasty deal to trade his stockpile of gunpowder and whiskey to the Indians for safe passage out of the fort. The deal was deemed not only unwise, but extremely dangerous to all whites in the area. Pressed by his subordinates to consider the error of his judgement, Captain Heald agreed to order all gunpowder, weapons, and whiskey destroyed. Unfortunately, the savages witnessed the secretive event and were quite angered.

"And so it was with false hearts that the red skins went on appearing agreeable to providing safe passage for the soldiers and their families. In fear of the situation, inhabitants living outside the fort having no wish to be left behind also joined the garrison for a planned retreat to Fort Wayne, in Indiana.

"The garrison of over fifty soldiers, their wives and children, along with the procession of civilian families were betrayed one and all by their Potawatomi guides and subsequently attacked in the open about two miles south of the fort. The result was a vicious slaughter. And as for Fort Dearborn—it was burned to the ground the following day."

"I can't imagine such a thing," blurted Rachel. "I haven' the wit to contemplate such horror. What possesses the Indians to act in such fashion?"

Rachel didn't wait for the answer. She suddenly dropped her eyes to the floor. I saw Caleb glance quickly her way. The room went silent. It must be said that irrespective of my feelings about Rachel and Caleb, they were introduced as my servants. I made every effort to keep them at my side so they might share in any comfort offered me. Of course, they would never be treated equally and they had little choice but to attend me in order to continue with the ruse.

The situation made me uncomfortable. In private, Rachel and Caleb assured me that they were in favor of this arrangement but for the protection it offered. At least by my side, I knew them to be in warm and dry quarters and well fed. I insisted on these things in their behalf as was my right.

I had no doubt that one of the reasons Lt. Davison never questioned my credentials was because of the impeccable service given me by Rachel and Caleb. Their refinement was evident, and the lieutenant understood that such service could be afforded only by the affluent. He was a man from the south and appreciated such things. As if to do me favor, he reinforced the fact of their slavery and sent a not so subtle warning their way.

"They are barbarians and the reasons are many," answered Lt. Davison. "Suffice it to say, should you run off foolishly, you will be numbered among the murdered."

There was brief silence in which the message was understood by all. "I assure you, Lt. Davison, my Rachel and Caleb are far too intelligent to run off foolishly. They have stood fast at my side for more years than I can count. I trust them implicitly." I looked at the two of them and smiled so all might believe the pleasure I gained by their presence.

Points being made, we then resumed our discussion of the massacre, but my hosts fell into disagreement about how many had died that fateful day.

"If my memory serves me correct, seventy or eighty were slaughtered, said Lt. Davison."

"I beg to differ sir," said one Daniel Clay, a militia man. "Folks that survived claimed nearly one hundred and fifty were butchered. They killed off all the children, most all the women and settlers. It was done in terrible fashion, grizzly it was, Mrs. Claussen. Those folks that surrendered were taken as slaves for ransom. Every last one of the injured was scalped dead or alive, their hairpieces taken to the bloody British and turned in for reward."

"I think that will do, Mr. Clay. Mrs. Claussen has no need to be affronted by your colorful but heinous details."

"Beggin' your pardon, ma'am."

"I thank you for your consideration, Lt. Davison; however, I am fine, Mr. Clay. I have heard many similar stories while in Detroit."

"I hear the slaughter still goes on." We all turned to look at Raymond Reeves another local militia man. "There's many a person about these parts that swears before God, they have seen ghosts running and screaming silently in the darkness of night. Nobody ventures by that way of a night." There was a moment of eerie silence as we studied one another in the flicker of firelight and contemplated the horror that had passed this way.

I broke the silence. "So tell me, Lt. Davison, the fort was burned to the ground, but here it stands."

"Yes, well as it was, the area was never resettled until well after the British were beaten once and for all. At that point the government saw fit to construct a new fort of wood and masonry in eighteen-sixteen. It was manned by troops until turned over to an Indian agency in eighteen-twenty eight, barely four years ago. And here we are again, manning the post because of renewed Indian hostilities.

"As we speak, I prepare this fort to receive two companies of the Fifth US Infantry and a good many Illinois Militia members. I expect all to begin arriving once winter eases its grip. Times are bad and trouble lies in wait. There will be plenty of blood on the ground before this year's out."

* * *

This news did nothing whatsoever for my peace of mind. It was with a troubled spirit that I called it a night and betook myself to bed. My last thoughts for the day coalesced into a belief that the sooner Rachel, Caleb, Taa, and I entered the safe harbor of St. Louis the better.

I made the best of time and bad weather by seeking out opinions and words of advice from those within or about the fort until mid-February brought the first break in temperatures and a long awaited southern blow.

Lt. Davison and his scouts advised us to head for Fort Clark at Lake Peoria and then on to Beardstown; it being midway down the Illinois River. It was a sizable port first settled about eighteen nineteen and now laid out. The town would possess good stores of supplies and provide a good measure of safety should we have a stay. His advice seemed to be well supported by others who also advised we not delay our departure.

In light of the Indian hostilities, few dared venture along the accommodating high ground of the Sauk trail. Lt. Davison warned us to travel any open ground with the utmost caution even though most Indians were south for the winter. He insisted we accept his offer of escorts to benefit us along either the high trails or through the bottomlands as far as Beardstown.

While seeking opinions and advice, I learned that the Illinois bottomlands were a dismal underworld unto their own. The river was a slow moving body of water that would soon thaw and overflow its banks to become a massive miles wide moving swamp. It was notorious for its ponds, its bayous, bogs, and quicksand. It was reputed to be overrun with wolves and wild beasts, and infested with serpents beyond count. The riverbanks would soon grow thick with vegetation that was dense and impenetrable. One risked cholera, pneumonia and consumption. Malaria would become rampant the whole of its length.

It was a picture worse than winter itself. Rachel and Caleb were fraught with the thought of traveling through such sinister landscape and urged me to heed the lieutenant's warnings and leave at once. I would not be the one to argue and so made arrangements to depart Fort Dearborn before the Mistress of Winter took her leave.

FIFTY-FIVE

Our preparations were well in order by the time we expressed our gratitude for the hospitality and escorts. In return for all done in our behalf, we delighted to carry for Lt. Davison letters and parcels to both Fort Clark and St. Louis.

Under the protection of his escorts and our heavy clothes, we bid Lt. Davison farewell and set out across a dormant field. I withdrew into my coat and scarves, for the damp late-winter wind met us head on and was as of yet a bitterly cold blow.

589

At the onset, we rode west following the bank of the Chicago River until it angled sharply north and left us facing our first miserably fearful looking swamp. It was necessary for us to traverse this forsaken place in order to reach the headwaters of the Des Plaines River. How thankful was I for the advice that prompted us to leave before the thaws of spring brought the melting ice and plagues to bear.

We managed well across the frozen lowland and made our destination without serious complaint, whereupon, we traveled nearly sixty miles along the course of the Des Plaines, home to the Potawatomi, Ottawa, and Chippewa Indians, all of which we had the pleasure not to meet.

Having reached a prominent sandstone landmark known as Mount Joliet, we were greeted by a number of settlers and voyagers who were quick to convey warnings of Indian movements and atrocities. The landmark was named by Louis Joliet, a French Canadian, who at about age twenty, traveled down the Des Plaines in the year sixteen-sixty-five while in search of his brother.

The mound was said to be something of thirteen hundred feet long, two hundred feet wide, sixty feet above the river bank, and 150 feet above the water's surface. It's top was table-flat and served as a place to calculate distances along the river. Mount Joliet was a well known gathering place, and barring harassment by Indians; it had all the makings of becoming a settlement in the near future.

With warnings of numerous Indian sightings taken to heart, we departed Mount Joliet and continued on within view of steep banks and cliffs that oftentimes closed in to form a narrow valley. The valley served to cradle the watercourse until forced back and away by the Kankakee as it made its appearance from the south. The convergence of these two rivers occurred in a vast lowland to form the headwaters of the Illinois.

Strengthened by the increased flow, the Illinois reentered that same steep and narrow valley for another fifty or sixty miles before turning southward to break free of the banks and spread out onto the plains. We were told that the river came to a standstill on that plain and simply spread out in all directions. It was supposedly impossible to discern the edge of the river from the edge of the earth.

In other words, a well defined river of about one quarter mile in width lost itself in a swamp reminiscent of the infamous Black Swamp and the endless marshes of the Kankakee. It was an unwelcome world, a place given to conjuring up quicksand and stories of the most ghastly kind.

The talk of Indians by the settlers at Mount Joliet convinced our escorts to climb out of the river valley. They believed it too early to be hearing stories of Indians in this area unless some had wintered over. It was rare, but if true, they would stay in the bottomlands where food was plentiful and protection from the winds far better than anything to be found on frozen trails crossing the high ground.

Bowing to their experience, we were removed from the river while at the union of the Des Plaines and Kankakee to strike out upon a shorter route across the plain. One only needed to look about briefly after emerging from the bottomlands to determine that Illinois was indeed a prairie state. These views were my first glimpses of what a treeless land would present.

Tall grass clearings might cover five or fifty square miles of earth with nothing but the sun of day and shadow of night falling upon their spaces. The oak clearings of Michigan were laughable in comparison. Only the river valleys remained faithfully forested to provide shelter from the winds and distant Indian eyes.

Stands of hardwoods would occasionally escape the river's valley and reach randomly into the golden grassy remnants of summer's season past. Except for these probing fingers of timber and scattered copses, the land was exposed to the universe. Across these featureless snow-covered plains, we quickly lost sight of the wooded watercourse I had thought to follow toward the Mississippi.

We camped on the trail for four days covering about eighty miles. It brought us back to a place where the Illinois River had opened into a large body of water some one or two miles wide. Some called it Lake Peoria, others called it Lake Illinois. We stopped briefly at a small settlement on the east shore called Little Prairie and made arrangements for ferry passage to the opposite shore. This settlement was near the south end of the lake and almost directly across the river from Fort Clark and the town of Peoria.

Fort Clark, long abandoned, was now undergoing refurbishments. Concerns over the increasing number of Indians moving through the area after crossing the Mississippi for the purpose of mischief had prompted the settlers to reinforce the old fort which was originally built for the war of eighteen-twelve. We delivered the first of our parcels to the officer in charge and remained in a nearby inn for the night. It was my first opportunity to bathe since leaving Fort Dearborn.

Whether one called the body of water Lake Peoria or Lake Illinois, it was expansive and from here the river was said to be navigable to the Mississippi. The watercourse was a centuries old route, with flat boats regularly plying their trade up and down, to and from, St. Louis.

The first steamboats made it to this port about three years back in eighteen twenty-nine. The trip could take as long as two or three months depending on water conditions, even so, steamboats were now testing waters farther upstream. And for good reason, this was the best place to build trade between St. Louis and Chicago. I was amazed to learn Chicago was actually closer to the Mississippi than any place of significance on the great lakes.

Peoria was still often called Fort Clark. It was the oldest settlement in Illinois. Joliet, wishing to pursue the rumors of the 'Mississippi' as the Indians called the great waterway, continued his trek down the Illinois River and passed through this place.

It was inhabited by a tribe of the Illiniwek Indians called the Peoria, which means 'Prairie Fire that Wanders About'. Ironically, the tribe moved about very little preferring to enjoy the bountiful supply of sustenance within the valley.

In sixteen and eighty, Robert Cavalier, Sieur de la Salle, Father Louis Hennepin, Henry de Tonti, and about thirty others paddled down the Illinois and erected Fort Creve Coeur on the southeast bank of the river just below the lake but soon abandoned it.

Meanwhile, Henri de Tonti earned the friendship of the Illiniwek and was persuaded by the chiefs in sixteen ninety-one to move a fort he had built upriver as a base for fur trading. The fort stood atop a sandstone tower called Starved Rock. Following their advice, he reconstructed his fort on the west shore of a much better location called "Pimiteoui", which meant 'fat lake'. He called his new structure Fort Pimiteoui. It became the first permanent village in the state.

France gave up the territory to Britain in seventeen sixty-three. British rule was not to last and lost out to the conquest of George Rogers Clark in seventeen seventy-eight. Peoria was governed thereafter under the American flag by Virginia, then the Northwest Territory, then Indiana, and finally Illinois when it attained statehood in eighteen-eighteen. Since the construction of a fort in eighteen and thirteen, the village was called Fort Clark. In eighteen and twenty-five if was officially renamed Peoria after the Indians that called this place their home.

A short distance south of Peoria, our escorts led us to the first for hire ferry across the Illinois River. It was operated by one William Clarke at the settlement of Pekin. The river narrowed at this place and made for a good place to return to the east shore where stood this settlement. The first steamboat docked here in eighteen and twenty-eight and so too was the first store established.

Setting foot ashore, I spied a vibrant village, two more stores, a hotel with tavern licensed to sell liquor, and finally to my pleasant surprise—a schoolhouse. Folks said it was founded just a year before. It was called Snell School. My joy was tempered only by talk of fortifying the structure to make it more fort-like.

We departed Pekin to head south on a trail that stayed close to the river. It would take us to Beardstown, but not before putting some seventy miles of swampland behind us. Aside from the fear of Indians, *or* breaking through swamp ice, *or* being devoured by roving wolves, *or* winter chills, *or* whatever else one could imagine, there proved little else of which to worry and so Taa'sooma'hane resumed riding out ahead as was his nature. Our escorts rode somewhere in-between.

The day was without wind and profited from a clear sky and proud sun. Our scarves were loosened and Caleb, Rachel, and I were left to talk freely in privacy about whatever took our fancy. The topic this day was of Rachel and Caleb, and their future. We had been given many miles to work it out.

"An orphanage?" Rachel stared down at her hands. She gripped the rein as we plodded along swaying back and forth to the step of the horses. "I don' know anythin' 'bout orphanages."

I laughed.

"Hwat's so funny?" asked Rachel.

"I was just thinking of Dorrie's reaction when I proposed she start a school. She expressed exactly the same sentiment."

"I was thinkin' I might get work as a cook. Now, that I can do."

"And I agree, but I fear you may forever face the worry of slave catchers and kidnappers. I propose that you and Caleb should become so highly visible and respected for your work in the community that no one would dare question your free state." Caleb grimaced openly. Rachel studied his expression and looked back at me with concern. She was worried I might have taken offense to his visual contradiction. Meanwhile, Caleb went on to speak his mind.

"I don' know, Miss Elizabeth. When hwite folk are of a mind to run you out o' town, that's pretty much hwere you're headed, like it or not. You might get tarred an' feathered an' live to tell 'bout it, or you might get dragged down the street on the end of a rope an' never utter another sound. Hwites don' take kindly to black folk movin' up from the fields—ain't our place. We'd be gettin' all too uppity. At least here in upper Illinois, we are in free counties. Rachel can find work tendin' and mendin', an' the same goes for me."

"Again, I agree. That is true most of the time. However, remember you would both be connected to Claussen and very few people would dare question his judgment and good name. Besides, it would be difficult to run out the overseers of an orphanage. Who would take care of the children? Would they just turn all those little thieves out onto the street? How many generous souls might you find to take in so many hellions? They are most assuredly brats, each and every one, but who else would step forward and put up funds sufficient to keep the children fed and clothed? I doubt there are few if any. Fact is, as long as I fund it and you two run it, I believe St. Louis will come to accept all of us and the orphanage with open arms and support."

"I don' know, Miss Elizabeth," Caleb repeated, still full of doubt. He shook his head with unease. "The world seen through your eyes is very much different than the world we see. It sounds good, hwen you say it. But, you can walk down the street with a young hwite girl without givin' it a thought. As God is great, I would get myself lynched for doin' something that foolish. A black man don' even look at a hwite woman or a hwite orphan girl *for any reason*, let alone walk down the street with one. You will never change these things, Miss Elizabeth. You mean well, but you don' understand. You can never understand. We live in an entirely different world."

"What is it you wish to do, Caleb? You tell me."

"Honestly, Miss Elizabeth, I have no idea."

"Do you feel the same way, Rachel?"

Rachel shrugged her shoulders. "We live in fear, Miss Elizabeth. I agree with Caleb hwen he says that you can never understand. Fear governs our every move, our every breath. It onliest takes one wrong word, one wrong look after a lifetime of righteous livin' to wind up swingin' on the end of a rope. We know you mean well. We know better than any, an' I will do as you wish, but I understand Caleb in my heart. He speaks the truth."

"Well, we still have time to think this out. You decide what it is you wish to do and know I will support you in every way. Otherwise, I will encourage you to pursue the orphanage with the promise I will remain in St. Louis for however long it takes for the two of you to become accepted."

FIFTY-SIX

The population of Illinois was moving upward from the Ohio and Wabash River Valleys, and northeastward from the Mississippi along the Illinois. It was for this reason that the farther we traveled downstream the more populous became the country. Americans were overrunning the land and because of it we seldom slept out of doors, but instead enjoyed basic shelter and the hospitality of numerous river towns most of which were outgrowths of ferry crossings. It was thus until our arrival in Beardstown.

In spite of the river being frozen and a lack of vessels plying their trade, Beardstown felt like a return to civilization. The cruelty of the north country was now diminished. Here was a place full of people, a place that presented the warmth and atmosphere of a town. True, the inhabitants had to fight this frightful winter, but they appeared wholly capable of overcoming its wrath.

We spent two days in Beardstown, taking time to rest, bathe, and enjoy the amenities. Caleb paid particular attention to the village folk and surroundings. He liked what he saw. The area wasn't overcrowded, yet there was plenty of work to be had. There were a number of inns, temporarily vacant, that stood to speak of summer traffic and the amount of business that would be realized once the river opened.

We took shelter in one of these inns, a small cabin with a number of holes bored into the logs that made up the walls. Poles protruded horizontally outward from the holes and were supported at the ends by posts standing upright off the earth. Across the poles were boards laid flat to make beds. In the nicer inns, a bag of goose feathers was laid across the boards and made for a supremely comfortable night's sleep.

Dinner fare was agreeable. Fish and fowl were plentiful, as were venison and wild game. Pork was especially plentiful as it was raised here in great numbers. It was said the animals took naturally to the prairies. Hogs were slaughtered and traded to the south in return for wheat and corn which was not to be found growing in the northern counties.

On our second day in Beardstown, we bid our escorts good-bye as planned and from there went our separate ways. We traveled south another fifty miles and arrived at the bustling community of Carrollton. This village was laid out back in eighteen and twenty and was well established. I was most impressed by the nearly completed courthouse, which I am certain had to be one of the nicest edifices in the state. It was obvious by the signs of civilization that we were moving closer to St. Louis.

I am grateful to say that the remainder of our journey through Illinois proved to be uneventful causing us no regret in parting with our protection. Fate spared us both wild Indian and animal, and that could only be considered a blessing. We spent our final days following Taa'sooma'hane south along the Illinois, sometimes through wood, sometimes across prairie, and sometimes sand as we closed in on the Mississippi. We also closed out the month of February and left it to memory along with the thick slabs of Lake Michigan ice and shores doomed to be chilled for weeks to come.

March fell into place with spring thaws and the first signs of life. The woodlands towered over those tiny but hardy herbs with heartening flecks of cheery petals peeking through disappearing islands of snow that bordered our softening path.

The sun was working its way down to the forest floor and encouraging the dainty pastels and whites of Spring Beauty, Bloodroot, Rue Anemone and upside down Trout Lilies to play peek-a-boo amid the miniature trees of Dogwood, Black Locust, and Wild Plum. Below Woodland Violets, fens were filling with warm water, yellow Marsh Marigolds, and cream colored Indigo. Wild Blue Iris, Golden Alexanders, Fringed Loosestrife and mint were to be seen sprouting everywhere across the marshes and moistening earth.

Away from the shadows of the forest, open spaces absorbed the spring sun's warmth and energy unencumbered. Disappearing snows left unsupported the skeletal grasses that now lay fallen and spread like damp soiled hay across a horse's stable. Through this thick matting arose a myriad of pretty violets, Milkweed, fluffy Pussytoes, Black Medic, and Pasqueflowers with petals that reminded me of nests of newly hatched chicks stretching upward with beaks wide open.

To be sure, there now appeared a few of those annoying insects that buzzed and swirled about the face, flying in dizzying circles and taunting us to swat the air in vain. And yet, they proved no match for the streak of beaks that snatched them up as hungry birds flitted back and forth in right angles to avert the trees. Here were the first signs of wood birds large and small, warblers, chirpers, and rowdy woodpeckers hammering away to end winter's silence. At risk of being left behind, the hard-headed tappers hastily pried up bark and perforated one tree after another while rushing past to keep up with spring's migration to the northlands.

Beyond the woods, in the western sky, collections of red capped cranes and geese counted by the millions rode the warm winds above the awakening sound of running water. Creeks were set loose by spring to find the same river which was now leading us to the banks of the Mississippi. We arrived together, flanking winter's residue of floating slush that the Illinois now vomited into the greater watercourse to be washed away downstream.

It was at this confluence that we surrendered our souls with trepidation and questionable judgment to the local Indians, who we employed to remove us by canoe to the western shore. The large ferries were pinned to their shores by floes of ice that moved to crush them. The watercourse looked woefully danger-ous, and I would have much preferred to backtrack around the earth in the opposite direction rather than cross this river in a hollowed out tree trunk. Instead, upon payment, we three were seated. Rachel and I sat side-by-side, legs straight out and hands locked onto the sides of a pirogue with the grip of death. In this frame of mind, we shoved off downstream to fall in with the threatening packs of ice.

The Indians paddled furiously then floated, paddled then floated, back and forth working their way through the maze of floating debris. We dodged and darted, raced and retreated. We bounced off bobbing obstacles that seemed bent to block any chance of reaching one shore from the other. We were often entirely surrounded by these large frozen chunks, which I observed to be heavily embedded with branches, leaves and rubble. So doubtful was I of our chances in the hollow log that my fears would have prevented me from noticing the passing of Missouri's mouth on the right bank had it not been for the river's icy belch of additional debris.

Nothing more than luck of the draw kept us from being crushed at any given moment. For twenty miles we were swept downstream, lost to our fate in the middle of a mile wide current now impossibly crowded with winter's leftovers. Only by the grace of God were we not added to the collection of rubble, but instead delivered to the wharfs of St. Louis dry and safe albeit mightily stressed and in need of a nap.

FIFTY-SEVEN

I was eager to enter into my diary that I had set foot on the shore of St. Louis, if for reason no other than to say I stood in another of those border places where story and myth were bred to run rampant through the gut of our country. Albany and Detroit in the north, Boston, New York, Savannah in the east, New Orleans in the South, all extents that marked the reach of our nation's spirit.

When it came to the final front, the frontier west, the *far west*, the west beyond the Appalachians that was little more than a wonder in one's mind, then the teller of tales could only be St. Louis. To an easterner, discussing St. Louis was like conversing about the dark side of the moon. It was the last outpost. It was *theee* place to capture one's imagination especially since the explorations of Lewis and Clark at the turn of the century.

St. Louis was always a place of refuge for those explorers driven to discover something of worth within the boundless spaces beyond the Mississippi. It was a favored location to regain contact with the civilized world. It was a geographical hub for traders, voyageurs and engages, who traveled by water to connect places as distant apart as New Orleans at the mouth of the Mississippi with its wharfs and seafaring ships, to the remote furring posts about the Great Lakes, Sault Ste. Marie, St. Lawrence and beyond.

From the southwest, by way of desert trails that struck out across the great expanses came those Mexican greasers, those Spanish merchants from Santa Fe and Chihuahua. Once or

600

twice a year, wearing large sombreros and carrying short brass shotguns, they rode guard alongside two wheeled carts hauling oaken casks filled with thousands upon thousands of large Mexican dollars ready to be spilled for the fineries that could only be found in St. Louis. After enduring the eight hundred mile trek, the rough looking troupe belied the civility and gentle character of their kind.

To the east, St. Louis called upon the shipyards at Jefferson and Elizabethtown to design and build vessels able to withstand the rigors of the Missouri. These vessels were much improved over earlier designs from the east coast that called for putting engines in the hold and ended up too deep-hulled for the shallows of inland waterways. Engines and boilers came from the machine shops of Louisville, Brownstown and Cincinnati.

There was always room for improvement, for unlike the more predictable waters of the Ohio and Mississippi, designers, builders and pilots had yet to unlock secrets of the Missouri. Much like the wild stallions seen running along its shore, the river refused to be tamed and so battled every intruder with its trickeries, twisted meanderings and mean spirit.

The old French settlement of St. Louis was incorporated as a town in eighteen and nine and now challenged both Albany and New York in matters of trade and significance. This bustling river town was not only nestled at the convergence of three great rivers, three centuries old routes of travel, but it also pressed the very edge of discovery. Beyond St. Louis lay only a great void, an empty treeless desert, a place of dangerous temptation for the curious, the unwary, and feeble-minded. It was said to be the land of lost biblical tribes, mountains of salt, prehistoric monsters, and of course last but not least; the land of Christopher Claussen.

The boldness of this land bled into the city itself, and if I had to evaluate the crowds about St. Louis by instinct, I would say that when it came to a communal sense of destiny and unfettered determination to move forward, these wayward souls were unsurpassed.

I felt as though every one of these foolhardy folks had arrived in the same manner as me. We came without invitation or direction, without any plan other than to face a final journey— one of unparalleled idiocy. That is to say, we aimed to press ahead along paths unproven for distances undetermined, all the while blinded by ambitions and goals to reach places that existed only in our dreams. To our discredit we were fueled by good senses gone afoul. Destination was clearly too powerful a term for those distant places unrecognized as mere mental mirages.

My impressions were far removed from those of Rachel, for she was searching for signs of another kind. She was looking for expressions that said nothing of dreams or discovery. She was searching for the unmistakable stare of hatred, poisonous eyes, frightful eyes that sought out the color of her skin like wolves sniffing air for the scent of blood.

"Hwat do you think, Miss Elizabeth?" Rachel asked with reserved excitement.

"It's not my decision to make, but yours." I responded.

"I like the looks of the place. I feel we could fit here. People don' seem to stare; they don' even know we are alive. I can' believe the difference from one place to another." She sighed with wonder. "Look at all these people, there's Africans, Indians, Creoles, French, Germans, Spanish, English—."

"Southerners," said Caleb.

"…Southerners," repeated Rachel after a pause, "*Northerners* as well, an' Easterners. Even the animals run freely. It's just like New York in that way, an' that I love. Don' you Caleb?" She turned to him. Caleb was wary and took a deep breath.

"Oh, I don' know, Rachel. No matter hwat you say this isn't New York. This is a slave state, no different than Virginee, but…." He looked over his shoulder. "New York was a free state an' hwere did that get us? I guess I felt safest back across the river in Illinois territory. I liked Beardstown, but I have no idea hwat we would do there. As long as Miss Elizabeth is offerin' to help us, I am willin' to stay an' work hard to make somethin' of St. Louis an' the orphanage, but if it wasn' for Miss Elizabeth, I would have been long since headed for Canada. I'll leave the decision to the two of you. Hwatever you think best."

I offered my encouragement and honest feelings. "I think it has the makings of a fine home, Caleb. I think an orphanage will provide you and Rachel with a secure framework to live in peace. I urge you to give it a try."

"I do too," said Rachel. "I think maybe we should stay, Caleb. This is a good place. I can feel it. Tell me we can stay. Tell me you won' mind if we give the orphanage a try. Miss Elizabeth is our best chance, Caleb. We can always cross back over the river. Surely, you see the truth of that."

"I'm in no position to disagree, Rachel. Don' worry about me. I can make do. I always make do. It's onliest about hwat makes you happy. It's about hwat is safest for you. If this is hwat you want then we stay. It's as simple as that."

"Oh, thank-you." Rachel squeezed Caleb's hands within hers.

She turned to me. "Hwat should we do next, Miss Elizabeth?"

"Well, let's stay the course, at least until the weather warms. We have comfortable rooms at the Planter's, we are settled in, and I am prepared to begin business at first opportunity.

"You and Caleb should walk the city, learn its streets and acquire a taste for your new home. At the same time, search for a suitable building to house the orphanage. Take note of those places far enough out of harm's way to accommodate us with reasonable rent and safety; yet close enough for the children to find work and earn money. And for the sake of us all, I beg you keep clear of the warehouses down by the levee. The smell of those hides is more than I can stand. Aside from that, I will leave you to your own devices.

"I'll be plenty busy presenting my letters of introduction, paying calls to announce our intentions, and laying the ground-work for solicitations. I'll need some time to arrange meetings with the leaders of their local charities and the ministers. I'll need to visit the bank, open our accounts and start the transfer of funds. We all have plenty to do, and Rachel—" I looked square into her eyes. "I believe we should begin our search for Isaac."

Just the mention of Isaac's name wiped all the glory off Rachel's face. She barely recovered from the sound of it. She nodded with an expression of shame, looking guilt ridden as though to feel happy for even a fleeting moment was sinful in the absence of her son. Caleb placed his arm around her shoulders and drew her in tight for support. He kissed her lightly on the brow. I knew eventually the boy would be located, and I did my best to reassure both her and Caleb.

"Money talks, Rachel, and Christopher's money screams. Believe what I say, for I have been witness to his influence the whole of my life. We will pretend Isaac to have been lost in our travels, and I will put out a reward for his safe and healthy return, a reward that will be too high to ignore. This time the slave traders and dealers will be used to our benefit, trust me. He will come home both fat and sassy."

"Caleb an' I will never be able to thank you. We will forever be indebted."

"You owe me nothing, Rachel, not now, not ever. You must understand that. By comparison, I am penniless and only a channel for someone else's generosity. Thank the Lord for giving us Mr. Claussen."

FIFTY-EIGHT

"Madame Claussen."

The clerk tilted his head to acknowledge me. He swept his hand with a flamboyance that prompted me to give up the comfort of my chair and follow him directly. He led me down a corridor cut short by a splendid set of expertly worked cherry doors that nearly reached the ceiling. The man twisted one of the bright brass knobs then stepped aside to allow my entry.

As I passed by the clerk and moved into a well-appointed space, I heard the door gently latch behind me. The office was very professional, a financier's room in every way and much like something I might find back east. Its occupant, a man of stature who was immaculately groomed, arose from behind an expensive desk. It was also made of cherry and worked in the same fashion as the office doors. Both the gentleman and his amenities exuded success through tasteful harmony and refinement. He followed his smile and came around to greet me.

"Madame Clows-sain." He extended his hand for mine. He leaned over and kissed it respectfully.

"Mr. Ledoux." I responded as I half-curtsied.

"Please, call me Franqua. I een-sist."

"Francois, it is then." The man was impeccably dressed and fragrant beyond his air of accomplishment. He took my coat and then ushered me across a luxurious Persian carpet laid beneath two beautifully crafted chairs.

"My word, sir. You are indeed a master of good taste. This furniture is exquisite and I am all but ashamed to sit upon such a piece."

"Oh! I *am* smeet-teen, an eentelligent soul weet' zee eye ov' an arteest. Sank you fair noti-ceen'," he responded. "Most peo-pell would nawt 'ave a clue. I 'ad bos shairs eempor-ted from France an' 'ave lived evair seence een fear ov unsheat'd

605

knives, brass but-tawns, an' belt buckluhs. Zee shairs are tawtal-lee eempractical, but I assure you zat zese shair was designed especial-lee fair a bottom sush as yours. Know eet rises to zee occa-shawn."

I looked at the man rather unsure of how to take his comment.

"I give you a complee-ment, madame."

"You make me blush, sir."

"So I 'ave. I must say I find your bloosh eentoxica-teen'. I 'ave won a small fortune wagair-reen' zat Frensh women are zee most beautiful een dee wairl', but I see now t'at I 'ave been fooleesh."

"You also seem a master of compliments."

"As are you a mas-tair ov men's 'earts to be cairtain. Please, seat yourself weet'out worry an' accept my 'ospeetali-tee. May I offair you someseen'? I 'ave coffee, tea, a fine rum an' meelk, or would you prefair someseen' fruity an' refresh-een'? I 'ave a splain-deed laymonade."

"Lemonade sounds perfect, thank-you."

Rather than summon a clerk, he served me himself. For the first time ever, as I watched the man take a seat in the matching chair alongside, I regretted my lifelong aversion to learning French. The two of us now sat before his desk. I was secure in my place, yet felt uneasy before his confident eyes, this for the way in which he studied me. I hesitated to strike up a conversation, sensing there was something the man felt compelled to put forth and of course there was.

"I must tell you, Madame, I am ama-zed zat anyone coul' keep sush beauty a se-crait. Whaireas, I woul d'ave deman-ded dat all ov hea-ven an' earts gaze upawn sush a pairfect crea-ture, Mr. Clows-sain men-shawned nosseen', nosseen' whatso-evair ov being a married man...."

The comment caught me completely off guard and I choked on my lemonade, which caused my host fair concern.

"Are you all right, Madame?"

"No, no!" I dismissed his concern with a wave of my hand, while the tart drink burned in my lungs.

"Ese eet too sour?"

"Yes, no." I gasped in an effort to catch my breath and speak. "You are—mistaken, or no, not mistaken, I didn't—mean to put it that way. I mean you are—correct, no—not correct, I mean...." I raised my hand to halt the verbal confusion and unscramble my nervous thoughts while I endeavored to clear my throat. "Let me attempt this one more time, I beg." It took several attempts to clear my lungs, regain my breath, and my composure. "What I meant to say, sir, is *no*, the lemonade is not too sour, *yes*, I am all right and *no*, indeed Mr. Claussen is not a married man. He is single as you supposed, a widower to be more precise." *Or so I hope*; I thought to myself.

"Zen I must beg you fairgive me my faux pas. I 'eard zee name an' was so taken by your pre-sence, I natural-lee assumed you to be nosseen' less dan zee absolute zjoy ov Mr. Clows-sain, a flaowless woman fair a man who 'as evairy-seen'. Yet, I freely admeet zat eef I am to make a mee-stake, zen zis ese surely a pairfect one. I feel vairy goot about bein' wrong."

Again, I blushed. The man was exceedingly flirtatious, but witty, appropriately respectful and sensible enough to be genuinely charming. I enjoyed him at once—what woman wouldn't. Who else would make me feel worthy of adulation? It was a sinful indulgence, a vanity I struggled to suppress. I sidestepped my conscience in order to avoid explaining—*this indulgence that only a spinster would understand.*

"I am his charge, his ward. A daughter by arrangement."

"Daugh-tair?"

"Adoption best describes it."

"Ah, *an adopted daugh-tair*. Steell—a powair to be reckoned wees I am cair-tain, fair you carry yourself most assured-lee. Tell me, as I 'ave already blundaired badly, eez eet Madame or Mademoiselle? Are you bound by mar-riage or nawt?"

"No, sir, I am not. And so you know, it embarrasses me that I should even answer such a question; it being unladylike and not a matter for your concern."

"Ov course. Ov course. Eendeed, you are correct, an' again zee fault ees mine. Not only 'ave I been fool-leesh, but rude as well, an' I apolo-gize. Yet, een spite ov all my mee-stakes, I feel dis might be a day ov goot for-tune. So, tell me, Madamoiselle Clows-sain, what breengs you to grace us wees your pre-sence. Ese zere someseen' I may do fair you to make up fair my ill man-nair? I pray you weell say yes. Please, do."

"Yes."

"Wondair-ful! Put me to zee test so I might repent."

"Two things, Mr. Ledoux—."

"Franqua," he corrected me. "Ask anyseen'."

"*Francois*," I repeated. "I am of a mind to establish a home for orphans here in St. Louis. It is a task in which I am well versed. I have with me two trusted freepersons, one Rachel and Caleb Cook, who will be running affairs during my times away, which could prove lengthy. Trust they both read and write fluently as is required of their standing.

"I have come to ask for your assistance in transferring ten thousand dollars into an account under my name with full access given to the Cooks for the purpose of withdrawals as they see fit. These monies will be used to fund the opening of the orphanage, to cover expenses and provide for their wages as well.

"I am in need of an advance until the funds arrive from Boston, and I am happy to give you whatever information you require to allay suspicions regarding my integrity. I present you now with these letters of introduction, which I trust you will find adequate, or if not, I would be happy to send for whatever public or private introduction from Boston that suits you.

"Of course you may contact Mr. Claussen directly, as it is he who ultimately covers my expenses. I work in his behalf to ease the plight of the poor and often handle large sums of money in his name. He is a very generous man in every manner save one— *the pen*. And because of this, his one and only shortcoming, I have requested to see you individually. You see, Mr. Ledoux, I am in fact searching for Mr. Claussen.

"I am distressed to say that Mr. Claussen departed Boston some years back to explore opportunities in the West, but never returned. Understand, I was fully forewarned by Mr. Claussen of this possibility along with the dangers he would face and the difficulties of keeping in touch; but I never assumed him to mean a scant dozen posts per decade. I've been left with little choice other than to travel the frontier myself should I ever hope to alleviate my concerns about his health and well-being. You might imagine how I could wring his neck for being so inconsiderate of my feelings."

"Ov course, 'ow could one not undair-stand? I am embarrassed fair Mr. Clows-sain. Mebbee, 'e ese looseen' 'is min', no?" Mr. Ledoux feigned indignance.

"I entertained ideas of finding him here in St. Louis although I am learning well the folly of such fantasies. I have called upon you, Mr. Ledoux, *Francois*, because of your reputation as a prominent financier. I know very few bankers or financiers who aren't connected to Mr. Claussen in one manner or another. I am told you know something of this man, and I pray, should you know something of his whereabouts, you would share such news with me and thereby hasten my efforts."

After listening with intent, Mr. Ledoux raised his eyebrows and let out a deep breath. "Hmm." He placed his cup back on the saucer. "I undair-stand your plight plain enough, mademoiselle, but ov all you might ask; you peeck zee impossee-bluh.

609

"Let me say ferst, een regard to zee trans-fair ov funds, considair eet done. Your lettairs are impecca-bluh, an' I believe myself an excellent judge ov charac-tair. I am happy to a-seest you. I weell forward you at once two sousand dollars een good fais. I also eemplore you to approash me at a latair date to discuss a donation toward your orphanage een behalf ov zee bank, zis fair zee good ov zee communi-tee. Eet ese dee type ov gesture zat offsets zee notion we bankairs are all blood-suck-een' money mon-gairs. I woul'd like to associate my name wees your cause.

"I might also add zat Bishop Rosati ese a close friend an' stands as one ov zee kindest spirits to be found anywhaire een zee ouest. Eash ov 'is accompleesh-ments seems miraculous an' you weell find 'is sair-veece invalua-bluh eef you weesh to realize your ambi-shawns. We 'ave a say-een' een St. Louis zat eef zee Bishop turns 'is eyes toward you, zee Almighty turns 'is 'ead.

"As fair Mr. Clows-sain—zat mat-tair ese nawt so ea-see. You are correct een assum-een' I might deal wees 'im. Een fact, I do deal wees 'im. I ovairsee 'is ouestairn accounts. Zey are numairous, an' een most cases siza-bluh to say zee least. E owns a boatyard 'aire een St. Louis. E also dabbles een min-neen' an' transporta-shawn. E ese heavily involved een zee peltry trade an' owns a numbair ov warehou-ses an' consairns fair keepeen' hides, processeen', an' workeen' leathair. E also 'as an insatia-bluh appetite fair land. I believe Mr. Clows-sain 'as a penshant fair railroads, but let us say fair now dat zis ese mere speculat-shawn. Fact would be 'e's intair-rests are varied; 'e ese an active man, an' I employ extra staff to maintain 'ees books, but een all honesty, 'ees books are zee only seen' ov 'im I see.

"I accept your comment about 'is genairosi-tee. Zere ese a zjoke ov sorts among zee local mairshant-men zat eef you want to meet Mr. Clows-sain, you must first find an orphan's addraiss an' feed zee shild in return fair an account ov zee man's wandair-reen's.

610

"Zee zjoke means many seen's to diffair-rent peo-pell. On zee one 'and 'e can nev-vair be foun', orphans 'ave no addraiss. On zee ossair 'and, evairybo-dee een zee street knows ov 'im, from zee powairful to zee painniless. I doubt 'e deals wees zee local mairshants pairsonal-lee, but oddly enough zere does seem to be a connect-shawn wees zee ur-shins.

"We are no diffairent zan any osair communi-tee. Shildren collect een St. Louis to beg an' steal. Waifs an' strays, zeir numbair can be foun' milleen' about zee levee. I 'ave often been told ov 'ow zese orphans lingair at ri-vair's edge een hopes ov meeteen' Mr. Clows-sain, believ-een' 'e will keep a promise to return at some point een time bear-reen' gifts.

"You know 'ow shildren can be. Zey get ideas een zeir 'eads an' pass zem on one to anos-sair like a cold. Troos be known, I've 'eard e's actually done eet a coupluh times, but regard-less, e's won zeir 'earts ov-air an' eef you listen to zee way zey tell eet, you'd swear zee man ees a god." Mr. Ledoux halted his conversation and a look of apprehension crossed his face. With sheepish reservation, he addressed me.

"Mademoiselle, speakeen' as a gentle-man who means you no offainse; might I ask your company zis aftairnoon fair din-nair. I say frankly, I am uttairly astonished zat a woman obviously accustomed to zee com-fawrts an' finair seen's een life 'as taken eet upon hairself to face zee pairils ov a journey to zee far ouest. An' wees-out an escawrt; eet ese a wondair to behold.

"I weesh to know more about you. In return, I promeese a fine meal, aftair a leisure-lee walk srough our cit-ee dur-reen' wheesh time I shall reveal all I know about zee activities ov Mr. Clows-sain een St. Louis. Zey are many an, maybe you weell find some parteecular seen' 'elpful. We might even speak wees some ov zee shildren as dey do go on about him an' zere ese genairal-lee some mairit een what zey say."

611

To see Mr. Ledoux tread lightly amused me, and I delighted in not answering him immediately. I chose instead to continue our conversation about Christopher.

"No offense taken, Francois. I must say I am happy to hear the years haven't changed Christopher's character. He has been fond of children as far back as I can remember. I recall during his days aboard the REBECCA, how he never put into port without at least one crate of gifts chocked in the hold. The children would stand waiting at the plank restless and impatient, excited not only for the gifts, but also in hopes of seeing his person.

"I would watch him lean against the gunwales for hours of an afternoon flipping coins to whomever could make the funniest face, run the fastest, dance the best or yell the loudest, anything that gave him an excuse to put a pittance into their pocket and raise spirits. He always used children to run his errands for pay. At times I might see twenty or thirty swarming about him hoping for handouts. Whereas most men were surely annoyed, presuming to be pressed for time, Mr. Claussen never seemed to be bothered. You would be astonished to know how many children he has helped with a heart."

"Eet sounds to be een zee sou-sands."

"A number not beyond reason. I often considered how certain it must be that those children, strangers in all, should go through life remembering to their offspring his good name and compassion. He must be unreservedly famous in his own right. They may never remember by what names we called our presidents and generals, but they will surely recall Christopher Claussen and his vermilion ship REBECCA till the day they die."

Mr. Ledoux said nothing further and merely sat back with his chin in hand looking at me with a most amused expression.

"What? Why do you grin? Have I said something to warrant such a look, or are you merely impatient for my answer to your question about dinner?" I felt the depth of his gaze. He chuckled.

612

"You are a sensational woman, Mademoiselle Clows-sain. Clearly, I am impa-tient. And yet, I was sinkeen' 'ow fortu-nate a man must be to 'ave not only a daughtair, but a *disciple*."

FIFTY-NINE

Mr. Ledoux returned to his side of the desk and produced an assortment of forms, which he brought back around for my viewing. He slid his quill and well toward me while pointing out the appropriate places to sign. Once satisfied, he collected the documents and handed them directly to a subordinate with whom he conferred momentarily. He had exercised patience, but now faced me with a most exuberant smile.

"Evairyseen' ese een ordair an' I am free fair zee remaindair ov zee day."

"Wonderful"

"Shall we?"

Much to Mr. Ledoux's delight, I accepted both his invitation to dinner and his arm. Eager to show off *'living art'* as he worded it, he frequently encouraged me to step out of the coach and stroll sidewalks that flanked the narrow paved streets of old St. Louis. Keeping firm hold of my arm, he humored me with an endless stream of flattery. He made every effort to introduce my project and me to everybody who was anybody in the city, whereby I gained a number of solid supporters for the new orphanage.

In and out of the coach, I walked close to his side for most of an hour. We passed many places of interest such as the Old Cathedral Catholic Cemetery on Walnut Street between Second and Third that had graves dating back to seventeen and seventy-one. When not walking at his side, I sat next to him as we warmed ourselves in the coach. Mr. Ledoux worked his way up the slope of the riverbank until reaching a favorite inn on the higher ground. As we ascended, I observed a weathered sign that stated five thousand residents now resided within the city limits. The sign amused him.

"Zat sign seems to pair-sist. It might 'ave been true last week, but I believe now zee count ese closair to seven sou-san'."

"Does anyone take into consideration the number of folks just passing through? St. Louis seems a city of transients if nothing else, and I can't imagine but it wouldn't double the number posted."

"I fully agree," he said

"The vibrancy of St. Louis reminds me a great deal of Albany and New York. It overflows with faces. Yet, unlike those cities, here the faces seem strange and there seems to be too many people walking about for the number of structures—unless of course everybody sleeps standing on their feet."

"I do not know about feet, but zere is leettle resairva-shawn about slee-peen' een zee saddle or on zee street. If you are fortun-ate enough to fin' free space on a front porsh, I guarantee you weell be asked to pay fair eet."

It became obvious to me while walking that St. Louis was full bodied and sophisticated. The soul of the city favored its French ancestry, especially the old parts of town where only lesser signs of Spanish sway were to be seen. Both countries influenced the region for centuries. The Spanish accent was the spice, as was the diverse and colorful sprinkling of missionaries, land speculators, cotton farmers, slaves, Indians, and immigrants arrived not only from the colonies, but also from the harbors about New Orleans and distant shores brought close to that southern port by sail.

Whereas the Spanish knew the land, it was the rivers that served to reinforce the city's French foundations. They brought forth the voyageurs, the rough and ready, the rustic trapper, the wild Indian and scout. These were the men peculiar to St. Louis that gave it an air of toughness not to be found elsewhere. Since the days of its inception, long before eighteen and three when Jefferson purchased the land, this breed of men painted the city's legacy with a French palette.

"Oh, evairyseen' about St. Louis ese steeped een Frensh tradi-shawn—" said Mr. Ledoux, "but one must concede zee Spaneesh waire 'ere first. Zey moved srough zis area back een zee mid fifteen hundreds. More recently, zey govairned us directly from seventeen seexty-eight unteel eighteen an' four dureen' wheesh time we answaired to seven diffair-rent Spaneesh Govair-nors.

"Fortunately fair us Frensh, zee Spaniards nevair really took to zee place. Only twenty or so Spaneesh families settled een St. Louis dur-reen' zeir last sirty years ov rule. Een zose days zee tairritory was considaired part of 'Illinois' an' eet passed from Frensh 'ands to Spaneesh control an' zen back to zee Frensh fair all of one day so Napol-leon coul' sail eet to zee Amairicans."

"It seems strange that Spain or France should give up their claim on such an enormous tract of land," said I. "I would have thought it worth a war for the winning."

"As would I. In fact, a war 'ad evairysing to do with eet. But zee war was een Europe not 'ere. No, zee seeds were sewn an' zee land was boun' to become part ov zee Union because neisair France nor Spain 'ad zee means to defend sush a massive hold-deen'.

"Zee Frensh waire exhaust-teen' zeir resources srough war wis England, an' zee Spaneesh knew first'and zat zey waire no matsh against zee English forces now well established een zee norzairn part ov zee country. It was zee Spaneesh who devised a plan to undairmine Breetish control by attract-teen' as many Amairicans possi-bluh eento zee Illinois tairritory. Zey accomplished zis feat by offairing Amairicans eight hundred acre tracts ov land fair a maire forty dollars, a fee only necessary to covair zee expense ov zee papairwork.

615

"It was a powairful incentive zat attracted many takairs, fair eet was a rishair offairing zan even zose lands being offaired in Kentucky an' Tennessee or by Congress. Zat's why Daniel Boone an' 'is lot came out to settle. Zee plan more zan met Spaneesh expecta-shawns an' successfully brought Amairicans to zee banks ov zee Mississippee an' St. Louis. It frustrated any Breetish ambi-shawn een zee region. Ov course zee plan, wheesh successfully foiled England also foiled Spain an' France een zee long run, fair zee land was now so settled wis Amairicans, eet was folly to sink eet would bypass statehood an' attashment to zee Union."

St. Louis was expanding, and there were now a number of smaller towns that surrounded it. According to Mr. Ledoux, originally the town had taken root upon a large bluff that extended about two miles along the western side of the Mississippi. A bed of white limestone laid flat at the river's edge then rose some forty or fifty feet in a set of natural terraces that simultaneously formed a perfect landing for boats and a solid barrier to protect the city from seasonal floods. In those days the bluff was well treed, hospitable, and flanked a narrows in the river.

Today the city was undergoing a fresh wave of growth and houses were under construction in every direction. Most were brick or frame structures common to accepted American archi-tecture, and although they were nice and even palatial at times due to the new wealth being generated in the furring business; it was the older houses that I enjoyed the most.

They were built during French and Spanish rule and were constructed of stone quarried from the bank. Limestone made them light in color and attractive. Normally they were one-story structures with lofts, and a good many of the dwellings sported porches or galleries built in the southern style. I was especially taken by the habit of building a common fence of wood or stone that surrounded an entire block of homes instead of individual lots.

Those oldest structures in the city that managed to survive the heartless pace of progress could still be seen now and then.

616

They were built of vertical timbers driven into the ground and plastered over in much the same manner as dwellings in the old crumbling French forts of the Great Lakes. These were now rare and only a few remained to reflect something of the earliest settlers.

The city and its progressive attitude impressed me. Mr. Ledoux and I discussed many projects underway for the public good and conferred in length about my plans for the orphanage. He was a stalwart supporter of good education for the young. He insisted on walking me to Ninth and Christy then along a block of Washington Street to show me a facility about to open as the new St. Louis University. The original building was built in eighteen and twenty-nine and was occupied, a second was just being finished. The institution laid claim as the first university west of the Mississippi; it being founded in eighteen-eighteen. He went on to tell me about city plans currently under consideration for a public school. In his position as a financier and lifelong citizen, he possessed an especially astute familiarity with St. Louis and its goings on.

I found the residents to be a garrulous lot and open minded to all variety of culture and ideas. St. Louis was no longer a French Catholic community of colleges and schools. There were also Methodist and Presbyterian congregations prideful of their newly built churches, and a whole slew of sinners that were welcomed to sit and eat with the most righteous of the lot.

Except for a common reference to all English persons and Yankees who came from east of the Mississippi to settle in the northern part of the city as *'Bostons'*, no one here seemed encumbered by deep-rooted traditions of culture or class structure still to be sensed back east or solidly embedded in the south.

It seemed only natural that with so many of the people in St. Louis just passing though, relationships were built on the 'here and now' without regard to one's past. You could be who you wanted to be in St. Louis, and that was how you were accepted without question or concern.

It was true that the Compromise of eighteen-twenty delivered Missouri into the Union as a slave state, but I felt strongly that the general temperance of its people made this place a potentially good home for Rachel and Caleb. As for Shadow Hunter, the word 'home' didn't connect to his character in any fashion and probably never would.

The city did have it's peculiarities, most notably the fact that water should be scarce even though we sat at our table surrounded by spectacular views of the Mississippi, but that was indeed the case. Springs were apparently far and few between, rarely bubbling up through the bed of limestone beneath the city. There was however, a fresh flow of water named Mill Stream that emptied into to the river at the south end of the city and thus far served to quench the needs of all. Mr. Ledoux pointed out quickly that a waterworks was in the process of being built.

Just prior to entering the inn, I stood atop a ridge, leaned into a yet cold wind while looking westward across a vast rolling prairie. It was a windswept plain of dormant grasses and common fields laid out neatly and nearly uninterrupted as far as the horizon. The land appeared level and might have been boring, but for those tiny misplaced islands of trees that were visible here and there. These flat and distant views gave me a preview of the enormity of the land. In a fashion, the country repented for its lack of visual amenities by giving one a sort of spiritual sustenance through its minimal but infinite expanse. It reduced existence to earth, sky, and God.

From within the warmth of the inn, I could see east across the Mississippi to the Illinois country from whence we came. I watched smoking steamers ferry people and parcel back and forth from one bank to the other as Mr. Ledoux and I conversed. The man fascinated me. He was an engaging host and openly revealed all manner of things about St. Louis and himself. To my surprise, I didn't find him at all narcissistic or arrogant. He was a confident man, truthful, and entertaining as he divulged stories of his past that I found quite interesting.

"You've lived here your whole life, then?"

"Yes, indeed. My family 'as been 'ere since zee day Pierre Laclede Liquest led a band ov tradairs uprivair from New Orleans. Zat was back een seventeen sixty-sree. He was searshing fair a place to airect a post zat might bettair profit 'is tradeen' activities. At first, 'is sole ambi-shawn was to find a site midway between New Orleans an' Canada zat possessed a bank solid enough to stand against flood-deen'. Zat was seventy some years ago when most all zee trappairs who traveled up an' down zee Mississippi waire eithair Frensh or Frensh Canadian.

"Mr. Liquest came upon zis site an' saw its poten-tial at once. Nawt only did he sink eet a pairfect place fair a post, being near zee confluence ov zee Missouri, Mississippee an' Illinois riv-airs, but he also believed eet might some day be a grand city rooted at zee intairsec-shawns ov sree important watairways, an' a place cairtain to produce wealth.

"Pierre returned to New Orleans an' placed sirty men undair zee command ov 'is lieutenant, 'is stepson een fact, a young man named Auguste Chouteau who was just sirteen years ov age. Zey waire to leave zee follow-een' spreeng wis provis-shawns to clear zee site an' form a settlement. One ov zose first tradairs who accompanied Pierre, an' who also returned zee second time wis Auguste was a man named Antoine Ledoux, my grandfathair."

"Mmm. Deep roots. Were you and your grandfather close?"

"As a mattair ov fact, we waire. He was an amaz-een' man, bos an outstanding huntair an' trappair. An' een latair years, a storytellair unsurpassed. He could hold me spellbound upon 'is knee fair hours at end, go-een' on about grizzlies an' Indians, fill-een' my 'ead wis visions ov craggy mountain cliffs zat towaired above zee clouds to lean ovair alpine valleys ly-een' silent an' sairene een zee shadows. He rambled on about enormous 'airds ov buffalo roam-een' across zee plains before tairrific sundairstorms, prairie dogs as far as zee eye could see, dens ov rattlesnakes ten feet long; stories wis'out end, some true some not, all exaggaira-ted.

619

"Eithair way, my grandfathair passed 'is stories on to me, but he passed 'is knowledge on to my fathair, an' although my fathair was a great outdoorsman een 'is own right, 'e mush prefairred business indoors. I like to say zat 'is forte was not so mush een ouest watair currents as eet was een east coast currency. My grandfathair trapped an' my fathair hunted. Only my fathair was hunt-een' fair zee best deals een zee buy-een' an' sel-een' ov furs, pelts, hides an' zee like."

"Did that cause them problems? I mean being so different in their likes and dislikes."

"No, not at all. I can undairstand you might believe sush diffairences ov 'eart waire bound to stir 'ard feel-eens', but een fact eet was quite zee opposite. My grandfathair was most proud ov 'is son, fair not only did my fathair look aftair my grandfathair's affairs; he fared far bettair zan my grandfathair evair might 'ave dreamed. My fathair made more money een 'is first two years ov business zan did my grandfathair zee whole ov 'is life. My fathair saw to eet zat my grandfathair fineeshed out 'is years een comfort.

"Grandfathair was nawt one to shange 'is ways an' so remained content to spend 'is final years trek-keen' freely about zee wildairness wad-een' waist deep een freez-een' watairs een ordair to set an' collect 'is traps. My fathair, on zee ossair 'and, remained pairfectly happy at home pour-reen' ovair papairs an' keep-een' a log on zee fire. My grandfathair came home wis zee fireside stories; my fathair came home wis zee profits an' zee best brandy money could buy. Zey drank 'eartily, toasted an' boasted ov zeir accomplish-ments. Zey lied beautifully to each osser an' got along zjust fine."

"Is your father still alive?"

"No. Zey are bos buried now. Zey 'ave left me a legacy an' I 'ave prospaired enormously by zeir fairesight. Zey died know-een' zeir lives waire productive. An' zat would be zee curse een all ov zis fair me, zee price I must pay. I lay een bed at night wondair-een' eef I 'ave lived up to zeir expecta-shawns, wondair-een' eef I am carry-een' my own weight. I feel zeir ghostly judge-mental eyes look-een' ovair my shouldairs all too often."

"Judging by what I have seen and heard, I'm certain you have but little for which to worry."

"Sank-you, com-een' from someone ov your background, zee compliment ese most meaningful. I must admit zere ese a great deal ov peace een know-een' my forefathairs 'ad a good sense ov humor."

"Tell me, have you never left St. Louis?"

"Not fair any length ov time—a few trips to New Orleans, Louisville, Cincinnati, Pittsburgh—rivair travel een behalf ov zee bank, osairwise no."

"Do you never feel alone or out of touch living here on the fringes of civilization? Have you no desire to travel east or abroad to see the rest of the world? I mean to say, I *just* received a letter from a dear friend in Boston and she posted it more than a month ago. It makes me feel as though I have dropped off the face of the earth."

"Zat ese due to your Bostonian upbring-een' wis eets rassair peculiar pairspective. You believe zat zee centair ov zis great land ese on zee East coast. Is zat because you folks feel Boston ese half way between England an' St. Louis or what? It often seems as sough nobody een zose harbor towns realize anyone exists beyond zee Appala-chians. Are zose peaks so high zat zey can't see us? Why do you suppose zee ol' frontiair nearly seceded from zee Union?" He shrugged his shoulders. "We Frensh 'ave been een zis country evairy bit as long as your English friends only we 'aven't been run-neen' amok. We 'aven't as ov yet become cramped.

"When I sink ov New York or Boston, all I imagine ese epidemics. I sink ov fires rag-een' out ov control. I sink ov rat infesta-shawns. I imagine all zee osair maladies ov congested

621

living. No sank-you. I mush prefair zee open spaces an' minds ov my wild an' wooly frontiair friends.

"Why would I shoose to leave zee one place on earth zat so many eastairnairs seem to dream about? I see no rush ov humanity going zeir way. I appreciate what I 'ave. Do you sink we suffair a lack ov divairsity because zis ese not New York? Your cities are made up ov many cultures, but so too ese St. Louis, an' I assure you zat een St. Louis not only are we ov diffairent stock, but by being 'ere, our peo-pell 'ave proven zat zey are unmatshed fair zeir sense ov adven-ture.

"Zis land ese excit-een'. It ese invigorating, an' I find zee peo-pell ov St. Louis fascinat-een', by far more intairest-een' zan any book written to describe zem. I am convinced most ov our citizens 'ave spent too mush time alone een zee wildairness, been too long out ov toush, an' zis makes zem a supremely odd an' curious bunsh, colorful, an' intairest-een'. It ese nev-vair dull 'ere. Craziness ese zee common bond zat 'as kept us connected seence zee vairy begin-neen'. Do you see zat build-een' ovair zere?" He pointed to a structure nestled in the center of the city that spread out below us.

"Yes."

"Zat was zee original post house built by Auguste fair zee company headquart-airs. It ese zee centair ov St. Louis an' zee point from wheesh zee city ese laid out. In zee begin-neen' zere waire only sree nors-sous streets an' a 'andful ov east-ouest streets zat crossed zem. Zee settlairs set aside one lot fair a shursh, anothair fair a public space, an' on zee high ground a place to build a fort. It was nosseen' more zan a sleepy trad-een' post.

"Zen one day, zese few settlairs received word zat zeir beloved king turned ovair all ov New France east ov ze Mississippi to our long time advairsary, zee king ov England. You must imagine what zey sought ov zat. He too was crazy, plain crazy, crazy like zee rest ov us.

"If you waire Frensh an' 'ad been liv-een' on zee Illinois side ov zee riv-vair, you waire left wis leettle shoice but to fairry your family an' belong-eens' across zee riv-vair an' take up residence 'ere een zee sleepy leettle post. To live undair Breetish rule was unthinka-bluh—genairally still is.

"My grandfathair told me zat when zey came across, zey came in sush a state zat zey nearly parted zee watairs wis profanity. He said some waire float-eeen' half zeir cabins to zis side ov zee riv-vair as zey blasphemed zee king fair 'is stupidity. Back zen nobody called zis place St. Louis, eet was refairred to as Laclede's settlement.

"I know zis place well, Elizabes. Zis ese an' always 'as been my home, my heestory, an' I love all ov it. I was a young man back een eighteen an' four, when we joined zee Union as part ov zee Louisiana Purshase. I steell remembair zee outrageous parties zat waire srown een honor ov France when eet flew eets flag fair zat one seengle day before turn-neen' our land ovair to zee Amairicans.

"I also remembair my fathair being bos angaired an' deeply concairned about zee mess caused by zee shange. He was not alone een 'is worry, zee whole town was een an uproar soon zereaftair, fair zere waire nearly two hundred houses een zee settlement when zee Amairicans decided to annul all ov zee propairties granted to zee ownairs by zee Frensh an' Spaneesh.

"It ese 'ard to believe as we seet at zis tab-bluh an' view zee univairsi-tee zat when I was a boy, we 'ad one bakairy, two tavairns, sree blacksmiths, an' a cou-pluh ov mills. We 'ad one doctor. Most ov zee mairshants een zose days worked out ov zeir homes an' whatevair stores zey sold waire vairy expen-seeve.

"Coffee an' sugar used to be two dollars a pound because eet 'ad to come hundreds ov miles uprivair by flatboat or ovairland by horse an' pack. My fathair was one ov zee few who could afford sush luxuries, but he nevair forgot 'is roots waire een povairty. He would scold me fair being greedy an' lack-een' any

623

apprecia-shawn ov our goot fortune evairy time my fingairs waire knuckle deep een zee sugar bowl.

"Fair zee longest time nossing shanged an' we wairen't mush diffairent come eighteen an' nine when St. Louis was incorpo-rated eento a town. Zee real growth began een eighteen an' seventeen when zee steamboats found zeir way to St. Louis an' shanged zee way business was done once an' fair all. Zee days ov cordelling flat bottom boats loaded down wis expensive goots waire suddenly a sing ov zee past.

"Sugar, coffee, linens, machinairy, zee price ov evairysing dropped srough zee floor. Life was suddenly easiair an' more peo-pell zan evair began to find zeir way to our village. Peo-pell genairal-lee liked what zey found an' stayed. Zee place began to grow steady from zen on until eighteen twenty-two when St. Louis officially became a city wis its mayor an' nine aldairmen. I weell wagair you whatevair you weesh zat someday St. Louis shall rival your New York or Boston een tairms ov trade an' ship-peen'. You mark my words, Elizabes, eet weell come to pass."

Once served, the food toned down Mr. Ledoux's exuberance and quieted our conversation. The lull gave me time to consider all that he had presented. The history of St. Louis was straight-forward, rugged, and truly an American story, but unfortunately for me there were issues about this promised land that were troubling, and as soon as my plate was cleared I pursued these concerns.

"I have heard you speak of many fine things, Mr. Ledoux, but I must tell you that Rachel and Caleb, who I have mentioned as being freed persons, are deeply concerned about their safety and well-being, for they are only now overcoming what was a terrible experience whilst in New York. I can't say that I blame them for their anxiety and reasons to question the principles of Missouri. They understand clearly, as do I that you elected to join the Union as a slave state. In spite of all you have shown me, wonderful as it has been, I for one don't find that a terribly progressive stance. I beg you explain your personal position on this matter."

My host was not nearly so quick with his response this time. His picture of perfection was suddenly blemished. He placed his napkin upon the table and looked across to the distant Illinois country. He looked back at me first out the corner of his eye and then he turned his head and faced me directly. His speech returned a degree of sharpness that hinted of distance between friends. It lost some of its joviality.

"Mademoiselle, I beg you nawt to confuse St. Louis wis Missouri or zee prefairences ov zee Sous. A great many immigrants 'ave come from sousairn states to settle Missouri fair zee purpose ov establish-een' cotton farms. Even if zeir conscience should turn zem away from slavairy, zeir sousairn ties force zem to support zeir hairitage an' defend zee livelihood ov zeir fathairs, brothairs an' families. Zee Sous cannot afford Missouri to be a free state an' zerefore presses hard upon eet fair support.

"I cannot deny what you say, eet ese true, but zere are many liv-een' haire who 'ave arrived from zee Nors an' zeir opin-yawns are exactly oppo-seet. As fair zee city ov St. Louis, eet ese steell vairy mush a home to Frensh trappairs an' voyageurs or zeir descendents. We are close to our hairitage an' embrace eet wis pas-sion.

"I tell you zis because France ese nawt a country inclined to harbor slave tradairs or promote zee practice an' zis vairy moment demands zee implementa-shawn ov an intairnation-al anti-slavair-ee treaty, wheesh your Washington politi-shawns oppose. Coffles, blocks, an' pens arra commonplace een zee mothair ov Amairican cities, fair eet ese zee vairy centair ov zee trade.

"A pairson would be fooleesh to believe sush demands called fair by France should 'ave no effect upon zee souls ov our peo-pell. Here, we steell subscribe to Frensh princi-pluhs as do most peo-pell ov Frensh background liv-een' or work-een' zee Mississippee between Canada an' New Orleans.

"I am zee first to acknowledge zat slavair-ree can be vairy profita-bluh. Howevair, just because I am a bankair, please do nawt discredit me by assum-een' I should favor sush practices when een fact I do not. Pairsonally, I oppose slavair-ree, yet zat does not mean I do not undairstand zee plight ov zee cotton farmair. It does not mean I will turn my back on 'im.

"Whethair right or wrong, zee fact remains zat zee Sous was built a century ago upon zee concept ov sheap land an' slavair-ree, an' done so wis zee blessings ov all. Now, to dismantle sush an economy weell spell disastair an' ruin fair half zee nation. It woul' take anothair century or more to transform zee Sous into somesing ossair zan zee agricul-tural society eet ese, hav-een' been built upon zee backs ov laborairs, slaves, or ossairwise.

"Congress ese keenly aware ov zis problem. Congress also knows zat by keep-een' a balance between states zat support slavair-ree an' states zat do not, eet avoids a potential civil war. It wants Missouri to be a slave state. I weell also say een no uncairtain tairms zat een evairy way zee Nors ese equally as guilty ov support-een slavair-ree as ese zee Sous, zis by zeir insatia-bluh appetite fair profit an' cotton to feed zeir mills at any cost. Mills, I might add, you shall find een greatest numbair about New York an' Boston—zat being your home an' your sin.

"Let me remind you, Mademoiselle, zat fish was not zee only profita-bluh commodity ov your Massashusetts port. As I recall, een eets day, Boston was principal een zee landing ov slaves, second to none. Allow me to stress my point by say-een' eet again, *second to none*. Embarrassing ese eet not?

"I am sure you undairstand eet woul' be suicide fair a norzairn politi-shawn to admit as mush, an' I promise you zat zee financial pain back home weell be sevaire should slavair-ree end an' cotton supplies fall short. Hypocrisy runs rampant een zee Nors, Mademoiselle, fair slavair-ree ese indeed zee disease ov our nation, zee entire na-shawn an' not just Missouri or your souzairn neighbors as you might weesh eet.

626

"Does eet not seem most peculiar to you zat while norzairn textile industries return obscene profits, souzairn plantations wis all zeir slaves an' free labor fail misairably? Souzairn farmairs fall to ruin as fast as rain falls to earths an' zey are washed away forevair. You must open your eyes an' see who really profits from slavair-ree. Zee Sous is only zee place where slaves are fed, bred, an' housed. Slavair-ree is visi-bluh een zee Sous, yes, but eets tenacity toushes all. It cripples, eet corrupts, an' eet taints even zee most innocent 'earts ov your beloved New England.

"You 'ave walked our streets wis me today, an' you 'ave seen zee faces zat pass by. Zey come from evairy nationality, evairy class. Zere are Frensh, English, an' Amairicans. Zere are Spaneesh an' Indian. Zere are slaves an' freed men. Did you not see 'ow leettle eet mattairs, 'ow nobody notices or cares? Nobody pays min' to sush diffairences because St. Louis has always been a place ov diffairence, a place ov strangairs an' strange faces.

"We best reflect zee na-shawn as a whole, many fair an' many against. Zee na-shawn made its compromise fair balance by split-teen' Massashusetts an' form-een' Maine so eet might be admitted to zee Union as a free state to countair Missouri as a slave state. Zee diffairence between zee nation, zee Congress, an' St. Louis ese zat een St. Louis we do not make a point ov cast-teen' zee first stone.

"Haire we maintain balance by recognizing all our diffair-ences an' keep-peen' an open mind to zose sings we do not readily undairstand. Zere ese a respect an' genairal tolairance pairmitted to all, fair suspi-shawns an' sympasies often do run deep on bos sides ov zee slave issue. Racial convic-shawns expressed fairvently sairve no one well een a city populated wis sush a divairse background. Ossairwise, who woul' be next, zee Swedes, zee Indians, zee Irish, zee Gairmans—who would be next, I ask you?

"Slavair-ree ese a fact ov our lives an' I cannot see a shange een zee foreseea-bluh future although I believe wis convic-shawn

627

eet weell end. It must end to ease our conscience. I woul' tell Rashel an' Caleb to put aside zeir trou-blud soughts een St. Louis. Fair one sing zey are fortunate to 'ave influential connections sush as yourself, an' me as well should you accept my offair to assist you een your cause."

Mr. Ledoux picked up his napkin to wipe his mouth. He took a breath and looked out across the river as he did before my reprimand. The man had proved himself to me, at least in spirit. I felt good about his character and I believed he would accept Rachel and Caleb for the fine people they were.

I was in the best of spirits when Mr. Ledoux sent for a coach to return me to the hotel. As the horses rounded a corner, I came upon a most bizarre scene. Alongside the road in front of the courthouse were a number of people lying about on the ground. My blood ran cold as I realized them to be negroes. A closer look revealed the chains that linked them together.

I yelled for the driver to stop. Needless to say, my first thoughts were of Rachel and Caleb. I could almost feel the sweat upon my brow. I studied the forms upon the ground as memories of Caleb's concerns echoed in my head. I turned to see a man strolling along the curb and so waited for him to come within earshot.

"Excuse me, sir."

"Ma'am"

"May I ask what it is that takes place here?"

He studied me carefully. Then answered cautiously. "An auction."

"Slaves?"

"Yes, ma'am. Are you an interested party?" It was a guarded question, his eyes awaited my expression. Just then a woman cried out and stole my attention. I saw her wail as she reached out for a black man from whom she was being pulled away. I thought of Rachel's separation.

"It is not a pleasant sight."

"No, ma'am. Did you wish me to summon a trader for you?" He pointed to a number of men standing in the yard.

"Are you are not yourself a trader, sir?"

"No, ma'am."

"Are you then a buyer?"

Again the man studied me and answered in the same guarded manner. "No, ma'am."

"Forgive me, my curiosity for I am unfamiliar with these affairs. What does one pay for such a slave?"

"The negress will fetch two hundred, a good field hand five."

"Does this type of thing go on often, I mean, right here in front of the courthouse?"

"Weekly, for sure."

"Were you just passing by, or does this activity interest you?"

"Are you toying with me, ma'am?"

"I beg your pardon?"

"I feel we are playing cat and mouse. Let me speak frankly. I am an abolitionist madam. I observe these proceedings with great disdain. Have you any further question?"

"Only one, sir."

"And that would be?"

"Would you join me in my coach?"

"Ma'am?"

He was taken aback. I opened the door, and after some hesitation, he entered the coach.

"Mrs. Elizabeth Claussen." I offered my hand.

"Mr. Henry Holton."

"Tell me, Mr. Holton, do you know anything of the financier Mr. Ledoux?

I spent half the next hour watching an auction take place while Mr. Holton remained seated as my guest. He knew a good deal about Mr. Ledoux and I was greatly relieved to hear Mr. Ledoux was reputed to be an abolitionist in heart if not so much in public.

On the other hand, I was greatly distressed to hear that St. Louis was not nearly the slave-friendly city Mr. Ledoux preferred to paint. In fact, as I listened to Mr. Holton, I learned that in seventeen hundred, Mr. Ledoux's French ancestors had slaves in their company, most often Indian squaws purchased as concubines. In seventeen-nineteen, the Frenchman Phillipe Renault imported five hundred slaves from the French colony of Santo Domingo to work the lead mines.

"Planters! My word, Mrs. Claussen, you couldn't have picked a worse place to board. The slave dealers are famous for sitting about drinking mint-juleps at the bar in Planters. Keep a close eye on your friends or they will surely disappear. Especially your Rachel, if she is as light skinned as you say. Quadroons and fancies command unbelievable prices. They are sold specifically to satisfy the cravings or maybe I should say the decadent depravities of rich men."

"Oh." I lowered my eyes. "I worry. I should have listened to Caleb. He was of a mind to stay in Illinois. Honestly, I thought that if I made the two of them visible enough, no harm would come their way."

"I suppose anything is possible, but only during Spanish rule was a concerted attempt made to end slavery in this area. That was back in seventeen sixty-six when the Spanish decreed that all Indian slaves were to be freed upon decease of their owners, and that all newborns belonging to Indian slaves were to be free persons. That was a long time ago and sadly their attempt was a failed one. There are now twenty-five thousand slaves in the Missouri, three thousand of them living here in the Mississippi-Missouri area.

"In fairness, I must say that the French are increasingly of a mind to do away with slavery. Their belief is much in line with Europe. In time I believe they will succeed, but for now it is the southerner who settles this land and he comes with a mind determined to promote his industry and this barbarity.

"Don't be fooled by the progressive façade of St. Louis, Mrs. Claussen. The support for slavery is both plentiful and profound. I suggest you encourage your friends return themselves to Illinois. That way, should blood be shed, it won't stain your hands.

"However, if you are determined to do otherwise, you might then contact one Reverend John Meachum. He is a black minister at the First Baptist Church. He has opened a school there for the education of negroes and may assist your friends in some fashion. You might look up Mr. Elijah Lovejoy. He is an outspoken abolitionist and has many connections. He may be of some service as well."

I dismissed Mr. Holton after being catapulted into deep cheerless thought. I wished to hear nothing more of what the man had to say, but reluctantly accepted his opinion as equal to that of Mr. Ledoux. Hopefully, Mr. Ledoux was as much of a mind to enforce change as he was empowered by his fortunes to do so.

I clung to my belief that through efforts to assist the orphans and the poor, in time Rachel and Caleb would earn respect and be accepted. They would especially enjoy the encouragement and support of the many who sided with the abolitionists. I felt positive they would again enjoy a place to put down roots, a place secure enough to call home and a point from which to seek out their son. And if not, then there was always Illinois.

SIXTY

The affect of our travels upon Taa'sooma'hane was profound. It was as though an ancient part of his soul had been resurrected. The transition became most notable during our passage through the Illinois Territory. The wildness of the country seemed to draw forth a similar wildness from his character, a part of him that had been suppressed in Albany for too many years.

It wasn't just my sensitivity to the killing. There was more. His eyes revealed an awakened inner spirit. He appeared more alert than ever, his step quickened by the energy and task now before him. Gone was the look of fatigue and distress, the look of hopelessness; he appeared younger with each passing day. St. Louis was saturated with wildness and the city not only nourished him, but the essence of St. Louis and Shadow Hunter were essentially one and the same.

Our journey to St. Louis opened up a window whereby I could glimpse into Taa'sooma'hane's past. He wasn't a man of many words, but many miles of hardship on the road could shake loose even the tightest of tongues.

According to Shadow Hunter's own account, he was the son of a French-Indian trapper and Delaware squaw. He was born in the Big Horn and Wind River Range and raised about the Upper Missouri in the midst of the Sioux and Cheyenne. Ironically, we were closer now than ever to the playground of his youth.

Taa'sooma'hane said that his father met his mother in the old northwest and from there they traveled to the Great Plains. The Delaware tribe had been badly beaten by the Iroquois in the eighteenth century and were forced west into the regions of Michigan, Illinois and Ohio. Even in those areas there was no peace, for his ancestors were persecuted by the white man who coveted their land. The pressure of European migration forced most all Indians farther west until there was no place left to go but deep into the barren desert.

As a young man, Taa'sooma'hane returned east with his parents to partake in the War of 1812 alongside Tecumseh against the AmKennethans who were encroaching into Upper Missouri trapping fields. He was then eighteen years of age and involved in some of the fighting.

Many Indians took up the British cause in this issue because they believed they would be given back the lands that the AmKennethans had taken by force and coercion. Many of his band believed the British would give them back some of the land they formerly lost in the Great Lakes area.

Taa'sooma'hane's father was killed in a skirmish unrelated to the wars, and left him and his mother to seek shelter with a mixed band of dispersed Indians. They were of many different tribes, mostly of eastern origin such as Cherokee, Creek and Potawatomi. There were also a good many runaway slaves. There were a few warriors from western tribes that had banded together from as far south as New Orleans to support the British, and who also were now displaced, abandoned or orphaned. It was a remnant of this motley bunch that I met while in search of the injured girl, Little Deer.

I was amazed to discover that Shadow Hunter also had a French name, which was Pierre DeWilde. Not only could Taa speak English, as did many from eastern tribes who had adopted white man's ways, like the Cherokee, but Taa also spoke some French, and in St. Louis he proved to be quite the interpreter among Indians about the city.

Taa'sooma'hane may have stayed with us longer than I expected in order to learn what he could from these Indians about the lay of the land, or it may have been to await news of his people, or dare I say it may have been out of concern for my own well-being in this far-away place.

I mention this because he remained vigilant and took no solace in the fact I might be lunching safely with Mr. Ledoux or dining with any of the influential St. Louis families. He was blind to their status and questioned my security whilst among them.

I might find myself looking up from the table to gaze outside from where I sat surrounded by a party of dinner guests, and there in the shadows I would catch a glimpse of him waiting and watching for me. My newly made acquaintances were always at first frightened by word of a savage lurking in the dark until I offered explanations at which point they became highly amused and curious about my guardian.

In the beginning, I laughed to myself thinking Taa'sooma'hane had too much time on his hands. I believed he kept an eye on me in return for the shelter and food I provided. However, in time my opinion changed as I came to better understand the man. He once made a comment that through Little Deer and Snow on the Ground, we were spiritually connected. If I failed to carry their amulet on my person, Taa'sooma'hane would become frustrated. I didn't have to wear it, just carry it to pacify him, for he believed it to be strong medicine and sound protection against evil spirits. It was ironic that the more I worried about a man who had lost everything, the more he worried about me.

Unlike my concerns for Rachel and Caleb, I always felt foolish worrying about Taa'sooma'hane. No matter what the circumstance, he was not the kind of man a woman could worry about with ease. I was like a mouse fretting over a cat. His Indian ways convinced me that nature gave him not only those wicked arrows, but also certain basic instincts needed for survival, much the same way it enlightens animals.

Taa'sooma'hane did his business with indifference to obstacles. Unfortunately, he was yet unable to uncover any reliable information about his people. It was uncertain as to whether they had ever made it as far as the Mississippi. They could still be somewhere in Ohio, Indiana, or Illinois country. But, it was common knowledge that the Congress was determined to rid all lands east of the Mississippi of Indians, and he felt that even if his family had only been driven out of New York, they would probably find no rest until they crossed the great river as did his ancestors.

In the meantime, Taa'sooma'hane was so taken by the wide-open spaces of the west and its sense of freedom, it became his goal to re-acquaint himself as much as possible with the place of his youth and possibly lead his people to live here in peace.

He was encouraged by a recent encounter with members of a Delaware tribe who claimed to live on a reservation some two hundred miles above the mouth of the Missouri. He knew the Delaware to be a peaceable tribe that now enjoyed good relations with the whites, for they were considered trustworthy and familiar with white man's ways. Because they had been an east coast tribe and shared his blood, he was assured they would welcome him into their camp as he traveled in search of his family.

When it came time for Shadow Hunter to go, he gave thanks by praying over me and making a vow to repay me for my kindness. He knew my plans were to travel the Missouri and not the upper Mississippi valley, which so interested him. In turn, I knew he felt more at ease traveling alone, and so rather than persuade him to join me, I saw to it that he had a good strong horse, a warm coat and blanket, ample supplies of pemmican and those things necessary to travel in comfort. I also presented him with a fine gun, lead, powder, and a mold. And lastly, a finely fashioned bow and two quivers of well made arrows. Taa'sooma'hane was overcome with surprise and gratitude.

"My heart hurts to see you go, Taa."

"I owe you many things, Ezlabeth. One day I will give back all you have done for me. You keep my word."

"I will pray for your safety and the return of your family."

"Thank-you. I know they will come. The gods hear your voice. Your spirit is very great. This I know. I have seen the signs."

"Good bye, Taa'sooma'hane."

"Good bye, Ezlbeth."

I watched with heavy heart as Taa'sooma'hane started down the street until I was distracted by a group of newly arrived Easterners. They were overreacting to his approach. I smirked after witnessing the way in which the men stepped between him and the women who were now nervously calling out to their children and rounding them up.

Exposure to an Indian who didn't feign submission had to be a first for many of the newcomers, for unlike most other places in the Union, in St. Louis, Indians were generally welcome within the city limits. Facing little persecution, they moved freely about, mingling with the crowds to trade their pelts and wares. On occasion one might notice an Indian or two acting a little contemptuous and unruly, but for the most part they wandered the streets doing nothing more than hoping to make some sense of sights and sounds belonging to a culture they could barely comprehend.

Not to be fooled or found partial, it must be said that these awe-struck Indians possessed no less an understanding of us than did the wide-eyed white man who found himself standing in the midst of a people he had been raised the whole of his life to despise, fear, and fight to the death. I myself battled to fight these misconceptions even after having traveled many miles with Taa'sooma'hane.

My thoughts returned to the women with their collected children now stepping back nervously to stare as Taa'sooma'hane passed. He paid them no mind, and no longer did I, for my concerns were fully with him as he trotted out onto the prairie. I could only imagine what distance or place his intrepid spirit might make its way. I knew he would face whatever hardship befell him with an iron will and a strength of character few men might muster.

Shadow Hunter was and always would be a stranger to me; a mystery, and my opinion of him could only come from intuition. And so it was, I sensed him to be a man of honor among his own kind, and seeing him separated from his people did indeed bring me sorrow as I watched him ride off to face the world utterly alone. I had no doubt as to how much his people missed him, for I felt my loss at having been left behind with only a hope that I might one day see him again. From far off, he turned to face me and waved good-bye.

It marked another of the good-byes, and a reminder that St. Louis was not to be my place. Rachel and Caleb were anxious about my leaving and hoping to delay it as long as possible, but having watched Taa'sooma'hane leave our company brought home hard the fact that I had business to conclude and a journey to resume.

I enjoyed my time spent in St. Louis. Still, my desire to find Christopher never waned. In fact, he had become even more of an objective for me as I felt closer to him than ever. It seemed I was filled with even greater reason to rise in the morning. I believed that to see him would at last fill a long suffered emptiness of heart in ways that the best of my new friends could not.

SIXTY-ONE

At the same time I worked to strengthen the foundations of the orphanage, I paid calls to most of the businessmen in St. Louis who were apt to have dealt with Christopher in one manner or another. Always, I came up empty handed.

No one really had any idea of his whereabouts, but each new meeting brought me farther down the ranks and into the midst of those folks who worked the levee and warehouses. It was these people who knew best the shipments of pelts and supplies going to and from the frontier. It was these people who sensed where were the trappers and explorers, and it was in knowing this that I walked down to the levee to pay visit upon one of the hide houses.

Mr. Ledoux had earlier brought me to the riverside so I might see the degree of development underway. He went on to describe the details of a future levee that he envisioned would stretch for miles along the river's edge. He pointed out a number of warehouses already under construction. Specifically, he showed me those that belonged to Christopher. I had been near the area a number of times, but avoided visits due to the disgusting odor. I preferred to think I might learn enough about Christopher in the fragrant offices of the financiers.

In stark contrast to the mouth-watering aroma of French cooking and sugar being boiled down in the mills, there was now this other smell, this one dreadfully obnoxious smell. For anyone not in the furring trade, instead of honeysuckle and lilac, this could be considered all too easily the true perfume of St. Louis.

The stench seeped out of large stone warehouses that lined the bank of the river. The massive structures housed and protected thousands of beaver skins and assorted hides that lie in wait suffocating in their own gaseous fumes. They produced a thick, choking, invisible cloud that reeked and remained potently refreshed with the arrival of each new raft of pelts.

It was often said that money was filthy, but in this case it was perfectly putrid, and the only way to thin the stench was to empty the warehouses by shipping the hides out of St. Louis and starting them on the next leg of their journey. Although much of St. Louis was made up of tanneries, cobblers and leather workers, most often the hides were tagged for a trip across the ocean to feed the fashion frenzy in England or the trendy vanities of other European countries.

Nearly every business in St. Louis was connected in some manner to the heaps of hides piled inside the riverbank warehouses. Only the indisputable wealth procured from such a malodorous treasure could be reason for any tolerance toward it. It was difficult enough to walk the warehouse streets let alone pass through the front door of such a place, but this I did with much distress.

Once inside, simply uttering the name Claussen from behind the handkerchief at my nose sent Mr. Williams rushing about behind his own mask, which was one of alarm. I was getting used to the frenetic response I received at each concern visited. To see full grown men practically drop to their knees, some of whom were too arrogant in their positions as managers, was something I found ever more comical.

I couldn't deny my playing games just to witness the power and effect I commanded by association with the Claussen name in St. Louis. Again I wondered what it must be like to travel through life as the real Christopher Claussen and experience these reactions on a daily basis. Maybe it was thoroughly frustrating to have everyone act like an idiot in your presence.

Mr. Williams' first move was to excuse himself in order to secretly warn a subordinate of my presence. From behind a wooden partition came a gust of staccato whispers, short bursts of hysterical intensity that mingled with a flurry of shuffling and sliding sounds. Cabinet doors clicked and drawers squeaked as they opened and closed. I envisioned a whirlwind of dust spiraling above the horrified head of a blameless assistant as he went forward frantically searching for whatever sins lie about. Left to myself, I listened to the commotion and a smile crept across my face.

"Forgive me, Miss Claussen. I di-di-di-did not expect a visit from you."

"I assure you, no apology is necessary, sir. I am embarrassed to have caused such commotion. I am not here on behalf of Mr. Claussen. I am here of my own accord, hoping you might offer me some information on where Mr. Claussen can be found. I am pressed to see him and I understand that you may be knowledgeable about his shipments and their destinations."

Mr. Williams was clearly relieved. This I observed by the way in which his shoulders returned to their original droopy position. As he sat in his chair, his spine seemed to fold forward and his posture was thereupon reduced by three inches at the very least. He struck me as a lonely man who determined many years ago he would never know the comfort of companionship, the joy of love. He reminded me of myself. The difference being he didn't entertain illusions, and cared little about his appearance or posture for my sake, whereas I sat straight up still living my lie.

"Mi-Mi-Mi-Mister Claussen hasn't b-b-b-been here for some time, at least a year or more. He is somewh-wh-where up the Mi-Missouri River looking for a pass through the Rocky Mou-Mou-Mou-Mountains. I ship his stores upriver. They are ferried upon his own b-b-b-boats. You might check with his boatyard."

I did my best to quell Mr. William's fears, but it was evident by his stuttering that I still made him very nervous. I decided to keep the conversation short for his sake, but when I was about to take my leave, I commented on my traveling up the Missouri to find Mr. Claussen at which point Mr. William's eyes grew amazingly large. He looked at me aghast.

"You can't be serious."

"I assure you, I am dead serious. I have already traveled this far from Boston and see no reason to give way to fear at this point."

He sat there speechless, not a solitary stutter, as his assistant placed two glasses and a cool pitcher of sassafras tea upon his desk. It was a state of shock that I was now growing accustomed to seeing among men.

"Miss Claussen. I do not wish to b-b-b-belittle your character or your ab-b-b-bility, b-b-buh there are innumerable risks in your p-p-p-p-p-plan. Mr. Claussen would not be p-p-p-p-p-happy to hear such things; of this I am p-p-p-p-certain. I urge you to reconsider, for such a p-plan is very dangerous and no one would forgive me if I said otherwise." He poured tea, which prevented me from getting up to leave as I intended.

"I owe you an apology for placing you in such a compromising position and for this I am sorry. Nevertheless, Mr. Claussen knows well, I am a woman of my own mind, and once set, hold fast. So let us not discuss the dangers of my plan, but dwell further on your thoughts as to his whereabouts."

"I am sorry, that is all I know. Even wh-wh-when in town, he is a rare sight. He does own a b-b-boatyard here in St. Louis as I said, and actively builds riverb-b-b-boats for freighting to and from New Orleans, St. Louis, Louisville, and P-P-P-Pittsburgh.

"As of late, I know he has b-been building b-b-boats especially suited for the Mmm-Mmm-Missouri trade. M-m-m-I assemble goods for shipment to the Upper Mmm-Missouri, receive cargoes of p-pelts to be stored in these hide houses. My last corresp-p-pondence with Mr. Claussen came this past winter with a request to outfit one of his boats with supplies and mmm-mules to be conveyed to the confluence of the Yellowstone. I enlisted the services of one B-B-Bernard Shaw, trapper and mmm-mmm-muleskinner, to p-protect the cargo, and to p-pack and drive the mules whatever distance remained."

"You don't know where Mr. Shaw was heading?"

"No, ma'am. He was to be met at the Yellowstone, so he said."

I finished my tea after hanging on Mr. William's every effort to speak plainly. I offered my thanks to him for his hospitality and exited his establishment. I had exhausted all but one lead, that being the boatyard, and to date everyone I spoke with aside from Mr. Williams served to reinforce the fact that Christopher was known by all, but unreachable by the civilized world.

It seemed if I was truly determined to find him, then I had little choice but to enter into the uncharted territories west of the Mississippi. The best way into the wilderness was by riverboat up the Missouri following the route of Lewis and Clark, and *'best'* didn't mean good. By all accounts I could expect it to be a difficult passage for the most part and dangerous the remainder.

I discovered through Mr. Williams that one man who enjoyed a good deal of Christopher's time was Luther Mendels, one of many Germans making their home in St. Louis. He was educated, well-spoken, competent, and the engineer who oversaw shipbuilding and day-to-day operations of Christopher's boatyard and fleet of riverboats. He had three steamers active on the rivers, and at least ten times that number of keelboats.

Unfortunately, for all of Mr. Mendels' dealing with Christopher, the story was the same almost word for word as the one told me by Mr. Williams. Christopher Claussen was unreachable. So, in spite of Mr. Mendels' way with words and his most convincing argument that I should abandon my notion to travel any further into the wilderness alone as a woman, I booked passage upon one his riverboats.

"Miss Claussen, please—."

"Your captains don't race."

"No ma'am."

"Your boilers don't blow up."

"Most certainly not."

"Your vessels are safe."

"Yes, ma'am. My vessels are safe."

"Then I see no problem."

"Ohhhhhhhh, God forgive me. As you wish. As you wish."

SIXTY-TWO

April, at last! Oh, how I had waited for winter's end. The sun now extended its daily round and encouraged temperatures into the sixties. Mid-March brought the first convincing signs of spring as millions of newly formed buds gave the riverbank trees a soft fuzzy look.

Everywhere was to be seen blossoms tripping across branches of fragrant Spicewood, and Mayapple along with pure white petals of Dogwood, and Chickasaw plum were not so unlike snowflakes left behind to stand bright against the darker barks of Cottonwood. Now came to view the palette of apple, cherry, and peach to compete with the colorful trunks of the Osage orange tree.

Below their overhanging branches, packs of passing river ice melted away into memory. Now, the freshest colors of nature, those vivid yellow-greens of new life flooded over the banks and across the countryside.

Blanketing the earth beneath the moving shadows of north-bound pigeons were the blue-purple spurs of violets, the pinks of doves foot, and the freckled yellow gold of cowslip—all precursors to the countless mayflowers about to rise forth. The entire plain looked velvety with its coat of rich green mixture of grasses.

Impossible to overlook amid this nearly perfect picture of nature's rebirth were the annoyed expressions of men, whose faces were veiled by a thick greasy coating of tallow, hog's fat, and sweat. It was a foul but effective recourse against the first horrific onslaught of mosquitoes that reminded us man was still being driven out of the Promised Land. The pests multiplied a thousandfold for each additional degree of warmth, and by unanimous agreement, they were deemed the devil's spawn on wing, for the wicked creatures brought to full measure sickness and the concept of hell on earth.

The warmer temperatures also brought an increase in river traffic. Canoes and smaller boats had been darting back and forth across the water since the earliest days of March even as the snow fell, but the speed of the current, floating debris, and floes of ice made casting off too dangerous for the larger keelboats and less maneuverable vessels. They remained tied up until the flooding began to subside.

The wait for safer waters was unbearable not only for me, but also for the many trappers and adventurers who had remained in the wild to winter out the severe snowstorms of January, February, and March. They would be near empty-handed and in dire need of the supplies that were now pouring in from across the country and rising in huge stacks upon the levee to await permission from Mother Nature and the Missouri to pass.

SIXTY-THREE

Mr. Ledoux was kind enough to escort Rachel, Caleb and myself to the landing in his coach. He had become a good friend and advisor. He dispelled my earlier concerns and left me only to trust him implicitly with my affairs, both personal and professional as did Christopher put faith in me. I trusted Mr. Ledoux not with pen, but with heart to watch over Rachel and Caleb. Leaving friends was never easy. This was evident by the sorrowful expressions about me, especially in the eyes of Rachel, but the time had come for me to say good-bye.

"Oh, Miss Elizabeth, I so wish you would reconsider. Our lives won' be same without you. Caleb an' I don' want you to go. I especially don' want you to go. We worry for you. Are you sure you can' stay longer, you know how we wish you would."

"I do, Rachel. And I appreciate your concerns as well as your affections. You must try to understand that I have seen many cities, and much of the country. It is not a new place that I seek, but rather an old heart. My needs are different from yours. I seek a place of comfort that cannot be found on a map."

"I respect that, Miss Elizabeth, an' I don' mean to meddle or dismiss your decision, but I can' help feel that if you jus' give some time, Mr. Claussen will come to you. By all you have said, I know he will come find you soon as he gets word."

"I have no doubt you are correct, Rachel. Even I believe it so, but when might that be, next week, next year, the year after, when? Christopher may well have found his mountain pass and now stands on the Pacific coast about to board a ship that sails for Boston. Do you see I have no choice? Do you understand? I could easily wait here forever. Tell me, Francois, when do you suppose Christopher might be back this way?" I turned to Mr. Ledoux for support.

"When does a fathair give up 'is daugh-tair?" He shrugged his shoulders. "One nev-vair knows."

"You'll be fine, Rachel. Caleb loves you dearly and will watch over you. Remember, Reverend Meachum and Mr. Ledoux are here to assist you in running the orphanage along with Mrs. Potter, and Isabelle, and all the rest. You'll be fine, I promise; and so will I. You have my word. Things will work out for the best."

The loud clanging of a bell interrupted our conversation. We all looked momentarily toward the boat and took heed to a warning.

"Awl aboooooord that's goin' aboooooooord!"

"Well, it is time; I should be going. I wish you all the best of fortune and health."

"And we you."

645

"I would wait to see zee boat off, Elizabes, but upon leaving my office, I was informed ov an urgent mattair zat requires my immediate atten-shawn. I regret to say I must return. Do forgive me."

"By all means be off, all of you. I insist. Everything is in order; there is no need to worry."

"Sank-you, I pray you will take care an' God speed. Remembair, eet ese dangair-ous enough fair a man to travel ouestward, let alone a lady. Be careful, be vairy, vairy careful." Francois reached for my hand with that combination of Southern-French gentility and kissed it warmly within his firm grip.

"I shall, I promise." Francois turned to Rachel and Caleb.

"I weell take you back wis me if you so desire."

"Yes, yes. You two go with Francois. Take her back Caleb. I will be fine, go, go, both of you, go."

"Very well, good-bye, Miss Elizabeth. Good-bye." There came a flurry of hugs and farewells.

"Good-bye, Rachel. And good-bye to you, Caleb. Take good care of your wife. She cooks second to none."

"Yes, ma'am. That I will, I promise." He patted his stomach. "Thank-you for everything. Thank-you for helping us to find Isaac."

"Shhh." I placed my finger upon my lips to silence him. "Think nothing of it, Caleb. He will be back before you know it. Word is out."

"I will pray for you every night, Miss Elizabeth."

"And I you, Rachel. Take care. Give Isaac a big kiss for me."

"I will. I will. God bless. God bless, and God speed."

"God bless."

SIXTY-FOUR

We finished with our good-byes and parted company. I turned to work my way through the proliferation of goods crammed into every available space at the landing until I finally came to stand at water's edge. There, I scrutinized the steamer I was about to board.

First impressions were important to me, and on examination, I felt at once that it was a sturdy vessel. It appeared well cared for, having received a fresh coat of white paint to face the new season. There was no visible rot or streaks of green residue from mold to be seen staining the hull planks. The red trim was refreshed and all the scrapes and scratches of a season past had been repaired and put in order.

The bow plate proudly displayed the name 'WAVERLY', and I was reminded of Mr. Mendel's mentioning how each time a new boat in Christopher's fleet was launched from the yard, it was named in honor of the farthest settlement established westward along the river.

One might have thought I chose Christopher's boats because there was no charge for my passage, but that was only part of it. I came to learn that unlike many of the steamers working the rivers, this particular fleet was built in St. Louis based on experience and designed specifically to confront the hazards known to one treacherous river—*the muddy Missouri.*

Placards along the levee, and papers and postings about town advertised the advantages of Christopher's distinctively designed side-wheelers. The placards pointed out that beneath the waterline, his boats were built with a heavy protective shield of double planking at the front of the hull to resist punctures and to draw the vessel lower in the water at the bows. It explained how this helped to stop the boat quickly when striking sand bars instead of allowing the hull to ride up and over, thereupon becoming beached amidships.

The placards boasted extra heavy paddlewheels to withstand blows against the rocks and floating debris. The gunwales were reinforced for 'grass-hoppering', a term I was at a loss to fully comprehend. Simply put, it had to do with raising the boat up into the air on poles that could be affixed to the bows like walking stilts so that it might be levered across sandbars when all else failed.

The fleet on whole was built lighter and of a shallower draft than the boats Christopher built for the Ohio and Mississippi. It goes without saying, for my peace of mind the most welcome sight was a bold-lettered statement that highlighted the use of extra heavy boilers. They were *guaranteed not to blow up when needed most to meet the extra demands of the powerful Missouri currents'*.

"Thank-you, thank-you, thank-you." I uttered under my breath with nervous relief.

Not only by plan was this side-wheeler built dissimilar from the start, but also in service it made no excuse for presenting itself as the ugly duckling of its kind. I noted the differences in its outwardly appearance at once, for unlike the other river-boats I had chanced to board, this one conveyed nary a sign of comfort nor pampering one fully expected aboard a steamer.

I noticed that unlike other riverboats, this main deck had been fitted all around with a rail. It might well have been a belt for the way in which it served to contain the mountain of materials and goods compressed on board.

This vessel looked every bit a workhorse. It was outfitted for business and little else, nothing frivolous about its decor, and there were few sounds of laughter or merriment. Instead, its lower deck was piled high with hay, bale upon bale, and sacks of grain stacked like sandbags awaiting a flood. There were long double rows of cordwood for the boilers. There were makeshift pens nailed as needed directly to the deck planks in order to confine sheep, goats, and hogs. There were stacks of chicken coops packed full of birds half dead from fright.

THE WAVERLY

I was delighted to discover a cage of bawling cats enlisted for service as 'mousers' at one of the military forts upriver. They were an adorable and entertaining lot and held my attention for a good bit as they went through their rough and tumble antics, each pressing hard against the bars and competing for a place in which to enjoy my affections. Mountains of trunks, footlockers, boxes and bedrolls surrounded the cats like castle walls. Over their heads, someone managed to strap a couple of wagons to the sides of the boat that protruded outward like unwieldy ears.

All this rummage plus a notable lack of neatness added to the serious, no-nonsense appearance of the vessel. At least it gave the steamer an impression of being a solid well-built boat worthy of its cargo and my confidence.

Having ended the hardships of travel through Illinois, I stored my Albany made *'travel clothes'* and returned to wearing the acceptable high fashion attire necessary for calling on the socially elite of St. Louis. Having no further use of such extravagant garments, I left those to Rachel, returning again to simple dresses and bustles and of course my immoral trousers, all perfectly suited for travel aboard a riverboat.

I found myself to be the only woman to book passage and as expected even in a simple dress I stood out like a sore thumb among the crowd of men milling about the landing to have a smoke, a chew, or a gander my way.

For my gender, life was often a collection of uncomfortable situations that only a woman could appreciate, and I wished I had hid my femininity behind one of my new pants outfits. Yet, even that had serious drawbacks; for once found out, being the only person in a dress was mundane compared to being a brazen hussy sporting pantaloons. Either way I would have regrets. Existing in a man's world was purely an exercise in exasperation.

Wishing to remove myself from the discomfort of the wanton stares, I busied myself by going aboard, where I was escorted upstairs to the cabin deck. There, I slipped unnoticed behind a gathering of men leaning mindlessly against the guard and watching the goings on below. I was shown to my cabin where I saw to it that my trunk and baggage were bestowed to my liking.

After dismissing the deck hand I took a few moments to relax and inspect my quarters. Feeling all was in order, I stepped back outside. I locked my cabin door behind me, and stood alongside the men at the guard where I was again stared at from below, but at a more bearable distance.

It was only moments thereafter that the bell on the hurricane deck clanged a second time and was promptly followed by the same voice heard before to call out across the landing. Only now, it came from directly over my head.

"Awl abooooroord that's goin' aboooooooord! Last call—last call!"

Instinctively, I looked back across the wharf and up along the streets for a sign of Mr. Ledoux's coach. Of course, there would be nothing of the coach or Rachel and Caleb to be seen. I felt a rush of loneliness that might have turned to depression had I not chosen to distract myself from my heart's yearning. I gazed down at the crowd for relief.

In contrast to the first call, those men still upon the landing took the second warning seriously and began shuffling toward the boat to ascend the plank as a few others hurriedly departed. Once cleared, the far end of the plank was drawn upwards and secured vertically against the railing near to where I stood.

The lines were cast off. Below the shadow of a huge black plume of smoke, wheels began to turn, driven by the thump-thump-thump of pistons hidden from view, yet present in the vibration beneath our feet. Nervousness crept through me as we moved into the deep murky water of the Mississippi and pressed against its current to make our way north for the Missouri.

SIXTY-FIVE

Even to the untrained eye, there were clearly notable differences between traveling this riverboat and one built for pleasure on the Hudson. Without describing further the barnyard similarity and smell, these boats were smaller on average, little more than a hundred feet in length.

There was also the matter of passengers, which for the most part presented themselves as crude and frightful figures severely limited in manners, and as a rule, rude and unrefined. I had little doubt that this was due to the fact there were no women or children to be seen who might have tempered some of the spitting, swearing, and actions in need of restraint.

My being that rare female passenger was made all the more obvious by a visit to the women's saloon, which was always positioned at the rear of the Hurricane deck, farthest away from the boilers for safety. Although small compared to any I had seen before, it appeared once to have been luxurious and accommodating. Having been long neglected and unwanted, it now emerged empty of anything other than cargo.

I felt a tinge of disappointment, for any woman asked, would have gushed when describing her experience or dreams of the lavishness, extravagance, and unsurpassed service to be found in this room. It represented the highest form of pampering money could buy, and to treat a woman to a steamboat holiday, even for just a weekend, to sit and socialize in the saloon as the scenery passed by was considered to be the most thoughtful gift a man might give.

As I pondered the length of my journey upstream and the time to be spent on board, the sight of cabin walls reduced to one lackluster coat of dust disheartened me to no end. I searched across footprints of dried mud that dappled the wooden floor, and would have rejoiced to see even the faintest glimmer of morning's light prancing upon polish long since obscured by the smear of sand and clay.

I yearned to hear the room resonate with conversation and music. I imagined myself immersed in the melody of an orchestra that flowed with the cool river air beneath shimmering stars on a misty Missouri night. I saw the dense river fog being stirred into whirlpools by the passing of high society ladies sporting their finest attire and brushing by one another in large embroidered hoops and tilters. I could see the angelic faces of hopeful young maidens blushing in the arms of handsome men as they were led across the dance floor in quick step to a lively Virginia reel or quadrille.

I recalled having once seen a Massachusetts doctor glare at a daring young suitor who, in spite of the doctor's moral objection, had nerve enough to ask a certain young lady for her hand in a round dance. It was after all a waltz and oftentimes considered to be as disgraceful as it was beautiful, this due to the closeness of the partners.

In the eyes of the overly righteous, the dance was considered to be a disrespectful union and generally raised eyebrows and suspicion enough to promote rumor and condemnation. However, to their dismay, this young lady had spent her youth battling rumor and not only possessed a mind of her own, but enjoyed the dance for all its worth in spite of their whispers and beady-eyed stares.

The recollection made me homesick for Mary and Allen, but I still laughed aloud at the memory and it was just then that the WAVERLY's captain disrupted my thoughts. I turned at the sound of his approaching steps.

"I hope that wasn't a laugh of despair," he asked.

"A small one possibly. What a shame. It was meant to be such a beautiful room."

"Indeed it was. And I for one, would much prefer the sound of ladies laughter to the grunt of pigs in a pen, but that too is a dream, for we seldom enjoy a woman's presence on board and what little space we have comes at a premium. I hope you will forgive us and try to understand."

"I understand, but isn't it just like a man to allow the one place designed for a woman's comfort and safety to fall into such disrepair. It's thoughtless; it's filthy. Just look, is it not a perfect picture of a man's world?" I chided him.

"Well, before I am forced to walk the plank, I implore you take my arm and allow me to escort you to the pilothouse. I shall then explain that contrary to what you might think; no saloon was ever built aboard a riverboat for the purpose of pampering women. Nor was it built for protecting them from faulty boilers and ill-mannered men, as you might wrongly assume. Quite the opposite in fact, it was built to assure the well-being and safety of the male passengers. *Imagine that!*"

"*Male* passengers? Why does that not surprise me?" I scoffed.

"It is true. In fact, if it had not been for the irresistible attraction of your fairer sex, captains would have had no need whatsoever to incur the expense of constructing such a frivolous place. However, they discovered early on that segregation provided the easiest means of eliminating jealousy, accusations of infidelity and issues of dishonor whether justified or not. All that brawling and bashing of heads, all those broken noses, broken jaws and knuckles too often led to something much worse. Duels—and that was especially bad for business.

"You see; it was so much simpler to confine women to a cabin and keep them off the decks. Of course, a captain couldn't just sweep them up and hold them under lock and key; no sensible person would stand for it. Instead, saloons were built to be chocked full of opulence in the same way one baits a trap. The ladies flocked to such a place and marveled. The door was closed behind them and any man lacking proper connection to a lady within was expressly forbidden to enter.

"He could spend his time in the main saloon or move forward to the Gentleman's room where he was welcome to gamble, get drunk, smoke, chew tobacco, argue politics or discuss business with others without fear of distraction or untimely death. But in no case was he allowed to enter the ladies parlor. It was a most effective guise, as you now know."

"I must say, captain, you have thoroughly discarded a great pleasure of mine."

"Please call me Kenneth—Kenneth Parker, and know I am at your service."

"And such service! You have already outdone yourself, Mr. Parker. I shall know you henceforth as Kenneth, my fantasy killer." The captain laughed.

"I beg you give me the benefit of the doubt. I am not so bad, certainly not a fantasy killer. In fact, to have a gracious lady aboard this humble vessel is more fantasy than any man could fabricate, and I will surely be keel-hauled if I disturb the dream of so many."

"I will keep that in mind."

"Please do, for I promise to afford you every convenience, every service I might muster to make your journey as pleasant as possible. I have already prepared to have your belongings transferred from your cabin into accommodations equal to my own, or you may have my own, simply say the word.

"Also, I have come to welcome you to the pilothouse. The views from that height are often spectacular. Our pilot, Mr. Thompson is a gentleman in every way, and I know you will find him good company. He has already asked if you would honor him with a visit."

I held little doubt that both the captain and his pilot had been well warned of the supposed close connection between their lone female passenger and one Mr. Claussen. Mr. Mendels was an efficient and capable individual who would have seen to that in short order. Any other woman would probably have been brushed off with a *"sorry about the accommodations, but this isn't Boston"* apology and nothing more. I, on the other hand, was given every attention no matter how petty my wants.

It was clear that Mr. Thompson and the captain both desired my presence at the helm. There, I was introduced to Mr. Mardeselle, a French cook, and his three French assistants, who seconded as servants and were kept on board primarily to attend the pilot, but also the Captain and any other dignitary or military officer that might buy passage upriver.

The proud staff of Frenchmen, although superb at their employ and wonderfully adept, was not held in nearly the high esteem enjoyed by the renowned Negro chefs and servants to be found on the more illustrious steamers. The Negroes were celebrated for both their cuisine and ubiquitous service, but the idea of slave labor being performed upon a vessel owned by Christopher was unthinkable.

My first lesson in travel along the rivers brought to light an amusing twist in the responsibilities of captains on riverboats and captains on sailing ships. On the open sea, the captain of a ship was the undisputed god and gospel except for that short period of time when a harbor pilot brought the captain and his ship to port. Only then did the captain turn command over to the pilot, but even so, the captain remained watchful at his side.

On the river, it is the pilot who is god and gospel except for those hours spent at the landings when the captain is temporarily in command. The captain assumes charge of the vessel only when it is secured. He then oversees loading and unloading of cargo, sets up the watch, and tends to the needs and safety of his passengers.

Once the lines are cast off and the vessel is set free to the current, it is actually the pilot who reigns supreme, and his decisions are never questioned. He is the man who knows the river and is ultimately held responsible for the safety of the boat and its cargo. He commands the highest wage, which often can be exorbitant; it being whatever the market will bear, and he always gets his way. It was because of this odd twist of responsibility that stories told and retold of famous or infamous characters and their adventures upon the great rivers were never of captains, but instead of river pilots.

It was Mr. Thompson, our pilot, who invited me to relax within the comparatively spartan appointments of his station and enjoy the service offered by his staff. The captain was obligated to convey his desire, and I felt obligated to accept such hospitality. And although I understood it could be nothing nearly as extravagant as what I would find on an Ohio or Mississippi riverboat, it was a world apart from life on a keelboat, or even the lower deck of the WAVERLY for that matter.

April 22, 1832

Dearest Mary and Allen,

I hope my letter finds the both of you in best of health and heart. Know I am doing well and ease your minds of worry. I am comfortably resting aboard the WAVERLY, one of Christopher's riverboats having just departed St. Louis. There is little to do beyond enjoying the scenery, and I fear I will be forced to endure more free time than I prefer. I determined it best to make good of my time by catching up on letters promised and long past due.

I am presently sitting alongside Mr. Thompson, our pilot. He is a good-natured man and well known for his sensibilities upon this river. He possesses an enviable reputation, proven experience, and, taking heed of Mr. Pennington's advice, no history of racing or tragedy. I have been impressed by the man's knowledge, not only of the land that I shall soon be witness too, but also of its history and inhabitants. He seems to know a great deal about western Indians of all tribes, and although I am able to observe the country clearly from the height of the upper deck, it will be some time before we reach lands where I might see these inhabitants in the wild. I am at the same time both impatient and hesitant, both excited and fearful to see tipis upon the plain.

I am embarrassed over all the fuss and attention being paid me. I have found that my objections to such pampering go unheard, and therefore am resigned to remain silent and accept their courtesies. It has been explained to me by Mr. Mardeselle, the chef, that his staff seldom has opportunity to practice manners and etiquette.

Since I made the mistake of mentioning that much of my youth was spent in service as a table maiden for the wealthy and elite of Boston, I have been confronted with questions for direction and improvement. I suffer under a burden of requests for advice and consul, and find myself amazed that past experience in tasks of my lowly origin now place me in such high regard. I can only say; if my advice serves them well then so be it. After all, there are worse ways to be welcomed into the western wilds....

SIXTY-SIX

Eighteen miles above St. Louis, I was introduced to Missouri's namesake watercourse. We left the easygoing flow of the Mississippi where began my two thousand mile trek up the Big Muddy.

As a witness, I was captivated by the activity of Mr. Thompson, who remained standing at the helm to steer us up the mouth of the Missouri. He called out a variety of commands through the paneless window openings while at the same time caressing the giant wheel back and forth in a constant motion as he held the WAVERLY steady midstream against the crosscurrents that coursed beneath us. He even smoked a pipe to make the perfect picture. My view from the pilothouse was advantageous as promised, and

I enjoyed the opportunity to see better than most the confluence of the great rivers.

Mr. Thompson was most friendly and ever ready to converse. It was with interest I listened to his descriptions of these waterways and their peculiarities. He was quick to point out the changes constantly taking place that only a pilot might readily detect.

"Did'jah notice how much yellowier is the Missouri?"

"I didn't, but now that you mention it."

"It's a fast flowin' river. Too fast. It steals everything that ain't nailed down or embedded in rock. It's dangerous, Miss Claussen. For every boat goin' upriver, I'll count a hundred wrecks comin' down. I've always said a whirlpool an' waterfall must o' bred this blessed river. It was born with a bad disposition, yes, ma'am, no manners an' a mind all its own. It keeps everything stirred up. That's why it's yellow—silt never settles. It stays on the surface as thick as on its bed. Most o' the silt comes down from the Osage. The Mississippi's always blackish green. The Missouri's always yellow an' thick with mud top t'bottom. It's colder water as well. Air always feels cooler on the Missouri."

"*That* I did notice."

"I thought ya might. There's an extra wrap there if ya need it."

Mr. Thompson nodded to the bench behind him. There I saw the wrap. He spoke as though he knew with intimacy each and every one of the three thousand miles of Missouri River that stretched between the Mississippi and the Rocky Mountains.

I was allowed to watch and thereby learned from Mr. Thompson what methods were best undertaken to overcome the variety of obstacles presented us—and there were many. His eye was truly keen and focused on reading ominous signs that I was hopelessly unable to discern, but which always proved his predictions of sawyers and sunken menace without fail.

660

In spite of our Mr. Thompson's wonderful accounts of the river and the wealth of information he freely offered, I had grown stiff upon the bench. I elected to break from my unexpected lessons and my letter writing in order to stretch my legs. Compelled to take my leave of Mr. Thompson, yet wishing not to be rude nor distract him from his duties, I mentioned politely that I intended to walk along the guard for a short spell and improve my circulation.

I was already on my feet and about to exit when Mr. Thompson gestured for me to stop and insisted I allow him to escort me down to the main deck and deliver me into Captain Parker's care. He expressed a personal motive to guard me against the insensitivities I might otherwise encounter before the more unscrupulous men on board. I welcomed the offer and waited briefly as he instructed his apprentice to take command of the helm.

Mr. Thompson was pleasant and considerate in every way, and after stepping out of the pilothouse; he immediately raised concern about the spring breezes and cool river air that confronted us. He saw to it that my shawl was bundled warmly about my neck before we descended to the cabin deck and strolled aftward.

We stopped and rested upon the stern guard where we watched the Mississippi recede into the distance. We spoke of the season and upcoming vistas, and made other small talk at which point he suggested I go to the bows on the main deck and hear Captain Parker's presentation on the Missouri River. For safety's sake and quite frankly, my own peace of mind, I insisted Mr. Thompson return to his station, but he descended the staircase at my side explaining that he was obligated to pay visit to the boiler room. And so we parted at the last step, I going forward, he going aft.

On my own, I walked forward to join a small group of men that had gathered to hear what Captain Parker was about to say. He had stepped atop a small crate at the bows in order to raise himself above his audience and smiled in my direction after seeing me approach. He faced us and joked with the men, holding their attention and keeping them amused until satisfied no one else would be attending. At that point, he sounded out with confidence.

"*Lady* and gentlemen!"

The comment brought a chuckle from the male passengers. Outwardly, I nodded. Inwardly, I too chuckled. For as God was my witness, there was indeed a lady on board; but aside from the captain, Mr. Thompson, and a small handful of others, nothing I could describe in good conscience as a gentleman existed among the scruffy lot of trappers, traders, explorers, or soldiers who were forever tripping over me, bumping into me and dreaming their futile dreams. A few of those characters now pointed out features upriver as Captain Parker took a deep breath and commenced to speak boldly.

"For those of you who have never before seen that infamous river of legend—that waterway which captures the hearts of the brave and foolish in a way no woman can—the waterway that leads them through these uncharted territories and the wilds of the Great American Desert—into the treacherous realm of the untamed Indian—that river, which so—."

The captain's voice faded unexpectedly amid an upsurge of unrest that raced through the crowd. No sooner had he started his presentation and spun around with an outstretched arm to capture a view of his legendary waterway, than all in attendance raised their own arms to point upriver with him at precisely the moment our boat flew into a fit of convulsions.

One and all were pitched forward as a group directly into the Captain, who was subsequently knocked off his crate and pinned hard against the guard. Without a moment's hesitation, he freed himself from the tangle, stepped rudely across the fallen, and bolted past the remainder to go aft beyond our view.

I was both dumbfounded and rather frightened as I regained my footing and saw those souls who managed to stay on their feet turn about in haste and disappear hot on the Captain's heels. Immediately thereafter, the men at the bottom of the heap jumped to their feet and likewise vanished. I stepped back from the stampede and in an instant found myself alone and confused.

I looked upriver to where all had pointed across deck, rail, and water without a clue as to what was happening. Surely, I too should be running.

"Am I blind?" I spoke aloud.

I strained to see something, but there was nothing before me except our bows, an island, and lots and lots of water. I stepped to the side of the deck and looked back along the boat where I noted signs of excitement, but nothing I could decipher. Apparently we had passed over something. Would we now pass back over it in reverse?

I stepped up to the bows, pressed against the guard and leaned over. I peered into the water expecting to see a giant sawyer or scaly monster emerge from the depths. I saw nothing. I then leaned as far over as possible and peered cautiously under the bows convinced more than ever that something would explode from the depths, for we were still running astern—full astern. There was a pronounced wake *before* me instead of behind but nothing more.

Not knowing what to expect, I stared into the turbulent wake ready to jump back at any second. It was obvious that a boiler hadn't exploded, for we were under full steam. I considered the possibility that the bottom of the hull might have been ripped out on a rock. That would have explained the sudden lurch forward and Mr. Thompson's attempts to back off, but why he was still steaming astern I couldn't venture to guess—unless it was to keep water from entering the hull or something of that nature.

All these thoughts passed through my mind as I hung out over the rail staring down into the water until I was suddenly grabbed from behind by my shawl and pulled backwards into the boat. I spun about to keep my balance and came face to face with a wide-eyed stranger who wasted no time telling me to move.

"Come on lady, lessin' ya wanna die up 'ere."

"Die of what?" Nervous of the stranger, instinctively I pushed his hand away. He pointed over my shoulder and across the bows toward the island.

"At that!"

"At what? There's nothing but—." I looked over the bow once again and my jaw dropped. The stranger didn't have to utter another sound, for as impossible as it might seem, an island was directly upon us. I was so surprised by the nearness of it that I clumsily stepped backward into the man.

"I reckon ya seez it now, eh? It's an islan' o' floatin' trees... call em' snags, an' they'z headin' right for us. Wasn't there yesterday, won't be tomorraw, an' either will we if the pilot don' get us the hell outta 'ere right now!"

It was all I could do to take my eyes away. I saw now that it was more like a bank of islands all combining into one. It was huge! A landmass in its own right, it appeared to be a hundred times the size of our boat and backed up the flow of water enough to push it along at breakneck speed. It was sweeping up all the debris before it like a giant pushbroom and now appeared fully prepared to sweep us away as well.

All I could do was stare in disbelief and pray Mr. Thompson knew what he was doing. It must have come upon us after he had taken leave of the helm to escort me down to the Captain and pay his visit to the boiler room. The apprentice probably feared taking it upon himself to turn and flee, and risked awaiting Mr. Thompson's return in hopes of leaving the situation to him. Evidently, he waited too long for there was now nowhere to go.

"I don' know if tha' pilot wuz sleepin' or what, but he shorz 'ell wasn' lookin' 'cross the bows. Ain't 'ardly time enough lef' t' turn this tub 'round now."

"Will we make it?"

"Can't rightly say. 'e's back paddlin' good n'ard, an' ya can bet 'e's stuffin' them furnaces full, but 'e'll be needin' a lot o' pressure t' keep us ahead o' that disaster."

"*Please* don't tell me we're going to blow up."

"Can't rightly say. Problem is, 'e ain't got no time to git 'round this one. I bet'cha we gits chased clear back ta the Mississippi 'fore we git room enough to go one way or 'nother. Ya know 'ow t' swim?"

"You can't be serious!"

"'If'n 'e don' get us turned about an' outta 'ere, an' get us up the Mississippi quick as a rabbit, or if she blows, then ya'll be swimmin' or drownin'. I can promise ya that!"

It seemed a tall order. No wonder everyone ran to the back of the boat. At least up to this point everything was moving orderly and sensible and that gave me reason enough to hope. Nevertheless, I cowered from the noise and vibration, the choking smoke, ash and cinders coming forward from the stacks to press on my worst fears of a boiler blowing us to 'kingdom come'.

The next few minutes were the worst for everybody because contrary to opinion, Mr. Thompson decided he did have time to bring the WAVERLY around. I have no doubt he did so in record time considering the cross currents and obstacles, which were never to one's advantage. As the bows moved to point down-stream, the stranger and I walked along the guard keeping the snags in view. We had lost precious moments that served to bring the island nearly upon our stern.

We moved to the back of the crowd where we watched nervously as the dense thicket approached closer on its high tide of water. There was, as the stranger said, no time to course sideways. The lost time brought the mass close enough for me to study the dreadful tangle of stumps, trees, bushes, sand, and dead animals that made up its bulk.

The island sounded out to us with an endless stream of cracking, snapping, and scraping noises as the mass encountered submerged barriers that pitted the unstoppable against the immovable. The groaning sounds seemed to mock our attempts to escape our demise as it dammed up more of Missouri's water to power the havoc it hoped to wreak. The swaying of trees and limbs at its leading edge reminded me of teeth grinding back and forth in frustration as it rushed forward to devour us.

By a lifetime of experience and possibly the grace of God, Mr. Thompson succeeded in keeping us ahead of the horror as we made for the Mississippi in all haste. Fortunately, as we headed back downriver, our *'extra heavy boilers guaranteed to withstand the demands of the Missouri'* were able to hold up to the certain strain put upon them long enough to keep us out of harm's way.

We were hell bent to cut north across the mouth of the Missouri and plow into the oncoming current of the Mississippi, which slowed us down considerably. It was with palpable fear that we prayed and watched as the minor continent came roaring upon us only to miss snatching our lives by a stone's throw before breaking away in submission to the swollen flow of the Mississippi as it raced southward. The faces about me showed a profound look of relief and fascination.

"Look out St. Louis!" A passenger yelled out.

"Hell, Look out New Orleans!" expressed another.

"Ooo-wheeee!" Everyone was yelling and whistling, and swinging their hats and waving it on by.

I breathed a sigh of relief and felt as though the Missouri had belched me out of its mouth along with half a plantation. I started to laugh. I couldn't help it. We had been afloat only a couple of hours before running like the devil in the wrong direction—backwards, east, of all things! We were back where we started, and this was only the beginning—two thousand more miles to go!

May 15, 1832

I am back to my letter for a while. Progress upriver can be incredibly slow at times. I find myself wishing away the hours as we fight our way for every mile. Better my time be spent thinking of you.

I must begin by saying that letters may be superb for conveying through pen, words of love that one finds difficult to voice in person, but it is sorely inadequate when one hopes to describe the likes of the Missouri River. It makes the act of writing difficult as one suffers the futility of conveying such a scene.

This river seems to turn the world inside out by churning its waters into whirlpools, whipping up a plethora of rock, trees, debris, and dead animals, which flow past abundantly between its banks. I have never seen anything like it.

Our first day out, we were no sooner upon its flow when we were nearly overrun by an island large enough to graze sheep. Imagine an episode whereby we are steaming full speed astern trying to outrun an island.

I am told that the smallest change in the river's flow can dislodge any number of small tangles of debris and cause them to suddenly collect into one enormous floating mass within minutes. It was just one such mass that put the fear of God into us all.

Mr. Thompson managed to get the boat turned about and to safety, but I assure you we were seriously in doubt of our chances. I was not alone in my prayers for redemption and my sighs of relief at our narrow escape.

Our second attempt up the Missouri was successful. We stopped first at St. Charles where we stayed over two nights and the day between. Maybe you can find it on a map. Most of the men went ashore to do business, little of it respectable. St. Charles seems to have been built on a foundation of taverns and brothels.

Mr. Thompson says this is where many of the river pilots and captains are found for hire. He says it is perfectly situated for Missouri river traffic, not too far from St. Louis, not too far from Franklin. A good place to wait out calls for employment, but a bad place for ladies to wander about alone. I had little reason to doubt him and so stayed on board. I was well entertained by the sight of those men returning to collapse.

After departing St. Charles, I began to learn something about the ways of life on this capricious river course. Everything about it is unpredictable, whereas much about us is becoming routine. We start each day with breakfast, and while we eat, a team of men go ashore to chop wood for the boilers. Meanwhile, a second team dismantles the boilers, opening the ends to clean out the mud. There is a sign that hangs in the engine room and reads:

Crusted, Rusted, Busted!

The boilermen know their business and are quick about scraping and washing out the sludge. They usually have the boilers reassembled and ready for the "woodhawks" to place the first load of wood directly into the furnaces, thereby getting them up to temperature by the time the wood is stacked and we are finished with our meal.

Mr. Thompson complains that the Missouri is too thick to drink and too thin to cultivate. He stands behind the wheel and contemplates whether the flow is one of water thickened with mud, or mud thinned with water. The latter I should think, based upon my observations of what comes out of the boilers each morning. Besides, water should be a healthy clean clear bluish-green, not dirty opaque yellow.

I think of the Missouri more as an avalanche than a river. I have never seen so much rubble come tumbling along. It doesn't look nor act as any river I have known. It is ill tempered and in a state all its own. I am told it learned its writhing mean-spirited ways from the snakes that crawl along its upper Missouri banks.

Ironically, the river has more trees between its banks than on them. Trees are becoming notably scarce in this country unless you are on a boat, then they come without end, each one floating past like a forty-foot pike taking aim at the hull. Their number equals that of a forest and so should anyone be surprised to see a herd of thousand-pound buffaloes bloated up and floating past like rotting carp? We outmaneuver them right along with the rocks, debris, and white water rapids.

All this dodging can get monotonous for real men, so for excitement there has been added an endless supply of shifting sandbars and swift contrary currents assured to explode our already stressed boilers. What better diversion could one provide for the cohort of gamblers on deck? Wagers on whether or not we make it upstream outnumber the poker bets two to one....

I put aside my pen and well, so I might watch Mr. Thompson take the WAVERLY to shore. The river had opened up to a wide bottomland where it meandered back and forth between sizable stands of cottonwood. Men known as 'woodhawks' often showed up in these places to chop wood and stack it for the steamers to earn a wage and a meal.

Once secured, Mr. Thompson stepped back from the helm and took leave of the pilothouse with me lagging behind. I had to think twice about following him out, for the mosquitoes were swarming in dreadful numbers. The pilothouse had no windows and now I realized Mr. Thompson generally smoked his pipe while at shore to fend off the mosquitoes. I did my best to cover up and spent a good deal of time seeking out breezes that crossed the deck and helped hold the pests at bay. In no way did I plan to go ashore where the air was still and the mosquitoes ravenous.

As I walked to stay ahead of the little devils, I spied the stranger who pulled me off the bow guard before the floating island. He was leaning on the rail at the opposite end of the boat smoking a cigar and watching the deckhands tie off the ship and pass news back and forth of St. Louis and the wilderness. I could hear some of the men laughing and others haggling over the price of wood for the boiler. They were all covered head to foot in tallow and bear grease.

As I neared the stranger, I noticed he kept shaking his head and snickering to himself until I found myself laughing with him from a distance. Fully taken in by his antics, I approached him and interrupted his thoughts to ask what was so funny. He turned to me, and breaking into a wide black-toothed grin, flicked an ash, and again shook his head.

"I wuz jus' standin' 'ere a thinkin' I'd gone plum' crazy, for I's cert'in, when I come down this river a month ago, this wood-pile wuz on the wes' bank. Not the eas' bank, as we're seein' it now. I's sayin' t' myself, geez-louweez, yer losin' yer brains. Afer'n a lotta head scratchin' I finally come t' the 'clusion, I din't lose nuthin' at'all. I knowz it wuz on th' wes' bank. So then I went on t' askin', why in tarnation would anybody go t' all the trouble o' movin' that pile o' wood from one bank t' th' udder. An' it hit me. Ya idjit! I said t' myself, they ain't moved nothin'. The damned river's in a diff'er'nt place again."

And so it was. Hadn't I just attempted to impress upon Mary and Allen that there was nothing at all conventional about this river? It was as stubborn and belligerent as the people who traveled it, a true communion of character. It was ornery and resentful. It resisted us every inch of the way, pelting us, scraping us, bashing us, pinning us down or leaving us high and dry. Its channels changed before our eyes, leaving us atop gravel beds, sandbars, or even worse—quicksand. Its banks appeared, or instantly disappeared beneath our feet leaving us reaching frantically for a firm handhold or scrambling for solid ground.

Mary and Allen would never understand, but I was certain that the WAVERLY's guardrails would be a testimony to life on the river, their lengths buffed smooth from days of hard gripping by white knuckled fists.

...We continue upriver, stopping only to replenish our ever-dwindling wood supply. The boilers are insatiable, devouring nearly twenty cord of wood a day as we fight the currents going upstream. We passed Point Labadie and the mouth to the Gasconade River. In particular, I was able to see one of the significant sources of the yellow color so characteristic of the Missouri. As Mr. Thompson said, it comes from the Osage River, which spills its effluent into the Big Muddy as one might squirt yellow ocher into a wash of water upon the canvas.

We passed the village of Cote Sans Dessien. It was positioned under a peculiar hill called the Hill of No Reason, named thus for standing alone and being so out of place. It knifes its way into the river from the north bank, where it juts out nearly half a mile.

Mr. Thompson is quick to point out each and every island, all of which seem to be named "Cedar". We managed our way past the Manitou Rocks and Split Rock where the river narrows down noticeably and put Mr. Thompson and Captain Parker on alert for more of those dreadful floating islands. All eyes were on the river and some on the bible.

After the narrows, the river changed noticeably. Now it wanders side to side, zigzagging back and forth with its underwater channels running contrary. The nature of the river is to attack us from the side with strong currents that pass underneath even though we are aligned with the flow. The boat is often jarred quite hard at times, its bows being suddenly swept away. It doesn't take long to understand how the Missouri makes its pilots famous for Mr. Thompson seldom has a moment to relax. I sit here and watch as he fights every moment to keep the boat centered upon the river and cusses at currents crisscrossing beneath us to undo his efforts.

The weather has warmed considerably and the heat of day is now something to be considered. Storms out here seem much more violent than back east. They always possess gale-like winds that blow across the open spaces and water to give us great concern. As the river changes from one direction to another, this brings the weather first to port then starboard and makes navigating the boat impossible. Often it blows with such ferocity, bringing with it a stinging mix of rain, sand, and hail, that we are left with no choice but to secure the WAVERLY to the trees along the bank and abandon the pilothouse to escape the thrashing.

We stopped for a day at Franklin. This is a most unusual place as it is a living community with the bizarre distinction of being a bona fide ghost town. That is because the original city of Franklin was a large community, second only to St. Louis and boasting over two thousand residents. It was the true start point of the Santa Fe Trail.

Mr. Thompson said it had some of the finest docks he had ever seen. According to him, it prospered handsomely on riverboat traffic, but right smack in the middle of its heyday, the river reared up its ugly head and washed everything away leaving nothing more than a flat field of sand covered with dead washed up trees.

The folks being strong of will rebuilt the town, this time a ways back from the river on much higher ground. They call it New Franklin now. The place looks nice to me, and I wouldn't know the difference, but Mr. Thompson says it never regained its former glory.

About three hundred miles upriver, we arrived at Fort Osage. William Clark had built it, and I am told it reflects his habit of building three sided forts. It was erected about five miles above a place called Fire Prairie and about a hundred feet above the waterline where it commands a spectacular view of the river in both directions. I found it intriguing after hearing so much about Lewis and Clark over the years.

From there we continued upriver past the Kaw, the Little Platte and Nodaway Rivers, which I understand probably means nothing to anybody in Boston. What I most want to say is look on your map! I have reached the place considered by all boatmen to be the beginning of the Upper Missouri, the beginning of the real 'wild west', the Platte River....

SIXTY-SEVEN

In a tradition much the same as one I recalled when a child, whereby we toasted the crossing of the equator, the men of the WAVERLY brought out the whiskey and offered it to all who wished to greet the Upper Missouri. It was both a commemoration and an initiation into that exclusive and most celebrated club of souls who claimed to have actually set foot in the 'far west'. It was an event to be recorded.

...On this one occasion, I was obliged to partake in downing that most distasteful brew, for I was told that the crew and passengers alike were awaiting word as to whether or not 'Lady Claussen' would join them in a toast. With so much attention being directed my way, I wouldn't have been worthy of the honor had I raised a glass of lemonade, so wishing to be a good sport, I braced myself and downed the whiskey in a gulp.

No doubt, the look on my face pleased the men to no end. I am certain that out of jest, I was not poured the watered down drink as promised and received far more than my fair share. And although my drink came directly from Mr. Thompson's private stock with assurances of its silky smoothness, it was a perfect blend of fire and acid that all but killed me. However, when my emptied glass hit the table, it put a 'whole lotta life' into a hundred men ready to raise the dickens....

After a riotous toasting to the passing of the Platte, the first signs of change were quick to come, beginning with the depth of the Missouri. Above the confluence of the Platte, the Missouri was suddenly much less a river and shallower to show for it. The whole character of the country changed as noticeably as the river and gave one the sensation of passing through a portal into another world.

This continent being formerly dense with varied forest that blanketed the lofty hills, now flowed outward to level itself. Immense plains transformed the world into wide featureless grasslands, where the sun pressed flat everything short of those copses of cottonwood that were instead squeezed out and compressed into corners formed by a break in the earth's crust or boundaries created by a rogue river's course.

The rocks that had been strewn about the countryside and collected into nightmarish rapids had all but disappeared. Now the banks were made up of dense walls of clay. Periodically a flooding river would work loose chunks of pumice and lignite from the vertical sculpted slabs to be washed downstream where it commonly bobbed past astounded passengers, many of whom lost more than their hats betting rocks couldn't float.

I was seeing a rush of new things for the first time. Some had to be pointed out, while others were overwhelmingly obvious. Horned toads and magpies made welcome introductions in contrast to rattlesnakes, which slithered along the banks in dreadful numbers to soak up the sun and cause my skin to crawl even from the safety of the boat. Mr. Thompson was unbothered by their numbers saying only that they were good to eat

Away from the banks, out on the flats of sage and mesquite, and often sharing dens with these horrible snakes were prairie dogs. They were adorable little furry creatures that lived in immense colonies, as could be verified by the mounds they built, which reached the boundaries of vision. Thousands of these little creatures could be observed carrying on, bobbing up and down, sitting on their haunches and barking out their conversation. Hawks circled overhead whisper quiet and watchful for the preoccupied prairie dog that was to become their next meal.

It appeared as though Mother Nature bred speed into some of her creatures to help them cope with the vast spaces, for I saw two animals in particular that left me thoroughly impressed with their ability to move. The first one was the white tailed jackrabbit, which leapt across the plain in bounds that approached twenty feet. It might well have been a bird for the time it remained in the air.

The second was the pronghorn, which began making an appearance in numbers out in the distance. On occasion we were able to near these creatures at waters edge and when startled they were capable of running at speeds too great to comprehend. I would wager five or six times that of the horse. Never have I seen anything move that fast across land. I have been told that the cheetah is the fasted animal alive. This I can't imagine after seeing the pronghorn run.

As we traveled farther into the desert, these marvels and all the trials and tribulations associated with our progress began to become routine, and as often as not wonders and woes alike slipped by the gamblers, the drunkards, and the unwary unnoticed. This was no truer than during passages through cliffs that blocked the open views across the prairies.

It was while pressed between these cliffs, that I heard a particularly sharp knock. In short succession, there came a second and a third much like the rap of a large woodpecker. My curiosity was aroused and I looked up from my writing in search of some magnificent bird heretofore unseen. Captain Parker was standing calmly behind Mr. Thompson and looking about. There came another and another at which point he looked down at me and smiled.

"What is that?" I asked most curious.

"An Indian game."

"Really?"

Again came the sharp raps, this time four or five in unison.

"What kind of game? I didn't even know there were any Indians on board." I was amazed that I hadn't noticed them straight away at the landings. I stood up for a look and see when Captain Parker answered.

"Shooting at us."

"Shooting at us!" I collapsed immediately upon the bench, rolling over onto my side in order to duck below the windows. "My god! Are we under attack?" The two gentlemen looked to be standing upside down from my vantage point. They both laughed at the sight of me.

"No, just a reminder that we are trespassing on their lands. You might say a game of Peek-a-boo. I wouldn't fear if I were you. You can sit up. They shoot down on us from this stretch of banks because the steepness of the shore allows their arrows to descend from a great distance. I think that is how they get rid of their old arrows. They save them up for us. Quite often, you can see them slipping in and out of view on the upper banks, but the overhang of the roof will keep anything above from entering the pilothouse. You can sit up. You're fine."

No further arrows fell from the sky, but that did little for my state of mind. I felt like a sitting duck, for there was no slipping in and out of view when it came to the WAVERLY with all its smoke and noise. The towering trails of black smoke could be seen for miles and the Indians were well aware of our presence. At last, like it or not, along the river's edge, I was seeing more and more signs of the savages that I had read about the whole of my life. I found the arrows and the encounters most stressful.

"Does this not bother you in the least?" I asked Mr. Thompson.

"Not really. Most of these Indians come to the banks in hopes we might stop and trade. As a rule they are friendly and like doing business with the settlers. They especially like our whiskey and wares."

His words rang true. I watched as Indians raced into view with waving arms in a frantic attempt to persuade us to land.

"It's the ones you can't see that you should fear. They are the ones who don't much care for white men or other Indians for that matter, but especially white men. They keep their distance. They come around now and then to remind us we're unwanted."

"See here?" Captain Parker picked at a small pit on the windowsill, and after brushing away some unseen splinters, he led me outside the pilothouse and went on to point out a couple of dozen more pits about the boat, places where arrows had left their marks. I was struggling to digest the sight of real life arrows laying about the deck as I followed him about. I had seen this odd scarring, but had never given it a thought until now, and now, it held some real significance that sent an agonizing cramp of anxiety clean to my marrow.

"See that one there, and all those over there. The boat is covered with them."

"You mean they just sit about overhead and shoot as us?" I was astonished.

"I wouldn't say it's that bad."

"And none of this makes you nervous?"

"Oh, it can get nervy at times, but a riverboat is pretty much like a floating fort, maybe even better as long as you keep it floating. Besides, I don't think that the Indians are bent on killing us. I mean we have been trading with them for years. Sometimes they just get annoyed at having nothing of value to trade for our goods and resent seeing us travel farther upstream to do business with their neighbors or worse, their enemies."

Captain Parker walked forward across the deck and bent over to dislodge seven or eight arrows that stood vertical on the deck. He returned and beckoned me to reenter the pilothouse.

"Sometimes, they get upset when they see us hunting their food or trampling over their sacred grounds. But, I will admit there are those days when they just plain don't like us. Usually when they're drunk. You might say this is their way of driving home a point." Captain Parker handed me the arrows and laughed at the pun. "No, to be honest, for the most part we ignore them and they leave us be."

"'Cept for the Sioux," injected Mr. Thompson. "They can get a little persnickety."

"True. Same goes for the Blackfoot. You have to keep a close eye on them as well or you'll be in a heap of trouble."

"When do we run into them?" I asked.

"Well, we don't," answered Captain Parker. "We don't travel that far upriver. They camp up beyond the Marias. But if you continue as far west as it sounds like you're going, you best get a good guide or you might end up barbecued."

My throat went dry.

...To an observant soul, our boat looks to be diseased. It is pock marked much as the face of those unfortunates who suffered the small pox. And no wonder, today it rained arrows. These marks are the result of arrow tips striking the wooden deck of our vessel. Is that not something to raise the spirits?

Indian sightings are now becoming much more frequent. Every few days we see them lined up along the banks of the river trying to persuade us to land. Neither Captain Parker nor Mr. Thompson seems concerned by their presence, but it troubles me terrible.

Instead, the men pay attention to movement in the distance, high up on the banks of the river or back up in the hills. I am told the Indians that are apt to give us trouble are Indians we don't see. Mr. Thompson can spot them right off, even while busy at the helm. He points them out to me and no matter how far off; a mere glimpse is enough to grip me with fear, for Indians are not reputed to treat women kindly.

I am confident I can stand up to snakes, spiders, scorpions, or anything but Indians. They worry me, and I find this queer considering the years I have spent working with people of every origin. Having read too many articles about scalping, disem-boweling, and torture must now be my undoing.

In contrast to my fears, I am surprised at the indifference both Captain Parker and Mr. Thompson exhibit toward the savages. Except for the Sioux and the Blackfoot, they pay them little mind. They don't seem to fear or despise these people nor do they possess the hatred in their hearts, as do most men back east. I suppose any danger becomes trivial when you live with it day to day.

At least I am happy to write that one advantage to shipping government supplies is that soldiers are always attached to them. True to form, they stand guard over their goods and unofficially watch over us as well, but guards, no guards, Indians, no Indians, no matter how I slice it, the Missouri is a far, far cry from the civility of the Hudson or even the Mohawk for that matter....

SIXTY-EIGHT

I happened to be in the pilothouse lost in thoughts about home, when Mr. Thompson had one of the Frenchmen deliver a message to Captain Parker.

"Tell Captain Parker that I wish to have word with both he and Captain Meyers." The servant disappeared.

Captain Meyers was in charge of the military contingent responsible for guarding the supplies aboard the WAVERLY. I looked up at Mr. Thompson who remained focused upon the river. I considered him with suspicion and uneasiness because I couldn't imagine there would be anything so important for Mr. Thompson to discuss with Captain Meyers and Parker that didn't involve Indians. My stomach went tight.

On the other hand, I considered it unlikely that Mr. Thompson should discuss something so unsettling in front of a lady. The two captains approached and yet, I hadn't been asked to leave. On second thought, it seemed my concerns may have been premature and so I settled myself until that time I would know.

"Good afternoon, Mr. Thompson—milady." The officer nodded in my direction.

"Good afternoon, Captain Meyers." I responded.

Captain Parker merely smiled. Although he, Mr. Thompson, Captain Meyers and I knew each other well by this time, Captain Meyers wasn't as close and still maintained a more formal air in my presence. Mr. Thompson addressed Captain Meyers as soon as he entered the pilothouse.

"Good afternoon, Captain Meyers. You have mentioned many times that this is your first trip along the upper Missouri, and so I felt it best to inform you of a problem that will most certainly confront us." Captain Meyers raised his head with interest. "After you have traveled this river a few times you will soon get to know her intimately and recognize such things

680

as her depth, which I am sorry to say is down. This is all too obvious by the number of sandbars and eddies that I have been fighting since passing the Platte."

"Do you fear we won't make it upriver, sir?" The captain interrupted Mr. Thompson out of genuine concern for his mission.

"I don't believe it will come to that, but in another days' time we will arrive at a stretch of white water known as Rapid Run, which is passable as a rule. I am certain that we will be able to manage the stretch, but not without delay. I know time is a matter of importance for you and so I am preparing you for what lies ahead.

"We will arrive at the lower end of the rapids where we will be obligated to unload our cargo and reduce the WAVERLY's draft. It is not an uncommon practice during low water at this place. I will then maneuver her to a landing safe above the rocks. Meanwhile Captain Parker will oversee the transfer of our cargo upstream. To consider anything less would be too much of a risk and surely you understand my priority is first to keep the WAVERLY afloat and everything else comes second.

"As a rule, the passengers aboard take responsibility for moving their own cargo unless weight or bulk prohibits it at which point there are always plenty of volunteers. Because of the amount of government supplies in your charge, you will have to enlist the service of the men at Rapid Run. They are always willing to trade a few hours work for common supplies.

"Barring any unforeseen problems, I expect to be delayed no more than half a day's time. We will be at Rapid Run for most of the day loading and unloading, but I will make up some of the lost time by running extra hours into the evening if the river appears safe enough to allow it. Have you any questions?"

"No, sir. I see no alternative. I appreciate the information, and I'll await your further instructions."

After some additional small talk both captains departed.

Most of my time spent traveling had been aboard sailing ships or stagecoaches. This journey into the interior by way of rivers and canals was unique and possessed peculiarities all its own. Most notable were the two major drawbacks.

Much to the glee of the stagecoach lines, rivers froze over every winter and that stopped river trade and transport for a couple of months at the very least. Also, rivers hardly needed to freeze over to become impassable. As the season grew late, or if there was a drought, water levels only had to drop inches to wreak havoc among the larger vessels. It only took one grounded vessel to stop all traffic on some rivers. There was a balancing act maintained between the dangerous high water of spring flooding and lows of summer droughts. No one knew this better than Mr. Thompson, and as he said; 'the summer was hot, dry, and the water low'.

I couldn't agree more, for since passing the Platte it was as Mr. Thompson testified; the sandbars were lined up one after another to thwart our progress. A constant vigil was maintained and because I spent most of my time in the pilothouse, he both encouraged and welcomed my attempts to help him spot rocks and unexpected rises in the river bottom.

From almost the first day aboard the WAVERLY, Mr. Thompson prodded me in jest to take the helm. It was friendly badgering that became a daily ritual until I finally mustered enough courage to do so and called him on his dare. I took a place at the helm, which to my surprise pleased him and his assistant. I ended up taking the wheel on occasion from that point on.

I must state that Mr. Thompson was extremely responsible and never left my side. Also, I am not the fool, and I realized early on that it was one thing to do such a task for a short spell in order to cross a river, a lake, or a smooth stretch of water, but to do it for hours on end battling the Missouri with little relief and carrying the responsibility of a large boat, its cargo, it commitments, and the lives of its hundred or so passengers upon your shoulders was something else again. It was nothing I envied.

And so this day was no different than most, and I for one believed Mr. Thompson earned every cent of his pay. It was long and trying, but it ended on the lower stretch of rapids at Rapid Run just as planned. He was relieved that the day was done, and I was relieved to know we were safe.

SIXTY-NINE

Louisville, Kentucky is probably one of the best examples of a place where a river obstruction becomes a gathering place and ends up becoming a settlement or even a city. It was this way in a hundred places around the country and Rapid Run was only one of the many.

Over the course of time, low water, delays, or wrecks at the rapids forced people ashore where they had little to do but give their thanks or bury their dead and set up camp to await help. As often as not, while waiting they might find themselves turned rescuers, taking part in saving survivors and cargo from the next unfortunate wreck to happen along.

There often comes a point when these river obstacles generate so much activity that people are soon drawn to the area for reasons of opportunity instead of rescue. So comes the early foundations for a permanent community. This is how it was at Rapid Run. A single permanent structure was built by some stranded party and used later by another, and then another and another. Then there were two permanent structures and so on.

Once steamboats began making more frequent trips, local trappers, furriers, and Indians alike soon learned that each visit brought with it a potential wreck or more often the need to lighten cargoes. Either way it added up as an opportunity for trade or wages. Wood hawks were soon stacking their labor in rows ready for the boilers. A post was raised in short order for frontier supplies, and as one would expect, an inn for voyagers and ever more frequent passengers was bound to follow. Later came the livery and a host of other merchants to buy and sell.

The shops and dwellings of Rapid Run were built upon a low plateau on the south side of the river that was easily accessible from the water, yet high enough to be protected from most flooding and shifting. It was an infant version of St. Louis.

Its residents were always thrilled to see an approaching boat certain to be carrying goods and the latest news about the world down river in St. Louis and New Orleans. They were also anxious to trade furs, but this was done primarily when vessels were on the return trip and looking to fill their holds. On the upriver trip they traded mostly services—helping to move cargo, supplying fresh game, vegetables, and fruits for simpler wares and whatnot. In fact it wasn't that much different than trading with the Indians, whom I was told were also seen frequently at the settlement.

Captain Parker was now in charge, and the men on shore welcomed him as an old friend. Along with Captain Meyers and some of the passengers, he set out at once to make arrangements for transferring cargo. Minor discussions on a plan, minor clearing of the decks, and the removal of a few personal items by the passengers was all that took place after our landing, for the heat of day was still upon us. The inhabitants of Rapid Run preferred to begin the heavy work during the darkness of night when the air was cool and less infested with mosquitoes.

To keep portage short, the boat landings were constructed as close as possible to either side of the rapids. And so, in place of the huff and puff of WAVERLY's steam engines, I stepped ashore amid a roar of white water turbulence that filled the air with sound and a mist that kept the surrounding vegetation thriving and lush.

What was most on everyone's mind at this time was being free of the WAVERLY's decks and enjoying the hospitality of Rapid Run. This was the first occasion in many days that we had an opportunity to wander unrestrained by guardrails and feel solid earth beneath our feet. What was most on my mind was a bath and a change of dress.

It was good to enjoy a rest in Rapid Run. Whatever these isolated inhabitants lacked in the way of news, they more than made up for in preparations for a good stay. They were in a festive mood before we even tied off, and the farther I moved away from the roar of the rapids; the louder became their laughter.

There was a lot of French influence in the settlement and the folks naturally took to music, dance, and drink. In no time at all they coerced those passengers among us who were musically inclined to join them and add to the merriment.

I enjoyed my bath at the house of a settler and decided to dress up for the evening more out of necessity than show. I employed a young girl to wash all my clothes other than the dress I sported for dinner.

Smiles abounded in the light of a roaring fire amid the aromas of roasting meats and baking breads. After a liberal amount of hard cider, wine, lemonade *and whiskey*, honey *and whiskey*, berry juice *and whiskey*, water *and whiskey*, and need I say, whiskey *and whiskey* or whatever else would mix with whiskey to ease it down, the crowd was singing outrageously immoral songs to the stars above.

The night was in full swing when much to the complaint of my companions, I elected to retire. My belly was full with a variety of hot tasty foods and too much alcohol for my own good. I quickly succumbed to its effects, and in spite of the ridicule I faced, I was drowsy and wanted only to curl up in my bunk and go soundly to sleep. Unable to persuade me otherwise, Captain Parker and Mr. Thompson volunteered to escort me back to my cabin where they bid me good night and paid a deck hand to stand watch outside my door.

Inside my cramped quarters, I suffered the influence of whiskey far more than I would ever admit. Between my unsteady balance and the jerk and sway of the boat against her lines, I removed my clothes and gladly fell into bed. I pulled up my blankets and let loose every worldly concern with a drawn out moan. I was utterly content. Aglow from food and drink, I thought fondly of Mary and Allen, of Christopher and all my friends back home. I gave thanks to God Almighty and drifted off to sleep with a smile, while floating in the air, a fusion of laughter and song slipped peacefully away.

For all purpose, any passenger who hadn't passed out from drink remained awake to revel without restraint. It was about one in the morning when Captain Parker finally herded them to the WAVERLY for the purpose of unloading.

The commotion on board was quick to stir me from my sleep. Having slept so hard for those few hours, but for the effects of whiskey and wine, I was remarkably refreshed and soon on my feet, dressed, and anxious to investigate the activities outside.

In passing, I bid the men good luck with their labors as I went ashore to join the wives of Rapid Run in preparing coffee, tea, and breakfast for the passengers. When presented with the opportunity, I took it upon myself to serve breakfast to Mr. Mardeselle, the French cook, along with Mr. Thompson and Captain Parker. I did so in my best form as trained in my youth. It was a tradition of sorts that the cook and his staff were to be waited on while in Rapid Run and freed of their responsibilities to feed the men for one day going upriver and one day going down. The three were wholly amused by my initiative. They ate heartily, complimented me profusely on my table service, and laughed without restraint at my curtsies. It had been a great deal of fun.

By ten o'clock the WAVERLY had been unloaded, and by noon most all the stores had been moved to the upper landing. During those hours which were the hottest of the day, Captain

Parker called for dinner to be served and so every available surface was fashioned into a table. Even so, by far the majority ate upon the ground.

I worked right along with the wives, which earned me the respect of the men and women alike. At the same time, in order to appease the crowd's demands, I again put on a show as a refined upper class table maiden. The whole place roared, for few had ever seen anything of the like.

How incredibly far I was from a table in the Barrington Hotel. I was now every bit part and parcel of the stagecoach inn business that I still believed to be utterly disgusting. My, but how things had changed.

As we downed our dinner fare, the boilers were opened, cleaned out and stoked. All but the minimum amount of firewood necessary to keep the boilers hot had been removed to shore. At a quarter to three, Mr. Thompson went aboard with Captain Parker to see that the boilers were reaching temperature and that the linesmen were ready to cast off.

Ignorance was bliss and one failed to realize how many small issues meant the difference between hallelujah and heartbreak, or in the worst case, life and death. I had come to learn how changes in the river's flow demanded changes of us that were seldom noticed; changes in the boiler temperature, changes in the amount of cargo, changes in the number of hands on deck to handle lines. They were all little things that assured our safety so long as they were paid proper attention.

Normally, they were carried out so smoothly that no one ever noticed, and my awareness was only due to the hours spent observing such work from the helm whilst sitting with Mr. Thompson. I watched the deck hands studiously, often nervously second-guessing or mentally guiding them in their duties, for I found it unnerving at times to realize how much depended on a flawless execution. At the helm it was most apparent that my only means back to the civilized world was this one boat and its pilot, who daily placed his all or nothing bets against a river that played for keeps.

By three o'clock the tables were cleared and most everyone was standing along the water's edge with Captain Parker to cheer Mr. Thompson on. The WAVERLY was riding visibly higher in the water, yet I for one still wrung my hands with worry. Maybe it was worse standing on shore witnessing instead of being in the pilothouse working. Regardless, I stood with all the rest and watched anxiously as he called for extra steam.

The giant paddles began to turn slowly and the lines slackened at which point they were unfastened and tossed to shore. The WAVERLY was set free to the current and the pilot's command. At first, the boat drifted downstream as Mr. Thompson aligned himself for the approach. Then the paddlewheels turned faster and the boat began to move slowly upstream as he set his course and carefully picked a way through the water swept boulders.

We walked along the bank following his progress toward the upper landing. I watched the ruffled waters slap at the WABERLY's bow. There was the occasional thud, but for the most part Mr. Thompson avoided the damaging rocks and snags. He reached the safety of the upper station and landed amidst the well-earned cheers and congratulations of a crowd packed tightly to welcome him back from his short jaunt. Mr. Thompson in turn rang the bell and picked up his horn to trumpet in appreciation.

SEVENTY

Captain Parker oversaw the last movement of stores to the upper landing at which point the roustabouts, passengers, and laborers stood ready and waiting to commence loading cargo back into WAVERLY's holds soon as the boat was secured.

The minute Mr. Thompson stepped ashore, Captain Parker gave the order to begin, and the charge was underway. Even with all the effort being expended, it was obvious that the rest of the day would be needed to complete the task.

For those of us who would only be in the way, there was little to do but relax, for our bellies were again full and the community of Rapid Run had nothing to offer for entertainment once away from the campfire. I shuddered at the thought of living in such quietude and isolation, for I was bred and born a city girl and preferred to drown in noise and confusion.

Content to mind my own business, I retrieved a piece of roast pig from the fire-pit and went strolling about. While daydreaming and nibbling away at the charred meat, I remembered earlier having spotted a message board outside the trading post. I now looked in that direction.

I imagined a message board would have to be *theee* social gathering place of Rapid Run, and as no one was presently standing before it, I thought it a safe place to visit and as good as any beyond the wanton stares of men. A little boredom, a little curiosity, and a lot of free time prompted me to head in that direction.

To my surprise, the board was well papered in scraps. I shouldn't have thought there was that much to say out here in the middle of nowhere. I started at the top and worked my way down, browsing through the collection of scribbles, the majority of which were messages handwritten on scraps of paper, odd sized bits and pieces, some fresh, most faded. A few adamant souls scratched their posting into the wood itself.

Increasingly common on these boards were steamship schedules for the Ohio and Mississippi and postings by parties traveling across land. They gave information about prices, boilers, boat sizes, types of teams, numbers of wagons if any, experience of masters, captains, and pilots, the departures and destination points as well as the expected dates of passing through stops along rivers and land trails alike. There were also the usual postings by scouts, English, French, and Indian looking to be hired. And of course I should have known as a smile crossed my face, in the middle of the mess, half hidden, another poetic posting from Dusty Peddler.

Even mountain men forget

that prairie storms get mighty wet

after which they'll dry and burn

when desert sunshine takes its turn

So be it cover, salve, or more

You'll find those odds'n ends galore

On trails of rut'n cuts'n cussed holes

Or wherever Dusty's wagon rolls

Dusty Peddler

By the time the stores had finally been moved back into the holds, and we were called to board the boat, the shadows of early evening were saturating the low spaces. Looking downriver, the mist from the rapids was no longer so quick to evaporate as in the heat of day. In protected places it remained visible long after wandering from water's edge. Where the river coursed behind banks of cottonwood and brush, the undergrowth appeared dark, indistinct, and secluded.

When the late call for boarding was heard, a number of the men had already put down their bedrolls and were off collecting firewood in preparation for another night's stay. There had been rumor of a late evening departure circulating most of the day, but even so, a few remained to be surprised and a good many were visibly annoyed at having to go about gathering up their belongings.

The crew was probably made least happy by the news. They had been making the best of the layover, it being nothing short of a vacation in spite of the work required of them, for once ashore they had room to disappear from their duties. They knew better than to voice their opinions too forcefully lest they draw attention from the captain. Mostly, they grumbled beneath their breath and expressed feelings about traveling upon the river at night.

Running after dark was usually done along the Upper Missouri only when the captain or pilot felt a need to hide from the Indians. The dark plumes of smoke could be seen for miles across the open plains, and offered evildoers plenty of time to devise their harassment while awaiting the boat's arrival.

After sunset, the smoke became invisible against the black of night and only the sound of high-pressure boilers remained to betray one's position. The boilers were loud by any measure and could be heard for miles in every direction, but at least sound couldn't be pinpointed with the same accuracy as smoke.

I already knew from my conversations with Mr. Thompson upon our arrival at Rapid Run that we wouldn't be steaming late into the night to make up for lost time. Also, everyone knew that it wouldn't be completely dark for at least a couple of more hours, for twilight permeated the river bottoms early and shadows resided between steep walls to choke out sunrises and sunsets for long periods of time.

The discussions did reflect disappointment, but word of Mr. Thompson's commitment to Captain Meyers was also circulating and there was a reserved acceptance of his decision. Most all of these people moved about the plains and would readily agree that nothing was worse than being caught up in the wilderness without supplies. Too many times it brought forth the final chapter in life, one of massacre or starvation. There was much pressure to reach the fort as soon as possible.

For more than one reason, I was among the first passengers to return to the WAVERLY. One benefit of boarding early was being able to select the perfect place to witness the drama of departing. I enjoyed seeing the emotion of friends and loved ones who were separating, for it was one of those rare times when people openly displayed their emotions.

I had never experienced losing a lover, and I had to admit that there were no lovers here to be pried apart by a wall of tears or kisses to be carried by the winds of Rapid Run. Still, there were the hugs and handshakes of old friends coming and going. Feelings were genuine and conveyed outwardly by their eyes and laughter. The emotions gave me a sense of hope for the world, a sense of relief knowing that we all have ties that willingly commit us to care for others. There was also the excitement of watching deckhands racing about double-checking cargo and holds, and last but not least, the final look at a place you doubted seeing again.

The more specific reason for my early boarding this day was the fact that my stock of washed clothes were still damp and unable to be packed. I had no desire to bring aboard my whites while men were standing about. It was a sure invitation for regrets. As a woman I could never afford to ignore the fact that anything feminine could instantly stir up an unwanted brew of activity among a horde of ruffians in a lawless land. To do otherwise would bring on certain ruin.

I was quick to find a place on deck that appealed to me rather than end up left to choose between the worst of a dozen uncomfortable situations. Tonight my place of preference was amidships along the main deck guard just ahead of the paddle-box and just behind the boarding plank. It seemed I wasn't alone in my choice, for another person followed along the deck in my shadow.

"Eve'nun, ma'am."

"Good evening." I eyed the man with suspicion. He stopped alongside me at the rail and removed his hat. He was about my age, worn looking, and possessed that rugged character that was an attractive feature given to even the most pathetic creatures roaming the wilderness. He turned to look west.

"Might o' bin a pretty sunset, hadn' we seen it."

"I suppose," I responded. "It might have been a sight warmer as well."

"That is so. Hard to believe how a hot day can become so cool at night. Wonderful lookin' skies though, wonderful lookin' skies." The stranger stared upward and looked about. "Come clear as English crystal, but they sure make ya pay a price for enjoyin' 'em. They're brittle hard on a man, brittle hard, and I agree, no matter what time a summer, no matter how hot a day, it can get a might chilly at night."

"A might chilly! You mean down right cold, don't you?" I corrected the stranger.

"Yes, ma'am. Seen that too."

Normally, riverbanks are too low to stop a robust sunset from shedding the last of its day's heat across the water, but not here at Rapid Run. Here the canyon walls rose upward steep and high to litter the river with chunks of their rocky skin.

It was still early in the evening and quite possible that my chill was more likely due to the anticipation of our departure than to the actual temperature. Yet, this night the air did seem slightly cooler, the gusts slightly stronger, and therefore it came as no surprise that I being a woman was the first to feel it.

I learned of a night when shadows appeared in the bottoms, they often ushered in breezes or sudden gusts, and this made for rare times when I actually preferred to press in against the crowd or even a stranger for added warmth. On this night, my companion stranger came across as one of those people who you instinctively knew to be a good person, someone you could stand close beside.

It may have been something in his voice, maybe a twinkle in his eye, or a certain way in which he looked at me. Who could say, but I stood by him to avoid the evening air and felt very comfortable in his presence. I would have thought he could read my mind, for without needing to be asked; he stepped back and positioned my shawl snug about my neck.

"Ohhhhh, thank-you." I shuddered.

He smiled, but said nothing more. We stood together and watched the shore.

SEVENTY-ONE

As soon as the boarding plank started its swing upward to be secured, Mr. Thompson called for more steam and the paddle began digging into the water to relieve the dock lines of their strain. The voices of the passengers, who were now standing shoulder to shoulder along the guardrail, arose in a chorus of final farewells behind a long row of outstretched hands that waved back and forth in the evening breeze.

Once slackened, in a single move all the lines save one were cast to deckhands aboard the WAVERLY. The deckhand that waited beside the stranger and me was also at the ready, but confused and empty handed. He remained focused upon the other end of the line, which failed to come his way. I was momentarily puzzled by the incongruity, for all lines were supposed to be cast in unison.

I had seen this routine performed time and time again from the pilothouse, and I knew Mr. Thompson avoided all distractions at the precise moment lines were to be cast. It was a critical moment whereby he attempted to afford the shore men just enough headway to break their ropes free before falling back and making way. It was not a moment for conversation, and should you bother him, he might advise you quite impolitely to hush.

Our linesman was becoming anxious, and for good reason. He knew better than I that timing was essential. I followed the line across the water and observed his counterpart on shore who was working frantically to unleash us.

The gravity of the situation was growing quickly. I was certain that by now Mr. Thompson knew he had a problem. I was also certain that he was having trouble holding the WAVERLY at bay in the stiff current, and much like a bad knot each time the line was jerked by the pitching of our boat, it worsened our predicament.

Few were aware of the seconds long crisis. Few paid attention, for the business of deckhands and linesmen was exactly theirs. Everyone else was caught up in the confusion of farewells and future promises made to new friends and old alike. But on shore men were now running in haste, hoping to lend a hand just as one of those bottom gusts came across, passed them by, and caught the WAVERLY broadside.

I saw the rope stretch thin. I watched as it twisted slowly around under the strain and although I felt nothing, I knew the gentle breeze was nudging the boat forcefully away from the bank and further burdening an already badly stressed line. Mr. Thompson was probably cussing up a windstorm of his own for being hindered by the rope as he fought to keep the WAVERLY under command.

These events were occurring in rapid succession and belonged to a collection of countless little incidents that cropped up unexpectedly, passed by unnoticed, and changed enormously the course of life. I was often compelled to say, they possessed the power to spell the difference between hallelujah and heartbreak.

The rope held, but in a most startling fashion the dock cleat gave way. It was ripped clean off the dock and sounded out like the crack of a gun. The rope, iron cleat, and a chunk of dock timber came hurtling directly toward us. Before anyone might even think to raise their hands for protection, it streaked through the air and slammed squarely into a railing post barely four feet to our right. The post snapped in half but for the cannon ball force of the strike. The anchor-like cleat dropped with a resounding thud onto the deck beside our feet, its rope still attached.

When our senses caught up with what had happened, we were first amazed to discover no one had been hit. It was nothing short of a miracle that one or more of us hadn't been killed outright. As the full impact of our fright began to take hold, many, myself included, failed to note how the trailing length of floating rope drifted quickly toward the wooden paddles. Within seconds, it was drawn underwater by the suction of the wheel that had speeded up considerably to regain control and get us underway.

The opposite end of the rope was still affixed to the WAVERLY's bulwark. Possessing more awareness than I, the stranger yanked me back from the guardrail in fear of the rope breaking with a similar consequence, or worse, cutting us in half. In the remaining seconds, we watched helplessly as the snagged rope now winding about the paddlewheel disappeared beneath the water. The line reappeared instantly as it snapped back up through the river's surface to tighten up with a hideous squealing vengeance.

The cleat at the rope's free end was whipped back off the deck and wedged briefly between the broken post and railing before ripping the entire structure off the boat. The now unsupported overhead walkway began to collapse under the weight of the crowd along the upper rail saying their good-byes. The upper deck's slippery planks now sloped dangerously toward the water in an attempt to shed itself of passengers. Everything was mayhem amid a thousand cries and visions of unfortunates dropping into the currents from overhead.

My eyes fell downward only long enough to witness the tremendous strain exerted upon the stretch of rope that was still attached to the forward bulwark. I cowered, turning my head into the stranger's embrace as he attempted to drag me away. Apart from the screams overhead, the air filled with the deafening sound of fracturing wood. I gripped the stranger's coat tightly, instinctively using him for a shield as the strained rope tore out a chunk of the boat, taking with it another cleat, a length of bulwark planking, and a ten or twelve foot section of guardrail.

The whole mess was summarily dragged into the paddlewheel. Wooden paddles were splintering and cracking and everything started breaking up. At that point the wheel bound up tight and stalled out, and I knew precisely the seriousness of our situation. We were adrift and heading toward the rapids with speed, for Mr. Thompson had just lost command of the helm.

As passengers above, and those of us below nearest the missing guardrail were leaping back against the cabin for fear of falling overboard, Mr. Thompson engaged himself in a race against time that made every second seem like hours. No doubt his attention had been fixed upon the line as it snapped in the direction of the larboard wheel. He had no choice but to throw the paddlewheel into reverse and attempt to regain his command and with luck unwind the snagged line. His decision put the WAVERLY at once sideways before the racing currents and provided all of us port side with an unobstructed view of the turbulent rapids down river.

WAVERLY's deck hands were trying desperately to work their way aft through the farewell crowd and scale across the paddle-box in order to reach the damaged wheel and untangle the rope. Fortunately for them, Mr. Thompson's gamble to reverse the paddlewheel freed it up and cleared out the loose debris without their help, but not before the current had carried us far down stream and fully into the run of the river. He was now struggling to bring the bows back and confront the river's churning waters head on with what remained of his damaged portside paddles.

How grave was our position became perfectly clear by the expressions of those people on shore who were now running

697

wide-eyed along the bank. They were swinging their arms, pointing downstream, yelling in the confusion to jump ashore, or hushing all sound by covering their mouths in disbelief.

I knew we were perilously close to the rapids. Frantic cries for more steam erupted from the crowd behind me like prayers in a church. The paddlewheels were turning full speed ahead. Ours was vibrating terrible, having been made out of balance and ineffective by the loss of a number of paddles. The damaged wheel was slapping broken paddles against the box and caused the deck to shake and shudder, adding immensely to the feeling of impending doom.

The stranger and I stood side-by-side in fear of the rotating mess but unsure of what to do next. We were trapped by a confused crowd both before and behind us. I feared something frightful about to happen and held on tightly to what small piece remained of the guardrail in preparation for the worst. I braced myself and waited with dread as the paddlebox beat itself into pulp. Its planks were now flying in every direction and as one sailed off toward the crowd at the docks it led my eyes to stare across the water toward shore.

Oddly, amid all the panic, the sound and movement of the crowd faded away momentarily, but for a distraction in the distance where I saw for the first time ever, Dusty Peddler's wagon. It appeared to be heading toward the lower landing. He was on the bank high above the shadows and highlighted by the bright reddish-orange rays of the setting sun. The sight of it prompted me to think of Lady Rebecca's vermilion coach, and for a fleeting second I felt calmed.

But only for a second before the noise and confusion returned. The shattered paddlebox prevented my seeing down-river and left me unsure of how close we were to the rocks. This was not the case for those standing at the stern, those who now understood in no uncertain terms the urgency of moving forward for safety.

Wasting not a second's worth of time they scrambled for the bows, and as they pushed their way forward, the WAVERLY slid back and struck the first large boulder. It sent a shudder through the hull and the feet of all on board. How much damage was done I could not know, but every bit as bad as the collision was the explosion of panic that blew through the crowd.

The men farthest to the rear rushed forward in full alarm casting all civility and common sense to the wind. With the rapids roiling at their heels, they became the driving force behind a mob with no sense of reason or restraint. Before them, unfortunate souls who were crippled, slow on their feet, or distracted, were knocked to the ground and run over by a wall of insanity. Within seconds they pushed past the paddlebox and stampeded into those of us crowded at the rail. It happened so fast we never saw it coming. The crush of mayhem was overwhelming and I was driven painfully into that remnant of the guard.

It could have been worse. Those standing where the guard had been ripped away were shoved overboard. Three men were at once pushed off the deck, two of which were immediately sucked into the paddlewheel and beaten to death, while the third hung precariously to a splintered piece of the bulwark.

As for me, I was trapped, pinned hard to the guard by the crowd and unable to free myself. I too panicked, but being unable to move I could only scream for mercy. At first, I screamed out of fear of being trapped, but that soon changed to screams of absolute terror as the damaged guardrail began to slowly give way under the strain.

My situation appeared hopeless for the crowd would not be calmed. They struggled instinctively to escape the suffocation of bodies crammed in too confined a space, and so pushed out in all directions as though fighting for their very breath. They were grown men screaming in sheer panic.

I heard none of it. I heard nothing but the a terrible splintering sound and the squeal of wood being wrenched off its nails. In a slow irreversible move, the guard eventually succumbed, losing its fight against the force of the mob that pressed upon my back. I felt my throat tighten as I leaned farther overboard, clinging to the collapsing rail and looking down into the froth churned up by the giant disgruntled paddlewheel that devoured everything in its path. I was paralyzed with fear, my thoughts both frozen and frantic as I searched for a means of escape from my horrid fate.

The guardrail finally gave way. I felt the hands of the stranger at my side grip my waist firmly and launch me far out from the boat. I didn't ask for help, but as before, he seemed to know and attempted to fling me out beyond the wheel of death. We parted in the air and my fate was cast to the wind or the water as I disappeared into the turbulence. I feared for the stranger's life as I fought for my own.

I thrashed about wildly, desperately trying to swim clear, blinded by froth and immersed not only in a boiling cauldron of frigid water, but also in a milieu of tremendous earth-shaking sound. The giant paddles came crashing down into the water and at once sucked me back into their framework. I felt as though my arms and legs were being ripped apart by the force of the wheel as it plowed through the river's current and slammed into my chest. Before any thought could be made, I was spit out into the wheel's wake as quickly as I was sucked into its path.

I surfaced only long enough to see 'WAVERLY' painted across the boat's stern. It left me lost to the currents and reaching up for help. As I struggled to catch my breath, I understood I had not instantly died. I had entered the rotating wheel where the paddles were missing and was spared being crushed to death. I also realized the speed in which I was being carried downstream and what lay before me. Whether I was to live or endure a prolonged death was yet to be seen.

In my favor was the fact that Christopher had taught me how to swim in the bathing nets hung from the yards of the REBECCA as a child. I would jump in with the sailors and the other children and have the time of my life. It was much like bicycling, a skill once mastered not easily forgotten.

What worked against me was my clothing. Once again I had foolishly worn a dress. My corset kept me from taking the deep breaths of air needed to sustain me while underwater. The river filled my dress and bustle like a ship's sail. My shawl remained wrapped tightly around me, restraining me. All the while, the weight of my boots drew me down.

I caught one last glimpse of the crowd on shore before I slid beneath the surface with only my prayers and a memory of their contorted faces that said it all. I was dragged down to the bottom by the current and held there for what seemed like eternity. I was floundering in hopeless panic as I struggled to rise. With only seconds of life left in me, I was catapulted into the air. My lungs exploded and I inhaled a mess of water, air, and hair. I wanted to choke, but there was no time, I went back under deep.

My chest slammed into a rock with such force that I expelled whatever air I had managed to gain. I was knocked nearly senseless, stunned. I surfaced. I gasped. Under, I went again. Another rock, this time I heard my ribs crack from the blow. I careened up into the air and gained a breath. The pain was excruciating. Under. The surface. The air, I couldn't scream for help. Under. I somersaulted. My head down deep, the pressure, I prayed for air, I had no sense of direction. My face dragged across the riverbed, ground into the gravel. I was upside down. I pushed away. Everything was froth. I couldn't breathe it. I reached out. Where was the air? Was I in air or water, was it up or down? No way out. Panic! Panic! Panic! My awareness faded. Into the rocks, my back, my head, too dark to see. Air! Air! Oh, god! Need air! Need air—need light.

As death closed in about me, my thoughts melted away. I tried to inhale the water, but it wouldn't go down and the intense burning in my chest finally began to subside. I was distant, traveling, looking through a long dark tunnel. The sounds were now beyond me, far from my ears. I thought of Mary and Allen. I reached out for Christopher.

701

SEVENTY-TWO

At last I was at peace and breathing the cool night air I so desperately craved, and then something went wrong, and I found myself choking again, gasping, suffering terrible from excruciating pain in my sides. I felt each of my broken ribs, the jagged edges grating back and forth with every insufferable breath. My mouth tasted like iron. It was full of blood.

I opened my eyes and looked up into the pale bluish-gray light of the evening sky. The stars were making their appearance. My shoulders had beached on the shore of an eddy, while my boots scraped the riverbed. My body floated dreamlike in the still water as I gazed through a veil of semi-consciousness at this wonderful stranger leaning over me.

I perceived him to be blonde-haired and blue-eyed. Swedish, I thought to myself. I cared not the least nor questioned from where he came, only accepting the peace he offered, then suddenly—.

"Christopher?" I was astounded. He wasn't focused clear. I could hear him breathing.

"— Dusty."

"Dusty," I repeated, now unsure.

"—save the children."

"Yes," I whispered. *"Save the children."*

It seemed the right thing to do, but for now I did nothing more than pass from consciousness. While drifting in that eternally dark state, from far away came sounds—distant sounds. I couldn't tell if I was moving toward them or if the sounds were coming to me. I heard someone say with a tiny voice. "She's alive, she's alive." At that instant the pain returned—terrible pain, pain from everywhere, my head and face, my arms, my legs, my ribs, especially my ribs. I could barely breathe.

702

Each time I inhaled it was as though someone twisted knives into my sides. My whole body shuddered from the hurt of it. I was being called, disturbed—slapped. I opened my eyes and there were four men standing over me. One was bent over me and had my face within his hands looking into my eyes, but it was getting quite dark by this time, and against the pale light of a night sky, he was only a silhouette to me.

"C'mon, c'mon, wake up, wake up. She's comin' 'round boys. C'mon, wake up. I think she's gonna make it."

"Thank you, Jesus," someone exclaimed.

"Ken ya hear me, Mrs. Clauzzen?" The man hollered.

"Yes," I whispered.

"Are ya all right? Anything broken?"

"Save the children." I repeated the message.

There was a second of stunned silence.

"What!" The man's lungs exploded. "Whad'ya say? Hey! Hey!" The man shook me. "Whad'ya say?"

"The children." I repeated softly, but I was losing my senses.

The man looked up and spit. "Ah, hail! Bart! Are ya tellin' me thar's kids! Damn! Nobody said nuthin' 'bout 'er 'avin' kids. Dammit t' hail! You guys run down the bank n' see if ya ken spot sumpin'". The others were off instantly.

He turned back to me.

"Don' leave me jus yet, ma'am. They yer kids?" He brought me back.

"He went to save them," I answered.

I was shaking badly from shock and the frigid water. The tightening of my muscles served to grind my broken ribs and cause me excruciating pain. I tried hard to slip away, as far

703

away from the pain as I could get. I didn't want to answer questions. I didn't want to be bothered. He shook me.

"Ma'am! Wake up! Who went after 'em, who went after 'em?" His voice entered my darkness then trailed off into the distance. I didn't want to talk. I wanted to be left alone.

"Dusty— Dusty Peddler," I whispered, and that was my last conscious sound.

SEVENTY-THREE

When I returned from the darkness, a dazzling bright light greeted me. It prevented me from opening my eyes so I squinted, trying to make sense of my surroundings. A small room began to take shape and I soon realized the bright light to be sunshine entering through an open doorway. With the light came the sound of river rapids, which at first made me nervous, but I soon realized that I was lying in a bed. The bed was soft. I was rigid. Memories flooded back into my head. I took a deep breath and was reminded instantly of my condition. I whimpered quite unintentionally and half longed for the darkness that had abandoned me.

A stirring in the room followed the sound of my moan. I rolled my head to the side and observed the form of a dark skinned woman who rose up above me. As my eyes came to focus, I could see that she had been sitting alongside the bed as she worked a loom and was now on her feet. I followed her movement as she stepped away, disappearing into the brilliant light.

Within moments a man entered the room, the dark skinned woman reappearing behind him. He pulled the chair away from the loom and set it alongside the bed where he seated himself. The woman stood behind him, placing her hands on his shoulders.

"'Ow ya feelin' ma'am?" I remembered his voice from the river.

"I hurt. I hurt too much to be dead." It took all my effort just to speak; my voice was raspy.

"Don' surp'ise me none. Yer 'bout as lucky as they git. The other three who wen' in t' the paddle wuz hacked t' death. Yes, ma'am yer a lucky one. Blessed." He held up two fingers.

"Close one o' yer eyes an' tell me if ya can see muh fingers clearly."

"Yes."

"Now th' other."

"Yes"

"'Ow many?" He held up three.

"Three."

"What's yer name, ma'am?"

"Elizabeth."

"Yer full name."

"Elizabeth—Dennison—Claussen."

"Clauzzen—Clauzzen." I opened my eyes to see him thinking hard on the name. "I 'member hearing it firs' time at the campfer an' thinkin' 'bout how I knowed thet name from somewheres. Ya got famlee out 'ere don' ya."

"Don't know." I took short breaths. "Looking—for Christopher Claussen."

"Christ'pher is zit? Christ'pher Clauzzen. Let me think on thet a bit. I might jes be able t' help ya with thet one. Sump'uns 'ere a rattlin' in muh mem'ry." He squinted his eye and rolled some tobacco around behind his lip. "Ah'll git it, you jes wait, Ah'll git it.

In th' meantime, Ah'm afeerd ya got cherself a heap o' brokin' ribs an' Ah woun't be thinkin' on movin' much anytime too soon. An' there's yer arm an' leg. Ah'm thinkin' ya might even have a coupl'a fractures there 's well. Th' swellin's a might fierce, painful, ah know. Best thing right now is ya git yerself some rest, but don' stay in thet bed longer'n ya have to. If ya don't git up an' move in a coupl'a days, you'll be down fer a month 'r more. I'll bring ya out some brandy. It's a hail of a way to start the day, but better'n how it'd start without it."

He pushed back the chair and stood up. He spoke to the Indian girl briefly and then stepped into the bright light. By the time he returned a short while later, I was basking in the misery of my full faculty. He placed a tray upon a small bedside table. I saw a bottle of whiskey, a decanter, a jar of honey and a spoon along with a few other items. He then retrieved the chair and seated himself a second time.

"Now, Ah'm meanin' t' ask ya t' listin' up. Yer lookin' purty wide awake. This 'n here's a bottle of whiskey. I cou'nd find the brandy no how. But, if'n I say so muhself, this is some damn good whiskey. Mix it up a little with this'n here water an' honey an' it'll go down a might easier. Ah don' reckin yer a drinker, but this is one time we'll all be a might bit happier if'n we see ya half in th' bag. But the choice is yers."

It didn't require much convincing on Mr. Crocker's part before I asked him to make it a tall tin-full, which he did with a laugh. I drank it down almost at once with great hopes and followed it soon after with another. I made no excuses for how I felt. I could barely move, and tried my best not to breathe.

"By the way—if I may—. I would like—to have the opportunity—of thanking the gentlemen—who saved my life."

"An' who might'n they be?" He asked?

"I don't know the name of the first one. He was with me— at the rail. He threw me clear of the—paddle. The one who pulled—me out of the river was Dusty Peddler."

The name brought a snicker of amusement.

"Thet's right. Ah 'member ya said sumpin' 'bout thet at th' river. Well, we'll git t' thet later. Right now, try n' relax an' do whatever ya can t' work them muscles loose. I had yer trunk put down at the en' o' the bed." He stood up. "Oh, an' I'd like ta mention thet I respected yer honor. Never was in 'ere alone without wunna da womenfolk. They undressed ya. I had t' look ya over fer breaks, but ah was a gentleman 'bout it." The man was serious, and I was touched by his chivalry.

"I have no doubts—about your honor, sir. Are you not—a doctor, after all?"

"Oh no, ma'am. Folks come my way cuz out here, all a man's gottta do t' be a doctor is not move fer more'n a year. By then, ever'one knows where ya are an' they come a lookin' fer help sooner later. Some we act'chlee do good fer, the others we bury out in back."

"I was never introduced." I lifted my left hand; my ribs wouldn't allow the other.

"Beggin' yer pardon, ma'am, Benjamin—Benjamin Crocker. Own th' inn, or the hospital dependin' on how ya come in the front door." He took my hand and shook it with care.

I started to laugh, but those ribs changed my mind real fast.

"It is my pleasure, Doctor Crocker. Either I'm getting drunk—or that has a really funny sound. Doctor Crocker. Like a magical—character in a fairy tale." I found this terribly funny in my state of mind, but I clenched my teeth, not daring to laugh. I was drunk.

"Mebbe. But sometimes ah feel like there's a li'l too much magic 'round here. Ah'll say this, Lord knows ya must be the chosen one, thet's fer certain. You bin givin' a second chance, ma'am. The Almighty's got sumpin' in mind fer ya cuz He had plenty o' opportunity ta take ya home last night. Lis'en, ah wancha t' rest up. Ah'm goin' back t' work, jus' speak up if yer in need a sumpin'." He walked out the room.

SEVENTY-FOUR

It took me a number of days in bed resting, and at least that many bottles of whiskey before I was able to get back on my feet. Life does go on, and the WAVERLY did too. I was left half dead in the middle of nowhere with many messages of regret, and no idea if or when another boat might venture this way. To be fair it must be said that there was nothing Captain Parker or Mr. Thompson could do for me, for the tragedy in Rapid Run would not postpone or even diminish the urgency of Captain Meyer's mission. Sudden death and injury were a fact of life that had to be accepted, regretted, and forgotten.

In the meantime, knowing more about medicine than 'Doctor Crocker' might ever hope to, I thought his advice to be sound, and I was on my feet struggling to face the world as soon as possible. Unfortunately, the world wasn't ready for me. I stepped outside my room and into the street for the first time and it seemed the whole settlement came to a standstill. I stood looking at them and they at me. Benjamin appeared.

"Ah see yer a braving th' out o' doors." He spit.

"Testing it, but I don't think it's ready for me." I looked at the passersby, many who stared, many who turned face to trade secrets. "Can't say I blame them. I looked into a mirror this morning, and I wouldn't believe it possible to look as black and blue and scabbed over as I without being a corpse."

"Give it time, Mrs. Clauzzen. You'll clean up, but there's more to it 'en just th' looks." He was clinging to a secret that cried to be let out.

"What are you saying to me, Mr. Crocker?"

"Are ya feelin' up to a walk 'roun' back?" He offered me his arm.

"We'll just have to see, I imagine."

I took his arm and allowed him to lead my stiff body carefully past the rows of stacked firewood, old barrels and lumber piles, until we arrived at the back of a large peddler's wagon, Dusty Peddler's wagon. He spit to the side.

"Have ya ever seen this before?" He looked at me. I looked over the wagon with its wide wheels and assortment of wares. I recognized it.

"Yes." I answered. He put his hand to his chin.

"An' where'd thet be?"

"Well, I saw it on the road headin' downriver towards the lower landing."

"When now'd thet happin'?"

"The evening of the accident, just after we hit the first boulder. I remember I was terrified. I was clinging to the rail and looking to shore for help. I saw him going down the road. He must have realized what was happening and headed for lower rapids to help. Why?"

"Ya never seen the wagon before?"

I thought about it a moment. "No. Never."

Doctor Crockter stood silent as he rolled tobacco around in his mouth and thoughts in his head. He studied me. He spat.

"You sayin' ya sawr him? I mean ya sawr him in person."

"I don't think so. I don't know, maybe I did. I can't remember. Why?" Again, I had to think about it for a moment; he remained silent. Then it came to me. "Not in the wagon, but I saw him at the riverbank. Seems like I remember him there. Why are you asking me these questions?"

"'Lizabeth, this here'n wag'n ain't moved from this spot fer three months 'r better. Not since the first days o' spring, when it was brought 'roun'."

I wasn't sure where this conversation was leading.

"Well, I'm in no position to argue with you, Benjamin. You would know. It was probably a different one."

"How d' ya mean?"

"Well, I mean to say, a different Dusty Peddler wagon, that would make sense. I've seen his postings all over. He probably has a number of these wagons. I don't understand; what are you getting at, or what's your point, Mr.Crocker?"

"Llizabeth, th' reason th' whole town's a lookin, at cha, isn't b'cuz of yer bruises. It's cuz ya said thet Dusty Peddler hauled yer hide outta th' river and he's bin deader 'n a nail fer the last three months. Ah no cuz Ah buried 'im muhself."

I understood what Benjamin was saying, but where did that leave me, I thought to myself. This was an utterly bizarre revelation to say the least, but what was I supposed to say?

"What about the children, he went after them," I said, knowing there was always an explanation.

"There weren't no children. We looked downstream fer nearly a mile. Nuthin'. Nobody reported any missin' kin, either."

I jumped in. "No, they were with me in the water. I remember them, they were ahh—." I couldn't put my finger on it. It was vague. But I knew they were with me, girls, a girl, and yet, how could there be children, I was the only person on board that wasn't a man. Maybe they boarded here in

Rapid Run. I thought back for a moment, trying to pry open dark cloudy memories.

"He said, '*something—save the children.*'" I nodded firmly having distinctly remembered that, and my desire to thank him for saving my life.

"Whud he say 'xactly." Benjamin was riveted to my every word.

"Not much. I remember him grabbing my shoulder and pulling me to shore. I looked up at him and I thought it was Christopher, you know, Mr. Claussen, the man I am looking for. I was surprised. I called him Christopher, and it wasn't right, he said '*Dusty*'. He said, '*save the children.*' and he left me."

"'Lizabeth," he spit. "Let me tell ya about Dusty. Dusty Peddler's real name was David Dusterwinkle. Said he got nick-named Dusty early on. Said he was a German Jew thet come this-a-way from Pennsylvania. He an' his kin were 'customed tuh hauling wares about in a wagon. I never seen nothin' like it till he come rolling in one day with his wife an' kids. I never seen so much stuff, chocked full of yankee notions an' whatnot." He spit.

"I got tuh know Dusty cuz he was in an' outta Rapid Run a lot. He liked the place an' hoped to settle down and buy a store. He kept talkin' 'bout how it was gonna have barrels of salt an' flour an' heavy goods in back, an' a high porch in front so's customers could stay in the saddle. He was gonna have a stove an' spittoon an' a coupla chairs for jawin' in the center, an' lots o' shelves. He said lots o' shelves. Upstairs, he wanted a place for his fam'ly to live. He was a good man, Lizabeth, good a man's can be.

"Anyways, in th' early part o' spring during th' meltin' season, he come back here from tradin' up on th' north ranges as was his custom. He was married tuh a English gal, went by th' name Roberta an' had two young uns, daughters, Eleanor n' Rachel.

"There's always been a rope raft, a ferry if ya will, stretched 'cross th' river, just there." He spit to the side then pointed. Following his outstretched hand, I was able to spot the rope high over the water. "Thet thar rope's kept high, so them boats can pass underneath. When someone's a wantin' to cross over, the rope's lowered an' ya wrap it 'roun' a crank on the raft. Ya see it o'er there by the stand a trees?" I answered that I did. "Yeah, yeah, an' as ya turn the crank the raft follows 'long the rope an' brings ya on 'cross the river." He put in a fresh chew.

"Well, th' fam'lee 'rrived ta the other side an' Dusty brought over his team. Then he went back an' loaded th' wag'n onto th' raft, chocked it sure, an' started on across. Th' next thing Ah sees is a coupla dead trees frozen in a chunk of river ice comin' right for 'im. It catches the rope and snaps it like a buggy whip an' th' wag'n n' raft start a headin' down river. At thet time, being spring n' all, the meltin' snow an' all, th' river wuz a might higher an' faster, not like it is now. An' Dusty know'd sure, their only chance fer seein' it thru was t' jump fer shore as the raft had nearly made it 'cross." Again, he pointed.

"T'wasn't but a spit's time for figurin' cuz the rope wuz still 'tached an' the ice 'n, trees be a pullin' 'em back inta the river. So he yells t' jump! Ah heard him clear over here. He went on in, only t' re'lize the fam'lee stayed put on th' raft, mebbe on 'count the water'd be freezin' an' all. But, there they be, sceered to hail, and him in the water beside 'imself wit' worry.

"He coun't go back, no way, so he had t' make fer shore. He ran down past th' front a th' landing here, following th' raft, worried sick, but he din't lose his head, no sir. He yelled at em' t' stay on th' raft an' ride it out, "Hang on!" he's a yellin', "Hang on!". The water bein' high an' all, might a worked. But th' mother, Roberta, seeing she's drifted close t' shore again, grabbed the kids an' jumped fer it, takin' 'em with her."

Benjamin stopped a moment and shook his head.

"'Lizabeth—" He spit to the side. "Muh heart jes stopped dead. Ah pray t' God, Ah never have t' be witness t' such tragedy agin 'n my life.

"Dusty know'd they were as good as gone. No better a man fer husband er father ever walked this earth. Ah'm here t' swear it. He dove inta thet godforsaken ice water knowin' full well he'd never make it back 'live an' went to 'em. I watched him struggle t' reach 'em. He made it sure 'nough, but they all drowned, beat ta death by the rocks. Terrible a thing as Ah ever seen."

He shook his head in sorrow and spit. "The wag'n n' raft shot through th' rapids, nah so much as a scratch, 'ardly even wet it wuz. We found th' bodies an' they were all buried proper right o'er there." He pointed to the handful of markers in the field a ways back. "So, now ya know." He spit.

I was lost for an explanation. I was sure though, it would turn up in time. I said nothing more and only looked at Benjamin, who was still lost in the tragedy and staring out at the markers. In the meantime, I found myself suddenly curious about the wagon. I broke into his thoughts.

"What becomes of the wagon," I asked. He raised his eyebrows.

"Not sure. Norm'lee, it woulda' been stolen clean out by now. But people b'lieve his spir't walks 'bout an' not a soul has even come near 'nough t' look at it. Ah'll make ya a promise o' this, after what you been sayin' Ah don't fear anybody goin' near it. Hail, when the sun goes down, it even makes my hair stand on end, an' Ah liked the man." He spit and I thought it over.

"May I look inside?" I asked.

"Ya wanna go in 'er?" Benjamin was astonished. "Ya ain't evin a lit-le spooked?

"No, I'm curious." He thought about it for a moment.

713

"Guess so. If'n it don' give ya the jeebies, don' see no reason not tuh. Hang on, an' Ah'll fetch a key." He walked back around to the front of the inn.

I walked around the wagon and noted its wide wheels. I approved of the awnings fitted both front and back, but now folded closed. I was fascinated by the layered stacks of goods piled atop its sturdy wooden frame and spilling down the side to be snagged upon the countless nail heads. In a settlement as remote and in need, as was Rapid Run, the town's folk must certainly have been afraid something fearful to have left all these valuables untouched.

Benjamin returned with the key and first opened the rear doors and then the fronts behind the driver's bench.

'I'm going to take some time and look through it, Benjamin."

"Help yourself. But if'n ya meet up wit' Dusty, don' tell 'im I let cha in."

I laughed. "I won't, I promise. Would you help me up to the driver's seat? My ribs won't stand for it just yet."

"Yes, ma'am, muh pleasure." Benjamin knelt down and grabbed my foot and placed it firmly upon his bended knee. I stepped up carefully onto the wagon, clenching my teeth to counter the pain.

"Thank you ever so much, Benjamin."

"Yes'm."

SEVENTY-FIVE

Everything on board seemed to be swinging about, as if suddenly awakened from a long sleep. Disturbed by my intrusion, countless items rattled out alarms of every pitch to announce a stranger was on board. I remained still until they hushed.

Respectfully, I crawled over the bench backrest and entered the small private world of the Dusterwinkles. I first took a visual inventory of the seemingly infinite assortment of odds and ends. It was a sight to behold. Beyond the pots and pans, pails on nails, washboards and whatnots suspended among a hundred other things on the outside of the wagon, there was inside, boxes upon boxes of everything imaginable.

There were needles, awls, hooks and eyes, scissors, buttons, beads unstrung, red, blue, and white, tangles of necklaces and bracelets. Jars of bright vermilion paint stood out in the light. There were blankets and cloths, calicos, flannels, shirts of cotton and linen, women's hats, men's coats, shoes for both, and children's booties. There were muskets and 'Northwest guns', balls 32 to the pound, flints of all design, fire steels, powder, potassium nitrate, sulfur, charcoal and molds. There were chunks of lead as well as wadding.

I found baskets, brushes and brooms, hatchets, scalping knives, (God help me) and even more vicious looking blades as well. I sifted through stacks of files and jars of fishhooks, strike-a-lights, lucifers, cowbells, tinkle bells, and numerous other trinkets. There was dried fish, and dry goods, flour, soda, baking powder, old sour dough in a jar, coffee, sugar, syrup, sorghum, jerky, tobacco, whiskey, a supply of dried vegetables and a tangle of dried fruits hanging in nets overhead. There was lye and sweet smelling lotion, soaps, scrub brushes, spectacles, medicines and horse liniments.

I was in awe of all I saw, of all I uncovered. An endless supply of goods badly needed on the frontier. The amount of inventory crammed into this wagon was deceiving. No wonder he wanted a store. The wares could only be memorized, for countless items were tucked neatly into drawers and boxes and packed deftly out of view.

The more I dug the more I produced. Every little corner was packed tightly. The wagon was better outfitted than most settlements. It must have weighed a ton if a pound, and now I understood why the need for such wide wheels. All anyone could ask for was here, all of it left untouched, all of it protected not by Benjamin or anybody else, but by its ghosts.

My attention was drawn toward the more personal items. I now began to sift through the private lives of a loving family. There were many items hanging from the ceiling. The sides were built as cupboards with doors that closed tight to stop everything from being jolted out.

Every square inch of these doors were covered with personal things that spoke of the family who lived here, a wallpaper of sorts that reflected the world of children. Concealing a back-drop of articles for sale were colorful drawings pinned perfectly in place, one butting up to the next. There were letters of the alphabet and lessons on reading and writing. There was arithmetic.

I had a strong feeling about the wagon that was good. It felt personal. It felt like a home. I was moved to emotion, realizing it felt like the family I had always hoped to have. It was easy to imagine the joy of children in the artwork hanging all about. It was so sad, but I felt very good about it and wished to have it surround me all the more.

I took my time, whiling away the afternoon, going through their personal belongings, learning about this family who's little public notices I had tracked since the headwaters of the Hudson River. I read through Dusty's papers and a stack of his poetic ads ready to be posted. It was apparent he must have had some schooling, for he also wrote poetry, pieces about his family, about his life or the land. He had a way with words, and I thought his writings were wonderful.

Mister Moon

Don't you fret my little one, my little one so shy
Don't you fear the setting sun, sinking in the sky

It goes to sleep, goes to sleep, just like you and I
It goes to sleep my little one, just like you and I

Close your eyes my little one, little one so dear
Close your eyes one by one, see if you can hear

Momma singing quietly, whispering in your ear
Time to sleep my little one, Mister Moon is here

He's naming all the stars tonight, each and every one
He'll work until the morning light, and then his job is done

Try hard now to remember them, tell them to the sun
So when he comes tomorrow night, he can continue on

Don't you fret my little one, my little one so shy
Don't you fear the setting sun, sinking in the sky

It goes to sleep, goes to sleep, just like you and I
It goes to sleep my little one, just like you and I

I was leafing through these poems; sheet after sheet, when I stumbled across one in particular that chilled me to the bone. Unlike the others, most of which were happy-go-lucky, this page had been soiled, its ink smeared as if by water or tears. Had a vision come to him? Hard to say, but to read it now brought me much discomfort as these words spoke for themselves.

TALKING WATER
by David Dusterwinkle

Blessed was my daughter, perfect in her way
Born to bring me happiness, she kissed me every day
I lost her in the talking water of Missouri's rapid flow
It raised a frothy head and said this that I might know

Never bring those things you love to the banks beside my face
And put to test my temperament, lest they slip from your embrace
Never take your heart's desire and flaunt it when I flood
Or you'll search for it eternally beneath my yellow mud

Shush! Shush! Shush!
Commanded the cottonwood
You always run in such a rage
Is there nothing in you good?

It pounded on the jagged rocks, it roared, and thrashed, and spit
Drop your limb within my reach and driftwood shall I make of it
We will, we will, we'll scratch you still, and stop you from our shore
Give up the child within your grasp, have conscience we implore.

The birds within the branches and rabbit around the roots
Bear and beaver all alike cried out with barks, and hoots
Implore! Implore! Say no more! He's mean right to his source
He runs wherever and whenever, and will never show remorse

I tripped and slipped along the shore, stumbling out of breath
As the river slithered through the rocks and swept her to her death
I fell behind, bereft of hope, and prayed to God above
To spare me Missouri's malevolence and save the child I love

But as the river filled with tears, I saw within the deep
Her hair about her peacefully, as though she were asleep
I thought I saw her wave to me, this daughter I adore
Beyond the trees that reached for her—*farewell forever more*

Sssshhh! Sssshhh! Sssshhh!
Whispered the cottonwood
We grieve for your beloved one
We did all that we could.

My eyes filled with tears as my blood ran cold. My skin tightened, chilled by the words. I read the piece over and over. Was it some kind of prophecy? I sat perfectly still, thinking about the tragedy, fully expecting Dusty and his family to appear before me. I felt beyond all doubt that the Dusterwinkles were with me at this moment, watching me, judging me, debating whether or not to give up their home, but I didn't feel afraid. Instead, I let the sensation sweep over me and subside.

Dusty's writings seemed to draw me deeper into the wagon. I felt invited. I felt the warmth, the coziness—the security. I felt the emotions that still haunted. I supposed after so much time traveling, a place that I could call my own had strong appeal. I wanted to take possession of it, ghosts or no ghosts, and if the Dusterwinkles would have me, or if they wished to stay on board that was fine, I wouldn't mind the company, for I was as alone as alone could be.

Life was after all filled with strange things, and who could say, maybe I did look into the face of David Dusterwinkle, maybe he did save my life. I knew I should have been dead as were three other men, and yet against all odds I was sitting here stiff and sore for certain, but alive nonetheless. He could have let me drown.

THE DUSTERWINKLE HOME

SEVENTY-SIX

After the passing of another week, I found myself much stronger and ready to resume my search for Christopher. There was nothing else in life for me to do at this point. I had decided to abandon my plans to follow the Missouri River to its head, and instead take up a southwesterly route along the Yellowstone. I made this decision based first on conversations with the explorers and trappers, and secondly on my concerns about approaching the lands of the Blackfoot Indians, whom I especially feared and wished to avoid at all costs. I was haunted by Mr. Thompson's remarks about being barbecued.

I handed over a note for twenty-five hundred dollars to Mr. Crocker on behalf of the folks at Rapid Run for the wagon and all its contents. It was a lot of money, but the wagon was chocked full of wares, and everything out west was priced at least five times higher than anything east of St. Louis.

I requested that the money first be used for improving the ferry and henceforth calling it 'Dusty's Ferry', and that a plaque be placed on the banks to commemorate the man's devotion to his family. My request was warmly received, not only because everyone was getting something out of the deal, but also because they seriously hoped to appease David Dusterwinkle's ghost.

My second request was for a portion of the money to be set aside for the purchase of books to educate the few children that lived here in isolation. I finished my letter to Mary and Allen and asked them to contact Marguerite for shipping the books. I left the letter with Benjamin to give to Captain Parker on his return trip to St. Louis. After that, the remainder of the money was to be used for the benefit of the settlement as best seen fit.

Once accounts were settled, I set out to collect my personal belongings and transferred everything including my diary and trunk into the wagon. It took all of two days to fully investigate the hundreds of odds and ends and then to rearrange the stores and bedding, but the wagon accepted everything without complaint, and still offered me a little room to spare. Having made myself a new home, I only needed to take it with me.

I proceeded to the livery for the purpose of purchasing a team. As soon as I determined to buy the wagon, I informed the stablemaster of my need for six strong animals. For some reason, Dusty arrived in Rapid Run with horses, which were eventually sold off to cover the expense of their upkeep. Those horses were still available and for sale, but whereas horses were great for riding and short-run stage work, when it came down to a no-nonsense work team, the choice was squarely between oxen and mules. Dusty's wagon was heavy, and I suspected the only reason he entered Rapid Run with horses was due to a trade. At this point, no one would ever know.

I did know horses weren't for me. I had learned from experience on the Erie Canal that mules were far better at pulling than horses. They were certainly more sure-footed and considered by many to be a great deal smarter, especially when it came to finding food and water. And so, I considered myself lucky to have been offered six Spanish bred mules that the stablemaster acquired in my behalf.

The animals appeared strong and healthy, and I purchased them with great satisfaction. I had them sent over to the inn, where I stood alongside a stableboy who showed me how to properly hitch them to the wagon. That was the last detail needing attention and now I was ready to go. Benjamin was standing along the wagon with a troubled mind.

"Missus Clauzzen, much as Ah'd like to see this wagon git, Ah gotta say Ah'm a might worried 'bout you goin' off on yer own the way yer thinkin' on doin'. It's true thet this wagin' does my bis'ness no favors. I swear, ever'time I let a room, I wake up to idgits howlin' and carryin' on 'bout ghosts and such. An all you been a sayin' ain't done a thing to improve muh situation, but ah'm worried for yer wellbein' an' I don't min' sayin' so. This ain't a good thing, ma'am. You sure ya don' wannuh be waitin fer the next boat thet can take ya up ta Fort Union? Them injuns are actin' jus terrible. Ya don' wannuh let 'em catch hold o' ya."

"It's most kind of you to be concerned, Mr. Crocker. However my mind's made up. I feel more secure and more in control of my fate sitting in this wagon than I have in a long time. This can never be a runaway stage, no island is about to sweep me away, and I hope never to worry about falling overboard again. Frankly, I've had my fill of water. Besides, nobody has a clue as to when another boat might make it's way this far upriver or when the WAVERLY will return if it doesn't first get wrecked. I could be here until winter supplies come through for the fort, or until next spring if the water drops."

I offered my hand in farewell. I was deeply indebted to Benjamin for his care. He spit off to the side. He rubbed his hand clean on his clothes and reached up to take mine. He turned to face me, his one eye squinted shut, and grumbled.

"Ah b'leive there's more 'an six mules Ah'm a facin'. They's stubborn animals, Mrs. Clauzzen."

I laughed, "Yes, they are indeed, but then they are also sure-footed and intelligent."

"Oh, an' Ah ain' a bit surprised t' here ya say it." He rolled his eyes. "Jez the same, there's mean country 'bout these parts an Ah'll be tellin' truth when Ah say, 't'ain't no place for a woman. But thet being what it may, ah got somethin' else, it's 'bout thet Claussen fellow . . .."

"What about that Claussen fellow?" I asked with great interest.

"Ah knew thet name ring a bell, an' so ah did a lil' pokin' 'roun." He spit.

"Seems he come thru here 'bout a year ago, mebbe a stretch more. Ah'm figurin' he come back from top the Marias, lookin'

725

for a pass t' Oregon. Ah'm rememberin', word had it he took t' south 'long the Yellowstone jest as you're thinkin'a doin'. Ah bet m' life on 'em goin' down t' the Big Horn. There's water off th' Yellowstone called the Big Horn flow an' it goes through them mountains. As fer myself, Ah never much got past them mountains, but Ah heard a good deal o' rumor 'bout a South Pass, a weeks' ride beyond. I been hearin' they found one an it jes seems there's bin a bit more traffic through 'ere ever since."

"Oh, Mr. Crocker! I can't tell you what that information means to me. That is as close as anyone as come yet to knowing something of Mr. Claussen's whereabouts and it falls in perfectly with my plans. Finally, I feel as though I wandering in a little less of a circle."

"Well, Ah'm sorry I couln't hep ya more, but thet's 'bout all I knows."

"No, you done fine. I can't thank you enough."

"I don' need no thanks, no ma'am. You jes 'member, if yer not of a min' to go t'Fort Union an' see McKenzie, then ya goes due west. Lil' south mebbe, but mostly west. You gotta hit water, be it the Muhsourri 'r Yellerstone. Once ya find it, ya goes upstream. No matter which it be, ya be goin' upstream. Thet'll getcha to them Rockies. Then ya goes south an' thets 'bout all I knows."

I thanked Mr. Crocker for everything he had done in my behalf. I was delighted that he had not forgotten my questions about Christopher after all. It was information that meant much to me. Those being our last words spoken, I coaxed the animals forward toward the trail. I started west along the Missouri's southern bank with the morning sun at my back.

SEVENTY-SEVEN

Once out of earshot, while fully submerged in the joy of my new home and the freedom to face the world on my own terms, I began to sing. I sang my heart out. I sang a slew of those crazy, senseless western songs all done to the same ol' tune that I heard men bellow out time and time again around campfires after dark.

At fist I was humming without notice, but in short time I found myself hollering verses at the top of my lungs just to prove how totally free of restraint was I here in the middle of nowhere. I screamed with a bolstered spirit and dared anyone or anything to shut me up. I could sing what I wanted fine or foul. I was the almighty power, the only power. I was supreme. I was fearless. I was free.

I was the master of my fate and for now, I was happy amid my collection of bottles and jars, all colliding into one another, clinking and tinkling away before a disconnected chorus of pots and pans that swung wildly every which-way to the erratic beat of a bad bone-dry road.

There's some land that's fer sale, down along the dusty trail
You can own it fer a drink o' dirty water.
It's the find of a life, if yer runnin' from a wife
Who gave birth to another useless daughter

The ground won't be farmed, but as long as you're well armed
You'll starve before you die from Indian slaughter
Its dry and its baked, an' it can't be over-raked
Or plowed under to produce the way it oughter

727

There's no law on the land, cept the gun held in your hand
But whose life would be worth the ball and powder
It's a hail of a plot, an' it don't cost a lot
It's all yers fer a drink of dirty water....

Every pelt I have smelt in St. Louis should be dealt
A dose of Rosie's fragrant water
I would swear when I'm there that the odor in the air
Is harder to breathe than drownin' water

One might wish it were fish found rotting on a dish
Or some other form of Frenchman's fodder
Say cheese in the breeze that causes one to wheeze
To choke and gasp like Old man Potter

But it's not and it's got a stench worse than the rot
'Tween the legs of Lizzie's bunch o' daughters
Nothin's helped what I've smelt
In St. Louis that's a pelt
Not even Rosie's fragrant waters

All that day and a second to boot, I sang the hours away until I made myself hoarse and strangely enough—nervous. It was nothing at first, nothing specific and only barely perceptible. And yet, I had to admit that my euphoria was dissipating to some extent, for I was beginning to realize a feeling of growing uncertainty. It had to do with leaving the rowdy lot of Frenchmen and the riffraff that populated Rapid Run. It was obvious to me that this was not a good sign so soon after my departure. In fact, this was *definitely* not a good sign.

The more time went on, the more I wondered if I had been too rash in my determination to get out on my own. Without so much as an echo, I realized at the very least, singing should be done in company. My singing solo was actually making me feel even more lonely, so I stopped the singing and went back to humming. At Rapid Run everybody sang, and if singing was going to become an issue, I might as well turn around and head back for the river.

Twice on my first day out, I stopped the team to give my bottom a rest. The first time, I extended the canvas awnings in need of shade. The second time, I stepped down from the wagon to stretch my legs and look back along the tracks. I could trace my trail straight to the horizon, straight to the river where everybody sang. Seeing it disappear into infinity brought me more than just a little anxiety. It added another dimension to my rising apprehension, one of distance.

The loneliness I felt growing in the pit of my stomach was nothing like the loneliness I had always known. It was nothing like spending nights in bed by myself or eating in a crowded inn without company. This was a disturbing sensation, one of being lost or deserted. It was a scary feeling that crept over me slowly and wrapped itself tighter around my chest with each passing hour. It raised a fear in my subconscious that was primitive; something that really bothered me, something I dared not even acknowledge.

I thought having a world to myself would be a welcomed reprieve from ruffians and white water rapids, but I was amazed at how bizarre it felt to be totally apart from everyone. There was absolutely nobody out here to annoy me, nobody to anger me, nothing to affect me, and the sensation, to my amazement, was profoundly unnerving.

My thoughts became troubled. I could be undone by a minor mishap and who would ever know. A little cut that festers and forever gets worse, and I might end up dead on the plain; a broken wagon wheel—*dead on the plain*; snakebite—*dead on the plain*; a leak in my water barrel—*dead on the plain!* These were most unsavory thoughts that did me no favor.

I worked to convince myself that these fears were mostly irrational and that there had been plenty enough to worry about while traveling in the company of men when one assumed it to be safe. It was always one eye on the road and one eye on men's motives. I knew this as fact; I knew it from experience.

I made an effort to remind myself how many things about river travel I loathed. I abhorred the crowds and clouds of suffocating smoke and soot that blackened my dresses. I especially despised those men guilty of unrestrained drinking and unwelcome advances, offensive in the way they followed me about the banks while I searched for some privacy in order to relieve myself. I thought of the whiskey and vomit, the cigars, the tobacco chewing, the disgusting sight of spitting and overturned spittoons. I recalled the nauseating stench of the filthy and unwashed.

I reminded myself that these were only the aggravations while on board the boat. Add to that, how the boat itself faced an endless barrage of rapids and cross currents, sandbars, snags and sawyers, and those infamous boilers that blew up to kill everyone within a country mile. There seemed no end to my mental list of worries and concerns, arguments that should have made me feel better but didn't. In fact, I was feeling worse in spite of a plague of disgusting male insensitivities.

By the first week out, it became painfully obvious that my greatest obstacle to surviving in this land wouldn't be overcoming Indians, snakes, or great distances, but rather facing down this formidable loneliness, this overwhelming sense of abandonment. Funny how this was never mentioned at Mary and Allen's table, no one had warned me, but then who would have ever imagined my traveling west of Albany.

I looked up to the sky and asked God would he watch over me, or would he watch a god-fearing fool wander to her death, a person who devoted a lifetime to watching out for others and abiding by His word. I lowered my eyes to earth afraid I might hear His answer. I glanced around me, I observed the enormity of this land and wondered what could my life possibly be worth in the scheme of things. What would my existence matter? What difference would I make? If I was, I was; if I wasn't, I wasn't. Who would know? Who would care?

The experience might have been different had I been raised the daughter of a pioneer who lived in Kentucky or Tennessee, or maybe atop some mountain range in the Northwest Territories. If I had grown up on one of those eight-hundred-acre parcels given away by the Spanish, possibly then I would have been better equipped mentally to handle the isolation.

Instead, I was misled by my past, for I saw only a history of traveling where as a child I crossed oceans, sailed coasts, and anchored in countless ports of call. It never occurred to me when I took it upon myself to strike out in a wagon, that there had always been a common element in all my childhood excursions—*people*, ordinary, everyday, obnoxious, pushy people—*God bless them all.* I overlooked the fact I had always been in the company of those who loved me, those who looked out for me, or at least cared enough to keep me safe. I had always shared the thrills and fears of far-away places with others who were there when I felt unsure and in need of a supporting hand or a consoling word. Now, comfort and consolation came only within the refuge of my traveling tinder-box of worldly wares.

Nothing I could do served to relieve me of the gnawing loneliness that was overtaking most of my thoughts and strangling my sense of well-being. Fact was, within that first week of leaving Rapid Run, I had gone from blissful relief to borderline hysteria. It was a rude awakening in a bed entirely of my own making. How many souls hadn't put forth every effort to dissuade me from such foolishness?

At last, I came to the full measure of my predicament and I cried. My tears came with a physical sense of doom. My chest succumbed to the pressures of hopelessness that engulfed me. I was suffering terrible attacks of panic and difficulties breathing even though I struggled to calm myself and maintain a level head.

At some point in my woeful state, thoughts of Christopher came to me. I longed for him in the worst of ways. I cried for him, hoping somewhere out there he could hear my pleas. As a child, I thought him a god, someone who could calm an ocean or settle a storm, someone who could read my mind. I believed it with all my heart until Lady Rebecca died, and even then I didn't dismiss it; I just didn't understand.

I wanted to be that child again, the one who never questioned his strengths. I desperately wanted him to be my savior. I focused upon his image. I concentrated on a certain memory of his eyes burned permanently into my soul from a time when I stared deep into their blueness aboard the REBECCA. It was a vivid memory of kindness and compassion, of understanding and hope. Just the thought of his eyes drove out all my heart's worry. I recalled the strength of character that ran through the lines of his face as he rested upon my bed in Boston. I remembered leaning over him ever so closely. Memories from so many years ago, and yet, still they could bring me solace.

These thoughts of Christopher not only settled me, but actually rebuilt my confidence and my determination to go forward. He always believed in my abilities; he always drove me to do the impossible. I concentrated only on my ambitions to find him. Thank god, I possessed something that held stronger sway over me than my fears.

I began to relax. I realized that the slow pace of my progress was a major reason for my suffering. Traveling by wagon was even slower than canal boat, and I had always thought of barges as the slowest going possible, especially after booking passage on a stagecoach and beating the roads to death.

Out here, hopes for a change in scenery or a sign of life seemed pointless, or rather *impossible*. I crawled across a landscape that showed no beginning or end. I might reach the horizon in a day's time or I might not. I had no way of knowing, and it made me feel trapped in time and space.

My longest hour was the one just after sighting another human, someone riding eastward or rafting down river in a flat-bottomed boat. Always, after spotting my wagon the strangers would seek me out unless I was already working my way down the riverbank with all impatience and high hopes of camping in their company.

Without fail, our encounters opened in the same fashion, men of every description staring at me with utter astonishment. Once over the initial shock of my being a woman, they took to acting like kids romping through fresh candy, enjoying themselves and eager to barter for supplies as they pawed through my many possessions within, without, and all about the wagon. Their glee ending only after a frank and hopeful 'to the point' question about my personal possessions, private services in particular, which I immediately answered by producing my staff and a promise of a severe beating should they persist.

On only one occasion was I forced to follow my words with a blow. This, due to the fact there were five men traveling in company, and their number gave them a false sense of security. I laid the most troublesome man out dead senseless, but their worst punishment came when I decided to take my wares and leave. At that point cries for forgiveness and a fresh start filled the air. They apologized wholeheartedly for letting down their manner before a proper lady. Believe when I say that although I made them beg with conviction and prayer, I needed their company much more than they needed mine.

Men who were returning from the wilderness were generally heavy with skins and light on supplies. Any weight they hauled east across country was pared down to pelts, traps, guns and powder. Items such as sugar, coffee, or dried fruit were not merely welcome sights, but relished pleasures that guaranteed me large toothless grins.

In high spirits, the men repaid my hospitality in a big way. More important than the furs, gold or grease they might trade, they offered directions, advice, and a feel for the land that lay before me. They went into great detail about places of danger where they wouldn't send their worst enemy without conscience or words of warning.

Although I enjoyed these wilderness meetings, they were far and few between with every man encountered giving me that same look of disbelief or high hopes upon discovering I was traveling alone. For the most part, these were good men with a common cause, and they held a full measure of respect for anyone male or female that braved the wilderness.

Even so, leaving camp was not always as easy as picking up and riding off. On occasion, arguments ensued whereby some characters were unwilling to allow me to continue on alone. In spite of my possessing a wagon and being well off, they honestly believed women to be feeble of mind and ill equipped to cope with the demands of the rough country. I couldn't be angry with them, they believed in earnest my death was imminent, and maybe it should have been. They may have been closer to truth than they knew.

In any event, at times it took a great deal of persuasion to remove myself from their company. For them, seeing to my safety was a matter of honor. Often, I came away convinced that I was better off avoiding these encounters, but I could never bring myself to pass up the promise of conversation and companionship. It was my only cure for desert insanity, which I dreaded above all else.

SEVENTY-EIGHT

There are no secrets on the prairie. It is too flat, too open, and contrary to logic, too expansive to hide anything. Even the dirt stands proud. And so it was, I could follow the flight of an eagle as it soared high overhead and far beyond the bluffs, or sight a herd of animals grazing miles away across a valley. On a clear day the course of the Missouri or the shadow of a cloud could be observed for distances so great it left me stupefied.

The one thing least likely to go hidden in this expanse was a prairie storm. I often found it the most intensely fearful, fright-ful, ten-minute ordeal one might experience short of a runaway horse. I was convinced a full-blown prairie storm could make a confessing Christian out of the meanest man alive, and I would be first to wager that after one or two encounters, the inexperi-enced would readily agree that Satan's fork might well have been forged from a triple-tongued bolt of Missouri sky lightning.

Bristling with malice, these wicked bursts of energy streaked through the air barely overhead. They would stand my hair on end while slicing open the underbellies of burdened clouds until some greater power finally drove them back to Hell. Cruel by nature, in this dry parched land a prairie storm was always a thunderstorm, but if you were hoping for rain then you were often disappointed.

Only souls long dead and buried, those deep in eternal sleep might be caught surprised by the approach of such an event. Forewarnings came far ahead and offered one all the time needed to size up how bad a thrashing was in store. I was doing some serious sizing up now, for I had watched this particular storm

735

rear its ugly head from below the horizon and blur the distance as it pounded the far away ground mercilessly.

Long before the storm arrived, I listened to its challenge. It sounded everything in its path with growls and grumbles similar to stacks of loosened barrels rolling recklessly across wooden warehouse floors. Evermore, it commanded my attention. The warnings were relentless and intensifying as the storm rumbled roughshod over the landscape scattering life like bees spun out of a fallen hive.

Aside from my instinct and stomach, I had no guide by which to measure such ferocity. My gut was good at making clear when there was nothing to fear, or when I should run away in panic and cower for all I was worth. On this day, right from the start I felt a need to run. This storm looked bad. It felt bad. It had fouled the western sky, turning it into dreadful and unsightly swirls of blacks, blues, and hues of gray. It appeared mean to the point of beating itself as severely as the earth below.

"This does not look good!" I yelled forward to my mules. "You boys are gonna get a bath and then some. Ya hear? You don't believe me? Huh! You just wait and see. You—just—wait—and—see."

The first casualty was a glorious sunset that never happened. It had been suffocated, stamped out, leaving little more than a trace of sickening grayish-orange residue. Its remnants could be seen bubbling through the face of an ominous and opaque precipice, a sheer vertical wall of flickering turmoil that was falling fast across my world like a giant black domino. As it collapsed upon me, it forced an early nightfall by shutting out the light of day and spreading a near blindness beneath its enormity.

I was heading straight for it, or more accurately it for me, and I was now seriously compelled to search for shelter. The pit of my stomach was telling me to hide without delay. I wasn't alone in my nervousness, for the animals were also reacting with unease, but now my concerns were growing less for the team and more for my own safety. The thunder had changed from that incessant background rumbling to sporadic cracking overhead that caused me to duck with each passing flare.

"Settle down. Settle down now. I told you we were in for some rough weather. I don't like it either, but we haven't much choice."

I continued to talk to my team. I attempted to console them. They were becoming spooked, but turning the wagon around in retreat had never been an option. There was no advantage to be gained, for the lay of the land behind me was identical to the earth beneath my wheels and the ground that stretched ahead. In all directions, the country was unchanged. Therefore, it remained most sensible to press forward in hopes of finding a haven where I might graze the team safely for the night.

Unfortunately, the lack of changing terrain was troublesome. The ground remained wind blown and barren, it being sun-baked stone-hard clay with scant vegetation for as far as I could see. There was little of anything the mules might consider edible.

I removed my attention from the tortured sky long enough to look around and consider my options. I had been following the river, although I only saw it on occasion. This was because the riverbed meandered back and forth in serpentine fashion across the bottomland, whereas I drove the team in a straighter line along higher ground. The river would leave me then return miles later only to leave me again and repeat the cycle. At this point it was coursing past me a few hundred feet to my right and a good hundred feet below the bluff I was traversing.

I intentionally brushed the bank's edge in hopes of spotting an accessible ravine that I might drive the team down in order to reach the bottoms. I had hoped the mules might spend the night grazing safely among the cottonwoods and grasses within the canyon, while I fished the eddies and foraged for fresh berries.

"That's enough!" I pulled back on the reins. "Let's just rest a moment while I have a look around."

The deepening darkness reminded me that I had but little time to make a final decision. I had halted the team close to a bluff where I then walked a short distance to the drop-off. There, I studied the banks below me for any sign of a passage to the ribbons of vegetation down at water's edge. I saw no access in sight upriver or down.

As I stared below into an already quick current, it occurred to me that this disappointment might have been for best. Facing the storm was going to be dangerous on the high ground for sure; its intensity increased by the minute. Its winds now pushed me about freely. Yet, as I spied the sheets of rainfall in the distance beyond the seemingly safe canyons, I was given cause to consider the certainty of flash floods already forming upriver to wreak havoc.

Washouts were commonplace, and so in spite of the animals being hungry and my mounting nervousness, I saw little choice but to hunker down on the high ground and take my chances. I studied the lay of the land, which was essentially flat as a tabletop. I urged the mules into the wind, driving them ahead to a place where a broad but barely perceptible depression offered scant if not make-believe shelter from lightning, wind, and worry.

The dark was now well advanced and the severity of the lightning most unsettling. Whereas the wind had been coming at a steady blow from the east for most of the day, it went slack in late afternoon and then reversed, building anew from the west to blow sand into my eyes with stinging force. I had thought to unhitch the team from the wagon and let them seek out what little food and shelter there was, but changed my mind for fear they would be frightened into stampeding off. I had no desire to awake in the morning and start my day walking circles for however many miles it might take to round them up—better to leave them hitched.

Sensing, I had run out of time, I at last drew the handbrake up firm and went about the business of re-tightening the straps securing my awnings to save them from being ripped away by the wind. I had no doubt that this storm would produce because I could see rain falling without interruption in a far-reaching veil of long wispy streaks.

Collecting water was always the first priority, but my oilcloth would have been lost at once if laid out. Instead, I unhooked some of Dusty's heaviest metal containers and set them about. Even so, I was forced to put hammers and other heavy items inside of pots to sufficiently weigh them down. Nothing would stay put in the wind.

Feeling anxious and having little more to do than wait out the last few minutes for its arrival, I walked up to the lead mules. I scratched their ears and fussed over them in hopes of settling them and me; but it was to no avail.

"I know. You want me to unhitch you and set you free, but if you had a grain of sense between those big ears, you'd high tail it out of this place and where would that leave me? I'm not going to spend a week walking about just to bring you back. Not this lady."

The security of the wagon was only twenty feet away, yet the sky was so threatening it made it seem unreachable. I both cowered and thrilled to see how this ominous heaven closed about me like gigantic black jaws of some snarling supernatural beast with terrifying white teeth flashing.

Every moment was a dare, as I forced myself to stand firm before both the wind that twisted through my hair, and the butterflies that fluttered through my insides. The jaws of the beast were closing down upon me and I knew soon the flow of its saliva would flood my being. The anticipation was unbearable and I squirmed with cramps as goose bumps erupted along my arms and across the nape of my neck.

Maybe the goose bumps weren't from fear, but from the sudden change in temperature. It felt to have dropped a good twenty degrees and continued on down until I found myself facing an uncomfortably cold and forceful blow heavy with the scent of water. Also falling with greater frequency were random raindrops, massive in size; scattered, one here, one there; all thudding onto the unyielding clay like the farthest reach of spray from a crashing wave on an ocean turned upside down. The jaws closed and a markedly diminished view through the dull foreboding twilight convinced me it was time to head home.

No sooner had I turned to face the wagon, when a cold mist rushed past me to pave way for the torrent that followed. It came first as a thrashing of radish-sized hail followed within seconds by bucketloads of frigid water thick with sleet.

I got a painful pelting in what few seconds it took to reach the wagon and climb inside. I wasted not a second as I dove for cover and slammed the doors shut against the punishing down-pour. Behind closed doors, I felt of myself and laughed, for I had most certainly lost the race.

"Good night! Look at me."

I had been doused, drenched to the skin. Ticklish drops of water worked free of my hair and slid down my face like a parade of confused tears.

I sat in the darkness of the wagon working to catch my breath while listening to the racket of hail hammering the roof and busting across the pots and pans. The noise was deafening, and I wondered how long I would have to wait it out. I was helpless to do anything but sit tight and worry for the mules. It made me sick to feel the way in which they were pushing and pulling against the wagon's brake. I rubbed a couple of welts on my skull and prayed the animals would fare better than I while out in the open.

The wind howled like a tornado and drove my stomach into my throat. I sat centered on the bed with arms outstretched as if to hold the shelves and wagonsides in place. Outside, pots and pans were swinging or slamming, or sliding in arcs across the wagonsides, or crashing into each other like giant cymbals.

It seemed certain that the wagon would be upset and so I held on expecting to roll over any second.

Added to this, claps of thunder scared the wits clean out of me and my mules. I was nothing if not lost in a world of utter mayhem, sitting in blackness under a raging waterfall. I was a nervous wreck and finally forced by fear to break open the rear doors of the wagon so I might look outside for a sign of sanity. I had to know that the earth was still beneath my wheels and the sky overhead.

In doing so, I glimpsed into the heart of nature's fury. The storm had forced out all sign of moon or stars; and it was now darker than night with the blackness haphazardly shredded by flashes of intense brightness. The lightning gave animation to what few discernible features were scattered behind the wagon. Rocks and small plants, these things flickered in and out, forward and back. They snapped side to side like barefoot children bouncing on hot summer sand.

My last vision revealed a rush of rain and sleet blowing by me in a straight horizontal fly. But for the sight beyond my doors, my drenching and the temperature, I was overcome by a spasm of chills that shot clean through to my bones. A further spectacular discharge of lightning left me so blinded and frightened that I immediately slammed the door shut, sealing out the weather with one trembling hand, while yanking at my blankets with the other.

In the coffin-like darkness that engulfed me, I spread an oilcloth across the top of my covers to keep them dry. I fumbled about, shifting tins back and forth beneath those annoying little leaks of which there were too many. I drew in my pillow and slunk down on the bed of the wagon where I disappeared into a curl beneath the blankets, the storm, and the metallic mayhem sounding out overhead. I closed my eyes, stuck my fingers into my ears, and relished the heat of my breath until I was about to suffocate.

When finally forced to emerge for need of fresh air, I opened my eyes to look about. Or at least that was my intent, for it was perfectly black inside the wagon; so dark I strained to make out the shape of any one of a dozen things that had fallen on me from the shelves above. I functioned with nothing more than my sense of touch, except when given the slightest use of my eyes by those splinters of lightning that slipped into my space after having pried their way through hereto invisible cracks and loosened joints.

I was warm and cozy within my blankets, but there was no thought of sleep. The wagon continued to shudder with each thunderclap. It continued to rock and pitch back and forth, if not from the wind then from the tug of the team as they lunged this way and that while attempting to retreat from nature's charge. My heart went out to them.

Although I was inside and free of their torment, I lay with clenched teeth and prayed for protection while the most unpleasant thoughts ran through my head. I jumped with fright at each lightning strike and considered how I was the only thing for miles around that stood higher off the ground than the few blades of scrub. I tried to find solace in knowing that if I were to be struck by lightning, I would die having never known. It was a noble thought, even scientific, but wholly unsuccessful at salvaging my peace of mind.

In dire need of something to allay my fears, I found myself sliding my hands along the shelf overhead.

"Where are you," I whispered.

I slid my fingers up and down along the draws and carefully past the numerous articles that packed the shelves full. Up and down, in and out, over a myriad of misplaced wares and whatnot until at last I came to what I sought.

"There you are."

I felt the leather lace. I fingered the feathers and beads. I pulled Shadow Hunter's amulet down and slipped it over my head before slipping back beneath the blankets. Such a superstitious move, so childish, and yet like a favorite doll, it brought immediate comfort.

I gripped it tightly as my mind retreated to a point in time long since passed. I found myself reminiscing about how I used to lay upon the seat of Lady Rebecca's coach beneath a thick woolen blanket. The wailing wind was fueling my memory of winter gales and frost covered panes of glass.

I remembered holding my ship's blanket above the foot warmers to catch the rising heat. Most of all, I remembered Lady Rebecca's embrace. I would lay with my head upon her lap as I now lay upon my pillow. I could almost feel her arm across me as she caressed my temples and urged me to sleep with a soft lullaby. A cheerless smile crossed my face, as I understood the humor and sadness of having grown up to be a woman who still very much longed for the loving embraces once given her as a child.

Now only the embrace of blackness surrounded me, and it was driving my imagination in the worst of ways. I had suffered through a good many storms, but this one stood out smartly from those of past. The wind was the worst I recalled, and I assumed it to be due to the lack of anything but dust to slow it down. I gave thought to lighting a lamp, but decided it was better to go without and not risk a fire should the wagon be upset. Twice I swore the wheels had all but lifted off the ground from the force of gusts to the vehicle's side.

Another troubling thought was that of the wagon moving about due to the lurches of the team. I was a good distance from the bluff and well braked, but just the thought of a cliff out there hidden from view by darkness was enough to destroy my confidence. I desperately wanted to reopen the rear doors and peek outside for reassurance, but had no desire to risk an additional soaking or let escape what precious little heat was in the wagon. So, I lay still and reprimanded myself for being such a measly and spineless scaredy-cat.

I had set the brake and double-checked it. The wagon was still hitched to the team. Wagons, carriages, coaches; they all had a common feel as they rolled along unforgiving ground intent on breaking bones and teeth in the process. I knew all these things to be true, but in the absence of light and the ability to reassure myself, I was slowly surrendering to my overactive imagination and a flourish of doubt. Feelings of doom were gnawing at me. Being closed in was terrible.

I tried my best to relax, to overcome my fears. I was warmer now and so to ease my stiffness, I stretched out to lie flat on my back hoping I might somehow fall asleep. I lay there for the longest time waiting either to sleep or die, but unfortunately it was neither. Instead, all my mental meanderings, all my random thoughts coalesced into one subtle realization. I came to notice that my feet, which rested at the front of the wagon were elevated somewhat above my head.

At first I thought it just my imagination, an illusion in the total darkness. It was a confusing prospect because my head was on a pillow, and I had to remove the pillow a number of times to rest my skull upon the wooden bed before I concluded this was a fact.

Something about this was not good. How *not good* wasn't at first apparent. It was more of a nagging intuition. Nagging enough, that I ended up focusing all thought on what direction I had been traveling when I halted the team. I clearly recalled that the ground sloped off to my right in a north or northerly direction toward the river.

In order for my feet to be noticeably elevated, the wagon would now have to be pointed somewhat southerly toward the rise of the slope. It was this realization that sent a horrific wave of panic through me, for that would have meant the wagon was no longer sitting alongside the cliff, but instead backed toward the cliff and able to roll into the gorge. It was an insane assumption. I knew for fact the wagon could not have moved because I would have felt the motion and jostling over ground. *But*—the wind had been bouncing me around pretty good. Maybe, I just didn't notice. As impossible as it seemed, I was certain the wagon now pointed uphill. How could that be?

I swallowed hard. Unable to wrestle with these thoughts any further, I climbed out from under the blankets and rose to my knees. I felt like an idiot and yet, I had no choice but to open the rear doors to assure myself all was well, for thoughts of rolling over the cliff choked out any hope of peace or restful napping.

The first ill omen was my near inability to open the door. The blast of wind and water forcefully held it closed against my will. I assumed without thought that the wind had changed directions, until there came that second wave of panic. The wind might not have changed direction at all had the wagon been turned about. One thing was certain, the doors were no longer opening entirely downwind.

I pushed the door open against the wind and strained to see outside through the narrow vertical opening. A bolt of lightning illuminated the ground and I saw that it was submerged beneath a vast sheet of silvery white water. The shallow depression I had looked to for shelter from lightning now appeared in every way a flowing lake rippled with concentrations of lace and froth.

I looked up from the ground into the darkness just as it was forced back by a wicked web of pulsating light. In the long seconds of illumination that branched across the sky, I observed the extent of this rippled lake until darkness closed in again, where after I sat sorting out the image before me by memory.

"Oh, my god! Oh, my god, *oh my god!*"

The pleas tumbled out of my mouth as quickly as my thoughts formed. I shoved the door fully open against the weather and leaned out to better see the ground. In the following flurry of lightning I saw a distinct black line across the lake and understood it to be the cliff, now no more than thirty or forty feet away. How the wagon could have been resting so close to the edge of the bluff was utterly beyond my comprehension, but it was so. I saw it for myself.

"What now? Oh, Lord, whatever should I do now."

I was frantic. There was no time to waste. If I were to lose the wagon I would die on the desert within days. I crawled across the blankets and pushed open the front doors. The wind ripped them loose from my hands. The rain streamed in as the force of the storm plowed into me like a cresting wave. I was instantly drenched.

I paid it no mind, for at this moment nothing else mattered. I struggled against the blow in order to climb over the backrest of the seat. I reached out for the hand brake and pulled it hard. To my surprise, it didn't budge. It didn't move as much as a whisker. I was momentarily lost for explanation. The brake was set firm and yet the wagon was turned and perched upon the cliff's edge. I hadn't expected this, and was suddenly unsure of what next to do.

The storm raged. It slung rain at me with a vengeance. It worked against me both physically and mentally. It most certainly clouded my thoughts, for I could give not one reasonable explanation for how the wagon was moved. I only knew the wagon had to be moved again. It had to be moved away from the cliff to safer ground and it had to be moved now.

This meant releasing the handbrake. The one thing I was most reluctant to do for fear the wind would drive the wagon backward down the slope and into the canyon. I knew this was an irrational thought for the mules would stand firm, and yet the laws of nature already appeared deceiving or at best contrary to what I was inclined to believe. It was plenty obvious the wagon rested mysteriously in a place some distance from where I halted the team.

I had little time to form a plan. I stared at the hand brake. The more I thought about it, the less I was inclined to sit on the wagon when the brake was released. I had visions of rolling backwards over the cliff because my clothing or something got snagged on the wagon. I much preferred to stand on the ground alongside wagon, but I knew if I didn't plant both my feet securely on the dashboard, I wouldn't have either the strength or control I needed to release the catch. Knowing this, I tucked in my loose clothing and positioned myself to jump clear of the seat should anything go wrong.

I snapped the reins to get the mules attention. I then grasped the brake handle firmly in hand. I said a quiet prayer, hollered out to the mules and released the catch. I attempted to simultaneously ease off the brake and goad the mules forward, but as soon as the tension was reduced, the brake gave up all its grip, and the wagon lurched rearward.

Considering that the brake block and wheel were wet, the wind was forceful, and there was bound to be some slack in the harness, I should have expected nothing less, and yet, the sudden move backward scared me positively senseless. Already at wits end and leaving absolutely nothing to chance, I instinctively leapt clear of the wagon. By jumping first and worrying about questions later, I put down any possibility of riding the wagon over a cliff this night.

I am not sure of exactly what happened next other than to say my world went upside down. Out of balance, my body wrenched, warped and twisted. I was out of control, but before any explanation, there came a devastating blow to the back of my head.

SEVENTY-NINE

It was a clap of thunder that drove me to open my eyes. I was laying on my back aware only of a terrific pain at the base of my skull. Then came the cold and the uncontrollable spasms. Lastly, there was the sensation of water rushing across me. I tried

747

to make sense of where I was and what it was I had been doing or was supposed to do. I tried to raise my head to look around, but the pain was so intense that I was immediately forced to lie back still. In my confusion, I thought myself to be at River Run and the rapids. I remembered slamming into the rocks. I remembered the pain.

It took time to gather my wits and reach my first question, which was—how badly was I hurt? I was too cold and numb to feel anything other than the pain in my head. I thought it serious. I moved my hand to the back of my skull and felt an enormous welt, but it was impossible to determine if I suffered an open wound or not. I couldn't feel blood but for the downpour and the rushing flow of water that washed over and around me.

In short time came the recollection of the wagon, the cliff, and my predicament. I remembered how the wagon had been too close to the cliff and how I was about to move it to safer ground. I opened my eyes and looked for the wagon. In the next flash of light, I noticed that it was a good hundred or more feet away. I had no recollection of walking away, so either I had been stumbling about or else the team had moved up the slope to put distance between the wagon and me. I didn't know which, but at least everything appeared safely away from the drop-off.

That alone was worth a sigh of relief, and now it was just a matter of getting myself back in order and out of the rain. The water had sapped all the heat from my body. I was so cold that my muscles wouldn't respond. I was barely able to push against the ground in order to sit up. I leaned back on my hands and let my head fall back long enough for the rain to flush away the dirt from my face as I adjusted to my headache.

I had no feeling in my hands. I noticed they kept sliding out from underneath me. I soon realized that is wasn't my numbed hands that were failing me, but rather the nature of the wet clay. I soon put together the pieces and concluded that I had jumped off the wagon and landed in this wet slippery goo, which caused my feet to slide out from beneath me. I must have caught my head squarely on the wagon wheel and clobbered the senses right out of me.

My thoughts were still cloudy at best, but they seemed logical. As for now, I had my fill of rain and mud and was determined to get back to the warmth of the wagon before I died of pneumonia. I never opened my eyes but for the pain in my head, and merely rolled over onto all four. Even with eyes closed, I noticed how incredibly greasy was the ground. My attempts to rise to my feet were futile, for the clay was slicker than wet ice, and every attempt left me face down in the mud and water. I could do little more than prop myself up on my elbows.

It might have been the funniest thing a soul could see if my head hadn't finally cleared enough to size up my situation and look around for something to grab. It was right then that I noticed there was nothing at all to grab behind me because there was nothing behind me at all. *I mean nothing!* I was only three or four feet from the edge of the bluff and sliding closer with every move I made. In fact the ground was so slippery and now sloped so steeply that I sensed myself moving closer to doom even when I remained perfectly still. The flow of water down the slope washed everything over the edge, including the earth beneath my body in order to carry me away as well.

I began fishing through the soil, frantically feeling for anything solid, but there was nothing to be found aside from more of the ooze that slipped through my fingers. And so, I continued toward the cliff in a slow and comical, but unstoppable downhill slide. The slope was much steeper here than at the wagon and increased markedly as I neared the edge. I stayed flat on my stomach and plunged my fingers as deep into the slimy substance as my strength would allow. It made no difference. It was as though I was clinging to a spread of butter that was slowly melting away.

I was at a loss. I was suddenly very alone. I stared at the wagon, which was my only connection with humanity and hope. In the flashes of light I saw the rain spill off its roof and fall to the ground where it blended in with the shallow lake that moved in my direction. The water passed by me and cascaded into the canyon. Slowly, very slowly, I was being washed over the edge by its flow. Then came the paralyzing wave of terror as I felt the ground give way beneath my toes leaving them unsupported in the sky. Without realizing it, I had already started crying and screaming out pleas for mercy.

Next went feet and ankles, then my shins. Out of mind with fear, I drove my fingers as deep into the soup as I could. I concentrated all of my weight upon my fingertips. I concentrated all my effort, but the futility of my situation was obvious almost at once, for my arms, which were exposed to the cold water were quick to cramp. I was losing control of my muscles to fatigue and against my will they quickly turned weak and worthless. I dropped onto my torso and drove my elbows into the grease keeping all my weight above them. I settled into the mud as far as possible. My face hovered over the goop as I spit out the water and hugged the earth for all I was worth.

So very slowly did I move. It could hardly be noticed. My death was being drawn out in the most tormenting manner. It was a hopeless situation whereby I was left to experience every prolonged second of my demise, every primal urge to survive as if clinging to that last breath before drowning.

At first I fought this finality with everything I possessed both mentally and physically, but this spirit was soon subdued as I came to accept my fate, and in those last moments, a very real sense of peace. I let loose what little hold I had maintained and it seemed to make no difference. I continued my slide to eternity until a dull pain cut uncomfortably across my jaw and the wound at the back of my neck and head.

This was not from the blow of my fall, but from the collar of my blouse or something other. It was a binding sensation that was in fact growing painful in its own right. As I lay there momentarily suspended in time and space, a flash of lightning arched overhead and lit the ground submerged beneath the water's flow to reveal the tangle of my hair drawn tight. A second flash revealed something more. Threaded within the strands of my hair was the talisman that Shadow Hunter had given me for good luck.

"Good luck," I said aloud with resignation.

I then realized it was my hair that was pulling painfully at the wound on the back of my scalp. It was the leather lace of the talisman that was cutting across my jaw and into the back of my neck. The amulet and tangle of hair had snagged on something in the mud. I had moved almost beyond the fear of death and giving little thought to any form of salvation, I reached for the talisman more out of curiosity than anything else.

The leather necklace had looped itself over the nubble of a root or stalk. I began to seek out this hidden anchor with my fingers. It wasn't much that I found, something less than an inch in diameter, but sufficient enough to stop my slide across the greasy slope.

I had sense enough not to dig for it. I doubted that the root was attached to rock or anything for that matter, but more aptly embedded in the mud of prior storms that had washed it toward the cliff and as of yet the deeper earth had not softened enough to give up its catch.

My situation had presented a dramatic reversal. I was still in grave danger for my legs dangled limply over the edge, and I hadn't slid one solitary inch uphill through the flow of water, but then I was supposed to be dead by now, so indeed things were looking up. I was as afraid to hope, as I was to die. And so I stayed put, not wanting to rush anything, not wanting to make the one stupid move that would waste this miracle. I took the time to think things out.

I began to dig a hole with my left hand, which went quite quickly because the running water cleared away the silt. I then formed a fist with my hand and twisted it back and forth as deep into the pit as I could manage. The pit filled quickly with silt and that caused a notable degree of suction that was sufficient to resist the pull of gravity on my body.

Keeping my fist planted firmly on the bottom, I was forced to muster every ounce of courage I could manage, because as I stiffened my left arm straight out, which slid me upward and away from the edge, I also unhooked myself from the root. My safety catch was no more.

I turned my body somewhat sideways to keep all my weight balanced upon my fist. I couldn't use my muscles but for the cramping. I then began to dig a second hole. I gauged the digging of a new hole against the reliability of the old. I repeated this process time and again, eventually slipping my feet in old holes as well. For whatever reason, God saw to it there would be a safe distance gained between the cliff and myself. I dug these holes for twenty feet or more up the slope.

Eventually I was crawling, sliding haphazardly on all four, for I never was able to fully stand up until very close to the wagon where the ground was level beneath the flow of water. I now understood that the wagon had never rolled toward the cliff, but instead simply slid in that direction while taking a buffeting from the wind and mules. Only one wheel was braked, and to think that would stop anything atop this bed of slime was preposterous.

The rain felt as cold as a Chicago winter, and yet I had no desire to enter the wagon for I was covered head to foot in mud and already too cold to ever warm up. Instead, I stood along-side the wheel and forced my fingers to move across my breast, button to button, unfastening each and dropping one article of clothing atop another.

They sank into the mud as I stood upon the pile perfectly naked, perfectly cold, perfectly exhausted. Only the talisman remained as the rain cleansed me, forcing the filth down my frame. I rubbed my face over and over and over. I rubbed my shoulders and breasts. I rubbed my eyes and massaged my hair until I no longer felt anything foreign trapped within.

Believing myself to be clean, I fumbled about in the darkness and retrieved my clothes from the mud. I climbed back onto the seat. With trembling hands, I released the brake and urged the team far forward, away from the cliff before setting the brake a second time. I looked a last time toward the river and feeling confident I was most certainly a safe distance away; I laid out my clothes to rinse and climbed back inside my box.

The bed of the wagon was awash in water and my blankets were soaked through and through. In my haste to jump, I had left all the doors open to the weather. Shivering miserably, I closed the doors and pulled the wet blankets over me. They were soaked and unbearably cold, but offered protection against the air. I craved the heat of my breath. I curled up in a pool of water and waited for the water to drain through the cracks. I pulled my legs up into my chest and lay there shaking until exhaustion forced me to sleep. It was restless and troubled, but it brought me through the remainder of the storm.

Upon my awakening, my first thought was of how supremely quiet it was. No rain, no hail, no wind, no pots and pans, no sound from the animals; it was perfectly still. I lay listening for the longest time. I should have been dead, I knew I wasn't. It was just quiet and nothing more. I wanted to look outside, but every time I moved a cold piece of the wet blanket would touch me and force me to shiver and hold still. Even so, unease about the cliff and my desire to look outside got the best of me, so I sat up and fought a relentless barrage of spasms as I moved quickly to cover myself in the driest clothes I could find. I then opened the back door to cold outside air.

Before me was a scene of such peace and serenity that I would have believed I had indeed died and gone to heaven. The night sky was clear, black, and thick with millions of stars. The moon was brilliant and it lit up the river valley for miles with a cold bluish cast. There wasn't a sound to be heard and the experience was profound.

I was overwhelmed by a sense of Divine intervention. Maybe, because I didn't go to Him on this night, He came to me. I felt He was here with me in every way. I was moved to tears by my close call with death and the stark beauty of the nocturnal world at my door. I felt myself a part of this beauty and all things made alive by His hand. I stared for the longest time across the desert before the cold drove me to close the door and lay back down. I was filled with a sense of awe. I realized I would never be more than a prayer away from His reach. I clutched the amulet.

* * *

The following morning brought with it a bright sun, a cloudless blue sky, and much cooler temperatures, thirty or forty degrees in the early hours. For this reason if no other, I slept late into the day, which was most unlike me. By the time I did finally awake, the sun was high in the sky, pouring down its heat and making the inside of the wagon akin to a steam bath. I was still wet and chilled and so determined to make the best of its warmth.

I opened all the doors, front and back to dry out the wagon. I studied the rain cleansed clothes draped over the wheel, but made no move to take care of them. Instead, I spread out my soaked blankets on ground that was already dry and intended to dry myself out as well.

Just before laying down beneath the warm sun, I looked around, especially in the direction of the cliff where I had nearly met my death only hours before. I walked in that direction and studied the ground. There was no sign whatsoever; no evidence to acknowledge what drama had taken place. My near death experience amounted to nothing more than a blink of meaning-lessness in the passing of time. I wanted to see tracks, scars that proved what I underwent, but the ground was washed as smooth as a clay plate and free of any guilt. It appeared hard, solid, undisturbed, virgin ground sinless in every way.

I looked out across the prairie. It emerged freshened and determined to forget about the night passed. Let bygones be bygones. No sign of the storm, no sign of the flooding, not a single pool of standing water to be seen. I grasped my amulet and brought it to my lips.

"Nobody knows," I whispered to the unseen spirits.

Two of my pots and pans had remained put. They had narrowly escaped a similar fate and now gleamed in the noon sun. I was pleased to see they were brimming full. In spite of my lingering chill, the sight of the fresh water heightened my thirst. It was cool and refreshing and I drank heavily of it.

EIGHTY

Benjamin Crocker had made it clear that I could follow the Missouri as long as I wished, and that I would eventually reach Fort Union. It was what he preferred. The Indians were on the warpath and the safest place one could find in these parts was in or about the fort.

Unfortunately, to follow the Missouri meant traveling weeks out of my way in the north country as compared to heading west across the desert. I was torn between safety and sweet water, or death by sun, thirst or Indian. It was because of my cowardice, my indecision, and the time I needed to work up sufficient courage, that I stuck by the river until I felt I was closer to the Fort Union than not.

By all been told, the flatness of the country would undergo a quiet transformation upon nearing the confluence of Yellowstone and the Missouri, and thus it happened as predicted. I could sense the gradual change and it was that recognition that prompted me at last to take my leave of the Missouri and the safety of Fort Union for better or worse.

In fact, I questioned what was more dangerous, Indians, or a fort full of whiskey and soldiers who hadn't seen a woman in recent memory. That thought alone was enough to drive me into the desert with a measure of relief.

One could easily believe that ages before man's existence there occurred a disturbance of the earth whereby great ground-swells were formed to rise and fall in long undulating waves of still motion as if flowing outward from some monumental prehistoric splash.

The wrinkled earth was surely caused by a range of mountains to the west, forcing their way upward to rise before me in disproportionate heights above the plains. They were ghostly in appearance, and yet striking, ragged, rough-toothed with crisp white edges. One might have thought an angry god had ripped off the bottom of a perfectly placid pale blue sky.

The mountains were deceptive, especially on clear mornings when they might lure you into believing they were but a couple of days travel. They became a permanent part of the landscape, and I studied them for hours upon hours. They seemed to keep their distance; and for me, they exemplified how remarkably immense was the space that separated us.

I was elated to have realized these changes with my own eyes, and also to have observed the tributary that until now had been nothing more than speculation and hopeful rumor. I sat a good while looking across the banks of the Yellowstone not only with a sense of success, but even more so, a sense of profound relief, for every mile ventured into the void was a mile of prayer; a plea to heaven that honesty might flow from the hearts of others who knew how a life could be saved or swept away by a statement simple as *'that-a-way'*. In the desert, one had little choice but to pay mind to strangers, to observe their outstretched hand and place faith at their feet while mustering all courage before moving on. It was most heartening to believe I might actually rely on the words of these outsiders and garner some truth to the whens, whats, and wheres of this mysterious unmapped land. Thank god for the Yellowstone.

I was now in the best of moods having reached the river and taking my rest for the night. I slept sound and awoke well rested. I set out bright and early the next morning in a southwesterly direction, driving the team parallel to Yellowstone's southern bank and ever closer to that frayed mountainous horizon.

As I traveled, entirely new and unexpected vistas opened before me. Here was a harsh land, dramatic, beautiful in its ruggedness. It was also entirely unreasonable. Ever more often, I confronted impassible chasms of erosion that not only astonished me, but left me disillusioned and bereft of all good nature. These great cracks proved impossible to traverse with a wagon and forced me miles out of my way and distant to the water that sustained life.

When I wasn't grumbling about the inconvenience and hardships, I was grappling with the enormity of a wilderness in which I had met only two other souls in more than a month's time. I suffered to think how my sanity might be eroding as much as the land itself.

My emotions became exaggerated. They grew strained and unpredictable. I blamed all my woes, especially my loneliness on nature, which I now personified. I felt it an entity that kept me on the defensive. I felt it a foe that threatened others and dissuaded them from seeking me out or coming to my aid.

I also felt uninvited. I felt rude to have left a trail with my wagon wheels, parallel scars upon an unblemished ground. I felt like an intruder with less right to exist in this place than the grains of sand upon which I rolled. At least they shared a history; at least they had a common bond. They might have sat a million years to experience twice that many sunrises and sunsets side by side in the company of their kind.

Compared to sand, I was little more than a puff of wind, a momentary gust of insignificance unable to affect my surroundings any more than those huge white fluff balls or mountainous black-bottomed islands floating by upside down in the blue sea overhead. And even the impressive size of the clouds was substantially diminished as I observed how small were the shadows they dragged silently across these same endless miles of settled sand.

Unlike those shadows that glided effortlessly across the land unencumbered by cliff or gorge, I never seemed to select or stumble onto a similar carefree route. If I traveled the river bottoms, I enjoyed plenty of water and game, but I had to fight for every foot of progress as I untangled my way through cottonwood, underbrush, steep banks, rocks and countless other obstacles that crowded the water's edge. When sick of the battle, I was free to take the high road across the baking desert, where I was certain to be forced away from the river in order to escape the deeply eroded ravines that cut their way across my path.

Sometimes separated by little more than a stone's throw, I was given two worlds in which to exist, two worlds as different as night and day. One world was easily missed, hidden from view at the base of fortress like canyon walls and vertical cliffs that sheltered the water. An abundance of life existed in these nearly subterranean havens. They were a place of botanical gardens, green shade trees, cool mists and comforts to meet every need and relieve every stress. In the other world, which stretched as far as the eye could see, there was only emptiness, hellish heat, and fear.

There were times when my attempts to stay focused on Christopher and my goals were not enough to stave off the more serious backslides into depression. My state of mind would undergo a marked change for the worse, and I could feel myself receding again into that world of hopelessness that had trapped me at the onset of my journey. It was akin to quicksand, drawing me down slowly, and although I could feel myself sinking ever deeper and realized the danger, I was incapable of escaping its clutch.

I tried hard to suppress the dreadful feelings for they scared me. I strove to assure myself I had every right to be anxious or depressed, and that it was a natural response to my prolonged isolation. But the land was taking its toll on me. It had no conscience and never relented in attacking my spirit. Instead of fighting the fears, too often I found myself succumbing to them, believing I was so far lost from civilization I would never return.

I saw death everywhere, and so one fear in particular was the thought of dying out here utterly alone. I envisioned my body entombed for eternity in the back of Dusty Peddler's wagon. I pictured myself dried into a mummified husk by a perpetual desert wind that would force the pans to swing endlessly, colliding and clanging like a bizarre collection of un-tuned bells; a melodic head marker to be heard by no one.

A morning finally arrived whereby I lost all discipline and purpose. I felt Christopher's memory was nothing short of mockery and a mirage of my own making. I was unable to bring myself to rise to the day, but unlike me, and in spite of what I did or did not do, the sun continued on with its upward journey. It moved to that place straight overhead, where it quickly baked the brains out of any living thing caught dawdling about below.

I lay lifeless upon the bed of the wagon and let the perspiration build on my face and forehead then run past my temples. It flowed down the valley between my breasts until my clothes were drenched in sweat. When I could no longer stand the heat, I stripped off every article of clothing and sat naked within the privacy and shadow of the wagon. I sat there leaning against the back of the bench seat and stared dully outside. The canvas awning mesmerized me, holding fast my attention as it rippled in an arid breeze that strove to dry me out like a discarded cob of unwanted corn.

I was constantly looking about so as not to be seen unclothed, and this I found absolutely pathetic. My modesty was so deeply entrenched that it made me irrational. I most certainly was out of my mind to worry about something as silly as being stripped in this desolate place, as if that would change my situation or influence time and space.

In truth, I would have cherished the embarrassment of an onlooker. I longed, I prayed for a river ruffian to gawk at me, to stare at my breasts and that crotch between my legs, which they craved with such boldness. I would have rejoiced at the humiliation of a groping hand. If only I had a brute to berate or a face to slap.

I climbed out of the wagon and stood tall and defiant upon the seat with spread ankles and outstretched arms. I screamed in frustration across the parched plain.

"I am perfectly naked! Do you hear! I am perfectly, *perfectly* naked! I was born perfectly naked, and I will die perfectly naked! And if I choose to be perfectly naked in-between, then so be it!"

Of course, it was all a lie. I could never *choose* to be *perfectly* naked. I was too self-conscience to enjoy such freedom. My life was one of restraint, and so I looked around just in case my yelling drew some unexpected attention, and that act alone thoroughly infuriated me. Like all my emotions, my temper also was exaggerated.

I dropped my arms and stood there upon the bench slowly scanning the country that surrounded me. I felt as though it were staring back and again felt uninvited.

"You don't like me do you?" I hollered. "You must wonder why I go on day after day, mile after mile, pushing forward when all the while it appears I have gone nowhere. Has anyone ever constructed a map that reflects the infinity of this place? Might a mark ever be made upon paper to show a measure of progress? I know what you want, you want me to go back, but that is impossible. I could never face all of this misery twice."

It was heartless, grueling country. Dumbfounded, I could only stand and stare across the distance and suffer through the oppressive heat.

"I will make my own map! It will be a map of misery, a map of loneliness. It will fit in the palm of my hand. One simple line pointing straight from heaven to hell! Whenever I get, wherever I am going, you can bet I will raise my hand and show all. I promise to tell all!"

I listened for a response, but as usual; there was nothing.

"God bless my mules!" I yelled.

I thought about how they faced the same overwhelming nothingness without complaint. I warned them as well.

"I hope you aren't counting on me to get you home!" I waited.

"Remember, I'm following you!"

The wind blew gently through my hair, past my ears, all the while talking to me. I slipped into a dream as it told me how it would fly eastward until it reached land's end, until it reached the ocean, the Harbor of Boston—the stone cottage of Mary and Allen's. I knew it would blow through the open window and past the curtains of my bedroom. The room would be fresh and safe, and from there I would smell dinner and listen to the boys carrying on downstairs. I would hear them slam the back door, and through my window, carried on a breeze, would come the sounds of their horsing with Allen.

There was nobody out here in this godforsaken land to soothe my anguish, so I would openly cry over such memories. I wasn't embarrassed to do that. I didn't care, after all girls were expected to cry, and there was only me, the mules, God and the wind; and most of the time I wasn't sure about God anymore.

I would sob my heart out for Mary and Allen. If only I could make them real. I was incredibly homesick. My friends in Boston would have thought little of me if they could have seen how spineless I had become, how I caved in to my fears and runaway emotions, how I babbled on like an idiot.

Was it because I was a woman? Did I underestimate my need for social intercourse with others? Was it as important to my gender as our food and the air we breathe? Why did I never hear of men suffering in such a manner? It was inconceivable to me that males could be immune to such desolation, but I never heard anyone ever say that Wilber was in yonder field having a good cry—*never once*.

I spent many hours reading the collection of poems in Dusty's wagon, they being my only connection to the feelings and emotions of another human being. I would scratch the outline of a stage in the sand with my boot and stand with the wind in my face and his poems in my hand. The setting sun was my limelight. With the mules as my audience, I would voice Dusty's lines with great passion across the endless spatterings of scrub brush.

After one such reading, I overheard my audience asking why hadn't I presented something of my own. I was speechless. Nothing of the sort had ever occurred to me. It was true that I had revealed my most personal issues. I had talked to them of my heartbreak, my beliefs, my struggle against depression and loneliness, yet I had never presented such emotions formally. It had never been an act.

I was honored. I took up the challenge, and committed myself by oath and promise. I was moved with purpose to pick up a pen knife, sharpen a quill, and present *my* suffering, *my* reflections, *my* feelings. It was a wonderful experience. It relieved me of much of my frustration, and I understood fully why men take to the pen. I called my work *Desert Wind*.

DESERT WIND

By Elizabeth Dennison Claussen

I am forever being haunted, taunted and teased,
Harried and flaunted by a delusive desert breeze
It stirs up a mess, seems to posses all the traits of a man
Kicking up dust, making a fuss, disturbing the sleeping sand
For my attention, it whistles endlessly, rudely as one can

Over drifts, bearing gifts, vows and promise of fresh water
It breaks them all, takes them back, one right after another
What care has he, my wanting lips are painfully cracked and dry
Unconcerned, he steals his kiss, no bliss, no care that I
Being so thirsty this far from home could just as easily die

Boyishly brushing against me, he innocently tosses my hair
Yet, take a chance, a whirlwind dance, he will lift my skirt with dare
He knows no shame, accepts no blame, will never stand up to face
Responsibility for his deeds, discourtesies, towards me in this place
He seduces me with blackened clouds and spurns me in disgrace

He swooshes me, pushes me, forces me to face a morning sun
Rising high over the Atlantic coast and Great Lakes of Michigan
Over forested mountains of Virginia, green meadows in Tennessee
Following the flow of the mighty Ohio to the banks of the Mississippi
He blows through all these places, which for me are now but memory

When temper shows, tempest blows sand into my eyes
He roars, screams, fights me, spites me, fills me with despise
For he knows it's far too dry for me to waste a shedded tear
I ask, beg, plead for want of rain, yet, he assails my wind-chapped ear
With howls of laughter while the sky remains as always perfectly clear

Still, for all his faults, his insults, for all his lack of restraint
He has stayed by me all the miles listening to my complaint
Over and over, and over again, as spokes on this wagon wheel
From prairie land to mountain peak, every emotion that I feel
His patience for my gibberish is tempered true as steel

And when shadows long, lie down at dusk, and blend into the dark
And sleep comes hard for the baying of wolves and lone coyote's bark
I feel his breath about me like a father's kiss at night
Murmuring whispers in my ear to blanket sounds of fright
The canvas flaps, the cradle rocks until first morning's light

It was a sell out.

After twenty-some shows, I had it perfected, but I shut down the act. I didn't want to abuse my audience or risk becoming old hat. More important was the fact I had performed flawlessly and enjoyed a personal victory greater than just my presentation. I had formed a shaky truce that stretched across the far-reaching turmoil of my inner conflicts. I was able to face the horizon and move on in peace with a fresh sense of confidence, and this was no small thing.

EIGHTY-ONE

My rejuvenation was timely, for I was obligated to leave the Yellowstone and its tributaries with much trepidation before being forced south by earth's towering enclosure. I left the security of flowing water within the shadows of mountains rising high above the swells of foothills. Their massiveness assured me that our continent would be split in half east to west as sure as slavery split it north to south.

In the shadows, the land rolled, and rolled, and rolled. The view remained unchanged like a centuries old still life rendered permanent in oils. The hours hung before me as did wild grape-vines in trees back east, impenetrable, confining, slowing my progress, holding back my hopes of ever seeing Christopher or a South Pass.

Time dilly-dallied without conscience. Out here, it knew nothing about the ticking of a clock, and undoubtedly wound down to prolong my misery during the scorching hours of long afternoons. Without a working timepiece, I was at a loss to prove such mischief, but I sensed the sun's determination to disallow me the relief of day's end. Late afternoons were the worst because it was then that the sun attacked me from below my awning. I was left to face it without relief. Late afternoon suns were terrible.

On this particular evening, even before the sun was finished with me, a blessing of no small measure came my way. I was keeping an eye open for a place to bed down. I searched for a low spot within the hills where I might hide my wagon and animals from wandering opportunists, for I especially feared roaming Indians who might watch from bluffs where they could see for miles across the open plains.

To my surprise, the mules swayed me toward a small spring-fed pond of sweet water. It was a splendid find. I halted the team and unhitched them at once. I thanked them profusely one by one with ear scratches and hugs, and wondered while I set them free if they understood in some instinctive manner how much they meant to me. I wished they understood my appreciation for their daily toil and the way in which they always seemed by their own merit to find enough to eat, drink, and get by.

I watched them wander off, and I worried for their return. I wondered why they returned at all, for the work of pulling Dusty's wagon had to be dreadful in this heat. I had the advantage of spending my day seated upon the seat if I so preferred, never having to pull a single pound across the desert, and yet even that was nearly unbearable.

To sit on one's behind from sunup to sunset might have seemed a life of leisure, but I would be first to dispel any such notion if it meant being seated upon the hard wooden bench of a drummer's wagon. It was a wonder I had any teeth left in my head for the constant jostling, jolting, shaking and shimmying. I never failed to smirk each time I thought of New Englanders who would complain should they happen to chance upon a mile or two of corduroy road while traversing the spring muds. Easterners had no idea what backbreaking travel was truly like. In order to comprehend this misery, a person needed to spend a month or two sitting upon a bruised tailbone or nursing a lower back and spine that knifed one with complaint. In spite of a plague of snakes, as often as not, I chose to walk alongside the mules. At least nothing was strapped to *my* back.

"Ignorance is bliss". I said aloud.

It took me less than a week of leaving the Missouri to learn that blazing trails was no fun. I drove the mules and fear drove me. I feared Indians; I feared wild animals. I feared broken wheels. I feared my team going down. I feared the unknown. On those occasions where I lost my bearings or thought I had gotten turned around, the fear that raked my soul was devastating.

The fear of never finding water was another terrible burden put upon the mind. It distorted both one's reasoning and perspective of even the smallest details of living. I saved my own urine in a large jar for reasons I couldn't begin to imagine.

It was very dark, very strong. My excuse was rooted in memories of old sailors who washed their clothes in urine to sanitize them, but I think the act was as much a matter of being unable to dispense with anything liquid.

Every sip of life saving water that passed my lips did so with a feeling of guilt. I always considered skipping a few drinks each day knowing I would be uncomfortably thirsty, but that I might stretch my life a little further if things went for the worse—a drink missed, a mile gained. It was always easier to be thirsty when you knew there was water to be had. I always thought it better I give my water to the mules. They certainly earned it. If they should perish, my own demise would follow shortly. Such reasoning kept me perpetually dehydrated.

If taking a drink was a soulful struggle, the idea of taking a bath was unthinkable. Who could waste precious water to rinse away dirt knowing full well that the filth would return within hours? I learned to live with my own stink, as did all traveling folk. I turned my head to breath upwind and avoid my odor.

The soap I possessed served as little more than a reminder of another time and place. The sight of it amused me, for it appeared to have never been used. It was shrunken, cracked, dried out. It was so hard I could have hammered nails with it, and I wondered if it would ever be able to dissolve in the pond.

Its dryness reminded me of my throat, which was also dry and parched. I swallowed to confirm the fact. I rubbed my fingers lightly across my face. I felt the roughness. I touched the hardened edges of deep wounds, cracked lips that I nursed with tallow to protect them in every way from the ravages of sun and wind.

I dropped my hands palms up and looked at the calluses formed by the reins. I turned them over slowly and observed the dryness of my skin and the rash of windburn. I lifted my sleeves to let the sand fall free and was relieved to see nothing of bugs or bites. My diligence in keeping my clothes and bedding aired out seemed to pay off.

The list of irritations and fears was long and lengthened daily. I acknowledged these things as realities that expressed a truth. This land was not a place for women, and this was not a woman's way of life. But for now, these troubling thoughts were to be put away. They faded as I stared at my reflection upon a surface of virtually invisible water.

I broke away from a blissful stupor in order to rinse out my barrels, leaving them in the pond to swell and freshen. I studied my wagon wheels with a thought to removing them as well for a good soak, but decided that work could wait until the morrow. Instead, I collected weeks worth of soiled rags and clothes and tossed them into the water.

I now only wished to relax and enjoy the mercy of this day's end, and so I went for one of those brick-hard bars of soap. With heartfelt sighs heard only by the mules, I peeled away each gritty, sweat-stained, dust-covered piece of fabric covering my chafed body and exposed myself so the wind might carry off my stench and ease my concerns of fouling the pond. I apologized to the pond anyway, knowing full well I was about to diminish its pristine waters with my filth. Then freely as might Eve in her Garden, I put all modesty aside and waded blissfully into the cool, clear waist deep liquid. I settled down to my shoulders and closed my eyes. It was indescribable.

The slow pace of time was now in *my* favor, and I was in no rush, for tonight life was good in spite of my menstruation, my cramps, and a myriad of other miseries that plagued me only minutes before. Tonight, I was camped on lush ground with an abundance of fresh water and a rare chance for a cleansing bath.

I was euphoric. I laughed aloud at the thrill of finding a suitable rock to work over all my dirty garments with soap. I probed the shallows for my clothes and one by one scrubbed each article in need with the utmost pleasure. Never had washing been such a joy. I was suddenly recalling worksongs from my days in service as a child.

Scrub, scrub, scrub
Master's dirty duds
Scrub, scrub, scrub
On a board beside the tubs.

Rub, rub, rub
Till my fingers feel like stubs.
Rub, rub, rub
Till I use up all the suds.

Rinse, rinse, rinse
Till I wash out all the lime.
Rinse, rinse, rinse
Till I hang them on the line.

Drip, drip, drip
Till mistress says they're dried

Pick, pick, pick
Till they're all put back inside.

I spent the remainder of the evening floating about lazily and looking up from the hollow at wisps of clouds tinted with pale oranges and blues. I was amazed to see so much water in one place, and I stayed as long as I dared until dusk deepened and the pond became spooky. I was made nervous by the constant threat of snakes and other unseen creatures that I could hear moving about in the shadows and sedges.

I emerged from the waters of tranquility, disturbing its surface as I walked away to stand wetted and nude upon the bank. Currents of air swept down into the hollow to dry me. The breezes crossed the pond, gently rustling the reeds to chill me after suffering so much heat. Suddenly, I wished to be covered and although I remained unclothed, the desire to dress was a welcome change.

How long it had been since I had washed and smelled like a proper lady; I couldn't venture to guess. I sauntered back to the wagon in very good spirits, and sought out an item nearly forgotten in my trunk. Holding the trunk lid ajar, I fished around until I located a jar of scented cream that I had received from Mary as a going-away present. I removed the cover and inhaled deeply of its fragrance. The scent of lavender seemed so misplaced in this dry desert air.

"Oh, Lady Rebecca, Lady Rebecca. How you've left your mark on me."

I slid my finger across the surface and removed a small amount of the cream. I spoiled myself with its smoothness, rubbing it deep into my elbows and knees. I rubbed it into the back of my hands. I tried not to fret over the dry lizard-like texture my skin had developed to defend itself from the high plain hazards.

Instead, I enjoyed my peace of mind as I gazed out across the still and silent pond. Reeds stood tall to conceal much of the water's mirrored surface that now reflected the more intense purplish blues and redder oranges of late evening light. The tranquility of my surroundings worked miracles in soothing my hardened disposition.

I continued to smile and sing with light heart. Who could be surprised at my decision to remain in this little pothole paradise for a few days to allow the animals and myself time to regain our energy. It was only fitting we might enjoy our lives for a change instead of fighting endlessly to save them.

I knew the mules would never leave the water, and so I left them to go about their business foraging while I retrieved my wash and paid mind to preparing my bed in the wagon. Although thoughts of dinner loomed before me, I couldn't bring myself to tramp through the underbrush in search of snakes to roast.

I felt pampered and lazy, and so placed a blanket upon the warm sand and dropped to stretch out across it. I felt glorious. I lay flat out and hoped, as I hoped every night that the joints in my back might straighten once again. I looked up toward heaven and noted the first evening star.

I was too comfortable to move even for a stomach filled with complaint. The air about the pond was quickly cooling and felt chilly upon my bare skin after spending a day submerged in the searing heat of a shadeless plain. Now, only sand retained the warmth, and for that reason I wiggled about back and forth, burrowing myself deeper into a cozy heated mold.

For the next hour or so, to move for any reason was unthinkable. Beyond that the coolness of night was upon me sufficient enough to force my getting dressed. Overcome with rushes of shivers, I donned a pair of my trousers and a shirt. More confining than a dress, it wasn't the most comfortable garment for a good night's sleep, but it gave me a sense of protection against snakes and most other uninvited guests. At least I wouldn't have to put up with accusations of immorality. The outfit served to ease the chill, but more than that was the fact it was *clean*.

The warmth of the ground was so inviting in the cool desert air that I resisted entering the confinement of the wagon. Instead, I returned to the blanket where I propped myself up against the wagon wheel. I covered up with my ship's blanket and sought out the comfort I enjoyed before feeling the need to dress. I had been dozing soundly and yet remained drowsy. I glanced warily about the shadows for anything appearing to crawl or slither and then released the weight of my eyes.

Behind closed eyes, I gave thought to my hunger and my lack of desire to do anything about it. I gave thought to all the things I would like to eat, and somewhere in front of a table covered with food that I could almost taste, I fell into a deep and restful sleep.

EIGHTY-TWO

The following days were days of bliss. I decided to read back through the pages of my journal and in doing so began to appreciate how different was my life. I had fulfilled my desire for change and then some to boot. I desperately wanted to express this realization to Mary and Allen, but that was impossible, and so I was left with no recourse but to make note of the desperation on the next page of my diary.

I moved unhurriedly about my camp making repairs, but most of my time was spent soaking in the pond and watching the mules forage. It was plain enough to see how they gained back their weight and strength, and even from a distance their looks were much improved, as were my own to be sure.

My evenings might well have been made to order, for they were nothing short of pure heaven coming as they did after long hot days in the hollow. To my surprise, I had spent most of them sleeping on the ground, which was most unlike me. I suppose the body of water served to temper the environment. So full of contentment was I that the feeling carried on through evening and night, spilling into my slumber and flowing freely through my dreams.

I dreamt of those familiar faces and far away places that I desperately longed for during my days and struggled to keep close to heart. Distance meant nothing in my dreams, and I traveled back to old haunts to relive memories of love and laughter.

And I did laugh, and I cried. I rejoiced within the embrace of good times. I was carefree, frolicking with family and friends until this night when quite unexpectedly they turned away. The lightheartedness, the cavorting, all of it ended abruptly as those around me crumbled into fragments of confusion.

To my dismay, there was no bliss this night, and I looked on disheartened as their nocturnal faces became twisted and contorted, their mouths stretching into freakish yawns. I strained to listen, to understand the sounds as they called out to me in ways I could not comprehend. I strained to make sense of what was taking place, but it was impossible, for they were yelling in discord and their disconcerting mouthings were indecipherable.

I was being forced from my dreams and the clutches of a sound sleep to face the cold of night and my irritability. I was stirring, perplexed and unsure of my place, but even worse, I suffered an overwhelming sense of sadness and disappointment. I was steeped in emotion, immersed in feelings that only a dream could deliver and for that reason I didn't wish to awake.

As though addicted, I refused to give up what I craved. I clung to wisps of people and places so loved and missed. I was determined to have them, to hold them, to keep them close, but my efforts were as pointless as putting smoke back into a fire. I was powerless to stop them from fading back into distant and dulled memories.

With eyes yet closed, I began to sort out what was real from what was not. The laughter and familiar faces were only dream; the longing and loneliness was real. The warm and loving embraces were dream; the hunger and cold was real. The noise and vibration—the noise and vibration—.

My eyes suddenly cracked open to meet the darkness and a spattering of white spots overhead. Half awake, I was hard pressed to explain the stars, for I thought myself to be in the wagon. I seldom slept outside; I disliked being on the ground. It was also normal for the wagon to shake and shimmy in a wind that never stopped.

It occurred to me that this sound was unlike the wind. I reached out and felt sand between my fingers. Then I remembered the hollow and a sense of peace returned. I remembered going to sleep on the ground, but—, but—, ground didn't vibrate. The ground should never, ever shake.

I lay motionless, working my mind to make sense of something inexplicable and wondering what was amiss. Was I still dreaming? My instincts said no. My senses were returning to me in a state of alarm. My stomach began to constrict, warning me there was indeed movement in the ground and that this was no dream. In fact, it was no longer a vibration, but now a rumbling.

An earthquake! I sat up at once. Fear and adrenaline shot through my body at the thought. My mouth felt dry as my stomach twisted tight. I looked around. It was one thing to stand upon an infinite ground, and quite another to have something that immense moving beneath you.

I rubbed the sleep from my eyes to clear my vision. The stars came into sharper focus. The moon was a cold thin crescent hardly to be seen, and everything about me was lost in the shadows of a dark night. The intensity of the rumbling escalated until the ground actually began to shake.

Badly frightened, I rose to my feet, preparing to face whatever might come. I backed up against the wagon and looked about. I saw my mules bolting off into the distance. My stomach sank at the thought of them leaving. I stood wide-eyed, and waited anxiously as I stared across the hollow fully expecting to see a ragged crevice split the ground before me, but it didn't happen.

Instead of splitting apart, the ground at the upper edge of the hollow disappeared beneath a wall of stampeding bison that washed over its rim and flooded down toward me. At incredible speed, hordes of crazed animals charged in my direction. Maddened, pounding, snorting and grunting, their hooves beat the ground to death.

Between the darkness of night and my shock, I saw the herd as a million strong and a mile wide. It exploded outward from within a dense cloud of dust and rolled toward me like a tidal wave about to break. The noise far surpassed any surf I had ever heard. It was deafening. I screamed in an instinctive act of utter absurdity, for amid this thunderous disorder no one existed to hear a cry that barely reached my own ears.

I forced my muscles to unfreeze so I might collapse. Terrified, I dropped to the ground and scrambled for cover under the wagon. Having crawled forward between the front wheels, I reached out for my ship's blanket, drawing it over me as if it were some magical shield. I then looked out from beneath the fabric and shuddered at the sight of these behemoths whose shadowy forms were as large as the wagon itself.

Too tense to breathe, I watched as I became swallowed up within their number. But for the grace of God and the pond that lie directly behind, in the last second, and in what little distance remained before I was to be trampled to death, the beasts split ranks and massacred the ground on both sides of me barely an arm's reach away.

I took in a single gulp of air, incapable of anything more, for the scene that raged paralyzed me. If only one of these enormous animals should fail to see the wagon in such darkness, it would assure my demise. I was at the mercy of fate, connected to life by little more than the light of stars, and helpless to do anything but remain rigid with fear and witness the madness about me. I cowered lower and lower, raising one hand over my head as if that might protect me from being crushed by these daunting creatures.

The dust in their midst was inseparable from the flying dirt, and this swirling soup suffocated me faster than the thick black smoke of a Hudson steamer. It was heavy and it settled upon my blanket with notable weight forcing me to hold the cloth tight to my face in order to strain out the stew of debris that blocked the least breath of life.

I struggled to maintain my sanity as I lie there on death's doorstep buried beneath the desert filth and the folds of my blanket. Afraid to look, my eyes were often closed, which heightened my sense of hearing, and maybe because of this, I took note of something else, something distinctly different from the rumbling, grunting, and pounding all about me. It was a sound I hadn't heard in ages—*the sound of voices*.

I had to see. I had to know, and so I dared myself to look into the darkness just as a party of Indians on horseback came storming down the hillside in hot pursuit of the herd. Boiling out of the blackness of night and contributing to the thunder and mayhem, they appeared and disappeared into the clouds of horror as they mingled with these horned monsters.

They rode hard down through the hollow, flying like phantoms in the night, occasionally barking calls between themselves and goading the animals onward. One after another, they flew past me atop their painted and patterned horses, leaping at break-neck speed, and whether in my mind or in reality, the savages appeared ghostly in the bluish light of the moon.

In the next passing second, it was over. The bison, the horses, the ghostly Indians, gone, all of it gone, vanished as quickly as had my dream. And just like my dream, I was left with that cloak of emotion, only this time instead of sadness or disappointment; it was fear pure and simple that drained me of my wit. Hardly was this the result of my dreams, but instead the wicked reality of my life.

Unlike my heart, beating as though it wished to break free, the earth was settling down and the vibration subsiding. I began to breathe again or so it seemed. I tried to assure myself that I was safe, and that the ordeal was over, but it was hard to believe. I looked about. It was black as pitch in this cloud of dust that blotted out the stars and anything beyond the wagon. The earth-shaking experience was nothing more than a memory now, and silence slipped back into the vacuum that remained.

I had but scant supper this day and nothing more for nourishment and yet, I found myself swallowing hard to keep my nervous stomach from unleashing what little it contained. In the blink of an eye, I was the center of a storm. In the blink of an eye, it passed, but not without leaving me to whirl dizzily in its wake, and so I did nothing more than lay flat on the dirt taking long deep breaths in an attempt to settle myself.

I had seen my first truly wild Indians. I could hardly believe it. Ironically, the intensity of the event entirely overshadowed all fears of the encounter, all except one, for I had heard something. I strained to see through the spokes. I tried with all my might to make out anything in the dusty darkness beyond the perimeter of the wagon wheels.

I heard the noise again, this time more pronounced, and I recognized it as the snort of an animal.

"The mules! Oh, my god, my mules!"

How had they fared? Could they have survived? Were they here, or had they been driven to eternity while running for their lives? I couldn't begin to know. Without further thought, I scrambled from between the wheels sick with worry.

I saw nothing in the shadows about the wagon or pond and so ran hastily up the slope to the rim of the hollow where I could see out across the plain. There was nothing to be seen, nothing at all. Even a part of the starry sky was missing like a lost puzzle piece, blocked from view by the drifting wake of unsettled earth. I called out for the mules time and again, hoping they might feel the desperation in my voice, but to no avail. I saw nothing; I heard nothing.

My state of mind at this point was frantic. I hadn't enjoyed a word with another living soul in two month's time and had convinced myself nothing could be worse, but now I was stranded in Indian country. Now, I wanted to be alone more than anything because now I realized that all the time I had spent complaining was time I hadn't thought enough about being held captive in the wrong kind of company.

I wanted nothing more than to pack up and head out fast. I needed to get as far away from the hollow as possible and hide from the Indians who discovered the wagon, but I had no mules. I could do nothing other than wait to see who or what returned first. If it were the mules, I would see to it that everything was packed and ready to leave at once. If it were the Indians—I was good as dead. I kept telling myself the Indians weren't Blackfeet. I was too far south; even so, I avoided all thoughts associated with campfires and barbecues.

The mules were my only hope, but where could they have gone? Would I be able to reach them on foot? What if they had all been trampled to death? I needed to retrieve all my mules if I hoped to make any speed with the wagon. All of these thoughts raced through my mind. I stood alone and increasingly concerned as I stared out beneath a barely credible star-studded sky.

I looked across the black vastness and understood at once that I was again standing alone to face God on his ground, on his terms. I was at his mercy and had but little left to lose, so I threw up my arms and cried out to Him with complaint.

"Please! Might I have just a few good days? Must it always be hardship and heartache? Must I always be sick with worry? Wasn't it You who saved me from the cliff? For what? So I can die at the hands of the Blackfeet? I thought at least for this short spell things would be different, a small pleasure. I had the pond, I had my baths, and…." I shook my head in disgust then let it drop, chin to chest.

I stared thoughtlessly at my clothes. I couldn't make out any detail, but I could imagine what they looked like—disgusting. I couldn't see the dirt on them, but I could feel it. I could feel it moving across my belly and scratching beneath my collar. I could feel the sand irritating the nape of my neck on its way down my back, rubbing on my skin, working to give me a rash. The dust was caked in my hair, making it feel course and ratty. I recalled how clean and fresh I had felt only hours earlier. I could still smell the lavender cream on my skin.

Exasperated and sick at heart, I started arguing with myself, debating opposing points of my predicament. I was considering the best and worst case scenarios and reviewing in detail every-thing on my mind aloud. This was my custom during times of stress. I did this in large part out of need to speak to someone, to obtain advice in troubled times, but in this land I had the only voice of solace and the only sympathetic ear.

The weight of dread swept over me as I walked back down to the wagon. I studied its shape as I approached and sensed it similar to a coffin that in no time would become my tomb unless I managed to get it rolling again. At first, the impression crushed me, but then I remembered the pond and its life-giving waters.

I glanced across the black void of its surface, and observed the way in which it reflected starlight. The pond brought relief. I felt even better once I considered the fact I had plenty of stores to tide me over even if I had to wait days or weeks for some of the mules to return. I was certain some had survived the stampede. Maybe, I could trade something to the Indians for my freedom—or—or—*maybe the savages would just kill me and take whatever they wanted—idiot.*

EIGHTY-THREE

My thoughts turned to salt. A simple block of salt that I used whenever I called out to my mules. It was one of the lessons learned during my time with Dorrie. *'Always give 'em a lick of salt when you fetch 'em home an' they'll be headin' your way before you call.'* Her advice and voice returned to mind. She was a strong person, the kind of person I should have been; the kind of person I desperately needed to be. Right now, she loomed real as life, walking alongside me as I started back down the slope toward the wagon utterly dispirited.

It was true that for the time being I would be fine so long as the Indians didn't show up, but the episode remained one more of those bad strokes of luck, one of those unnecessary events that worked to make my life intolerable. I was suddenly consumed by frustration and my complaints flowed aloud. I wouldn't directly blame God, but He was certainly on my mind, and I was bleeding cynicism.

"Thank-you, thank-you so very much. Thank you for watching over me. Thank you for seeing me through these trials and tribulations. I am forever grateful. I am forever yours. I never stop praying. I never stop giving thanks. I pray all day; I pray all night. I am here to serve, and not to question, but as long as we are talking, might I mention that I am very upset, and I would just like to say—."

Before my tongue could get me into further trouble, I was interrupted by the snort of an animal. It was the second time I heard this sound, and now it stopped me in my tracks. Before, in a state of blind concern for my team, I had charged to the top of the hollow and completely forgot about the sound that had set me off. This time, I stopped on the slope and stood quietly listening, quietly peering about the pond. I waited and watched. I dared not move.

At last, I could see something, or at least I believed it so. I certainly thought twice before moving toward the indistinct form. The closer I approached, the more I assumed I was looking at a large animal on the ground, a fallen bison no doubt, but as the dust settled, I determined different. I was horrified to realize I was looking at the rear quarters of a mule.

Putting my fears aside, with a heavy heart I sped to its aid, never imagining it could be anything other than one of my team. It was only as I stood nearly upon it that I observed the pattern of its hide. It wasn't a mule after all, but rather a downed horse. I should have been elated at having not lost one of my animals, but instead I was hard hit with a blow of anxiety, for a downed horse surely meant a downed Indian. The thought absolutely petrified me.

I swallowed hard. I looked about cautiously. I settled slowly upon my knees to assess the creature's condition with measured concern. It was a large dappled horse and seriously hurt, for it was panting hard and irregular, and making no attempt to get back onto its feet. There was much froth about its mouth.

In an unconscious act of sympathy, I placed my hand on its side, but instantly snapped it back in revulsion. What I assumed to be a dapple of color was a saturation of blood, and my hand was heavily coated with the thick warm liquid. I took a closer look in the dim moonlight and determined that the animal had been badly gored by a buffalo.

Nothing about my find was pleasant. I remained quietly perched upon my knees and waited. I watched. I listened beyond the heartrending sounds of the horse as it descended into its dying throes. I grieved for it, but I wasn't ready to risk my life by shooting it and drawing unwanted attention in order to put it out of its misery, especially not when I feared an Indian to be lurking nearby.

I fully expected that at any moment one or more of the savages would sneak up behind me and slit my throat or something worse before stealing away my wagon. And so amid the choking sounds of a horse drowning in its own blood, I listened for any hint of their return. I knew they had seen the wagon and that knowledge heightened my worries. I was scared through and through.

It wasn't long before my ears picked up that expected sound, that peculiarity which stood apart from the stillness of the night, that unsettling sound which failed to blend with the buzzing harmony of pond creatures, croaking frogs, and crickets clicking underfoot unseen.

It was the faintest rustle, yet it might as well have been a blaring trumpet in the way it gained my attention. I turned my head toward the pond and shut my eyes. I listened intently while trying to control my breathing and quiet the pounding in my ears. I heard it again, very faint, and then again.

After such a horrible night, I concluded that my months of solitude and prayer hadn't increased my sanctity or chances for special favor in the eyes of God. As much for that reason as any, I scampered over to the wagon, crabbed around to the driver's side, and without a second's thought, grabbed my gun.

Quietly, very quietly, I crawled beneath the wagon for security. I again peered out from between the wheels. Hidden behind the spokes, I looked toward the pond and studied the sedges and darker region of reeds and grasses from where the sound emanated. I intended to sit still and wait things out, no matter how long it took.

That turned out to be about a half an hour. By then, I was fairly convinced that I was listening to an Indian who was injured in some way and trying to escape through the growth surrounding the pond. In time, I grew confident that I was in better condition than he, and so crept out nervously from beneath the wagon with gun in hand and at the ready. The firearm went a long way in giving me the necessary courage needed to follow my ears toward the quarry. I moved forward ever so slowly, step after step after step, and then—I found exactly what I expected.

There, within the taller grasses lying before me in flesh and blood was an honest to goodness wild Indian, a throat-slitting, baby burning, head scalping, disemboweling savage. The real thing. I stopped short to confront all the fear instilled within me since my earliest childhood, a lifetime of revulsion. I was both terrified and mesmerized. I couldn't determine much except that if the savage had been able to move, he most surely would have been long gone by now, and so I turned my back on him. I walked back to the wagon and fetched a lantern for a better look.

I lit the wick and returned to the fallen foe. This time he had stayed put. I moved in as close as I dared, and observed that he was both conscious and in a good deal of pain. At first I didn't see any wound. It wasn't until I glanced down and noticed that his left leg looked to be deformed. It was twisted. Then I saw the bone sticking out through his skin. He had loosened his leggings and the wound seemed to ooze out from the parted leather. It was bloody, and grizzly enough to turn my stomach with ease.

I looked into his face. It was dripping with perspiration. His eyes followed my every move. He had covered a fair amount of ground in his attempt to escape into hiding, but it was pointless. I turned away from him and walked over to the horse to assess its condition.

Whereas I was indifferent to the Indian, I felt terrible for the horse. The animal was bleeding to death, and I wanted to cry. I knew what had to be done, but could not dwell on what I was about to do. I backed away and lowered my piece in its direction. I cocked the gun and fired a ball into its head midway between the eyes. The horse shuddered then released its last breath.

In all my years at Allen's side, I had never put a horse down, and although I understood this to be an act of mercy, it made me feel filthy and empty of compassion. I didn't like it. My shoulder ached from the recoil, and somehow I felt deserving of the discomfort, if not a bruise.

I went back to the wagon and reloaded, all the while thinking about the savage. I was torn between helping him and running for my life. I was a mental wreck and talking to myself openly without reservation. If the Indian possessed just half of his senses, he would know soon enough that I had probably lost my mind.

With questionable common sense, I approached the man and sat down to study him in the dim light of the lantern. I wasn't sure why. At first my thoughts were only of him and his pain, but I kept drifting off into my own problems. I was worried and wanted nothing more than a fast way out of this hollow before his friends came nosing around. Unfortunately, without the mules that was impossible. I sat there with a sense of inescapable doom, and so, with a spirit both defeated and resigned, I spoke to this other creature, this heathen that appeared to be more animal than man in my eyes.

"Why are you in my life? I don't know you. I don't even want to know you—. I come from a completely different world than you—. I don't live like this, groveling in the dirt. I don't belong out here. I come from a place of law and order, a civilized place, a place where people wash and eat at tables with forks and knives, but that means nothing to a savage—. It means nothing to someone like you, does it?

"Of course not, I mean, why would it? Law and order has no place out here. What does sun or savage care about civility? Here, it's only life or death, and I'm good as dead without my team. Do you understand? Thanks to you, my mules are some-where east of the Mississippi. There is no way out of here for me—no escaping you and your kind." I stared at him. He stared at me. He uttered not a sound. He could do nothing but listen.

"You are a savage. You probably have one of those names that means 'he scalps bears with his bare hands', or 'the one who barbecues women', you know, something like that—something boastful, something horrible to reflect what you are, something to strike fear into the soul of your enemies before you roast them alive and eat their hearts, or drag out their intestines to play jump-rope while they watch.

"My name, on the other hand, is Elizabeth. And you might know, that it is a refined name. That is the name you can put on my marker when you're done with me. It's the way we do it where I come from....

"You can't even spell Elizabeth, can you? I don't get a marker, do I? Savages know nothing of dates—when one is born, when one dies—records. In this land you kill or get killed and no one knows the difference—you just disappear."

I could see the Indian was delirious. I wondered if I was also. I kept my gun pointed at him and rambled on until I noticed a knife nearly hidden at his opposite side. I looked at him and back at the knife. It was nasty looking. I looked at him again. His eyes never left me. I viewed him as an injured animal, a dangerous wounded animal. I moved around to his other side

784

and slowly reached for the blade. I kept his head perfectly centered at the end of my barrel. He was in no position to resist, lest he wished me to send him off headless to his happy hunting grounds.

I studied the knife. I studied the Indian. I studied my situation and tried to overlook the fact that most likely I was every bit as dead as this Indian. The mules were gone and the Indians knew right where to find me. The thought of what might become of me made me nauseous. There were plenty of stories to recall, should I forget my probable fate. I gave thought to loading a pistol and keeping it by my side in case I had no choice but to take my life.

"I am not a bad person, you know. I don't go around killing and kidnapping people just because it might be Wednesday and I'm bored."

The Indian remained silent. We sat and watched one another, unsure of what would come next, for fate had forced us into each other's company. After a good deal of soul searching, I elected to play the only card I had; a good deed for a good deed, or so I hoped. I returned his knife to him. I laid it upon his chest then stood up and walked back to the wagon.

I set my gun aside, understanding now how false a security it truly was. It might buy me an extra day or maybe a week by keeping the savages at bay, but they had only to keep my mules and wait. I would die of hunger or insanity without the Indians ever having to look down into the hollow. My heart sank deep into a sea of hopelessness.

I entertained no idea of further sleep. I reached up on the bench seat for the pieces of dried wood and dung that I had collected during the day. In this treeless land, burning buffalo dung was about the only way to have a good night's fire. In time, I had one burning alongside the wagon that helped force out the chill and illuminate my surroundings.

I returned to the Indian and sat down cross-legged, this time close to his side. He had placed his knife back into its sheath and seeing this improved my state of mind immensely.

"Well, Mr. Indian, I guess it's just you and me. I would say we are both in some serious trouble, but at least I can do something for you. I might just be able to set that leg. I've been mending fractures since I was a kid. Maybe in time, if you live, you can do something for me like—set me free."

I needed to move him closer to the fire. No matter how well he stood up to the pain, he was probably in a state of shock. He was too sweaty to be exposed to the cool night air. About one thing I was certain, if he died, so would I.

"Give me your hand."

I held out my hand for his, but he didn't take it.

"I need to bring you to the fire."

Mustering up all the courage I could, and making no sudden moves, I reached for his wrist. He let me grasp his arm without resistance. I could feel him shaking from shock or chills. I began to pull for all I was worth—which turned out to be nothing at all. I hadn't considered how long it took for ribs to heal and mine were hardly ready for such strain.

I let loose and gave thought to some other means of moving him. In no time, I was back at the wagon, where I tied one end of a rope to the rim of the wagon wheel and walked the free end to where he lay. I handed him the rope.

"Pull yourself to the wagon. Pull. Pull." I motioned my meaning. "You are too big. I can't drag you. I broke my ribs. Pull. Pull."

The man seemed to be listening. He looked at me and at the fire. He then raised himself onto his hands and crab-walked backwards, dragging his broken leg as he went. He never touched the rope, much to my embarrassment.

"Well, I beg your pardon. It seemed like a very good idea to me."

I walked alongside him and coiled the rope as he inched his way toward the fire. I winced each time I saw the bone slip in and out of his skin, causing more blood to flow. Just the thought of it made me queasy. The side of his foot lay flat on the ground. How could anyone stand such pain without crying out, without dying right off? Was it pride, another one of those manly things? I couldn't imagine possessing such strength of character, and it did me good to hear him groan under his breath. I was afraid I would next discover that he was immortal. I directed him to sit up against the wheel, after which I fetched blankets and pillow to make him comfortable.

In the light of the fire, I was able to get a good look at my first Indian in the wild. I couldn't help but to stare. I packed the pillows in behind his head and tucked the blankets around his frame. I felt myself to be an emotional boomerang, my feelings circling out past the attractions of his handsome features, his bronze complexion, his dress and paint, his untamed nature, his capacity for pain, but then I would circle back to fear dying a horrible death by his primitive hand.

"I must say, Mr. Indian, you are dangerous, but you are beautiful."

I felt that as far as Indians went, he was a model specimen. At least he wasn't covered in the grease of animal fat or some other foul smelling extraction. There was no excessive self-mutilation, no distended ears or noses. I guessed him to be a somewhat older than myself, probably mid-forties. He appeared incredibly healthy. He was trim and muscular for his age. His hair was black and collected into braids that were folded back and fastened with rawhide strips.

On each side of his head, separate from the braids, strands of hair were threaded through a collection of bleached bone chips and teeth. They became smaller in size the lower they were fastened on the strand. He had a small parcel of herbs tied to a lock as well. Along with these, he was adorned with feathers. The back of his neck appeared to be covered in down.

His eyes were as black as his hair. Under his right eye, three diagonal stripes of white paint cut across his cheekbone. He wore a vest of leather, possibly deerskin that was decorated with dyed porcupine quills, teeth, and fine roots or twigs. It had no sleeves, and in the firelight I could see six or seven scars that crossed each of his forearms in parallel bands. They looked like perfectly shaped soldier stripes, a quarter of an inch wide and spaced evenly about half an inch apart.

His vest covered him to just below his waist, and there he wore a breechcloth covering his manhood. Coming up high on his leg to mid thigh, were his leggings. They were also made from skins and had a flap that was as long as the leggings themselves and hung to the outside of the leg. He wore moccasins with soles.

He struck me as being very clean. Although he was covered in sweat, he had no foul odor about him. This surprised me for it was always said Indians had an odor different than white men. It was said horses accustomed to one scent often disliked the other. I had assumed that the smell of Indians must have been unbearable after knowing the stench of white men who believed washing was unhealthy. This was not at all the case.

I leaned over closer to his leg and studied it. It was badly fractured about four inches below the knee. The bone was protruding through the lacing of his legging. I motioned to him that it was not good. He watched me, from some distant state of consciousness.

I thought about the pain he must be suffering and wondered how Indians dealt with these types of serious injuries. He should have been in deep shock. This kind of injury often killed a man by shock alone. Maybe he knew this was his call to death. Maybe that was why he let me approach him. He would not be able to walk for many weeks and would have to be cared for.

Maybe savages just left their injured to die. I didn't know. Maybe things were as hopeless for him as they were for me.

What I did know was how to set a broken leg. I had not only seen it done, but had helped Allen do it many times in his office over the years. I could help this man if he would allow it. I decided to make the offer. I picked up a stick and sat down close to him so he could see me clearly in the firelight. I placed my hand on his chest. His face was wet with perspiration. Anybody else would have been unconscious by now, but this man remained coherent. It was incredible. I pointed to his leg and then I snapped the stick in two.

"Do you understand? Your leg is broke. Yes?" I nodded my head. He only watched me.

"It's broke!" I repeated myself. "Do you understand?" This time he nodded slowly.

"Good." I nodded. "He understands. Oh please, Elizabeth. Of course, he understands. It's *his* leg that's broke, you daft dolt." I shook my lowered head and chastised myself aloud for being such an idiot. "Elizabeth, Elizabeth, Elizabeth, the sun has finally baked out the last of your brains." I looked back at him.

"Don't worry. I'm not really that daft, and I do know how to set a leg."

I pointed to his leg, and I slid the sticks along themselves, drawing them apart in opposite directions to their ends, which I then butted together repeatedly. I tried to show him with the sticks what I wanted to do. He seemed to understand my meaning, and I felt it might go better than I had anticipated. I rose to enter the wagon.

Inside, I retrieved a bottle of whiskey that I kept as a back-up should I run out of brandy, which I still used on occasion for easing the pain in my ribs. I opened the bottle, and in a most unladylike manner, brought it to my lips and took a healthy swallow. It knocked the breath out of me, burned all the way down to all but kill me. My eyes flooded with tears as I reminded myself exactly how much I hated the stuff.

I was still gasping when I stepped down to pass the bottle to him. He was reluctant to accept it. I then took another swig so to encourage him. I found it necessary to keep prodding him to drink as much as possible even after he knew what it was. I was greatly surprised by this, as I thought all Indians took to whiskey like children take to candy. It didn't appear that way now as I watched him.

After persuading him to take considerably more swallows, he began to chant in a low voice. I suspect it was his prayer. In any event, his eyes appeared to grow heavy. The whiskey was taking hold, and I figured in short time he would be well on his way to feeling little pain, if for no reason other than the way in which he began to grin at me.

"You just keep on drinking and grinning, and stay put until

Elizabeth gets back."

I re-entered the wagon to obtain the items I would need. In all the mess about me, I was amazed that I could not find any suitable pieces of wood to use as a splint. Eventually, I ended up prying off the top two boards of the backrest on my bench seat. With a hatchet, I split one board in two, lengthways. The other I sawed in half.

I grabbed a pair of scissors, some bandages, an extra blanket and a bolt of cotton, which I planned to wrap firmly around leg and splint. I cut and formed cloth pads to tuck between the splints and his leg to avoid chafing. I prepared poultices for the wound, Peruvian bark for infection and onions for swelling. By the time I was finished, the Indian was extremely drunk. I gave him fifty drops of laudanum for good measure and prayed the medicine along with the whiskey would knock him out sense-less or at least bring on a deep sleep.

I waited and waited. He was no longer grinning or chanting, mostly mumbling incoherently, but he refused to drink further and always stayed a short step ahead of sleep. I was afraid the effects of the drugs would wear off and so decided I could wait no longer.

"Mr. Indian! I am going to pull this leg into place and set it. I don't dare wait on you. The longer we sit here and wait the worse this will get. Now's the time."

I motioned my intent, but he never noticed me. I moved down to his leg and placed my foot squarely into his crotch, an act of which I was supremely conscious. I grabbed his leg firmly about the knee and calf, and began to pull with all my strength. Pain shot through my ribs, but nothing like the pain put upon the Indian. He sat up stiffly and looked at me wide-eyed, then closed his eyes and went back to mumbling.

The task of setting his leg was much more difficult to accomplish than I imagined. Although the whiskey was working its magic, his leg muscles were well developed, aggravated, and contracted. They were not easy to stretch, and my ribs burned with complaint. I pulled and held, pulled and held, trying to work his muscles loose.

I refused to fail in this work in spite of the sharp pain in my ribs. It was a matter of strength and stamina. I pulled and held until at last his muscles allowed me enough movement to position the bone back into place. I held my breath as I let loose of him and then exhaled with relief. I rotated my arms to extinguish my own pain and looked up to see if he noticed that I had succeeded in setting his leg. He hadn't. His head had toppled over and the chanting was complete. I couldn't hold it against him, and was actually grateful he no longer felt anything. I could not get over the fact he never cried out once.

At least I knew Allen would have been proud to see how his teaching had stayed with me. All those times during my youth when I cornered him with questions, pestering him to satisfy my curiosity, all those times added up to this one moment. Yes, I could see the look on his face; he would have been proud, indeed. I continued the business of dressing the Indian's wounds and applying poultices, bandages, pads, and the splint. With my last turn of cotton, I disproved the notion that medicine was too indelicate for women.

In the still of darkness, I sat back and stared at my patient. Men were ignorant in so many ways, I thought to myself. It was obvious that too many of them shared too much stupidity for their own good. I wondered if this man had broken his leg out of stupidity. I wondered what he was like. Was he the 'Christopher Claussen' of the Indian world, or brother to one of the thousands of unrefined savages that made up my world?

Why couldn't more men be like Christopher? He was everything I wanted, generous to a fault, kind, respectable, well mannered, well learned, well everything. He was perfect in my eyes, and the reason I spent much of my youth building my knight-in-armor around his likeness. I waited for that knight. I waited and waited. I learned the hard way that I had set my sights too high, for men like Christopher Claussen came far and few between, if ever at all. As a spinster, I had proven the truth of it.

"And so I ended up alone." I muttered to deaf ears.

I conceded that much to the sleeping Indian. Whether the Indian passed out from pain or whiskey, I didn't know. Either way, he was where I wanted to be, for I was tired. Dawn was but a couple of hours away, and soon thereafter the heat would be back with a vengeance. Until then, I hoped to get some sleep. I reached down for my ship's blanket and shook out the dirt and dust. I grabbed my gun and crawled back under the wagon. My last thoughts were about how nice it was to fall asleep with someone near.

EIGHTY-FOUR

The night had exhausted me. I had slept hard only to wake up to a world of mayhem. Whether it was worse than a herd of buffalo stampeding in the night or not, I never decided, but before I had a chance to open my eyes, my body was yanked straight out from under the wagon. It was a violent awakening with all the surprise one might imagine after surfacing from a deep sleep tethered to a galloping horse.

I was clearly on the wrong end of a rope wrapped tightly around my ankles. My first fleeting view was that of sand billowing up into a cloud through which the image of my wagon was receding at great speed. I was then dragged along the ground in a giant circle around the wagon amid the sounds of savages whooping and hollering in my ears.

I had not a single morning thought before I found myself scrambling to piece together this blur of a world that swept me away. Whatever was happening to me, I couldn't imagine until a rush of memories about buffalo and savages came to mind. It was a recollection that instantly made sense during my final blurry image, which was that of an Indian slapping the hind-quarter of his pony.

Large clumps of earth were being pitched at me by flying hooves through an upheaval of smaller debris. Because I had been sleeping on my stomach, I started this day skidding on my face. Instinctively, I spread my hands outward to protect myself, to raise my head and then to flip over onto my back so I could breathe dust free air.

I found myself eating dirt off the desert floor. The leftovers were being pressed into my eyes and ears or passing through me like a curse of cholera. Repeatedly, I reached for the rope to free myself, but every time I made the effort, I began to roll uncontrollably and so was left with no choice but to ride out the torture as best I could. I rolled over onto my butt and took the beating.

I was unable to see anything as I bounced along the ground, but for the sand streaming across my face. Yet, as I neared the upper ridge, I glimpsed the passing of many more horses headed in the opposite direction, they galloping down toward the wagon. At their passing, the horse to which I was tethered came to a halt.

I lie there stunned, motionless, my world spinning about me insanely. My eyes, ears, and mouth were filled with sand. My hair felt ripped out. I could feel the sticky flow of blood moving across my exposed skin, now scraped raw by the rocks, rough grass, and cacti.

Then came another sensation, one of tingling pain, one of terrible tingling pain that was creeping up upon me to send chills all through my body. Unlike leather, my corduroy trousers offered no protection against the needles of the prickly pear that grew in great numbers across the plains. These needles, many of which were driven deep into my flesh, had penetrated every square inch of my body.

Whereas, I was numb with shock at the start, I now openly cried, and I cried hard knowing there was no one to help me. My time was surely at hand. Everything happened so fast I never thought of death until now. Now, I was totally immobilized. My only movement was that of sobbing and the shaking of shock. Every move served only to drive the needles in deeper.

The sudden gush of tears allowed me to at least open my eyes, but I was only able to make out the light of morning and nothing more. My eyes were flooding themselves clean, and I fought to keep them open out of fear in order to watch an abstract shape approach through my tears.

I listened as the Indian dismounted his horse. He walked back to where I lie, and stood at my head looking down upon me. I heard the voices of Indians in the hollow near by the wagon, yelling to my captor in a strange tongue like nothing I had ever heard.

"Aenôheso! Nóxa'e!" (Little Hawk! Wait!)

The Indian turned to look down toward the wagon.

"Hénová'e?" (What?)

"Nóxa'e! Ho'neheveho, éhávêsévetano. (Wait! Chief Wolf, he's feeling bad.) Éé'êškóhta. Éónêšeohtse. (He has a broken leg. He's in pain.) Nenáasêstse!" (Come back!)

The Indian looked at me oddly before his eyes grew wide with surprise.

"Hĕ'e? Huh!" (A woman?)

He walked back to the horse and tossed his end of the rope to the ground, after which he rode down into the hollow. I was left lying on the ground to suffer. It gave me a moment to realize I wasn't yet dead even though it might have been for the better, for I couldn't believe the misery generated by the needles. I raised my hands and looked at them. They resembled pin cushions. Needles protruded from every inch of exposed quivering flesh.

I thanked the Lord for one consoling realization. The herd of bison had pounded the prickly pear to pulp only hours before and softened the earth with their hooves. Not that I didn't hurt in every way imaginable, but it could have been even worse.

I thought of the Indian with the broken leg. I tried to be strong like him and hold myself above physical pain. The Indian never cried out once. I concentrated on his strength, but realized in short time I didn't possess anything like it. Knowing that fact only served to make me feel worse, and so I cried all the harder.

It wasn't long before the Indian on horseback returned and dismounted a second time. He unfastened the rope about my ankles, and then grabbed me by my jacket. With no regard to my condition, he yanked me up onto my feet. I whimpered in agony, which only prompted him to give me an unfriendly push in the direction of the wagon. He mounted his horse and nudged me from behind with his foot, directing me to where his comrades were gathered.

"Nóheto!" (Let's go.)

Once we arrived at the wagon, my captor left me to my own devices. I stood in a daze alongside the bench, rocking back and forth on my feet as I studied the numerous needles and splinters protruding from my arms. I looked like a porcupine. If for no reason other than to shut out my fears and focus my thoughts, I selected the first needle and pulled it out with a badly trembling hand. It sent a shiver clean through me.

While the Indians were having a discussion among themselves, I was slowly regaining my wits. Their stares shifted back and forth between the injured Indian and me.

"Hénová'e há'tóhe, hë'e?" (What is that, a woman?)

"Héehe'e." (Yes.)

"E-ono'aha." (She's beautiful.)

"E-tóhtahe." (She's afraid.)

My captor walked over to the injured Indian and studied his leg and my doctoring. He stooped down and poked at the splints.

"E-toneto-mohta-he?" (How is he?)

"E-hosotomoo'e." (He's resting.) Éé'êškóhta. (He has a broken leg.)

To them, I must have appeared like a frightened animal, trapped with no place to go, cowering and preoccupied with my pain. Who could blame them, I was all of those things and more, but I did possess one objective. I wanted my pistol. The gun had been removed from beneath the wagon and was in the possession of a brave, but no one as of yet appeared to be brandishing my pistol.

The Indian I had doctored was now beginning to stir and muttering in a low voice. The others hushed at once and gathered tightly about him with great interest. It occurred to me, they might have thought him dead, but for all the alcohol and opium I gave him. In any event, his stirring commanded their full attention. The injured Indian was still leaning up against the wagon wheel where I left him. The others moved away from me and toward him with much excitement, and no longer paid me mind. That was good.

Seeing this, and having been given an arm's length of freedom plus a sudden now or never impulse, I jumped for the wagon seat. My sudden move didn't go unnoticed and two or three of the Indians dove for me. I kicked at them like a grouchy goat and escaped their reaching hands long enough to fall back through the door and cower inside my wagon.

None of their party chose to follow. Instead they added insult to my injury with loud laughter. Why wouldn't they laugh? They knew I could hide in the wagon all I wanted, but I wasn't going anywhere. To them I was a rabbit that backed into the coyote's mouth.

What they didn't realize was I only wished to reach my pistol. Unable to understand or observe the activity brewing outside the wagon, I could only imagine my fate teetered upon the whims of their mood. If they were busy, I might be left alone. If they were bored then I might be raped and tortured for amusement. I would use my pistol to take my own life, providing they hadn't already stolen it.

I glanced about quickly and was relieved to discover that although the Indians had rummaged through some of my things, most were left in place. Encouraged, I went straight for the cabinet where my pistol and powder horn were kept. I retrieved them. I flipped open the flash pan, pulled the stopper out of the horn and poured in a charge of powder. I then pulled back the hammer and calmly placed the barrel to my head.

At once, my emotions settled. There was no longer the frantic rush to gain an upper hand. I was now in complete control of my life, my destiny was my own. I was unable to sit down, but for the needles, and so I remained ready to die on my knees. I wasn't afraid of death. I was afraid of how I would die, and I hoped this would be quick. It was a road taken by many before me. I reached around to my behind and pulled out a needle.

"Oh!"

The Indians began to whoop and holler and were evidently overjoyed at finding their man alive enough to carry on. They spent some time conversing and laughing in their tongue, and I heard two horses ride off over the crest of the hollow and out of earshot. The Indians then became very quiet and spoke in muted conversation. Something was about to happen. I listened nervously and pulled out another needle.

"Ouch."

I whimpered beneath my breath, lord that hurt. I began praying to God for forgiveness. I regretted some of my earlier thoughts and cynicism, and knew in the next moment I might very well be speaking to Him in person. I was trying not to succumb to panic, trying to stay in control and clearheaded. The sweat was running off of me as I asked for the courage needed and not faint from fear before I could pull the trigger. I recalled all the horrible stories I had ever heard in order to bolster my courage. I only had to pull the trigger. Death would free me in a split second. My chest felt heavy, my mouth dry. My breathing was constricted. My time was at hand, and I was trembling something terrible. I reached for another needle.

"Mmmph."

I winced from the pain. I then felt the wagon tip to one side. An Indian had placed his weight on the step. I tightened my grip on the pistol. I began to apply pressure upon the trigger. I felt myself float away from reality. The world seemed to be empty of sound as I stared out into the early morning light. This was it; I thought to myself, this was it.

"Forgive me Lord. Please, forgive me."

Very slowly, the face of an Indian came into view, rising up from below to peek inside. He looked at me briefly then eased out of view before stepping back to the ground. I released the pressure. I heard him speak to the others, and his words generated a conversation among them.

Again the wagon tipped and the same Indian appeared cautiously as before. His face was painted. He looked at me and spoke in that foreign tongue. He held up his hand. He waved it and shook his head. His expression was one of objection. He addressed me quietly.

"Hová'âháne. Éneoestse." (No. Put it down.)

By his tone of voice and actions, it was obvious he didn't want me to kill myself. Why, I wondered. Did they need me for a sacrifice? Of course! That was their plan. I had read about these things. Indians were famous for sacrificing women to the sun or some pagan corn god. It was the curse of my gender. I knew it!

The morning was cool, but my hands were sticky. The Indian stepped down from the wagon to initiate another conversation. This time a voice spoke to me in English.

"Né'áahtovêste." (Listen to me.) Elizabet—no shoot."

I was astonished. I was also too scared to respond. It had to be a trick. How could a savage know English words? How could anybody out here in the middle of this hell possibly know my name? These thoughts totally distracted me, and I eased off the trigger.

"Elizabet?"

"Elizabet! Né'áahtovêste! (Listen to me!)" Someone called out to me again.

"What?" My voice cracked as I forced it through a throat dry as flour.

"No shoot."

I let out a sob and my tears ran. This was too much. The people must be possessed by the devil in order to taunt me in a wagon that was for all-purpose and intent a coffin ready to roll. I couldn't believe what I was hearing. I pulled out another piece of prickly pear, and another.

"Oh! God help me, this is worse than death."

The Indians talked some more amongst themselves.

"Elizabet, no shoot. Yes?"

"How do you know my name?"

The wagon tipped and the same Indian as before again showed his face. He spoke to me, motioning with his hands. He was pressing air down with the palms of his hands.

"Hová'âháne! Hová'âháne. Névé'nêheséve. Éneoestse." (No! No. Don't do that. Put it down.)

He did not have the same voice as the one who spoke to me in English.

"No shoot, yes," came the stranger's voice.

"I'm afraid." I said at last.

"Why afraid?"

"You'll kill me."

There was a moment of conversation amongst them.

"Elizabet, no kill, no kill."

I started crying again. The tension was unbearable. I pulled out another needle. This time I felt nothing. I was now ready to accept death by my own hand, but they were confusing me. I knew if I gave up my gun I would face a much worse fate than the instant death of a ball. I knew if I gave up my gun, I gave up all control.

"Elizabet."

"What?" I sobbed.

"No kill."

"I'm afraid! Don't you understand? You are all savages, and I'm afraid of you!"

"What afraid?"

"I'm afraid! Scared of you! Just look at me. I'm a mess. I'm bleeding everywhere." I searched for a place on my sleeve to wipe away my tears without getting poked. My legs were quivering from holding up my weight and my knees ached terrible.

"Elizabet no scared. Elizabet have gun."

Why would they say that, I wondered? I wasn't sure what they meant. Why would they remind me that I had a gun? That made no sense. Was it time to pull the trigger or should I wait? Could I keep my gun? Should I see what happens? Could I trust Indians? I didn't hurt them. I helped the man with the broken leg. Would they consider my good deed? Did savages care about such gestures? I could have killed him just as easily.

I heard more riders enter into the hollow. The men started talking among themselves and became very excited.

"Elizabet, come."

I waited, uncertain, distraught.

"Elizabet, come."

"I'm afraid you'll kill me."

"No afraid, no kill. Come"

The conversation went on in this manner for some time, but the Indians seemed ready to wait for however long necessary to persuade me to leave the wagon.

Three braves, believing themselves to be in no danger, took up a seat upon the wagon bench and watched me suffer through my indecision and the pain of removing needles. They winced at every yank.

Although, they finally coaxed me into removing the gun from my head, they made no attempt to take it away or enter my wagon and reach for me. They acted without fear even though I now kept my gun cocked and pointed directly at them.

It took all of the morning for me to settle down enough to even consider stepping out of the wagon as they asked, but they were persistent and patient. In the end, I agreed, but before I turned myself over to them, l reached for the amulet given to me by Shadow Hunter. I placed it around my neck and prayed that they would find something good about it. It must have had meaning indeed, for the braves immediately showed surprise and began to announce my actions and mimicked my fastening the amulet, about their own necks.

"I'm coming out, now."

"Come, Elizabet." The voice answered.

With that announcement, I released the hammer and moved cautiously forward. I crawled awkwardly and it was with great difficulty that I climbed over the bench seat, for my legs were full of needles and locked up from the strain of kneeling so long. The braves jumped clear of the seat and backed away.

As my view forward widened, I could see many Indians sitting about on the ground or bathing in the cool water of the pond. When I came into view, the Indians quieted. Some pointed at me, all turned in my direction. Their faces expressed curiosity and interest. They were fingering and fussing with their hair. It seemed they had never seen a blonde-headed woman.

I had overcome the worst of my initial fears, and now dared to look at these people. I saw scores of black eyes and bronze faces, some young, some older and weathered, most adorned in paint and decoration. They sported feathers and beads, and held on to dappled horses and quivers as they stopped their business long enough to study me. My life was in the hands of fate, and I was now resigned to this fact. I still had my gun, but I doubted I could ever use it.

"Elizabet."

I looked down and was amazed to discover that it was the injured Indian who had been speaking to me in English. He didn't look good, but he was still sitting up against the wagon wheel. I couldn't imagine how he knew my name?

"Nenáasêstse. Come. Hámêstoo'êstse." (Come here. Come. Sit down.)

He looked up to me as he patted the ground next to where he sat. I stepped down from the wagon, but conveyed that I was unable to do as he bid but for the quantity of needles in my behind. This brought forth a good deal of laughter from the others once they realized my predicament. Two of the Indians stepped toward me. I backed away at once, frightened by their advance. I raised my gun.

They stopped at once. The injured Indian made an effort to calm me with gestures and motioned for me to turn around and face the wagon. This I did. Another Indian stepped up behind me and reached around my sides. Slowly, carefully, he unfastened my trousers and pulled them down around my knees. I offered no resistance. I don't believe embarrassment is often a term of relevance in the desert. I hugged the rim of the wheel with all my strength and clenched my teeth as a second and then a third Indian joined in pulling needles from my flesh in rapid fashion. They removed what they could see, clearing my back, my arms and legs, but especially my behind, which took the brunt of it.

They were not what I would have called compassionate. They openly laughed, thinking my situation was extremely funny. In short time they plucked my bottom clean of what could be picked until the injured Indian motioned them away. I reached down to retrieve my trousers, but every move no matter how small was excruciatingly painful.

I stepped across the Indian's broken leg and attempted to sit the best I could. It proved impossible and so I positioned myself on my knees and leaned up against the wheel alongside him. He looked horrible. His pain must have been unimaginable. I watched the sweat pour off him. Still, he reached under my chin and after taking hold of my jaw, he twisted my head back and forth to look over my bloodied face. He pulled me in close and smelled my hair and shoulders.

"Ve'kee heséeo'ótse." (Sweet medicine.)

Whatever he said made the others laugh. He reached for my amulet. He looked it over carefully. His eyes remained fixed on mine as he turned his head to direct his words to the rest.

"Éma'heóneve. Ma'heono." (It is spiritual. Sacred powers.)

His words raised a stirring among his companions. They seemed to be impressed by Shadow Hunter's amulet. I wondered if it could save my life twice.

"You good spirit, yes?" He spoke with a weak voice.

"You speak English?" I stared at him disbelieving.

"Small." He grinned as he held his fingers together.

"How do you know my name?"

"You talk much. Talk, talk, talk. Talk spirits, I listen—you tell me you Elizabet." I pondered over this for a moment and then realized, he was telling me I talked to myself. Any other time in my life I would have shrank with embarrassment, but as I learned, out here embarrassment meant nothing. Now, I simply accepted the truth of it. After two months on the trail, I talked to myself all the time.

He looked up to the men and spoke as though giving a command. "Éxanénêstse! Nóheto! (Get ready. Let's go!) We go, Elizabet."

He reached for the spokes of the wheel to lift himself off the ground. Others moved forward at once to assist him. He winced with pain as they raised him by his arms. He was weak and in no condition to be moved. It must have been terrible, and I was embarrassed at all my fuss and crying over the needles. He looked down at me.

"Épéva'e. It good."

He patted the splint. It held fast and so he motioned toward the wagon seat after having said something to the others. The men raised him carefully onto the bench. Then, in a somewhat rougher manner they grabbed me by my arms and raised me to my feet. I was walked around to the opposite side of the bench. I started to pull myself up, but not before one of the Indians ran his hand fully up my leg and squarely into my crotch.

Instinctively, I jumped, but was unable to let loose of my grip on the wagon, lest I fall. I spun around hissing like a startled cat and lashed out with the heel of my boot. The flash of my temper painted my face crimson before I could hope to conceal it. I shoved my gun into the brute's face, which delighted the others enormously and fed a roar of laughter among them. The piece wasn't cocked and I didn't have a free hand to attempt it, but the Indian was too busy ducking to notice.

"Taasêstse!" (Leave!)

My injured companion barked at the man, who seemed to laugh at everything including himself, but he backed away and returned to his horse. As the others mounted their horses in preparation to leave, my team of mules appeared on the crest of the hollow. They were being herded toward me and I was instantly overjoyed.

"My mules! My mules! Oh, thank god!"

No more wondrous sight could I have imagined. I jumped off the bench at once and hobbled in their direction to see for myself that they were all right. I wrapped my arms around them, I scratched their ears, I talked warmly to them. I walked back with them to the wagon where I retrieved my block of salt and let them lick it. With a sigh of relief, I fit the harnesses and hitched them without interference from the Indians waiting on me. As I returned to the wagon I happened to notice my ship's blanket wadded up in the dirt between the front wheels. I reached for it and shook out the dirt and dust as before. I folded it and placed it upon the bench. I was suffering terribly, but doing so in much better spirits.

EIGHTY-FIVE

When I returned to climb back onto the wagon, the brute jumped off his horse to assist me once again. I made it clear I would have nothing to do him, and my eyes and gun conveyed a second warning. The Indians seemed to respect my defiance, but continued with their laughter nonetheless. They carried on until the injured Indian gave me a sign of support and motioned for the man to mount up. The brute didn't take instruction well.

"Ótahe! Né'áahtovêste! Taasêstse! Taanáasêstse! Hetsetseha!" (Pay attention! Listen to me! Leave! Go! Now!)

The injured Indian turned to me and shook his head.

"Éhé'heetovánove. Énâhahe." (He's crazy, mischievous; he bothers people. He is wild and uncivilized.)

I had no idea what he said or uttered under his breath, but he rolled his eyes with an expression that I assumed meant the bully was less than intelligent. Some of the others nearby overheard him and nodded in agreement. He spoke to the man, but it seemed as though the man didn't communicate in the same fashion as the others. There was a lot of sign language used. The injured Indian then looked back at me.

"We go now. Yes?"

"Yes."

He called out to his men.

"Nóheto!" (Let's go!)

I came to realize quickly that the Indian I had helped was the only one giving orders and seemed to be in complete command of this party. Maybe God hadn't forsaken me after all. Maybe this man was sent to deliver me from something worse. At his word, the Indians mounted their horses and headed up out of the hollow. I reached for my whip.

"H'ya! Heee-ya!

I cracked the air and started my mules off. I didn't believe the man next to me had ever rode in a wagon. I could see from the expressions of the others that this was quite an event and that it brought him much esteem. He drew constant attention. The jostling was painful for both of us, but the experience was apparently worth it, because he laughed a little here and there between gritting his teeth. He looked at me, pointed at my butt and at his head and moaned.

"Me'ko." (Head.)

I looked at him momentarily puzzled then to my surprise, I broke into a grin. The man was in pain, he was suffering, but if was from a headache—the effects of the whiskey and opium, and not his badly swollen leg. That was indeed funny. Contrary to all I had heard about Indians, this man was definitely not a drinking man.

Once out of the hollow, a party of forty or more Indians on horseback made my wagon, my injured companion, and myself the highlight of a parade. They grouped tightly around us and I was given my first opportunity to get a good look at these people without as much fear that they find me bold or confrontational. I made a point of not meeting their eyes intentionally, or else doing so with utmost caution.

They and their horses were patterned, painted up in vivid colors and adorned with ornaments and trinkets. For me, traveling in their company was akin to moving through a field of snakes. That is to say, aside from the danger I faced, aside from being kept wary and unnerved to the point of falling sick with fright;

their colors and patterns, like scales of a snake, made it impossible not to succumb to their hypnotic beauty.

The Indians, on the other hand, were not at all bashful about staring at me. At some point along the way, each one of the braves made an effort to ride up close enough to get a good look at me and my collection of clanging pots and pans. Quite often they would rotate their wrists back and forth very rapidly and then speak to me. Getting no response, they would then address my companion.

"Why do they do this?" I asked as I rotated my wrist in similar fashion.

"It sign. To all people, it mean question, how, where, why. They ask you go, one? They ask, why you go one?" He raised one finger.

"Oh." I nodded in understanding. "Yes, I go one."

"Hmmmph."

I gathered that, like most of the men I had met, he thought it amazing that I was traveling alone. I believed he conveyed this fact repeatedly to the others who shared in his amazement by raising one finger in astonishment. I had long since learned the expressions of disbelief men would exhibit just before falling into private conversations. Like others, these Indians must have thought I was either crazy or with the Great Spirit. Either way was fine with me, just as long as they didn't think I was a sacrifice.

As for me, I imagined I was to become their slave, which made me think of Rachel. I was developing a taste of what it meant to feel terrified at the hands of others, to have no say in my future, to be completely at the mercy of someone else. I wondered if I had felt something of the fear Rachel had experienced, and these thoughts made my respect for her all the more pronounced. Like Rachel, I was in no position to make demands or barter for my life or the goods in my wagon, for they could kill me at any time and take possession of whatever they wanted.

Like a slave, I now existed in their world, but would never be a part of it. Unlike Rachel, I didn't live it the whole of my life.

Right now, it made sense that I should drive the team, the wagon, and the injured Indian back to their camp. Right now, I served a purpose. At least I could say for certain that I was still alive and unharmed in a manner of speaking, and for this I continued to thank God profusely. I begged Him not to let me enjoy a false sense of hope then lead me to a fate much worse than the pain of the prickly pear.

From the hollow, we rode southwest for the next four days. The terrain was growing rougher, the grass shorter, and the ground drier. The going was slow in the wagon, but it gave the two of us a chance to get acquainted. The Indian was very curious about me. He exhibited an extraordinary amount of patience as we traded words back and forth. We were building a vocabulary between us. It was my good fortune that he knew a number of English words.

As we talked, we passed both time and rolling plains that now flattened out and sloped evermore upward to merge with foothills that propped up the most majestic mountains I had ever seen. During this time, by means of pillows, blankets, and laudanum, I made my companion's journey as comfortable as I could. In return, he eased many of my fears. It seemed every minute of every hour was a learning experience for me, and I came to realize first and foremost that this injured Indian was not nearly the heathen I originally thought.

In spite of his pain, or maybe in an attempt to be distracted from it, he proved quite willing to converse, and so I worked up the courage to ask him by what name he was called. His told me he was called Ho'neheveho, which he translated into Chief Wolf. His people were called the Tsistsistas. I had never heard of them. He then said Cheyenne.

"Cheyenne!" I was immediately unnerved.

Yes, indeed, I had heard of the Cheyenne. Lewis and Clark among other trappers and traders had made mention of the Cheyenne, and Mr. Thompson, the river pilot, had mentioned tribes of Cheyenne and Sioux being settled along the upper Missouri. I had thought of them more a people of the Michigan Territories or the Northwest Territories, but most of all I had thought of them as being fierce warriors. I had thought of them as being ruthless and ritualistic. I knew they did not associate with the white man.

My throat went dry. I believe he noticed the sudden expression of unease on my face. He must have realized how close to the surface was my fear, for he looked at me quizzically and then began to tell me about his people. He spoke with his hands.

"My father, and father father, come from—." He rolled his hands to express generations and then pointed.

"East," said I.

"East—great water. My father, and father father come here hunt. My brother live—east, great water. My brother live here. Brother there, brother here."

Ho'neheveho attempted to explain to me how his people originally came from the upper Missouri River area. Some, not many, still remained on the great river. There had been much trouble with the Hóheeheo'o, another tribe of Indians who were armed with guns they had received from the English. He told me how many of his people had been killed by the guns, and how dangerous it was to remain in those places. His people decided to move where there was less death and more buffalo. They gave up farming and became hunters.

We conversed for many hours, which eased my worries. I finally asked Ho'neheveho why he spared my life. The question seemed reasonable to me in view of how I had been raised. He looked at me very strange.

"Why I kill you?"

"I don't know. Indians kill white people."

He laughed.

"No. Indians kill Indians."

He went on to say that most of his people had never seen a white man and those that did liked white men because they had good wampum, good trade, strong medicine. He swept his arm across my wagon, to illustrate his point. He told me that for many years his people were forbidden to make contact with the white man because their prophets claimed the white man would bring an end to their kind. He said he had never seen a woman with hair the color of the sun.

He also told me that Cheyenne never treated women badly. He said his men were confused by his drunken state and thought that I had injured his spirit. They thought I was a man sleeping beneath the wagon because I was hidden from view underneath my blanket, and because I wore trousers. They were worried about me killing them with a gun, and so slipped a rope around my ankles to yank me out before I could shoot.

He made it clear that he regretted my being dragged across the ground, and expressed sympathy for my rump. Everyone seemed to understand the consequence of prickly pears and the thought of it along with his laughter and a few words to the riders had them laughing heartily. To see him laughing did them good. To see them laughing did me good.

EIGHTY-SIX

In time, we crested the last rise of dry scrubby ground, beyond which opened a beautiful valley. Just to see such a place set one's mind free of the torrid desert temperatures. I was calmed by its gentle flow downward from between the steeper

811

slopes of the mountains. It was a sight for sore eyes, an astonishing change from the infinitely flat and arid plains at my back.

As if to accentuate its difference, the valley absorbed a short-lived but ample cloudburst that left me heady with the perfume and fresh fragrances of dampened earth and wildflowers. The moisture-laden air soothed my sinuses, dried skin, and chapped lips. The fleeting shower was enough to glue the dust back to the ground and enrich the greens of juniper and pine that reached down from the heights. This high plains valley was a haven, a beacon that rose above the desert floor to attract life. This was evident nowhere more so, than at the bottom of its fold, where an enormous collection of tipis came into view.

At first sight of the camp, the riders in our troupe started howling and yelping. They raised their spears and bows high into the air as they made known our arrival from across the fields. Unseen faces in the distance echoed a response. The sudden explosion of spirit and commotion that crisscrossed the valley unsettled me. Ho'neheveho was weary, yet he thought to console me. He looked my way and smiled.

"I say, *Na venovo*. You say, *my home*."

I said nothing. I was nervous. I looked at the numbers of tipis spread out across the valley, and the sight of so many dwellings strangled me with apprehension. The tipis ranged in color from bright white to light browns and drab gray. Their number was split roughly in two, parted by a stream that broke free of the mountain to run crazily downhill where it fed a pond and later disappeared in the lower levels.

The tip of each tipi had an opening crowned by a dark brown stain, a residue formed by an almost invisible column of smoke rising lazily until evaporating into the late morning sky. The tipis all faced the same direction—east. They were all the same shape, but differed in height and diameter. Some were constructed with ten or so poles, others with twelve or fourteen, or even more.

A few of the lodges were considerably larger than the rest and heavily patterned with decorative symbols. They were adorned with stars and circles, stick figures, animals, weapons, and smaller designs of which I failed to readily identify from our distance. Some of the larger tipis had poles and stands next to them that were draped with feathers and various items. They reminded me of parlor room coat racks being used as a 'collect all'.

There were numerous animals about. At first glance, it looked as though there were half-a-thousand horses grazing the upper valleys and slopes above the encampment. There also appeared to be countless additional mounts staked in front of tipis throughout the camp. Aside from horses, there were dogs.

They could be seen everywhere frolicking, sleeping, or nosing around for food. They followed the Indians about, played with the children and got chased out of tipis. Now and then I would hear a loud yelp and see a poor animal speeding across the field with its tail between its legs as it fled a beating or cruel prank. I also saw dogs laboring along well-worn trails between the tipis and the trees upon the ridges. They followed the women and were fitted with harnesses and travois that were burdened with stacks of firewood to be dragged back to camp.

As we drew in closer, I could see the people moving about. In the fields surrounding the tipis, women were gathered into many small groups of four or five. Some were kneeling or sitting upon blankets while weaving and working clothes. Others were bent over hides staked to the ground, attacking them with tools of one kind or another in order to dress out skins. Nearer the camp, I could see mothers caring for their young inside tipi-like structures where the sides had been raised to enjoy a breeze. They also sat in the shade of skins and grass mat roofs that were draped across arbors of a sort to ward off the sun.

Children were playing in groups separated by gender, all running helter-skelter like little hellions. I determined one group of boys to be playing a hunting game where an older youth appeared to be acting out the role of a buffalo, and the rest the role of hunters. Other boys were raising havoc in the riverbed, some splashing and swimming in the cool water, some drawn to fence-like structures bridging the flow to catch fish. There were toddlers sitting naked at the water's edge and covered in mud as they fashioned articles out of clay while under the watchful eyes of nearby mothers wringing out clothes upon the bank.

I spotted a small gathering of girls about nine or ten years of age playing in and around a miniature tipi. It must have been the Indian version of a dollhouse. As we entered the camp, I watched the girls dismantle the tipi, strapping the poles and hides to a large dog with a wagging tail. They moved the tipi a couple of hundred feet to the side and then erected it a second time and set up house anew. I only saw one group of girls that were older; they were playing a game of football. I watched as a couple of adolescent males walked toward them to join in the fun.

This appeared to be unusual, for most of the boys stayed together and played rough. The largest gang visible to me was engaged in a fast paced game whereby a person would roll a circular wooden frame at great speed down between two rows of contestants. The frame was about waist-high, made from a sapling or something similar and held its shape by means of a net that stretched across it like spokes on a wheel. As the wheel rolled between the two rows of boys, they would whip sticks at it. The best I could determine, where the net was struck determined the value of the strike, for I saw them taking a tally of the sticks that were snared.

Amid the tipis, I saw clusters of boys and men seated upon the ground listening to speakers who I assumed were giving lessons. Beyond the tipis, beyond the women weaving upon their blankets, older boys and young men improved their skills by playing games on horseback. I watched them gallop back and forth across the valley at breakneck speed. They rode horses as though they were born upon them.

Parties of older men could also be seen on horseback, fanning out in the distance, heading in different directions with extra horses in tow. I watched them pass through many smaller herds of horses, which were tended by young boys lying about then suddenly springing to their feet as the riders passed them by. At the very fringes of the valley, high up on the ridges, were solitary individuals, men who I assumed to be sentries.

It was hard enough for me to believe that anybody was able to survive in this godforsaken land, let alone a community of such size. It occupied the entire valley before me. It was the first congregation of people I had seen in ages since leaving St. Louis.

As the wagon approached, it drew more attention. All the inhabitants, young and old alike, girls and boys, women and their men, those in camp and those far out on the plain halted their activities and turned to observe our party. The wagon was something that apparently many of these people had never seen before, and it drew them toward us like a magnet. They were clearly overwhelmed with curiosity.

Their numbers made me uneasy, and as they multiplied before me, I grew inwardly tense. I felt very much the outsider, for in spite of Ho'neheveho's attempts to alleviate my misgivings; I was still most apprehensive about what was to become of me once the wagon stopped. This was not my home; this was not my place. This was a culture of which I knew nothing. Apparently my fears were again visible, for Ho'neheveho placed his hand upon my thigh and gave me another word of consolation.

"Come. No afraid."

The sight of our approach stirred up a great fuss throughout the camp. The young Indians interrupted their field games and came riding out toward us fast and furious, whooping, hollering, and making great sport of it. The women folk emptied out of their sunshades and rose from their blankets. It seemed everyone stopped whatever their activity and began to swarm in our direction. I watched as they sifted through the tipis and merged

815

into a large wave of smiling faces ready to meet us. They spoke excitedly amongst themselves and filled the air with gibberish.

The wagon held the crowd spellbound. The young riders were galloping around us with much pomp and ceremony. The warriors traveling in our company hovered close about the wagon as though jealous, as though wanting to protect their place and be seen as party to this wondrous vehicle. They closed ranks as if to shield us from the young riders and the rest of those who were crowding in to get a better look.

Because of the wagon, the spectacle of articles hanging upon it, and the sight of Ho'neheveho seated upon the bench, as we entered into their midst, the crowd exploded into a frenzy of emotion. He held out his hand in an attempt to greet them and calm their unrestrained behavior. His actions further convinced me that he was a man of esteem, for his every move had an effect upon the crowd. A wave of his hand was like watching wind move across a field of tall grass. It appeared that all revered him.

The warriors escorted us through the crowd and moved to stop the wagon before a great lodge. It was much larger than the tipis that surrounded it and also carefully painted in the symbolic fashion I mentioned before. There were numerous horses staked in front that were disturbed by the hullabaloo of a mob pressing in tight to satisfy curiosity.

The warriors attempted to shoo the crowd away in order to safely remove Ho'neheveho from the wagon to his tipi. With arms spread across their shoulders, he was lifted off the bench and carried down between the rows of staked adornments that led to the flapped entrance. Family and friends surrounded him until he disappeared inside.

When Ho'neheveho vanished, so too did my courage. To be left alone on the wagon amid a mob of garrulous Indians was more than I could bear. All the fears I had buried since my capture were now resurrected to suffer me. I held my head high hoping to rise above them, hoping to present myself as confident and fearless. I hoped to conceal my anxiety, and prayed they might not dare me to meet their eyes.

My gaze swept back and forth above the crowd, above the faces until I noticed one woman in particular who not only stood separate, but seemed gripped by my presence. She made it difficult for me to look away. I recalled that she was one of the first to approach the wagon when the warriors removed Ho'neheveho to his tipi. They hadn't shooed her away like all the others. She was now standing at the lodge entrance in the company of the braves. Her attention made me most uneasy, and I felt as one woman to another, she could see straight into my soul and sense my insecurity.

It was apparent that Ho'neheveho held a high position and she seemed to share his status. She moved in and out of the lodge freely and was shown a notable amount of respect from the others. I avoided looking in her direction and concentrated instead on the activity immediately surrounding the wagon for any sign of malice. I felt completely out of my element and watched warily for a sudden change in the mood of these people.

While I sat waiting for whatever would happen next, a quick glance now and then revealed that a troupe of warriors were giving the woman an account of what had taken place and how I had gone about setting Ho'neheveho's leg. I determined this by the gesturing of the braves and by the way in which the woman kept looking in my direction. It was clear that she was judging me by her own set of standards.

After hearing the men out, she stepped back briefly into the tipi and then reappeared with her eyes set squarely on me. This time I didn't look away. She held my full attention as I watched her walk toward me. She was a confident woman. She never wavered. She stopped before me to look up and offer her hand.

"Peveešeeva, ne tonéševe he?" (Good day, what is your name?)

I could only watch this woman, believing her to be asking me a question, but having no idea how to respond or react.

"Nenáasêstse. Nenáasêstse." (Come. Come.)

She was beckoning me to leave the wagon. I didn't move at first, instead staying put to study her face. In doing so, I discovered her expression to be compassionate, her eyes to be kind. Nevertheless, my fears governed my actions and my hesitation was apparent, but she seemed to understand. With repeated waves of her hand and a gentle voice of encouragement, she persuaded me to step down and follow her lead.

"Nenáasêstse. Nenáasêstse."

EIGHTY-SEVEN

In spite of my fears, I was in no position to be contrary or rude. I was a stranger in a strange land, and I prayed these people would know and remember that I had worked to save a man's life. I prayed that they might feel grateful and let me be on my way, but that didn't appear to be happening. Instead, the woman took my hand firmly into hers and led me through a gathering of curious whispering women who all turned to follow.

"Etónėsóotse?" (What happened?)

"E sáa ame hne." (He's not walking.)

"Nevaahe ta'tohe?" (Who is that?)

"E ve'ho'a'e ve!" (It's a white woman!)

In a procession, we passed between the rows of staked adornments and reached the entrance to the lodge. Just prior to entering the tipi, she suddenly stopped and then turned about to face me. She studied me for a moment, and then with a look of concern she said something to me while patting her abdomen.

"Ma'e? Ma'e?"

I sensed there was an issue, but I was at a loss to understand the meaning behind her gestures. It sounded as though she was asking a question of me, and although I had no idea of what she asked, I did notice the other women were taking her words seriously, and so I paid close attention.

"Ma'e? Ma'e?" She repeated, again patting her abdomen.

"Ma'e?" I mimicked. Whatever did she mean? Hungry? Pregnant? I was gesturing my inability to comprehend her question when without warning; she reached down and pressed her hand between my thighs. Instinctively, I jerked backwards as my face blushed with embarrassment. At the same time, a quiet giggle floated among the women crowded about me.

My self-consciousness was made all the worse, by their sudden interest in my crimson color. A number of hands reached to touch my face. They were completely taken in by my blushing. I realized that this was something not easily seen in these dark skinned people. They thought my glow was very amusing. For a moment the focus remained on my face and not my privates, but it soon returned to the original issue.

She confronted me again in the same manner, but my inability to placate her in this matter only served to increase the confusion and my anxiety. I felt awkward and plenty embarrassed. The women were quick to sense this and after a brief discussion, they relented. However, the plan to lead me into the lodge was changed, and I was led away from the lodge and brought instead to another tipi alongside the stream. This one we entered without further ado.

Inside, there was lying about seven or eight women, most of them completely nude except for a diaper-like cloth. All had one obvious thing in common. They were menstruating. Right then, everything fell perfectly into place and I understood the fuss and commotion. I too was menstruating and could only imagine how they might have known. I used to be obsessive about keeping myself clean and free of odor. The desert had a way of changing that.

Enlightened, I acknowledged that it too was my time of month, and to my surprise, admitting as much greatly relieved all present. Their sudden relief revealed to me that they hadn't known after all, but instead had been inquiring for some specific reason. They spoke seriously among themselves for a moment, while I stood before them uncertain of what was expected of me.

Then came another one of those horrible thoughts. Maybe they wanted to know if I could get pregnant. Maybe they had some unsavory plan for me. Maybe I would be offered to the men for some religious ritual. Maybe they knew I was a virgin and that was important. Then came a second thought. *My word, Elizabeth, nobody in his or her right mind would think a thirty-four year old woman could still be a virgin. Give it a rest.*

My escort then turned to me and smiled. She patted me on the shoulder and pointed to one of the women sitting down. She said one last thing to this woman who was some years younger than I, and then stepped outside the tipi leaving me alone within their company. The woman looked at me.

"Ne tonisėševe he?" (What is your name?)

She addressed me, but I could only stand there and stare at her. I was in a bad situation. I looked at the other women and then back at her. She smiled and suddenly spoke to me in English.

"Please, sit."

I was astonished as before when Ho'neheveho spoke in English. I was instantly drawn to her, instantly hoping to become her slave, instantly wanting to be under her command, to answer her beck and call—to prove my worth for protection. This was someone with whom I could communicate. I dropped at once to sit before her.

"I Haonovahe. You?"

"I am Elizabeth."

"Elizabeth—. What Elizabeth mean?"

"I don't know—chosen one, I believe."

I wasn't sure where that came from. It just seemed to roll off my tongue. She turned to others and commented at which point they all appeared surprised and humored.

"What does Haonovahe mean?" I asked in return.

"Talk a lot."

"Talk a lot?" This time I was amused. I smiled.

"Yes, I talk much. I talk English. I talk French."

"What does ma'e mean?" I asked, thinking of the incident at the lodge.

"Sang. Blood." She answered in both French and English.

How sweet and to the point, I thought. She promptly cleared my confusion.

"How did you learn English?" I asked.

"When I small, I live on Missouri River. I know man that speak English. I learn much English. I talk to trappers. I learn some French, Qui?"

"Where is the man now?"

I was allowed my hopes, but she only shrugged her shoulders and changed the subject.

"Many winters past. I hear you good spirit. You good for Ho'neheveho. We happy. We thank you."

"You are welcome. Is Ho'neheveho a chief or what?" I was curious about the man. What was his social status? I was certain he was someone important. Talk-a-lot looked at me momentarily puzzled, possibly in disbelief, and then answered my question.

"Yes, chief. Ho'neheveho brother. Big chief. Big chief. Soon, he give you horses. Soon. Now, we wait." She pointed at my crotch and showed me the blood on her cloth.

821

Her frankness took me aback. My face flushed anew. I understood that all the aversions I possessed regarding sexual matters were due to the culture in which I was raised, and yet the awareness of this fact did nothing to help me overcome my discomfort. I wished to put forth an appearance of control and found myself to be exceedingly annoyed by my inner sensitivities and the embarrassment it caused to be seen upon my face.

Why did I blush over nature's announcement of womanhood? Why, did I have to be embarrassed when no one else in this tipi was? God produced me according to his holy design, but thanks to the puritanical men in my New England background, I didn't defecate, urinate, nor menstruate.

Talk-a-lot and the other women were visibly excited to have me in their midst. They were openly curious about my fair complexion and my blonde hair. They pulled at my clothes, impatient that I remove them so they could look at me. Maybe for the first time ever, I found myself far more afraid to displease these women than to undress before them, and so I stripped down as they bid. They were visibly upset by my rash of wounds, many now infected. Yet, they paid mind most to my skin and hair. They stared at me with awe. I dropped my face into my hands to avoid their eyes.

The women surrounded me and took turns stroking and studying the skin on my back, my arms and legs. They were particularly drawn to white skin of my breasts that least tanned by sun, and the light pink color of my nipples. They dissected my features and discussed my differences, and the fact that I was so different from them made the situation for me all the more unbearable. At least they held my modesty in high regard and this brought both acceptance and consolation, which helped me adjust to the openness of their ways. They comforted me with laughter and soothing voices.

They were mesmerized by my blonde hair, which they unfastened, flipped, twisted, lifted, fanned and combed through with open fingers. They braided it, unbraided it, braided it again and decorated it. Each person demanded a turn. They competed and judged among themselves, who could fashion it the prettiest. They laughed endlessly about my pubic hair being blonde and brought me to impossible levels of discomfiture. During those moments, I could have made the ripest tomato look pale by comparison. Bashful as I was, this was one of the most uncomfortable experiences I ever endured.

They pampered me, fussed over me, washed me, and sent my clothes out to be scrubbed. They expressed unending dismay and sympathy over my skin's show of festering pimple like infections caused by the countless prickly pear needles still embedded. While half the women played with my hair, the rest worked to remove what needle fragments they could. They all ridiculed their men for being so stupid as not to know a woman when they saw one.

The intentions of these women were nothing if not good and forthright, and I was calmed enough to begin taking notice of my surroundings. The outer skins that covered our tipi had been raised a few inches above the ground, which allowed for light and cooler air, and the occasional breeze, to enter from below and then rise up to exit through the opening at the top. The floor was swept clean. Circling the inside of the tipi, a safe distance back from the fire pit was a thick covering of freshly gathered grass. It filled the air with a pleasant fragrance and provided comfort while lying about isolated from the confusion and heat of the afternoon.

Over the next few days, I spent all my time conversing with Talk-a-lot and the other women in the privacy of the tipi. They were full of questions about me, my life, and wanted to know from where did I come. They also were eager to know all about the rumors of the wagon and its wares.

I answered the best I was able, and in return I learned a great deal about their way of life. Most importantly, I learned amid an outcry of laughter that no one was planning to prepare me as a sacrifice. I had to admit that such a notion seemed absurd within the friendly confines of the menstrual lodge. However, in my defense it must be said that I carried a great deal of mental baggage—a head chocked full of horrid tales about Indians that I refused to believe could be all lies and exaggerations.

In any event, for the time being, I cautiously allowed myself to enjoy being pampered and having people back in my life after so much time spent alone. I did feel safe in this company, and entertained no thoughts of escaping or wandering off from the tipi and my newfound friends without good reason or well-laid plans.

From Talk-a-lot, I learned how highly respected was Ho'neheveho within the tribe. He could not thank me at this time, for I was menstruating and this was considered very bad medicine for him. I was informed that while I sat with the women, Ho'neheveho, and a number of other braves were going through a purification ceremony in his lodge. The men were compelled to do this, lest they be wounded or killed in battle. There had already been some accusations alluding to the fact that if I hadn't been menstruating, Ho'neheveho would never have encountered his misfortune. Fortunately, there were those who came to my defense. Either way, I was expected to remain in the menstrual lodge for four days or until my bleeding had passed. This was no small matter.

I learned that during menstruation I was not allowed to cross the path of any man. I was not allowed to enter the lodge of any warrior or chief. I was not allowed to be near any medicine or sacred items such as amulets, war bonnets, or weapons of any kind. Women were expected to remove themselves to the menstrual lodges in order to preserve the well-being of their men.

I first found such customs amusing and occasionally demeaning, yet I kept my opinions to myself and accepted their explanations and guidance with due respect. I came to understand through our conversations that although men were the lords and masters in this society as in most, and that at first it might

824

appear as though women were banished for being women and crowded into menstrual tipis, this was not as it seemed.

The attitude of the men towards the women of the tribe was respectful and significant. Women were held in high regard. They seldom partook in the meetings of council, but rarely was a council meeting undertaken that didn't address their concerns. It was they who maintained the harmony and preserved the well-being of the tribe. They were less likely to fly off the handle and rush off into battle or make rash, revengeful decisions. They did not hesitate to impress upon their men or their chiefs what they expected of them, and it was not wise to disappoint them.

It would have been easy to assume that the men spent their time sitting around eating, betting, smoking, and being lazy while the women worked their fingers to the bone. The women were always dressing hides, making clothes, gathering firewood, cooking, and raising children, but I was taught to view it from a different perspective.

The women assured me that every time their men left camp they lived in quiet fear, worried about their safe return, worried about what might happen while their men were away. Out on the plain, the lives of the men were fraught with danger. There were often encounters with warring tribes. There was hunger and thirst. There was serious injury and death. Hunting and killing buffalo was extremely dangerous work, but the men had to bring back food. The lives of all depended upon it, and risks were a large part of assuring success. To have their men sitting about relaxing and gaining strength, to hear them laughing, was a time free of worry, a time of plenty—to have them gone was the opposite.

Ho'neheveho was a perfect example of all they said. They were greatly relieved to have him back, and the fact that I had attended to his wounds placed me in a position of respect. They were determined to repay me for my kindness. I was told that as soon as I was free to leave the menstrual lodge, Ho'neheveho would hold a dinner in my honor. Preparations were already underway.

During my stay in the menstrual lodge, I noticed on a couple of occasions a certain ritual that struck me as very peculiar. During the evening, some of the visitors in our company stood before us in the tipi and produced a sizable length of a rope, which they centered at the small of their back. They then pulled it forward around their sides, to be tied off in front just below the navel. At this point they drew it down and passed it back between their thighs. Next, they separated the two halves, and wrapped each around a thigh, sometimes as far down as the knee, where it was then tied off.

About this, I was very curious and I discovered at once from their explanations that although sexual issues were readily discussed and openly accepted, chastity was absolute in unmarried women. Any girl who failed to maintain her respect was shunned throughout her life and often was unable to marry. She brought disgrace to her family, and it was not uncommon to hear she had hanged herself in remorse. Most all women wore this protective rope at night. They also wore the rope during the day if they were traveling away from the tribe.

If any man should violate the protective rope, it almost certainly meant his death. If not killed by the men of her family, then he was often beaten mercilessly or exiled by the women of the tribe. The fact of rape wouldn't save a young girl from dishonor, but fortunately the occurrence of such a crime was virtually unheard.

Any illusions I may have harbored regarding heathen immorality or the wanton sexual activity of savages was soon put to rest by these women, at least as far as the Tsistsistas were concerned. These people abided by laws that were chaste, strict, and generations old.

Talk-a-lot fussed over me endlessly by offering me drink, food, blankets at night, or other items of comfort. Without tiring, she demonstrated a concern for my contentment. I accepted all her efforts with appreciation and allowed her to tend to me as she saw fit, for it was explained to me by her and the others that I was an honored guest, and I bought them all much esteem and good medicine by association.

And so, Talk-a-lot was thrilled to answer my many questions. She was a willing conversationalist and exhibited the enthusiasm and patience required to teach me some of the useful words of her language, and even more important, the customs of her people. The fact that I showed an interest in her life, as well as that of her people and their ways, pleased her immensely. Fortunately, she would never know that deep down inside I came from a place of nearly insurmountable fear, and how these questions I asked of her helped alleviate long nights and bad dreams.

It was fortunate that I made a friend of Ho'neheveho's younger sister. If Talk-a-lot had been his older sister, custom dictated that she would have been forbidden to speak with him for life after reaching the age of about fifteen. Instead, by being the younger sister, she witnessed all and was able to tell me most everything about her brother.

In our conversations about Ho'neheveho, Talk-a-lot revealed to me information about him that struck a warm chord within my heart. Rather than living the ferocious life of a warrior who commanded raiding parties across the plains for the purpose of stealing, scalping, and letting blood, as I would have supposed, his primary purpose as a chief was to care for the widows and orphans.

I was amazed to hear this, finding it nearly inconceivable that such concern for the welfare of others existed within a tribe of supposed savages. Sadly, Talk-a-lot could not appreciate the coincidence of my life and that of her brother's, each paralleling the other in our convictions and devotion to pursuing a similar mission in life.

While in the menstrual lodge we bathed twice a day, once first thing in the morning and then again last thing before retiring. While we were indisposed, other women in the camp brought our food, washed our diapers, rags, and also our clothes so that we were prepared to leave the menstrual lodge dressed presentable.

Compared to the civilized life of the white man, where a woman had to keep to her chores and labor sunup to sunset no matter how severe her cramps, no matter sick or miserable she felt, I found myself preferring the 'unenlightened' manner of the Cheyenne. These women retired from the trials and tribulations of daily life to rest for whatever time necessary until they felt well enough to face the world anew.

There were so many revelations, so many aspects of these people that had never once been mentioned during the hours of storytelling that only depicted death, destruction, and dismemberment. Their lives were hard, but to say that they were uncivilized or savage seemed extraordinarily incorrect. After only a few days spent with these women, many of my former notions about Indians seemed ill advised and began to crumble.

I waited in the menstrual lodge for two days more than need be, for I had no desire to venture outside before Talk-a-lot was herself ready to leave. Normally we would have left the menstrual lodge early in the morning, ready to be free of our confines, but because I was to feast at the chief's lodge, we instead waited until his summons arrived, which happened late in the day. This was not unexpected nor considered rude, for all feasting and merriment was usually done at night after sundown when it was comfortable to be outside gathered around a fire.

Word of the feast was everywhere, and so when Talk-a-lot and I finally exited the tipi, we were prepared to be engulfed by a large crowd of curious women that had gathered to await my appearance. Many had brought their blankets and mats to sit upon and work while waiting the day out for a chance to see me and my blonde hair.

I still readily blushed over the purpose of my stay in the lodge, yet I was not now nearly as embarrassed as before, even in spite of the fact that the whole world knew why I was there. Nothing was subtle about being a woman in this place—no secrets, no hiding facts, no escaping inhibitions. Here, these truths about women were accepted and expected to be well understood by all. Fortunately, in front of this evening crowd I had some help from the reds and oranges of the setting sun, which effectively masked my reticence.

EIGHTY-EIGHT

Talk-a-lot lived up to every letter of her name, and as long as I was willing to listen, she was willing to speak. I didn't find her obnoxious, but bubbly and engaging, and I understood that I gave her the opportunity to improve her English, which she seemed to learn at a remarkable speed. In only days of conversation, she was learning new words almost as fast as I could teach them. It was quite a contrast to the way in which I struggled to learn even the simplest words of her language and it made me feel stupid.

"Haonovahe, does it bother you that I always call you Talk-a-lot instead of your real name? I'll stop if you wish."

"No, we have much names. Two, three names together. My father say Haonovahe. My friend say a name different. I like Talk-a-lot because you say name. A gift. My family hear you say Talk-a-lot. It is a good name. It sound good."

"I can't believe how fast you learn English. I try so hard to learn your language, but it is not easy. You learn fast, you speak good English."

"Yes, before, I say much English. Before, I live with white man. Before, I know much English, but I forget. Now, I know more because I hear words more."

"You never told me that you lived with whites. Why have you never told me this before? I can't believe you never told me this."

Haonovahe shrugged her shoulders. "This bad memory. I very young. I say I live on Missouri River. I play with boys in…." She looked at me as she searched for the word.

"Semo—semo…."

Then her face lit up and she started paddling in the air. She was clearly showing me the motion of propelling a canoe. What a strange thing to see in the desert. I felt a fool to ask.

"A canoe?"

"Yes, a-canoe. We play in a-canoe. You understand?"

"Yes, yes, I understand."

"The water is high, very fast when snow go. The a-canoe go in water. Not good, bad. The boys leave, but me, no. I afraid. I see boy die in water. I stay in a-canoe. I afraid many days. I go far, ho hae'še, ho hae'še, very far. A white man, Louis Ward see me in semo. Louis Ward good man. Give me food. I live with man two seasons, many moons, long time. Louis Ward take me home. I learn much English words and French words. I tell words to others. I tell my brother words."

I believed all she said, for if nothing else, Talk-a-lot was a natural born teacher. I guess it was common sense to bring me to her. She was the translator. With me, she began at the beginning and for the three days we spent together in the tipi, she explained many of the basic customs of her people so I would act with respect in her brother's lodge.

"The entrance?"

"Yes. The entrance. Always look east. Always look rising sun. Always. The man always sit at back. He sit at back and look east. Always. Ho'neheveho always sit at back. He bed there. He always look east. He look out entrance. When you go in tipi, you see fire you see Ho'neheveho at back. He look at you.

830

"Family always sit this side in tipi. Always. This custom. Family live this side of tipi. You no go there. Only family go there." Talk-a-lot had indicated the south side of the tipi, the area to my left as I would enter. "When you go to tipi, you stand the entrance. Ho'neheveho say 'come, Elizabeth, come, sit with me'. You go in. You go this way——." She indicated north.

"To the right."

"Yes, to the right. People go to the right, family not go to the right. You see fire. Elizabeth not walk here. Man here, fire here. Elizabeth not walk here."

She motioned in the middle, between the person sitting and the fire pit.

"This no good. This bad. This——."

"Rude?"

"Rude?"

"Not nice."

"Yes, not nice. You say, rude. No walk here. Not nice, rude. You go here, not here." Talk-a-lot at first walked behind me to show proper passage, then before me to show what was rude. "Much time people say 'walk here'. Then good, when people say 'walk here'. You understand?"

"I understand."

The teaching never stopped and by the time Talk-a-lot led me from the menstrual lodge to Ho'neheveho's tipi, I had learned a great deal. His was one of the large lodges I saw when we first arrived. The outer skins of the tipi were coated in a whitish pigment of clay or mud. They were covered with painted symbols of bison and hunters with their weapons. There were symbols of other animals that I assumed to be sacred or special in some way. Stars and circles portrayed the heavens and other scenes appeared to depict battles.

I took closer notice of the six poles embedded near the entrance that suspended strings of feathers, shells, and beads. There were two prominent tripods situated amid the poles. One supported a headdress of feathers; the other a shield fashioned out of thick leather and adorned with the same assortment of decorative work.

A travois was leaning up against the lodge, and I couldn't help to notice that my wagon had been moved to a position close by. I also noticed much to my surprise that after my three-day absence, nothing appeared to have been taken from the wagon. That alone revealed something about the character of these people.

As was the case of the menstrual lodge, the chief's tipi was not the perfect cone I had come to expect by all I had read and seen as a child. In fact, I noticed that all tipis actually leaned over instead of pointing straight upwards with the peak in the center. Its footprint upon the ground was not circular in shape but oval.

The entrance was positioned opposite the blow of the wind, that is to say, on the east side or leeward. Drafts and flying debris were further sealed out by means of a protective wind flap. Because the weather side of the tipi stood nearly vertical, it made the family area in that half of the lodge more accommodating. The opening side of the tipi, considered to be the front, leaned over into the vertical side, and became a strong support against the hard blows that nearly always came down out of the mountains to strike the tipis from the west.

These were small and meaningless details to the ordinary white man, but I was taken in by such subtleties. It revealed to me a sense of pride, a need for perfection. It reflected skills and refinements in tune with their ways of life. In other words, in this very different, this very wild and dangerous world, I readily saw the signs of a profoundly intelligent people that possessed traditions, morals, civic minds, and survival skills that were finely honed.

As we had heard in the menstrual lodge, Ho'neheveho kept informed of our progress and prepared his feast accordingly. Once we arrived at the chief's lodge, Talk-a-lot threw back the wind flap and the full aroma of roasting meat escaped to swirl about us. She stepped aside.

"You go."

"No, you go first."

"No, you go! Go!" Talk-a-lot pushed me inside.

I wasn't about to argue my preference while standing at the open entrance way where Ho'neheveho could see me, and so I entered nervously.

Ho'neheveho was seated at the back of the tipi just as Talk-a-lot said he would be. He looked up, and when his eyes met mine, his face broke into a wide comforting smile. He was visibly pleased to see me. Promptly, he signaled me to enter and be seated to his immediate left as his guest of honor.

"Né'éstséhnêstse, né'éstséhnêstse, come in. come in."

Showing respect for the private area of the family, I walked around the lodge to the north, to the right of the tipi as instructed by Talk-a-lot. I was pleasantly surprised to discover how roomy and accommodating was the interior. Ho'neheveho attempted to reposition himself in order to greet me, but I objected. Instead, I immediately dropped to my knees and lowered myself to his level. He was wearing a broad smile.

"Népévomóhtâhehe?"

He was asking me a question that I did not comprehend. I turned to Talk-a-lot feeling embarrassed for my ignorance. She jumped right in before the chief could begin his own translation.

"You feel good", she said?

"Yes, thank-you. I am not afraid now." Talk-a-lot relayed back my response, which drew a good laugh.

"Hámêstoo'êstse. Sit, Elizabeth."

He used what English he knew, mixing them with his own language as he patted the floor beside him. I took my place at his left side as guest of honor, close to the bed and mat upon which he rested his leg. Talk-a-lot seated herself behind me upon the next bed. The rest of the family and tenants remained to his right, on the south side of the tipi and occupied the space between him and the entrance.

I was reacquainted with Hotoomee'e (Shelter Woman), his wife, and introduced to his sons, Ho'evanestoohe (Howling on the Ground) and Hotoa'ôhtšêhe'kêstaestse (Short Bull). They were all warm with their welcome. Afterward, I asked Ho'neheveho if he still suffered much pain and how was his leg healing.

"Épéva'e, good. I not afraid."

He was teasing me, and the remark brought a smile to my face. Through Talk-a-lot, he conveyed that he had received a fitting punishment for his foolishness. Indians never rode at night, but an unexpected encounter with a herd of buffalo clouded his better judgment. They had stumbled upon the herd and weighed the risks. They elected to sneak up on the animals with the intention of frightening them closer toward the camp.

I asked and received guarded permission to look over his injury. The wound was draining, and this was good. I was perplexed by a notable show of opposition to my returning to the wagon for fresh bandages to redress the wound. Likewise, I perceived concern over my work and looked to Talk-a-lot for an explanation.

From the moment we entered the lodge, she explained every detail, every activity that took place. She explained that there was bound to be hard feelings because their medicine man had not been called upon to perform his work when the leg was first broken. Now, he might see fresh dressings and be further insulted. I had no idea how to respond. I looked at Talk-a-lot and shrugged my shoulders.

"You no worry. My brother make it good. You no worry."

Shortly after we returned to our places, Ho'neheveho instructed an orphan who lived with them to take a message to a certain old man. It was an invitation to receive food from the chief's lodge. This was done to show the generosity of Ho'neheveho, which earned him respect and at the same time set a good example for others in his tribe.

Instead of going directly for the old man, the boy stepped outside the tipi and immediately began to shout at the top of his lungs as he moved off into the distance. At first, I thought his yelling typical of children all over the world, and I laughed to hear such commotion from the lad. Talk-a-lot looked at me quizzically and a discussion followed whereby I learned that acts of generosity were announced loudly for all to hear. It served to set example.

The old man soon arrived and stood at the entrance. He was greeted and then invited to seat himself across the fire from Ho'neheveho. He stepped forward and sank to the ground. I was told that the man was now old, but that he had been a great hunter the whole of his life and fed many through the years. He was favored by the Great Spirit and honored by Ho'neheveho for a lifetime of giving.

Along with the old man, I was expected to remain seated and be provided whatever my need as the family went about their business preparing to serve the food. The chief and the old man conversed, which momentarily removed me from the center of attention and allowed me time to relax and collect my thoughts. I retreated from the talk in order to look around and take note of all the articles and possessions that described this family. I reached back to touch Talk-a-lot, drawing comfort from her being near and questioning her on much that I saw.

I first studied the tipi. I counted nineteen poles sunk into the ground and lashed together at the top. They were covered over with at least fifteen or sixteen tanned hides, taken specifically from old buffalo cows for their particular properties. Surprising to me was the discovery that the inside of the lodge was also covered with hides from the ground to about a third of the way up the tipi. This provided extra insulation from both the heat and the cold. It also stopped all dust and sand from blowing inside. The bottom edge of the inner hides were laid inward across the earthen floor and held in place by a carpet of grass and the weight of the beds. This effectively stopped all drafts across the floor that might interfere with the fire or cause discomfort.

There was an opening at the peak of the tipi fitted with two wing-like appendages that controlled the upward draw of air, which entered the lodge from behind the inner hides. By this means, the lodge was continuously purged of smoke and freshened with outside air, and yet because the inner hides acted as a screen, at no time was anyone exposed to drafts.

There was no lack of space in the larger of lodges. In fact, there was sufficient room to bring prized horses inside at night for safekeeping if need be. The size of the lodge was needed to house the many people living with the chief. I was told many of the larger lodges housed the owner, his immediate family, possibly some animals, but also quite often a number of people from his extended family. Many widows and orphans could also be found within, providing some small service in return for shelter and food.

The size of the lodge was dependant upon the wealth of the owner. It was obvious that more poles and skins were needed in the construction of a larger lodge, but that was not what necessitated wealth. What was not so obvious unless pointed out by someone such as Talk-a-lot was that any man could build a large lodge, but only a wealthy man owned enough horses to move it.

It required two or three horses to drag the poles and another horse or two to carry the lodge skins. But, this was only the beginning for the owner required additional horses to move his family and all their possessions. These people were nomadic and every aspect of their lives—every decision, every activity, reflected this fact.

A central circular portion of the ground had been cleared of grass and carved away to within about four feet of the sides of the tipi. It was lowered about three inches. This formed a circular ledge of sorts all the way around the tipi. Upon this ledge grass was laid down as a cover. On top of this grass was placed the bedding.

The bedding as with all other items belonging to the Indians was designed to be transportable. It was made this way by laying down a mat of willow stalks. Each stalk was cut about four feet long and placed in a neat row, side by side and tied together with sinew until the row reached a length of seven or eight feet. Once fastened and completed, the bedding could be rolled up tightly and placed upon a travois for journeying.

Another type of grass was woven together loosely and laid down as a mat upon the bedding of willow stalks. Atop these mats were placed two, three, or even four softened buffalo hides, some thickly covered with hair to make up the bed. These beds were placed around the perimeter of the tipi, about four feet apart. In this lodge there were six of these hide-covered beds, enough to sleep the Chief and his wife, Talk-a-lot and her sister-in-law (by our way of speaking), two sons, two widows and two orphans. The remaining bed was free for guests, in this case for me.

In the space between each of these beds, there stood a three-legged tripod or a four-legged stand hinged to spread open from the top. Tied to the top of these stands and hanging down to either the head or foot of the bed were backrests constructed in the same fashion as the willow mats for the beds, only made with lighter weight stalks.

The backrest was shaped roughly like the letter 'A'. It was narrow at the top, the stalks being only about a foot in length. At about shoulder's height, it spread out to a width of four feet, and thus continued on down at this width to meet the bed. Also tied to the top of the stand, and draping down to cover the backrest was yet another hide.

Each end of the beds was outfitted with a backrest and hide as described. When assembled and in place, the bedding and backrests offered the occupants a very comfortable area to lounge about and relax. They also provided the only semblance of privacy within the confines of the tipi, something like stalls in a livery.

Packed tightly between the legs of these backrest stands was the food. The majority of which appeared to be dried buffalo meat, and this stored in great quantity for times of scarcity. There was another food described by Talk-a-lot as a pounded meat. There was an abundance of dried corn, squash, turnips and beans, these staples being cultivated by the tribe and now coming to harvest. There was also an assortment of dried roots and fruit, most of which were berries dried and formed into small cakes. All of the bowls, eating utensils, tanning utensils and ornaments were neatly placed between the legs as well.

Lastly, there were a large number of rawhide bags, some big and some small. The Indians often called one of these bags a 'parfleche'. This was obviously a French term and undoubtedly learned from the early French explorers and trappers that traversed these lands. Now the term appeared to mean most anything made of rawhide.

The most common parfleche was generally made to be about three or four feet long and a foot to foot and a half wide. Talk-a-lot noted my interest in the bags and told me that when they were filled, they rested comfortably across the rump of a horse. The bags provided a means for transporting the possessions of the lodge when the camp was moved. In these bags were kept items of all descriptions, all the goods that a household collected during their years of travel.

The fire pit at the center of Ho'neheveho's lodge was bigger than most. It was dug to a depth of about eight inches and shaped like a cross. Each leg of equal length, each leg directed toward one of the cardinal points. A man never started the fire, which burned continuously. Custom dictated that only a woman perform this ceremony.

In the coals of the pit were two copper pots, two clay pots, and three pots made of hides. Above the fire pit was a skewer of roasting buffalo meat. The tipi was filled with the aroma of the meat and after so many weeks of eating out of a pot in the open air devoid of any culinary ambience, I could say I felt myself seated for a banquet. My mouth watered and my stomach growled with impatience.

Three other men, all chiefs, were also asked to join Ho'neheveho in my honor. They arrived and sat across from us as well, but in spite of their rank and social position, they did not request the old man to move back from the fire. Instead, he was given all the courtesy of one of the chiefs. They were introduced to me as, Eše'he Ohmo'ôhtavaestse (Black Moon), Eše'henâhkohe (Sun Bear) and Hahpêhe'onahe (Clenched Fist). The old man was called Haa'êstoo'onahe (Longjaw). At that point, all were present and the meal was to begin.

"Néxháóénâtse!" Ho'neheveho called for prayer.

I learned from Talk-a-lot that her people always preceded their eating or feasting with prayer, an offering of thanks to the Spirits for their generosity and the hunter's good fortune. This was no different than being back at home seated around the table with heads bowed to thank the Lord for his blessings.

Ho'neheveho removed five pieces of meat from the roast buffalo and placed them in his hand, palm side up. The pieces represented the four directions called Nivstanivoo. Each of four pieces was positioned on his hand to symbolize one of the four directions, and the fifth piece, placed in the center of his palm, the sky.

He then chanted a prayer of thanks, at the same time thrusting his hand to the east to offer his food, then the south, the west, and finally the north. After this he raised his palm upward to the sky and finished his prayer. He then placed the food down alongside the fire pit, where it remained untouched.

Talk-a-lot explained that the meat was no longer considered food, for the Spirits had partaken of it, and now it was nothing. It would be swept away. The prayers and offerings took time to complete for they were recited with reverence and repeated without haste for each vessel containing food. If Ho'neheveho hurried the prayers in behalf of my growling stomach, I would never know, but the moment I awaited finally arrived.

"Mésehe! Eat!" Ho'neheveho demanded of everyone seated about the fire.

"Méseestse, Eat." He urged me with a smile.

Hotoomee'e, the chief's wife, moved forward and began to fill the bowls with stew. The old man was fed first. He was given a large bowl of stew and as much food as he could carry in his hands. Having received enough for himself and his family, he removed himself from our company and stepped outside to announce in a loud voice that his dinner was provided to him by the generosity of Ho'neheveho. He walked through the camp and repeated the announcement many times before retiring to his lodge.

As the old man's voice became fainter in the distance, we all began to eat. All except for Ho'neheveho, who touched no food, for he was our host. Instead, he prepared his pipe. I was encouraged to take what I wished. Aside from the roast buffalo, we also had buffalo stew and corn. The stew was rich with meat, gravy and an assortment of roots and beans. Ho'neheveho looked up from his pipe to observe me.

"Etóne'éno'e?"

"How taste?" Talk-a-lot asked me.

With a mouth of filled with food, I attempted to smile. "I like it. It tastes good, very good, thank-you." I spoke to Talk-a-lot, but my eyes remained fixed upon Ho'neheveho. She was my mouth and I watched his reaction as her words carried my gratitude.

"Nápêhévé'áhta. Epêhéveéno'e"

Ho'neheveho smiled broadly and nodded his head with satisfaction. Meanwhile, I discovered that as my life became reduced to the basics of fear, friendship, hunger and sleep, so to was my palette adjusting to the basic and simple dishes of the land. I found my meal to be every bit as delicious as it smelled.

While we ate, a warrior of high honor was summoned and soon made his appearance. He was invited to sit and eat with us. After satisfying his hunger, he was asked by Ho'neheveho to count coup. Because it was difficult for me to understand what was taking place, Talk-a-lot took the time to translate. The result of my ignorance was to receive a much more graphic and detailed account of the warrior's response to his chief's request.

I struggled to keep my appetite, for I discovered to give or count 'coup' was to relay one's personal accounts of bravery and accomplishment while engaged in battle or during raids. War stories in short. In an attempt to make sure I wasn't deprived of any detail, the warriors gestured freely, showing precisely how they scalped their victims, how they slit their throats, how they disemboweled them and kept them alive to watch their own innards writhing upon the ground.

One might think four hours of this type of thing might get boring, but nothing could be farther from the truth. In fact, I never appreciated how many ways a scalp could be fastened to a shirt, or the variety of patterns that could be made up with human teeth. All of which was displayed to best advantage for my benefit.

These accounts of bravery were relayed to me with great fervor by at least six or seven warriors all told. It was a far cry from the dinner theater I was accustomed to in Boston. But, believe me when I say, between the oratories, the intensity of the delivery, and the vividness of the gesticulations, it equaled anything I had ever seen before. Sadly, nothing was left to my imagination.

I continued to nod with amazement and false approval, all the while strangling myself in order to keep my food down. To my dismay, there was indeed a darker side to these people, but for now I felt safely distant from ever seeing or being a part of those activities.

The warriors ate alongside the chiefs and myself, and upon finishing their counting of coup; they left the lodge when deemed appropriate. Other than being somewhat brutal, as far as dinners go, the night progressed on smoothly, everyone about me appearing to have a good time until the medicine man announced his presence. He had grown impatient after waiting hours outside to be summoned by Ho'neheveho, which never happened. Ho'neheveho did not wish to be rude, but understood once the medicine man entered the lodge, all other activities would be disrupted. He was not mistaken.

The man was introduced to me as Ma'heo'ôhme'ehnêstse (Medicine Comes In Sight). I could see at once that he was not pleased by the acquaintance, and by his state of agitation I could also see that he was very concerned about the healing I had performed without his guidance. I also understood he was not at all happy about my presence in the chief's lodge, for he had brought many sacred articles to drive out bad spirits.

Whatever it was he was saying, it was having an adverse reaction upon my hosts and their guests. Ho'neheveho listened patiently to every one of the medicine man's complaints and then paused for a spell to show respect by taking an appropriate amount of time to think about what he had been told. He then spoke up with a wonderful air of authority, appearing to go into a lengthy defense in my behalf, explaining things to the medicine man that I could not begin to understand.

The family members remained still and wide eyed, listening intently to the conversation now taking place between the medicine man Ma'heo'ôhme'ehnêstse and the chiefs seated with me at the fire. The expressions upon the faces of the chiefs made me more than a little apprehensive about what was being said. Visions of human sacrifice were springing up afresh in my head as I considered how badly the medicine man wanted me out of their lives.

I tugged at Talk-a-lot who said nothing, but looked at me with grave enough concern to put the fear of God into me. Suddenly, Ho'neheveho reached for the amulet about my neck and made great issue of it. He gestured vigorously back and forth between his leg and me, attempting to obtain good of it. This quieted the medicine man down, but his eyes turned in my direction. They remained filled with suspicion, as if to say *'I will be watching you. I'll be first to roast you alive. It will be I who disembowels you. I will eat your heart!'*

I learned from Talk-a-lot that although I had nearly worked a miracle in my doctoring of her brother's leg, the medicine man argued with conviction that the accident would never have happened in the first place if I had not been menstruating when Ho'neheveho encountered me at the hollow. It was a bad omen and there were certainly more to follow.

Talk-a-lot said very little to me during these events, but I understood. In my lessons on basic customs, I learned that one never interrupted a speaker under any circumstance. Because I was not considered to be in the conversation now taking place, no opportunity to speak would be afforded me. So, I motioned with my hand to draw attention and was thereby recognized and allowed to speak. I looked to Talk-a-lot for a translation.

"Talk-a-lot, would you tell Ho'neheveho and Ma'heo'ôhme'ehnêstse that I would like to leave the tipi so I might get my gifts of strong medicine? Tell them that I was not able to give them my gifts before because I was in the menstrual lodge."

This she did, and the announcement brought silence as fast as the fall of an axe. I imagined their minds were racing, for the items hanging all about the outside of the wagon had been viewed for almost a week by a thousand coveting eyes. Talk-a-lot urged me to do so quickly, and I arose from the fire remembering to step behind the chiefs and the medicine man as I walked around the tipi to exit.

There was an audible gasp when I threw back the wind flap and suddenly appeared from within the lodge. At first the people backed away quickly, obviously frightened by my sudden and unexpected appearance. It was a large group of people that had gathered outside Ho'neheveho's tipi.

One reason was they wished to see 'Heova'e'e', the 'Yellowhair Woman'. Another was most assuredly the knowledge that the medicine man was most upset about me. A final reason, and undoubtedly the one most enticing, was the wagon, which had been brought alongside the lodge. They looked at the tin pans and kettles and the myriad of metal items, all of which were greatly desirable, for they had only wood, leather, bone and stone for tools and utensils.

They watched me closely, but I ignored them, and climbing into the wagon, went quickly about my business. Once inside, I collected an assortment of decorative beads, a selected length of fabric, some ribbon, a steel knife in particular, a steel file, nails, a hatchet, and an assortment of other odds and ends, most of which I placed into a large steel pot.

I returned, lugging the large pot filled with gifts, and presented it to Ma'heo'ôhme'ehnêsts. When I did so, I determined it best that I not cower nor take the position of an inferior. I looked the medicine man straight in the eyes as an equal. He viewed the gifts before him, and he studied me, but said nothing. He then turned his attention toward Ho'neheveho and the other three chiefs.

The gifts seemed to stir up a second discussion as intense as the first. There was not the heated nor agitated gesturing of before, but nevertheless there was a great deal of debate and the gifts were studied and scrutinized. Ma'heo'ôhme'ehnêstse made a couple of final comments, which visibly pleased Ho'neheveho and the chiefs. He then opened his parfleche and produced a bundle of sage grass, which he lit and waved it back and forth across the gifts. At the same time he began to chant. He rose to his feet and paraded the burning sage about the tipi while praying to the spirits. He circled the burning grass over my head many times.

Talk-a-lot broke my concentration on the medicine man when she placed her hand upon my shoulder from behind. She still sat upon the bed and along with the others; she expressed a silent sense of relief.

"You good spirit. All good now." She whispered only these words and nothing further, but it was a speech to me.

The medicine man occupied himself with either expelling evil spirits or blessing the lodge; it made little difference to me either way. What was important to me was understanding I wouldn't be staked to the desert floor, and also learning that the medicine man was no person to cross under any circumstance. The look upon the faces of the family, including the worry visible on the face of the Ho'neheveho at the beginning of the discussions made this fact very clear.

The medicine man eventually left and the stress of his visit wore us out. Ho'neheveho even stopped struggling to speak to me in English. It wasn't worth the effort as long as Talk-a-lot was in our presence. Besides, he understood that she enjoyed using the language and he allowed her the prestige that translating brought before the chiefs. He would occasionally say a word or two, first in his language and then in mine when he saw fit.

"Elizabet."

"Yes?"

"Népévomóhtâhehe? You feel good?"

"Yes."

"You sleep here, yes?"

"Yes."

"Épéva'e. Good."

We finished our meal with a prayer, just as we had started. I felt bloated and sluggish. Food was plentiful for the time being and there was little want to be found. I was in a lazy mood and ready to lie down for a peaceful nap, if not a secure worry free night's sleep upon the luxurious hides in Ho'neheveho's lodge. He on the other hand, had an entirely different idea in mind.

EIGHTY-NINE

With the exception of Talk-a-lot, the chiefs, and myself, Ho'neheveho commanded all those in the lodge to take their leave. As soon as they departed, he lit his pipe. He raised it to the sky, moved it to acknowledge the four directions, and then passed it to me.

I placed my mouth over the stem and drew in a breath that immediately started me into a fit of choking spasms. My lungs protested, my eyes rained tears, and I felt as though I were blowing smoke out my ears. Talk-a-lot was quick to my rescue and immediately spoke to Eše'he Ohmo'ôhtavaestse, who was seated to my left, and who promptly relieved me of the pipe.

The incident was embarrassing to say the least, but my apparent frailty warmed the chiefs to my presence. They grinned with expressions that I instantly recognized as universal for affirming that I belonged to the weaker sex. In another place, another time, I might have protested, but at this point I was more

846

than happy to let it go. However, when the pipe was next passed, I was a good deal more judicious.

The smoking of the pipe was a sacred ceremony, and it was for this reason Ho'neheveho had commanded his family and the others to leave. Their departure was only one of many aspects to the ritual. I noticed there was a specific positioning to the pipe when it was placed on the ground, its stem pointed east. There was also a specific manner in which the pipe was passed; it never went around in a complete circle.

It was first passed to me, and then on to my left, clockwise, until it reached the opening of the tipi. At that point, rather than pass the pipe across the entrance of the tipi, it was returned counter-clockwise in the direction from whence it came, past me, past Ho'neheveho, and on to those seated at his right. It was always done this way.

As we ate, smoked, and talked around the fire, a number of things were explained to me regarding my gifts, my wagon, the wares, and more. In these conversations, I learned that the reason nothing had been stolen from my wagon wasn't so much due to the righteousness of the tribe as it was due to their fear of possessing white man's belongings. They believed that it was dangerous to do so and could bring them great spiritual harm. For this reason, they crowded around the wagon to marvel at all its enviable goods, but dared not touch a thing. The medicine men contributed heavily to their fears.

It was this belief that prompted the discussion earlier in the evening, after I offered gifts to the medicine man, Ma'heo'ôhme'ehnêstse. Everyone wanted the gifts in the worst of ways, but the fear of evil spirits caused great consternation. In the end, the medicine man determined as long as he first sanctified the articles, then they could be given and received without concern.

On another matter, I was astounded to hear the reason why Ho'neheveho wished me no harm, and in fact saw to it that I was well fed and protected. Through the translations of

Talk-a-lot, I listened as he declared that in 'matsé'omeva', the season of spring past, an Indian had foretold of my coming.

Ho'neheveho called the wayward Indian, Hestoxehnêstse. The name meant 'Walks Last', and was given to him because the man was traveling alone without his family. He was searching for them when he encountered the braves and followed them back to camp. He claimed to be the last of his tribe to leave the land where the sun rose beyond the great waters.

He brought with him many stories of sorrow, many stories of evil spirits that lived in the hearts of the white man. He told of how white men put up fences and prevented others from walking and hunting the land. He told of the white man's cruelty. He advised the chiefs to be wary, for the future was not promising. He said the white man could not be stopped, but even worse, he could not be trusted.

The Indian also told Ho'neheveho and the chiefs to watch for a pale skinned woman with hair colored as the sun, and to befriend her at all cost. He said she would travel through these places, and advised that she be protected. In return she would teach them well the ways of the white man and bring with her the blessings of the Great Spirit.

He spoke of her as having strong medicine. He said she came to his village and sought out an injured girl. He said she put her medicine into a brush, which was used on the dying girl's hair, and in that way drove out the evil spirits that lived inside her head. Afterward, the girl opened her eyes, arose, and walked. He said the Great Spirit spoke to this woman in dreams by night, and guided her by day. He said she wore an amulet given by the girl's mother for protection, and that she was called Elizabet.

"You say you Elizabet, yes?" He smiled.

"Yes, I said Elizabeth, and that it was a refined name. I remember."

"Yes. I see sun hair. I see good." Ho'neheveho made a motion that referred to the amulet and then patted his broken leg.

Upon hearing all of this, I looked at Talk-a-lot with an expression of sheer amazement. I could hardly accept that Shadow Hunter might have traveled this far west, but in one fashion or another he had made contact with these people.

Ho'neheveho went on to say that he wished I would tell him and the other chiefs more about the white man and how to avoid their anger. He wished to know how to obtain their medicine so his people could live easier lives. And so to please him, I spent the following hours telling stories both good and bad about the white man and their ways until the chiefs no longer knew what questions to ask.

They were baffled by almost everything I said. They were mystified by the white man's ways, which made absolutely no sense from their point of view. They had great difficulty comprehending the ownership of land. To them the earth was a living spirit and could never be owned by a mortal. They laughed at such a notion, looking at me with sorrow for being so foolish.

Bathed in the glow of the fire, we discussed many things and smoked many times while sounds of Indian song and dance echoed in the night. I had reached a point where my mouth tasted terrible from smoking of the pipe, and I was yawning repeatedly. I was far past weary, but concealed my discomfort. I wished only to stretch my legs and lay back upon the thick furs in the bed.

At first I thought I wasn't alone for Ho'neheveho asked the chiefs to help him to his feet, but rather than move back to his bed, or indicate his intention to call it a night, he instead rose to his feet and prepared to leave the lodge. He ushered us out before him. In spite of my distress, I made no complaint and walked with the chiefs. As soon as we stepped outside, the ceremony was concluded and Hotoomee'e, her family, the widows, orphans, and the rest moved back inside.

I followed the chiefs and Talk-a-lot to the center of camp, where earlier in the day Ho'neheveho had directed a large fire be built. This was done, and as we walked away from the tipi to join in the activities I began to sense that the chiefs who walked with me were more than average leaders in the camp. I came to realize this after observing many more chiefs about the campground who suddenly began to move in our direction. Once we exited the tipi, these unknown chiefs appeared out of thin air, drawn toward my hosts until we stood in their midst, their number being all of thirty and then some.

After we had taken our places close to the fire and with a good view of the dancers, I began to question Talk-a-lot on this issue and she confirmed my suspicions. My hosts were men of special status indeed. They were the four chiefs who presided over a council of forty lesser chiefs. The four had no special powers, but were held in the highest esteem by all the people. Such prestige was earned through a lifetime of bravery, and even more importantly, generosity. Talk-a-lot was very proud of her brother and wished that I knew what kind of man he must be to have earned such rank.

She told me how Ho'neheveho had taken seventeen scalps in his days as a warrior. He was fierce and brave in battle, and could count coup for the whole of a night if asked, but he was modest. He was also a loving man, generous of heart, patient, and good to his family and people.

If a woman should come to him for food, he would give her all she wished. He would give her fire. He would give her a horse. All of this even if it left him to starve, holding nothing to eat, and no horse with which to hunt buffalo. If he met the same woman on the plain and she was returning home with a broken horse, he would give her his horse and walk back to camp with hers, even though she was nothing in the eyes of others, and he was the leader of his people.

If a man of the tribe held a complaint against her brother, and if the accusation was wrong and unjust and the man chose to whip Ho'neheveho, he who had it in him to take those seventeen scalps would raise no hand in defense. He could be beaten and abused unto the point of death, but Ho'neheveho would raise no objection.

If his wife should fall in love and run off with another man, he would find no fault in her action. All of these things were beneath him. If a man asked to borrow his buffalo robes in the dead of winter, he would freely give them with no expectation they be returned. He was a man who gave himself wholly to his people and expected nothing more than further word of their needs. His life was devoted to leading, caring, and serving his people.

Of men, two things were expected among Tsistsistas, unquestioned bravery and unlimited generosity. To become a chief over average men who held such high standards was no easy task. To become a chief of chiefs meant Ho'neheveho had to guide his followers as a lesser chief for ten years, living above and beyond the virtue of all other men. It was a seemingly impossible undertaking, but these he had accomplished and his people were loyal to the death in his honor.

As I listened to this and more, I found myself growing numb with ignorance. Such civilized manners could barely be found in the world in which I lived and yet I had never heard of Indians having any virtues at all. I felt as though I would explode from a desire to tell everyone back east that these people were hardly bloodthirsty savages of Satan's brood.

These people lived simple lives, and simplicity brought clarity. There was life and there was death. In this world the two were blended together. And whereas 'Sudden Death' was a harsh reality back east, out here the meaning became vague. Out here, the need to survive was the same, the need to eat, sleep, take a mate, and raise a family in peace was no different than back east except that these basic truths were not masked by the clutter of civilized trappings and greed. In this land, life often appeared brutal, but also beautiful, and above all else it was nothing if not honest.

I kept looking over at Ho'neheveho and considered that the man couldn't have been that much older than myself. Yet, I sensed he had lived a thousand more lifetimes of experience. I began to see the wisdom gained from those years of experience as it emanated from his being. It showed in every measured and well-thought move he made. I was filled with admiration for the man, and for this reason I wished to perform some deed that would enhance his standing among his people. I already knew how to do this even as I was thinking of it. I also realized that my gesture would assist me in leaving at my will.

I asked Talk-a-lot to tell her brother that I wished the medicine men to purify all the wares on my wagon. I asked her to tell Ho'neheveho that I wished to make a present of my belongings to him, and that I only wished to keep my trunk, those things close to my heart, and what else was needed to travel in safety. These things only would I set aside. I asked her to tell him that I wished all to know his generosity and that I believed by giving these gifts to his people he would earn great praise. I wished to thank him for my care and I asked to be welcome in his lodge forever more. I asked her to tell him that not all white men were bad medicine.

Talk-a-lot grew very excited and did all that I asked. I could see by the expression in Ho'neheveho's eyes that he was both astonished and overwhelmed by my generosity. He asked Talk-a-lot to tell me that he had never seen such generosity. He said his people would have no way to return such a deed. He said he didn't know how to accept the enormity of my gift.

I asked Talk-a-lot to tell him that I could never be as generous as he, for I could never find it in my heart to give up all that I possessed to another. I asked him to understand that I was just the hand of a much greater spirit that wished this gift be given. I hoped some day he might meet the great white man that gives his heart freely to all, as does Ho'neheveho. He asked by what name was this man was called.

"Claus."

852

"What mean, Claus?"

I had to think about this need to know what was behind a name. How could I describe the integrity and generosity of Christopher?

"He is a saint, a chief who gives to those in need. He is like you."

After this having been said and translated, Ho'neheveho appeared somewhat perplexed, as if holding back questions, but mostly he looked pleased. He assured me that I would always find shelter within his lodge and food at his fire. He signed with his hands to say that his heart and soul were mine.

Ho'neheveho asked if he might be excused, and returned to his lodge with the other chiefs assisting him. He instructed me to await his return and so Talk-a-lot and I remained to watch the festivities. I would have guessed it about three in the morning when the crowd began to move apart. Ho'neheveho and the other chiefs were working their way toward the center of the grounds near the fire. As soon as they stepped free of the people and could be seen by all, a hush fell across the camp.

Ho'neheveho began to speak and Talk-a-lot turned to me.

"He speaks of you."

"Why?"

"He say, you sent to us. He say you help Indian child;—he say you are with many spirits. He say, spirits bring you with many gifts, good medicine to the people. He say, you brave. You ride as one. You not afraid of bear—."

"What bear?" I asked with concern. Talk-a-lot looked at me puzzled then returned to listen.

"He say, Ého'néhevêhohtse. He say you have wolf footprints."

"What does *that* mean?"

"It means you smart. You more smart than men. He call for you, now. Come. We go."

She stood up and bent over to pull me onto my feet. The people stepped back from where we sat and gave us room to walk ahead and join Ho'neheveho. I stood with Talk-a-lot, centered amid hundreds of strange faces, their eyes staring and sparkling in the flicker of the campfire.

Above the crackle and roar of the fire, Ho'neheveho began to speak again. Talk-a-lot listened, glanced my way and smiled. Hers eyes darted back and forth between her brother and me. There was more to what Ho'neheveho said, but I didn't understand. For a split second I thought of the fire and sacrifices, but I put that idea right out of my head at once.

"What is he saying? What is he saying?" I asked Talk-a-lot, while burning with curiosity.

"He'kotoo'êstse! Be quiet!"

"Haonovahe, please. What is he saying?" I prodded her under my breath.

"Vehona'e. He say, you, *Vehona'e.* Chief woman. Vehona'e. He say, you show brave, you show heart. You now, Chief Woman, Vehona'e. Yes, Vehona'e."

It was then, Ho'neheveho called for a headdress, which he raised into the air to show all his tribe. Talk-a-lot urged me to step forward, and he lowered it upon my head. It was a beautiful cascade of eagle feathers, bird feathers, beads and bones. The feathers were fastened to a rawhide crown, and were splayed outwards like the outstretched wings of a bird. Underneath the wing-like spread of feathers, more of the same fell away in rows, hiding the flaps at the sides of my head upon which they were mounted. Narrower straps decorated with hawk feathers and down, fell along my back. A number of rawhide laces were fastened to the crown just ahead of my temples and fell along my breast. These were decorated with colorful beads, shells, and stones among other things. It was unlike a war bonnet in the sense that the feathers did not rise upward over the head and fan out backwards.

This was a scene never envisioned in the wildest of my imaginings. I had to convince myself that I wasn't dreaming, that I was indeed being honored as a chief among a race of Indians that terrified me to death only days before. I looked deep into a mob of faces set aglow by the light of a roaring fire that burned on the edge of a western plain far beyond the awareness of Mary, Allen, my friends in Boston, and most all white men.

I turned away from the light to stare into the darkness of night, into the distance where stars met the eastern horizon. I was overcome by emotions that went unnoticed by Talk-a-lot, Ho'neheveho, and those around me. I reached out to another time and place.

"You wouldn't know me, Mary. I don't know myself anymore, but I'm still alive—I am still very much alive."

NINETY

Talk-a-lot and I stepped back from Ho'neheveho and the fire. We returned to our places where we remained seated as persons of significance for the remainder of the night. Talk-a-lot relished her opportunity to introduce me to the lesser chiefs and the medicine men of the camp, not to mention the throng of ordinary Indians who wished only to connect with a good spirit or see blonde hair.

I met most all the chiefs, and my initial belief that the camp was enormous was confirmed when I learned from Talk-a-lot that this meeting of the tribes was the largest to be held for the year. According to her, all of the tribes, which comprised nine or ten divisions, had come to sit around the fire.

The number of people gathered at this camp was in the thousands. The chiefs came to discuss the future of the people, but just as important, they came for entertainment and an opportunity for young men and women to socialize. Single people such as Talk-a-lot were forbidden to take a mate from their own tribe, no matter how far removed. This was strictly prohibited amongst the Tsistsistas unless it was a union with one of the Arapaho, another tribe of Indians who traveled with the tribe and added their numbers to swell the ranks.

This year, the gathering of tribes was of great importance because of a profound difference in opinion over what region of the country the Tsistsistas should secure for their permanent home and hunting grounds. For generations they had traveled north and south with the seasons to enjoy favorable weather and follow the herds of buffalo as the animals sought fresh grasses to graze upon.

Now, half of the tribes wished to leave the north for good. They felt that too many unknown tribes were entering northern ranges and causing trouble. Even worse were the attacks by the Hóheeheo'o, which I understood to be a tribe of Sioux that possessed white man's guns and slaughtered Tsistsistas on sight.

These invading tribes often became unfriendly because of misunderstandings or when the need for food and shelter increased. It was my understanding that the number of tribes entering the historic hunting grounds of the Tsistsistas was increasing dramatically. These strangers were fighting for their own survival after being forced from their homes and pushed onto the plains by the white man or Indians he supplied with arms.

Tribal warfare had uprooted the Tsistsistas twice before in the east and there were those who wished now to take a firm stand and face the Hóheeheo'o and their guns, and fight them to the death in order to protect the hunting grounds. But there were just as many who wished to avoid further confrontation with the Hóheeheo'o, preferring instead to remain forever at their winter camp far to the south and do business with William Bent, a well known trader who was constructing a permanent fort and trading post. They believed there was a lot to gain by trading buffalo robes with the white man and were not so afraid to break with old traditions.

For now the gathering was a good time for all, but the camp would be forced to break up in short time. Ho'neheveho explained that when the camp was so large, it could only stay together briefly because their number kept buffalo from roaming near, and this meant that the braves had to ride out farther and farther to locate the herds. It made feeding so many people difficult. That is why if at all possible, the hunters drove the herds into the area of the camp so they might avoid the difficulties of transporting the meat. It was much easier to have dinner stampede home.

As an older chief Ho'neheveho no longer went on raids as frequently as he did in his younger years, but he still kept his skills sharp and his body firm by taking to the hunt on a regular basis. He was on just such a hunt, driving a herd back toward the camp when startled by the sight of the wagon so near his people. This was something most Indians had never seen in their lives and a cause for much concern. Ho'neheveho said at the moment he turned his attention toward my wagon, his horse was gored and tossed aside to fall onto his leg.

Although I apologized profusely for being a party to his injury, he would have none of it, insisting it was the result of his own stupidity. Indians knew better than to chase buffalo at night. In any event, I was compelled to make good on my promise of the night before and spent the day sorting out the goods in my possession. Aside from personal keepsakes, I kept about ten percent of the stores. This included all my food, my guns, powder and packing, a few pots and pans, the barrels for my water and a small collection of items for bartering.

Ho'neheveho accepted my gifts graciously and living up to his reputation, he set out at once to distribute everything to his people with the exception of a few items held aside for gifts to the lesser Chiefs. The grounds about his lodge were riotous with hopeful recipients. The hunting parties stayed at home and joined in ranks with those hoping to leave with a treasure in hand.

The atmosphere was festive with the sounds of people exclaiming aloud the generosity of Ho'neheveho as they paraded about holding their gifts high in the air. Food was plentiful at every lodge and games sprouted up everywhere. Everyone went home that night more than satisfied, for even receiving something as insignificant as a nail was considered good fortune as it could be used for an awl, a scriber, a spear tip or a weapon.

Over the course of the following days, Ma'heo'ôhme'ehnêstse, the medicine man continued to pay particular attention to Ho'neheveho. Seeing his improvement helped him to accept me as possessing a good spirit. I don't believe he had much choice in the matter if he wished to remain in favor with the chiefs. I suspect it was for this reason that he elevated me to a spiritual position of high regard amongst the tribe. The act pleased the chiefs enormously and kept him in both good standing and control of the situation.

NINETY-ONE

The Tsistsistas were unable to agree on a place to call home, so the tribes decided to separate into two camps. A smaller faction would head south, hoping to profit on the furring trade with the whites at Fort Bent, while the majority would head back north toward Black Hill country.

The large communal lodges had all been dropped and packed up. The women had been busy finishing up the tanning and scraping of hides, the making of pemmican, and now were dedicated to packing their parfleches.

There came the final morning when the camp appeared barely a remnant of its former size. It was early in the morning and the last of the tribal chiefs had already struck their tipis and started their journey south. We watched them heading far out across the plain, poles and travois strapped to their horses and dogs. They were trying to beat out the midday heat.

A group of us had been collecting firewood and buffalo chips up along the ridge and from that height the view of the exodus gave me the butterflies. I was contemplating my own future and discussing my thoughts aloud with Talk-a-lot while returning to camp from the hills. She sensed I wished to move on and was pleading with me to stay with her and the tribe, and although I knew that was impossible, I was unsure of what would shape my own destiny.

Talk-a-lot and the other women carried their loads back to the lodges in the customary manner, which is to say they strapped bundles of wood about three feet long across their shoulders and upper back. I was not used to this and found it painful, so preferred to collect buffalo dung, which I placed into sacks suspended at the ends of a stout pole. This I could span across one shoulder or two, lift waist high behind my back or to my side, or drag like a travois.

We took our time hauling the loads and talked all the while. I was telling Talk-a-lot about my life back east, her favorite topic, for she was very curious about our ways and generally insisted we discuss such things. She marveled at the descriptions of material things that filled my life, a life that seemed both complicated and dream-like to her. It was all beyond her comprehension and although she didn't believe I would lie to her, she had to put my stories into a spiritual context in order to make sense of what I said. I believe she rationalized in her own mind that these mysterious and wonderful ways were the ways of gods, and somehow I was connected to the spiritual world in a very special way.

Talk-a-lot viewed me with reverence. In fact, I had come to be treated with more respect than ever by everyone except for Vonêstseahe, the brute that accosted me at the wagon. I was asked frequently to overlook his persistent groping by the women who freely offered apologies in his behalf. They repeatedly reminded me that he was an Arapaho, and that he was filled with unlucky spirits, which caused him to do very strange things. They also offered up the fact that he rarely ever bothered ugly women.

Translated, Vonêstseahe meant 'No Brains'. Everyone knew he was attracted to the women and fondled them often, but he had never hurt anyone. The tribe put up with his unacceptable behavior because of his low intelligence and excused him from being punished for acts that would never be tolerated in a society as chaste as theirs. He was so outrageous at times the men would watch and laugh with disbelief—and he made everybody but me laugh. All to often it was the men who put him up to no good for the sake of their gambling or entertainment, all at the expense of the women.

At first, I accepted what my friends said, because aside from the actions of the brute, there truly was a high degree of respect for all women of the tribe; myself included. This was no more evident than at this gathering of the tribes where I saw first hand much of the courting done by young men toward the girls. The men always made known their intentions in a socially acceptable manner that was quite strict in nature, and according to Talk-a-lot, could last as long as five years.

To my way of thinking the humiliation would have been unbearable, for I had seen men waiting outside lodges for seven or eight hours in order to speak with the women of their desire and not be given the time of day. I had seen men return to the same lodge day after day before friends and neighbors without ever being recognized. This might go on for weeks, but no matter what, respect for the woman was always observed.

If a woman chose to shun her suitor, he removed himself from his cause and left with a badly bruised ego, but he accepted his rejection without belligerence. For the lucky man who was accepted, he then spent hours standing with the woman of his desire beneath a blanket. Thus, their relationship would begin innocently enough as a couple standing amid the crowds with a blanket over their heads for privacy.

Unfortunately for me, whether it was due to my blonde hair, my fair skin, or the fact that Vonêstseahe was an Arapaho, my lone suitor lacked any hope of mental normality or morality. He didn't subscribe to the appropriate manners of the Tsistsistas. Instead, he dogged me relentlessly and tried my patience to no end. It became obvious to all that he was fascinated with me and now no longer spent time harassing other women at the far ends of the camp. He was always around.

To be polite, and to respect the wishes of the women, I bit my lip and exercised restraint when my every impulse was to slap the man silly. I endured his continuous groping and affronts, always allowing the other women to chastise him in my place. For the most part they chased him away and kept him at bay, but too often he got away with murder. In my opinion, he was mighty quick for a moron.

Every bit as annoying was the laughter that erupted from the other men, who often encouraged him to stir up trouble while they stood around waiting and watching his advances. For this reason more than any other, my patience was wearing thin and the laughing at my expense made me bristle with irritation.

It may have been because everyone was leaving, that Vonêstseahe had become much more aggressive than usual. It may have been that he thought he would never see me again and that drove him into being all the bolder in his attacks. Whatever the reason, it was irrelevant to me and I knew only that it had to stop, even if it meant going to Chief Wolf to put an end to it.

Oddly enough, I had just interrupted my conversation with Talk-a-Lot when returning to the lodge so I might make mention of this very issue, for I had seen Vonêstseahe darting about. There was no longer a crowd of tipis for him to hide behind.

She supported my decision then drew me back into telling her further of my life back east. We had entered the camp when

Vonêstseahe slipped up quietly behind us. I looked away from Talk-a-lot for only a second, about to question her on why so many men were standing about looking at us. I had hardly begun to ask, when a pair of arms reached out around me from behind and pinched both my nipples painfully hard.

Instinctively, I dropped my load and folded my shoulders inward, crossing my arms to protect myself. Thus my behind was perfectly exposed when he made his second attack. He thrust his hand between my legs from behind and pinched me mercilessly on the tender part of my inner thigh. I cried out in pain.

I knew instantly what was taking place and lurched forward to spin around and face my tormentor. I was furious. I had reached my wits end with this brute. My reaction brought forth a boisterous round of laughter from those idle men who obviously put this mindless soul up to no good once again. They were falling all over themselves, squealing like brats in their idiocy.

Game or no game, it mattered little either way, for the pinches were not kind. They were painful and I found no humor or honor in his prank. I was seething with anger. Talk-a-lot stepped in to intervene, but I blocked her advance with my expression of fury.

In my fit of rage, I bent down and reached for the pole that suspended my sacks. It was now second nature for me to possess only the finest poles—poles of pride, strong and straight to keep in my reach. I was fully ready to accept whatever the consequences of my intentions. While the idiot was looking about in the direction of the men and relishing all the attention, I slipped the pole free of the sacks and brought it around with all my strength. Feeling the solid pull of its weight within my grip. I laid it square into the back of his knees.

Vonêstseahe landed flat on his back with a resounding thud that was heard by all. The laughter about me came to an abrupt halt, to be replaced with wide-eyed stares of disbelief. The brute lay stunned for a moment and then the moaning stopped, and regaining his senses, he shot up to his feet. He had the look of a wild cat in his eyes, for he had been dishonored before his peers. It was the same look I saw in the man at the canal. He may have been a moron, but he knew anger.

Before the crowd of braves could move forward, the brute, who was no longer laughing, charged toward me in a dead run fully intent on revenge and regaining his honor. It was certain that he was bent on attacking me, something the Tsistsistas would never consider. The other men knew this incident had immediately grown out of control and may have worried about what their pranks might bring in the way of reprimands should I be injured. They moved at once in my direction to intervene, but the brute was well ahead of them.

I stood perfectly still with my staff vertical as Dorrie had taught me. At the last second, I flipped the shaft horizontal and held it firm as he plowed into the business end of it. It nearly punctured through his breastbone. I could only imagine the pain, by far much worse than a pinch. The wind rushed out of him, his ribcage making a hollow drum-like sound.

Infuriated, he reached for the end of the staff, but Dorrie taught me well what to expect, and I had already retrieved the pole. I let it slip through my hand until I had hold of the end once again. I spun around quickly and brought the staff about full circle. I felt the proper force of its pull, and landed it across the back of his knees a second time. He crashed to the ground with a great 'ummph!' as the wind again was knocked out of him.

By this time I was looking for blood and praying that he would get back on his feet. I was shaking with anger. All at once the men charged in and grabbed the brute by his arms, raising him off the ground and back onto his feet. He tried to grasp what had taken place and was now glaring at me with murder in his eyes, and I loved it.

"Come on, you pig!" I screamed. "Let him go! Let him go!"

The others held him as he struggled to free himself. I was blind with rage and began to chase off the men who held him from me, threatening them with my staff, which they now took seriously enough to back away. I was not to be deprived of my revenge. The men accepted my wish with amusement and let the man loose. They quickly began placing bets. He charged directly for me just the way I hoped; full of anger and void of brains. I wanted him in the worst way.

This time I held the staff horizontal along side my waist. I looked down the shaft as he approached knowing he would try to grab the end and strip me of my weapon. He made his play and I rotate the far end up over his head. Instinctively, his arms went up as they followed his eyes, while down below, the other end of the staff came around and up full force into his breech-clout. Only luck would keep him a male after that blow.

With a terrible scream, he clasped his crotch and fell to his knees. The staff arched around and stopped dead across the back of his shoulders, knocking him forward, his face slamming into the ground. He left me with the one target I couldn't resist. I swung around with all my might and brought the whistling staff to meet his ass. It drove him flying forward to be fully laid full out across the spilled sacks of dung.

I stood there praying he might have even a little fight left in him, but I soon settled down to the point where I realized he was in terrible pain. It had been covered up by his blind rage, but now it totally engulfed him. He lay motionless upon the ground, crippled with agony and holding onto his manhood. I left the dung where it lie beneath him, and walked back toward the lodge with Talk-a-lot, who for the first time ever had nothing to say.

Neither did a peep come from any person to be seen. Chastity and respect were conventions strictly adhered to, and the only reason Vonêstseahe got as far as he did was because a few unscrupulous Indians had put him up to it and then stood by to watch. I had challenged them as well and knew that Vonêstseahe wasn't the only one who learned a lesson. I also knew it was time for me to leave the Tsistsistas.

I entered the lodge both agitated and ashamed. As a chief I had failed miserably. I could never command the discipline these people acquired over a lifetime of training. It was impossible for me to accept the irrationality of others when it adversely affected me and mine. To be wrongly attacked and turn a cheek, to rise above the injustice was not my nature, somewhere deep inside I was driven to defend, to claw, and to spit back.

Ho'neheveho, who was under a great deal of pressure to stay off his feet and rest in preparation for leaving, had been watching through the opening of his lodge and was witness to the entire incident. The confrontation had occurred almost directly in front of the tipi. To my surprise, he looked up at me and broke into a broad grin. He motioned for me to sit beside him, which I did, so he could put his arms around me. He embraced me strongly and held me until I settled down.

"Névóomâtse (I saw you.). Vehona'e. You brave. I see. Yes." He went on speaking to Talk-a-lot, who in turn translated.

"He say, you no afraid of bear. You smart. He say you teach boys no touch women. This good. He very happy."

"It is time for me to go, Ho'neheveho." I looked at him with the truth in my eyes. "It is time for me to go. I must go." I gestured with my hands the need to leave.

"Yes," he said with certain sadness.

I let out one last deep breath and felt myself relax. It was over. I was free.

The following morning I packed up my belongings and hitched up the mules. This was not a welcome sight to most, and the Indians were very remorseful of the brute's deeds, believing his indiscretion the reason for my departure. They believed I moved with a great and powerful spirit, and did not wish for me to go.

"I want you stay."

"I must go, Talk-a-Lot. I have things I must do. The Great Spirit tells me it is time."

"It because Vonêstseahe. He bad."

"No, it is not because of Vonêstseahe. He is not bad, he is only stupid."

"Please, stay."

"I can't, Talk-a-lot. I can't." I leaned over and warmly embraced her. I had grown fond of my younger companion; she had done much to my advantage.

"You tell everyone that Great Spirit told Vonêstseahe to make me restless, to keep me from getting lazy and fat and spending too many days around the fire. He was told to pinch me so I would stay on my feet. The Great Spirit pushes me to move on. I must go. I must find another great spirit."

Talk-a-lot never doubted what I said, for in her eyes everything about me was mystical. I left Haonovahe with a hand mirror, a brush and a large snuffbox of crushed nutmeg wrapped in a splendid red ribbon. The gifts thrilled her beyond words to describe.

"Oh! Mé'konáséto. (Oh! A braid tie.) Oh, thank-you, thank-you, Elizabeth. Thank-you for my gifts. Thank-you."

"You are welcome, Haonovahee. Nêstaevâhosevoomâtse. (I'll see you again.)" I did my best to say good-bye in Haonovahe's own language. I made a mess of it, but she understood and took my farewell to heart. We let loose our grip and I moved away to take my leave.

As I headed up the team, the Indians came first on foot with many items of food and clothing. Ho'neheveho had turned my wagon into one large fur lined bed. He had wanted to give me horses in return for my help, but understood my explanation for declining such a gift. I wasn't able to care for horses without

866

knowing when and where I might find water. I often could hardly quench the thirst of the mules. To show his gratitude he had the wagon lined thick with his best buffalo hides to make a soft bed. He sent along dried fruit, pemmican, his finest furs and robes for my comfort. I had emptied the wagon of most everything it contained and Ho'neheveho had filled it back up.

I headed south out of camp along the eastern edge of the mountains. Vonêstseahe was still lying in the same spot where he fell the day before. He had been given a blanket and pillow for his head and sympathy for his manhood. He was conscious but in enough pain that he preferred to sleep where he lie. My statement about him being used by the Great Spirit had absolved him of his sins. The other Indians came collectively to offer their apologies and determined to fast and meditate on their foolishness and lack of respect for women. This was undoubt-edly the advice given by Chief Wolf.

As I looked behind me at what remained of the camp, I remembered the state of fear that engulfed me when I was first arrived. I remembered trembling at the sight of young braves riding out in force to meet us, watching them circle about on horseback like crazy people, a whooping and a hollering. Now, they appeared entertaining, wild with life, giving me a show of their horsemanship and their attention for my amusement along with a safe escort across the highlands. They rode alongside my wagon for the whole of the day then spent the night. We sat and signed. We ate, drank, and laughed until finally overcome by sleep in the warmth of a fire.

The next morning we arose before the break of day. Amid a flurry of farewells and affections, I headed out leaving the braves behind. They would return to camp and join the warriors that stayed to protect those families yet dismantling lodges. They remained long enough to watch over me until one final ridge rose high enough to separate us.

I had left my mark on these people, one not soon to be forgotten. As for myself, I had been permanently changed.

God had presented to me the same lesson as always. Knowledge brought friendship and fortune, ignorance brought hatred and fear.

One way or another, I had expected always to be haunted by a lifetime of European prejudice and ill advice in regard to Indians. And so it was to my surprise, I should be far less happy to leave than even I might have known. But then, once the Indians dropped from sight, I was left to face those dreadful feelings of desert loneliness that were instantly back to feed on me.

NINETY-TWO

Attitude was everything. I say this because during my short stay with Ho'neheveho, Talk-a-lot, and the Tsistsistas, I nearly forgot about my weeks of blistering battles against the same sun, wind, and sand.

During my stay, when I looked toward the horizon from Ho'neheveho's lodge or from the upper ridges while gathering wood, I found myself beginning to view this vastness with a sense of awe and respect—no, not respect—reverence was a better word, a sense of reverence.

I considered how whites always warned me to have 'respect' for the desert. I understood now that it was because the white man was the invader, because ignorance meant fear, and one 'respected' something fearful. Settlers couldn't imagine living in a place void of trees. Without trees there could be no homes, no fences, no fire, no animals to hunt, to trap or corral. A life without trees was a life without sustenance, a short life indeed.

The Indians on the other hand offered living proof that the white man was wrong. They were perfectly matched to this treeless terrain. They understood it. Their knowledge came from generations of venturing, generations of adaptation, years of learning to live in harmony with their surroundings.

I realized that if a woman truly wanted to know the beauty of this land, she would have to see it through the eyes of the natives, for I seldom heard a white man voice anything good about it. In fact, most influential Easterners did little more than share emotional rhetoric and dire warnings of certain death or insanity from venturing into such a desolate expanse, the exception being specific waterways where beaver thrived or money might be made.

Maybe they were right, and yet, the intimacy between the Indians, the grasslands, and the foothills, left me warmed to the heart. I observed how successfully they managed their lives in this place, how perfectly efficient was their every move. There were no excesses. They were not blinded by greed or the material distractions that belied the reality of life married to death. Theirs was a perspective entirely different from my own. Whereas my life recognized a spiritual realm, their lives thrived in one. They seldom differentiated between the natural and supernatural, for they were woven into the fabric of life and land by a myriad of spiritual threads that presented a perfect pattern.

These were sons and daughters swayed by mystical forces since times unknown. To the Indians, the earth, the sun, the moon and stars, the wind and water, all were sacred facets of their existence. The ground, which we so despised, they worshipped at every meal, at every activity. All of nature was a living spirit in their eyes as real as the horses they rode upon, and so they took from it only what was needed, careful not to be greedy. They were grateful for whatever gifts were bestowed by their gods, and quick to show appreciation by giving thanks and sharing in their success.

Ho'neheveho never disputed that their lives were often difficult, but he never blamed the land or described it as an adversary. He might express it as being hard, but hard like a parent, or being moody like a spouse, or even disagreeable like a child, but never as a force to be feared like an enemy. Like family, he accepted the many faces of nature as they presented themselves, overlooking the faults and cherishing the virtues.

Unfortunately for me, a few weeks spent with Ho'neheveho and the Tsistsistas was not nearly the lifetime needed to mold my heart into feeling the same endless love for the land. And so, now that I was back to traveling alone, my so-called civilized prejudices were back as well, and my outlook quickly collapsed into that of an east-coast white woman fighting for every inch of ground gained.

It was again oppressively hot. It was again dry and barren with any water found to be often intolerably alkaline and cause for nausea. Again, distances grew impossible to measure and time slowed to a halt. My lips were once more becoming chapped and in need of grease and my eyes soon grew blind to the beauty that had surrounded me only days before. In short time, I came to view my occasion with the Indians as hardly more than a sweet and memorable break from the monotony and boredom of my crawl across a dirty floor.

The mules worked hard at pulling the wagon sun-up to sunset, nothing like my mind, which barely worked at all. It was all I could do to simply stare ahead and stay upright on the bench as I sank deeper into an overheated hibernation. Nothing ever changed and I had no reason to wake up. I was reduced to a single dream, my desire to find Christopher, and only that one goal kept me pressing forward farther into the unknown.

The blowing wind and clanging of what few pans I still possessed made noise enough to stifle any sound, especially the songs of birds, the buzz of bees, or anything that might come as a pleasant distraction to the ear. There was nothing else of any magnitude to hear in these miles of wide-open spaces. So, needless to say, when the head of a horse appeared from behind me along with a boisterous *'How-do!'*, I nearly dropped dead from the fright it gave me.

The very last thing I expected to see was another face. The idea of watching my backside by scouring a hundred square miles of emptiness in order to know if I were being followed was utterly beyond reason. It was insane. Nobody was ever that lucky.

Yet, against all odds, and sitting forward in a saddle directly behind a set of chestnut ears and a blowing mane was this sandy haired, blue-eyed man with boyish features and a wonderfully infectious smile. He had a guitar slung over his back, a smart looking overcoat, and a perfect row of gorgeous white teeth. They were now spread wide across his face. I was also quick to notice that within inches of his hands were a long arm and two holstered guns lying securely across his saddle. On the surface, everything about him smacked of trouble.

I had little doubt that he noticed the way in which I nearly jumped out of my skin at his greeting. It was a miracle I didn't fall off the wagon. It was embarrassing to say the least, and I felt like a supreme dolt for being caught entirely off guard. I got exactly what I deserved for spending all my time submerged in a mindless stupor. The man tipped his hat.

"Afternoon, ma'am."

He worked that smile effectively. I said nothing, but acknowledged him with a guarded look as he paced his horse alongside.

"Wasn't meaning to startle you like that, but I didn't think it wise to discharge my pistols in order to announce my approach. You might have gotten the wrong idea, maybe thought I was out to rob you and your...." He stopped short. His eyes darted about.

"Are you traveling alone, ma'am?" He stretched his neck to peer about me.

"What concern is that of yours?" I responded, not trusting him in the least.

"Merely an observation, a question and nothing more, I assure you."

"In that case the answer is no. I never travel alone. *Smokey!* We got company!" I hollered out.

871

I lied. This was one of those times when lying was smart and not sinful in spite of the fact that I liked the way the man spoke. First impressions were important to me, and he sounded educated or at least well read. Even so, I kept my eyes on him, for this was perfect country for no-good drifters and opportunists alike. Only the cunning and conniving survived, and a man had to be one or the other in order to be alive and sitting in a saddle.

"Smokey? Is that a dog or somethin'?" he asked.

"It's a somethin'." I answered, as I produced my pistol and pointed it directly at him. His eyes opened wide with surprise.

"So it is, indeed! Maybe, I should have been introduced through a friend."

"What is it you want, mister?"

"A moment of your time and nothing more, I swear."

"You men are good at swearing. Oaths and lies are generally about the same when uttered by your kind. I'm not much fond of anybody who comes sneaking up from behind. Now I'm asking again. What is it you want?"

"Begging your pardon, ma'am, but we've really gotten off to a bad start. If you would just halt that team a moment, I could ride off a couple of rods and then we could yell back and forth a spell and maybe get to know one another."

A smart-ass. My luck never changed. If there were but one man, I guarantee he would pick, polish, and present his gift, then blame me eternally for eating it. Without taking my eyes off the stranger, I pulled on the reins and brought the team to a halt as he suggested. He stopped as well. I was now free to grip my pistol with both hands and so sighted him in squarely down the end of the barrel.

"I like it just like this, you being nice and close. Keep your hands on them reins or I will blow your head off," I threatened. "Now I am going to ask you one last time, what is it you want?"

"Very well." He raised his hand to tip his hat.

"Hands!" I hollered. He dropped it instantly and exhaled with exasperation.

"*If*—I may introduce myself—I go by Lucky Laredo. My friends call me that, and you may also if you wish, otherwise, I started out this life as Luke and you can call me that as well. Or you could call me Lucky Luke if you prefer, or for that matter—."

"Can you not hear me?" I interrupted. "I have asked you a simple question. What in god's name is it that you want? Or am I to assume you are asking me to blow your brains out and end your miserable existence."

"Lord, no! I ain't askin' any such thing. Life's short enough already. Really, ma'am, I mean you no harm. You must try and settle yourself. I would be foolish to provoke a lady such as yourself equipped with a gun, such as that one—pointed at my head, such as it is—out here in the middle of nowhere, such as we are—out here where there isn't a soul to sit with over a good cup of coffee on a cold morning for ten thousand godforsaken miles. Out here where it's easier to swim in a mirage than say nothing to a passing stranger, and I mean to say."

"Oh, for god sakes, *shut up!* Do you never stop rambling on. I got your point. Unfortunately, you didn't get mine." I cocked the hammer. "I am impatient and nervous, and that is not good because I'm told I shoot like a scared rabbit when I get that way. I get jumpy, and instead of squeezing the trigger like this;—I jerk it, so it releases when I least expect, and…well…. I reckon you can imagine where that leaves you—you and all your guns."

Again, I lied as I looked down the barrel at him. I prayed he would believe my every word, because I could never shoot anybody who smiled with such allure. For that matter, I could never shoot anybody under any circumstance. The stranger sat atop his horse in silence. He said nothing for a moment, choosing only to stare at me until finally asking with caution.

"Are you a little more relaxed now?"

"Not very."

"Speaking frankly and to the point; I am out of water and supplies. I was given some bad directions for a short cut to Santa Fe and stumbled into a party of Blackfeet returning from a raid. They looked pretty beat up, and I guess they figured on taking their whipping out on me. I don't mind telling you, I barely escaped with my scalp. The fact I'm here is proof I outfoxed them, but it says nothing about how they chased me half way across this godforsaken continent before giving it up."

"I applaud your good fortune, but it all sounds like your problem and has little if anything to do with me."

Again I lied. Just the sound of Blackfeet put the fear of God into my heart. I gulped, yet I had no desire to get friendly with this man. My comment did little to slow him down.

"I refuse to believe that a woman as comely as yourself can be this mean spirited. Whether it be imagination or misunderstanding, I'm not sure, but I swear I mean you no misfortune. I am merely disoriented."

"Is that a man's way of saying he's lost?" There was another pause. This time he looked a little annoyed.

"I reckon it *could* be put that way."

"You reckon. I see. Have you anything else you would like to reckon? If so, I suggest you spit it out and be quick about it! I wish to be on my way."

I allowed him the use of a hand to rub back and forth across his chin. When he resumed his story, his speech started out slow and deadpan.

"You are one *hard* woman. I was about to say that the Indians kept me zigzagging back and forth for a good three or four days until I finally gave them the slip. Unfortunately, I gave myself the slip as well. *Lost*, if that's what you prefer. Anyhow, I saw your wagon tracks, and by god, I have never seen the likes of those out here before. I couldn't believe my eyes, and I knew for fact they weren't there the day before so I made for em' straight away. I was mighty surprised at the sight of them. I don't believe I have ever seen a wagon in these parts. I don't know that anyone has.

"Anyways, not that you would care, but I haven't had a drink in two days, and I was hoping you might at least spare me a bladder of water. Aside from that, simply point me to the nearest outpost north of here and I'll be gone, out of your sight forever. On that you have my word."

Under his breath, the man mumbled something certain to have been insulting, but said nothing more aloud much to my amazement.

"I don't have a clue where the nearest outpost north of here is." I responded.

He studied me a moment. "What!" This time it was he who looked surprised and so I repeated myself.

"I said, I don't have the faintest idea where the nearest out-post is. Does that seem surprising to you out here in the middle of *ten thousand godforsaken miles*, as you put it."

I could see he was confused. His eyes narrowed into slits. His mouth broke open as if preparing to voice a thought.

"Aren't you a peddler that goes from place to place?"

"Mmmm. Well, not exactly. I feel more a traveling side-show, I think."

"You're telling me, you have no idea where *you* are?" He studied me then twisted his head around to study the sur-rounding country.

"Nope."

"Well, where are you comin' from?"

"The Missouri."

"The Missouri! Holy mother of Jesus! You come all that way by yourself. Good lord!" He paused momentarily. "Pardon my curiosity, ma'am, but what exactly are you doing out here?"

"Minding my own business. What do you think?"

"Mmm." He grew silent. "Well, I don't believe you give a damn one way or the other about what I think, so how 'bout I stock up on some supplies and we'll go our merry ways. I won't dicker, jus' name your price and I'll gladly pay it to be outta here. I'm beginnin' to think you're even more ornery than that party of Blackfeet."

"I don't have any supplies."

"Wh—wh—no-no-no, you can't be *that* upset with me. You're sayin' you won't sell me a handful of goods. You'd actually leave me out here to starve or die o' thirst! My god, woman, I'm not that bad! Trust me, you don't know me. I'm not…."

"I don't have any supplies, simple as that. It's nothing personal."

"But you're a peddler for cryin' out loud."

"I never said that."

"Said what?"

"That I'm a peddler."

"You sayin' you're not a peddler."

"I'm not."

"Your not what? Your not a peddler or you're not saying you're a peddler."

"I'm saying, I'm hardly in the business of drumming."

"Of course not—of course not. I wish I knew what the hell business you are in."

The man could be irritating. He swung his head back and forth as he sat on his horse struggling to make sense of our meeting. I could see he was frustrated. He was a beautiful man and although I never took my gun off him for a moment, I enjoyed looking at him across my sights as he bit his lip and studied the wagon. I loved the sound of his voice. He let out a deep sigh.

"Ma'am—I know I must be pressing upon your good nature, your patience and all, but you can understand how the average, or possibly the *only* passerby might make the wrong assumption. I mean to say; the side of your wagon is painted up in big, big, bi-ig bold red letters that say 'DUSTY PEDDLER'. Surely you must see how easily one could be misled."

"The wagon came with them. Does that surprise you?"

He dropped his head. He rolled it about then spoke mostly to himself giving great emphasis to individual words as he spoke.

"What *doesn't* surprise me is how a woman back east, a woman up north, or a woman out in the middle of ten thousand godforsaken acres all act alike. I didn't get it then, I don't get it now. Who would believe this? Who *could* believe this? I'm so lost I can't find the horse I'm sitting on and finally by the grace of God, or so I thought, half way across the continent, I spot an honest to goodness wagon.

"Angel of Mercy, I say to myself, this is too good to be true—*a peddler of all things*—and I'm off riding hard out o' the hills for a day an' a half trying to catch you before the sun turns me into toast. I use up the last of my water basting myself in all this miserable heat, an' for what? So you can tell me that you have no idea where you are, where we are, that you're no peddler, that you have no supplies, that—that—ugh."

Again, he stuck his knuckle into his mouth and bit down hard upon it. I thought for sure he was going to cry and I waited. Instead, he poured out one final rush of exasperation.

"I should have guessed. I should have known! Only a dim-witted woman would be out here in the middle of absolutely nowhere doing absolutely nothing but going around in great circles on ground even the snakes have abandoned—."

"Are you finished?" I interrupted, not at all happy about his remark regarding a dim-witted woman.

"What?" He turned to face me after having made great swinging motions over the horizon with his hands that I chose to overlook.

"I asked if you were now finished. I suggest you not say one more thing about the stupidity of a woman going in great circles, especially in view of the fact that the only thing I can envision being of greater stupidity, is to see the all-knowing man following the dim-witted woman going around in great circles. Don't you think? Not to mention, this dim-witted woman has no problems going around in great circles by herself with her dim-witted woman's barrel of fresh water, if you get my point."

He studied me for a moment, and then abruptly changed the subject and attitude.

"Is there anything I can do, to get you to put that gun away?"

"Not much, it relaxes me, and that's more than you do."

"Obviously. How about this? I get off my horse and walk out a ways. You come to my horse, take my guns, and put them in your wagon. I get back on my horse, and we ride together until we find a camp or something. Two is always better than one. Besides, you might do well to have a man around, especially with Blackfeet about. Who knows, we might even become friends. All I ask in return is enough water to uncurl my tongue." He thought a moment, and then with a look of great suspicion, he lowered his head and peered at me through the corner of his eyes.

"You *do* have some water, yes?"

"Friends? Your brain is burning up, mister. And for what it's worth, I don't lie, but that's not the point. The way I see it, you might be better off without your tongue, and why would I want your company in the first place? Why should I share my water with you? I don't know you from Adam and I can travel twice as far on my water if you're not drinking it. I can't imagine any benefit in having you around."

Again, I lied as I thought of Blackfeet, but he must have found humor in what I said, for he smiled and my heart melted immediately.

"What you say is true. I'll be the first to admit I have little to offer, and that I am in need. But—it is also true you didn't shoot me at first chance, so might I dare to venture that you desire some company? Possibly a face considered handsome by many of your gender, possibly a little laughter and some song to boot, hmm?"

He might as well have shot me. The words wounded me in the worst way. The temptation was so very persuasive that I was forced to give it serious thought. He was working my greatest weakness. I studied him carefully. He was so egotistical, a grown up brat to be certain, but wonderfully devilish in his way. The one big, big advantage he had in his favor was my desperation to have someone with whom to speak, and I believed he knew it. Anybody out here would know that.

This need may have been the only thing remaining that was truly woman in me, or was it? Maybe I just needed to periodically engage with another human to measure what sanity I still possessed. Maybe, even though he was a man, he suffered the same gut wrenching loneliness that so often laid me to waste. Maybe, I was being to hard on the man. He seemed all right, sensible, somewhat obnoxious, but clean-shaven and presentable. Anyone who would take the time to shave out here had to have some decency of character. I thought it over and decided to take the risk.

"All right, I'll trust you as far as that. Go over there and keep your hands on your head." I pointed out away from the side of the wagon.

"Great! I knew you were an intelligent woman the moment I laid eyes on you." He stepped down slowly and put his hands up in the air. He began walking backwards, away from his horse.

"Intelligent woman! *Intelligent woman!* Did you not just say I was stupid to the core—going around in great circles?" I couldn't believe this man, what gall.

"I never said anything about stupid to the core. I simply said dim-witted, nothing more, just dim-witted. Don't turn it into something it wasn't."

"And that should make me feel better?"

"I meant it in a affectionate sort of way. You know like when you talk to your dog. Sometimes you say, 'hey, you, you dim-witted mutt'...."

"Oh! So you're saying you were talking to me like you would a dog?"

"Nnn-nope."

He clammed right up, turned around and walked away uttering not one additional word. Good thing for him.

Once he was a fair distance off and I knew he had no chance to beat me back to the wagon, I rested my gun on the seat and eased myself down. I never allowed my eyes to leave sight of him as I moved toward the horse. He turned to face me, his hands clasped atop his head.

"Go easy, he's skittish." He offered a warning as the horse backed a few steps away from me.

"Stay there, Bender!" The man looked at me. "Just talk to him, he's skittish that's all." The horse was again moving toward him and away from me. I didn't like it.

"You move back farther." I warned. I glanced back at the wagon and my gun to reassure myself.

"Back as far as you wish." He continued to move backwards. I took a few more steps in the horse's direction, and I could see that the animal was shy of me. It was about to step away a third time when I decided to make a lunge for the reins.

As if to anticipate my move, the man yelled out.

"Bender! Skittish!"

The horse bolted toward him guns and all, leaving me standing out in the open. I wasted no time waiting to see what would happen next. I spun around and lit out for the wagon and my gun. Only two steps short of my goal, I was just an arm's length from the pistol grip when the ground before me exploded into a cloud of flying sand.

The shot rang out and scared the daylights out of both my team and me. I jumped backwards and the mules jumped forward, moving the wagon far enough away to stop me from grasping my gun at first reach. It was over in an instant. Oddly, I wasn't nearly as frightened as I was infuriated. Maybe, I was a dim-witted woman after all. A man could certainly make you feel that way. I turned to face the victor and my sentence. He stood there as calm as ever working that smile for all it was worth.

"Never, never, never, leave your gun," he scolded me. He looked at the ground and shook his head with disapproval. "I know—it's heavy. I know—it doesn't go well with lace. It's all true, true blue, true blue." He raised his head and met my gaze. His long arm was leveled in my direction.

"You did." I protested.

He looked at me for a moment.

"Well, not really." He opened his coat and produced yet another pistol. "I don't use the ones on the horse, I won them in a poker game. Hate carrying all that weight," he grinned. "Oh, and by the way, my horse thinks '*skittish*' means '*come*'. Don't ask me; it must be the breed."

The man really could be smug, I thought to myself. I felt like I was looking into the eyes of a beautiful animal that was about to devour me. He walked up to me then stepped aside, turning his back without fear—or maybe he was just plain foolish. He moved over to the wagon seat and picked up my pistol then turned around and looked at me with discernible pity. Holding it by the barrel, he handed it to me. It was still cocked and ready to fire.

"Here's ol' Smokey. I give him back in trade for a name, fair enough?"

He looked directly at me and grinned. I couldn't turn away from his eyes. They were clear as crystal. Blue, icy blue, they chilled me even in the heat of the sun.

"Elizabeth," I answered. "Thank-you very much." I felt foolish, immeasurably relieved, and excited all at once.

"Don't jerk the trigger."

"You ask the impossible." I released the hammer.

"I mean you no harm, Elizabeth. Yet, I wouldn't expect you to believe that out here in the middle of nowhere, being that it's just the two of us. Anyhow, I think I have gone a long way toward proving my honest intention. I could have easily held you at gunpoint, had my way with you, and afterwards taken whatever I wished."

"Maybe." I thought about my staff lying in the wagon.

"*Maybe? Maybe?* Lord you women are all alike. You never know when to quit. You woulda whipped my ass, no doubt. Have it your way; who cares. I'm just saying this. I respected you and your things. I have proven myself to be a gentleman, but that doesn't mean I have any reason to trust *you*. Remember, *you* drew on me first, and you can't deny that. So, if it's all the same to you, I'll be holding on to my guns to keep us both honest. And now—*puh-leeze* may I have a drink of water?"

Luke, or whatever his name, was always smiling, whether by grin or by glint. He was the worst kind of man a woman could meet; for he had the ability to make all her decisions go his way.

"Go on in and help yourself. There's a barrel inside. The ladle is on the shelf."

"I trust you won't shoot me in the back."

"I'm not that kind of woman."

"Could have fooled me."

"You really don't want a drink do you."

The Indians saw to it that I had plenty of water and a generous amount of dried meat and fruits. In all honesty, the stranger made every attempt to be pleasant and respectful of my belongings as promised, and for those reasons I encouraged him to drink as much as he wanted.

There was no denying, he possessed a powerful thirst. I sat back upon the bench and watched him inside gulping down water ladle by ladle. After seeing the way he drank; I began to lower my guard. I determined there was little point in traveling any farther this day, and gave thought to making camp earlier than usual. Truth be known, the stranger held sway over me, and while I tried hard to conceal my hopes for having company, I wanted nothing more than to sit at a fire in his presence for an evening. I desperately wanted someone to talk to.

"Listen, Luke, I wish to apologize for my behavior, but a woman just can't take a chance on any count out here when she's alone. I—."

"Please, don't say another word. I can't begin to believe you are out here by yourself. I'm afraid I find it irresponsible, fool-hardy, and perfectly dim-witted, but I understand you must have your reasons and so I take no offense by your manner. If I hadn't been so thirsty, I might have been a good deal more mannerly and soft-spoken myself. I had all I could do to keep from busting through your wagon in search of this barrel. I'm convinced I was dying of thirst."

"I was uh—thinking about making camp for the night, and uh—well—I was wondering if you would like to stay on until morning. I must confess that your offer of conversation was most tempting. If you're still of a mind, I can't think of anything I'd like more."

"Well, Elizabeth. At last we're of the same mind on something. It'd be my pleasure."

Luke gave me a hand unhitching the mules and relieving them of their traces and collars, after which he collected wood to start a fire. I crawled inside the wagon to freshen up. I was humming to myself as I washed, when suddenly there came this heavenly caress of chords and melody—music to fill my heart and soul. It was followed by a full and resonate voice that stilled me, causing me to listen and pray there be no interruption to this stream of sweetness.

I reached over for my shawl and stepped down quietly from the wagon wishing not to disturb a single stanza of this desert serenade. I sat down next to him and when he finished, I poured tea.

"Such a sad song. How beautiful."

"Mary of the wild moor. A lovely Scot-Irish piece."

"You know, if you had serenaded me with that song instead of sarcasm, you would have gotten a great deal farther, a great deal faster." He strummed the instrument. The strings rang with pristine clarity, each singing out in harmony with the next.

"How much farther?" He asked cheekily without missing a note.

"Oh, god help me, you men are all alike, born of the same seed, I swear." I was exasperated by the entire gender. I moved to stand, but he reached out and held me in place. He stopped playing.

"I am sorry. I am sorry; I apologize. The comment was uncalled for. It's obvious you are a lady and deserve better. I promise to stay on my best behavior. Forgive me. Please, say you will forgive me."

I slid my jaw to one side and gave him that *'you are a worthless immoral pig and have offended me'* look. I knew only an idiot would accept his apology, and there I was.

"I will overlook your misjudgment this one time—only."

"Thank-you. I can see that you are kind."

It seemed as though everything he said had a trace of sarcasm to it. Never enough to get him into trouble, but sufficient to make me feel like I was being toyed with. He began to strum more chords.

"Do you like the guitar?"

"I love the guitar, yes. But it isn't the guitar that I enjoy so much; it's the music, the song. I love the music. I don't understand some people. This country is supposed to end oppression and yet I know a good many people out there who profess singing and dancing to be sinful. It amazes me how anything so pleasurable can be defined as the devil's work. We're supposed to be escaping religious persecution, but I often think we are living to prolong it."

"You must be a New Englander."

"Yes, I'm afraid so, Boston."

"Ah! That explains a great deal."

There it was again, that hint of sarcasm, which so effectively got under my skin.

"What exactly does that mean?"

"Excuse me? Did I again say something to offend you?"

"That bit about *'that explains it'*. That explains what?"

"That explains *it*. I was just inferring that you were probably starved for music as you said."

"I'm sure that's what you meant. Funny how I almost missed your meaning." My own sarcasm oozed forth to hide my eternal sensitivity to sexual matters. "Anyway, if I may continue—I was about to say that when I was a child and lived by the sea, there was this man named Darin who sang to me always. He was song itself. He would work on the docks or high up in the rigging and sing to anyone who might listen. And the whole world listened. At least my whole world did." The memories brought a smile to my face and comfort to my heart.

"Well—we're a long, long way from Boston's harbor, and out here there are no boats, few women to serenade, and fewer still worth looking at. So, all that's left to soothe a man's heart is imagination and a good song. Needless to say, I do a lot of singing."

"I hope so. I like the way you sing."

"Well, thank you. You should hear me howlin' with the boys when we start up a 'sing-in'. That's fun. When it's a group, it gets down right rowdy; when it's one, it gets sad. Unfortunately, out here it's almost always sad. You can listen to a man sing and hear his thoughts, see his soul, his conscience, his hopes. You can listen to him tell you about his love, his family and friends, good times, bad times, you can hear it all in his voice or the strum of a guitar."

"What about your family? Do they all sing?" I asked.

"We sing bawdy, we sing gospel. We just plain sing to hear something that drowns out the wind and nosey women."

"What about your—. Nosey!"

Before I could get in a retort, Luke broke into another song. It was his way to shut me up, for his voice caressed my ears like velvet to a cheek. I watched him and wondered whether it was the Good Lord or the devil that sent me this man. Either way, he sang all evening before the fire. I last remembered wrapping up in a blanket against the chill of the night and curling up close by his side before drifting off to sleep with the echo of a lullaby in my ear.

Reach up for your mama, child,
and pull her close to you.
Whisper how you love her,
and kiss her when you do.

Thank her so, for all she does,
the way in which she cares.
Remember her to Jesus
when you say your bedtime prayers.

For mamas need the lovin'
only little ones can give.
It fills their heart with all the reason
in the world to live.

Tell her how you love her,
although you know she knew.
She'll never tire of hearing this
when it comes from you.

Reach up for your mama, child,
—and kiss her for me too.

NINETY-THREE

The following days were undeniably some of the most thrilling in my long solitary life. This man found me attractive and didn't hide the fact. I could see it in his eyes. I noticed the way he studied every inch of me from head to foot, the way he glanced at my breasts, the way he toyed with my temperament.

He resurrected feelings and emotions within me that I thought long since useless. I was glowing in his presence, and embarrassed by the way in which I involuntarily rose to the occasion. Of course, I was also sinking into my quagmire of puritan morals, pushed down to drown beneath the weight of my views on virginity, virtue, and values.

These were inescapable struggles, private battles waged within. I was morally anchored in crosscurrents of desire, and yet I knew I would never allow this attraction to get out of hand. Still, it was so euphoric, so very euphoric to be the object of a man's desire. Not only did I want desperately to feel his arms about me, but also I knew he wanted to hold me with the same passion, and it was this awareness that clipped my each and every breath.

Every morning my awakening thoughts were only on how I might look and how I would act in the light of all this attention. I spent twice as long making myself presentable. How freely I used my lavender lotion. From the moment I awoke, I felt waves of anxious intoxication course through me. I was not at all myself. I was overly conscious of my every move even when only sitting to sip coffee. I was sensitive to every interaction.

I understood there had been no time for infatuation, so I believed this to be as close to passion as I might know. This had to be passion, pure and simple. It was sweet, innocent—dangerous. My word, it was so very dangerous. I realized at once how these feelings blurred the distinction between right and wrong. I tried hard not to worry about it, not to think about it. I just wanted to enjoy it.

"You know what?" He asked, while we sat at the fire.

"What?"

"I like you."

"I like you too."

"I like you more than you like me."

"How would you know that?"

"Because I can't take my eyes off of you, that's how."

"Well, I must tell you, it's very impolite to stare. It makes me uncomfortable. Besides, you don't even know me."

"That's true. That's also what makes it so nice. All those terrible shortcomings you have, all those embarrassing things in your past you've kept from me. Until I discover them, there is nothing about you that isn't perfect. There's a lesson to be learned here."

"And what might that be?"

"Kiss me, keep your mouth shut, and we could live happily ever after. What a life. Can you imagine?"

"I would say, you've left me speechless. Would you care to know what *I see?*"

"I don't want to know what you see. You're too apt to ruin a perfect dream."

"I see a slick talking Romeo."

"Oh, not nice. I think I'm hurt."

"I don't think you've ever been hurt. Hurt might do your ego some good."

"Ouch! You're really touchy this morning. I feel like I'm walking barefoot in a briar patch."

It took Luke's comment to point out how bizarre I was acting. It wasn't at all like me to wish ill upon anyone. It was as though I were trying to determine if he would stick around if things got a little rough. Was I giving him a first test of loyalty? Was I insane! My god, how embarrassing, I thought to myself.

"I'm sorry. You didn't deserve that. I guess I've just been alone for so long that I've forgotten how to appreciate a kind word."

"I forgive you. I'll tell you what. I am going to give you a present that will improve your opinion of me."

"A present? You can't be serious. You rode up with nothing but your horse, a guitar and the sand in your boots."

"And you can't play a guitar, is that what you're about to say? Oh ye, of such little faith."

He stood up from the fire and walked over to the wagon, where I permitted him to store what little he owned. He retrieved a pistol and its holster. He came back to where we were sitting.

"I give this to you."

"A gun?" I wasn't exactly thrilled.

"No, not *'uhh gun'*. A Gun!"

"That's what I said, a gun."

"The trouble with you desert women; second only to having a poor sense of direction—is you don't kill enough people to appreciate a really fine weapon."

"Oh! Now that is truly a failing. Slaughter is my shortcoming. Yes, sir, you can see right through me. I'll give you that. You read me like a book."

"It's nothing really. The female mind is a simpler facility. Whereas, sound reasoning has never been one of my shortcomings."

"Simpler mind? Sound reasoning? Oh, this is special! You must have been lonely as a boy, the sole possessor of the one trait your gender entirely lacks. Let me see was it intelligence or humility."

"Well, admittedly, I may not have attained your own qualities, quite perfected—and demonstrated by your sharp tongue and aimless wandering, but I did move to the front of my class."

"Class on compass reading, no doubt; obviously an all boy school. I can see you now, following the other boys in great circles to find your desk. Funny, how history repeats itself. Let me think, was it I with the simple mind who was lost? Or was I happily minding my own business and enjoying the countryside. Was it my simple mind baking to a crisp while I sat on a horse begging for a drink of water? No, as I recall, I wasn't even thirsty. On the other hand, I noticed you begged rather admirably, certainly with great conviction. I assume its one of those admirable skills you mastered while in school. Front of your class, I'll bet."

Luke looked at me with astonishment, and I realized I had just attacked him again. What was the matter with me? He was only teasing me, toying with me, but I was striking out. I was shocked by my behavior.

"All right. All right, you win. Forget the gift. I'm too stupid to realize I can sell it for a small fortune instead of giving it away to save your ungrateful hide. Once again, it occurs to me why you might be traveling alone."

He rose to his feet and started to walk off. I quickly reached over and grabbed the back of his coat, pulling on its tails to stop him. I refused to let go.

"I'm sorry. I was mean. I was mean; I was very mean. Don't leave. I really do want my gift."

"You have a funny way of showing it."

"I know. I'm peculiar in every way, believe me."

"Well, you went too far. My feelings are really hurt this time. I'm taking my gun and going home."

"Where are you going?" He was back to kidding again, but it was funny how my stomach tightened with sudden concern as he got up to leave.

"I'm going to sit and lick my wounds on the other side of the wagon. Over there, the people are friendlier, and it's a lot better view, thank-you." I loved the way he kept his spirit in spite of my mouth. I was genuinely relieved.

"Poooor boy." I purred. "I'll make it all better." I reassured him.

"How?"

"How what?"

"How are you going to make it all better?" His eyes sparkled afresh.

"By letting you spend another night in my camp. And you better be careful or you are going to sleep outside on the ground."

"I already sleep outside on the ground."

"Good. Then you know what it's like, and it isn't fun is it? Everything down there crawls. Now, where's my gift. I think you owe me one after getting me so upset."

"Getting you upset!"

"Come along little boy, sit down, right here, right next to me." I dragged him back to the campfire. "So why are you giving me this? I already have a pistol." He puffed himself all up and strutted about for show.

"Well, only because you ask—two reasons, neither obvious. First, I think you are the most enchanting woman I have probably ever met, and second;—I would hate to see anything happen to you. You need a good firearm. This piece is not your everyday lock, stock, and barrel. This is a work of art, a true piece of genius and craftsmanship. Take a minute and think about your pistol. Is it not a common piece with flint, striker, and flash pan?"

"Oh, yes sir. It is very common indeed." I acted like a student.

"Un-huh! Just as I supposed, and that means—too many things can go afoul." Playfully, he shook his finger at me like a true headmaster. "It may be the wind, the rain, your powder, who knows? All things unpredictable, that could cost you your shot—and maybe your life."

"Oh, no! Is this true?"

"Yes, ma'am, as God is my witness. But, with this gun, not only is your shot nearly guaranteed, you also get a second chance, and a third, and a forth, and a fifth. And if you haven't made your mark after five shots, you deserve to be dead anyway. Don't you agree?"

"Absolutely."

"You see this?" He held up a small brass plug of sorts.

"Un-huh."

"Do you know what it is?"

"Nope." I played along, but in this case, I really didn't know.

"It is called a percussion cap. It changes everything. It will revolutionize the gun, as we know it. Do you want to know why?"

I started to laugh. "Yes, yes, I want to know why."

"This is why." He removed the gun from its holster and placed it in my lap. I looked at it with some surprise.

"This is the oddest looking gun I have ever seen. Is it a prank of sorts?"

In a complete change of attitude, Luke became serious. He looked at the gun and he looked at me. There was no laughter left in his voice.

"I assure you this is no prank. It is odd, isn't it? It is called a repeater."

"It doesn't have a trigger. How do I shoot a gun with no trigger?"

"The trigger is in the handle my dear. Watch. You simply ease the hammer back and let it loose. It is held in place by the trigger, which now has appeared below. See? Pull the hammer, pull the trigger. Boom, boom, boom, the gun fires away.

"It is a remarkable piece. There are only a handful of men, who are experimenting with this design and fewer actually building this style of pistol, but the design represents such an advance in gunsmithing, they'll soon be everywhere. Let me explain." Pinched between his thumb and forefinger was the percussion cap, which he placed in the palm of my hand. "You see by using this cap instead of flint and flashpan, you can keep the fuse fixed in position at the chamber, directly behind your charge. Watch this." He pulled a pin forward on the gun and the middle of it fell out to one side. He handed it to me.

"This is called the chamber."

I observed it was cylindrical with five large holes in one end to take the ball and charge, and five small holes in the opposite end. He took the piece from me and fitted it back into the gun, then slid the pin back in place. I took hold of the gun.

"I don't like this. It's too heavy for me. Besides, I am only just now getting used to mine."

"Oh, you can get used to this easy enough. C'mon lets shoot it a bit. You should practice anyhow."

"I don't know. I'm not much for shooting guns. In all honesty they scare me more than anything."

"Come on now, be a sport." He pulled me up to my feet. I followed him reluctantly and watched as he went about making up charges and fitting his caps.

"Now pay attention." He held the gun in one hand and brushed the hammer. BOOM! He gave the gun a slap of sorts and brushed the hammer again. BOOM! And again, BOOM—BOOM—BOOM! After firing the rounds he turned to me and smiled like a proud father.

"Five rounds in fifteen seconds. Do you now see my point? After the first shot, a person would assume you must sit down, unstop your horn, fill the pan or fit another cap, and ram another ball. They would walk up to you and laugh. An Indian could have a quiver of arrows in the air by that time. You'd look like a pin cushion, but imagine his surprise to see you grinning then sending a second ball his way, and then a third, and a fourth." He beamed with pleasure.

"Do you not like Indians?" I asked.

"Let me just say they keep me on my toes. Them Blackfeet are a bunch to contend with. I think Rudman was dreaming about Blackfeet when he designed this piece."

"Who's Rudman?"

"Paul Rudman. Clever man—gunsmith by trade—one of the best—he also liked to play poker. Sometimes he found it easier to trade his odd looking guns for poker chips than to sell them. That's how I come by this one."

"You're a poker player, a gambler?" Luke stared at me with that look, which said I have no business judging his calling in life.

"If it makes you feel any better about me, then allow me to say it took years for me to raise myself from the life of a drifter to that of a gambler. You might like to know that I'm the kind of person who has always set goals for himself, and I put my heart and soul into achieving them."

He stared directly at me, daring me to say something disapproving. I decided to keep quiet, which was immediately evident. We moved on.

"Come on now. You try it."

895

He handed me the gun and I must admit, I had never seen anything near the likes of this pistol before. It looked odd, it felt odd, but it was impressive as it filled the air with a thick cloud of smoke and fire. It certainly gave one a sense of power and security.

I allowed him to give me his lesson in the art of shooting. We stood there together, he instructing me on how to hold this heavier pistol straight out with both hands. He stood behind me and wrapped his arms around me, taking my hands into his. My heart raced.

"Now take aim for that piece of wood. Look across the sight on the barrel."

"Like this?"

"Well, not exactly. Here, more like this."

He kept squeezing me and holding me in different positions. He was dragging the lesson out longer than need be, I was certain—this for his own benefit. It wasn't that I minded. It saved me the trouble of finding my own excuses to prolong his embrace. Besides, it was obvious he was paying a pretty stiff price for the honor. It was very nice, this piece of his.

"Now am I doing it right?"

"Let me see." He placed his head on my shoulder and nuzzled up to me. I noticed he was looking in the wrong direction.

"Are you looking at the target or at my breasts?" The second the words rolled off my tongue, I was astonished. I couldn't believe I dared say such a thing. I just thought it very funny and out it came. He released me at once and stepped away fully ashamed.

"Oh, for crying out loud! What kind of man do you take me for? I suppose you think all gamblers are womanizers."

"No, I think all womanizers are gamblers."

"What does that mean?"

"It means you're going to lose."

"Just pull the damned trigger, would you please. Just—just pull the—."

BOOM!

"Oh, darn it! I missed again. I know I can hit it; I just need to practice."

Luke looked at me for a moment, unsure where I was taking him.

"Yes, well, I'll give you that. Practice makes perfect. Who knows maybe that's why it's called a repeater. I never thought of it that way, but in your case it makes sense." He walked up to me slowly and wrapped his arms carefully around me once more.

The best I could do in this situation was to intentionally miss the target as often as I could, allowing a hit now and then to keep Luke encouraged. It was so unlike me to act helpless, but I wanted the feel of his arms around me and if that was what it took, then so be it. I loved the way he made my body tingle. He was thrilling and unbelievably arousing.

NINETY-FOUR

Luke handed me a freshly loaded gun. I took it reluctantly and then handed it back to him.

"I can't do this anymore. My ears are ringing so loud I can't hear a thing. My wrists hurt, my arms hurt, my shoulders hurt. I can't even hold it up. I'm done, finished."

I can't say for sure how many times we shot the pistol, but I too was paying a steep price for passion. Luke holstered the gun.

"Fair enough. You've been a good sport, but I gotta say, I have never seen anybody have that much trouble hitting anything. Lucky for you there's no barns out here. The killer instinct is not your forte."

"I'll take that as a compliment."

Luke walked off and started searching the ground for dimples and spent balls. I joined him and after collecting dozens we gave up trying to find more. He gathered up his pistols and returned them to the wagon, afterwhich, to my horror, he reappeared with my large glass jar of urine.

"What's this?" He held the jar up high.

"Oh no." I was utterly lost for words. I couldn't begin to come up with a reason for keeping a jar of urine. There was nothing I could say that might even stand up as the feeblest of explanations.

"Don't ask me. Please, don't ask me."

"Is this urine?" He asked almost gleefully.

"Oh, no."

"This has great color."

"What!"

"Good color." Suddenly, he unsealed the lid and smelled it.

"Whoa! That's potent! You have some mighty powerful pee there, Elizabeth."

I just stared at him. Was he crazy or what? The man was making me nervous. Maybe this was one of those hidden secrets he was talking about, some sort of male perversion. I stood silent.

"Why are you saving this?"

"Why are you smelling it?"

"I know good urine when I see it. So, why are you saving it?"

"I have no idea. Believe me, I wish I hadn't."

"It's dark. Strong. You've been conserving your water—not drinking enough. You shouldn't do that. It isn't healthy, but for now, it's a stroke of good luck."

"What do you mean?"

"Ammonia. You have high quality pee, Elizabeth, and I aim to make the best of it."

Luke went for his saddlebags and produced a couple of sacks. One was filled with yellowish green clumps and the other with black powder. For the next few hours he worked to crush and crumble both substances then dissolve them in my urine. As if to upset me, and in spite of my loud complaint, he poured the mixture into one of my pans and the set it out to dry. He kept an eye on a bank of storm clouds approaching from the west, but as for now the sun was hot and bright and quickly dried out his concoction. Luke was bent on driving me crazy by not telling me what he was up to. He looked like a practiced alchemist as he carefully gathered up some of the dried powder and placed it on a rock.

"Is that what I think it is?"

"What do you think it is?"

"I know it isn't gold."

"Nope, but out here it's worth more."

Luke grabbed a second rock and slammed it down upon the powder covering the first stone and immediately there was a bright flash and explosion that produced a large cloud of smoke. He gave me a good scare.

"Gunpowder! And this is high quality. I knew it would be when I smelled your piss." He teased me.

"Stop it."

"Stop what?"

"You know what. Talking like that."

"I thought you were educated, a chemist and all."

"I don't care what you think. You don't need to talk like that. It's rude."

Luke looked up at the sky.

"I think we better get this packed into your powder keg before the rain hits." He arose to his feet and went to fetch the keg from the wagon. I looked up to the sky and observed the dark line of clouds about to blot out the sun. The plains ahead were fully shadowed.

I began to gather up our belongings from around the campfire. Luke poured the freshly made gunpowder into the keg until it would hold no more. He then began making charges for the repeater with what powder remained.

"You better put this stuff back in the wagon before it gets wet." He warned. "This is high quality powder. You'll be able to count on it."

"Whatever you say." It all bored me. There were more important things to contend with. "C'mon, you can help me spread the canvas. The way you drink, we need all the water we can get."

I gathered up our belongings from around the campfire and climbed onto the wagon bench to hand them inside.

"Oooo, I hurt. I'm going to be sore tomorrow."

"Turn around."

"What?"

"Turn around and sit still."

I turned around on the bench seat as he asked. His large hands gripped my shoulders from behind and he began kneading them, working out the stiffness.

"That feel better?"

"Oh, yes, yes, yes. That feels wonderful." I closed my eyes. The wind suddenly picked up and his hands slowed to a halt. My eyes were still closed. "Don't stop, don't stop," I pleaded.

"No, I think we better stop and get that canvas stretched out. Looks like we're gonna get it any second."

I opened my eyes to see the silvery veil of rainfall moving our way. Luke began to nudge me.

"C'mon, c'mon, let's go."

I jumped down to the ground with him directly behind. He snapped the canvas out to unfold it, and we stretched it out, raising the corners to collect the water.

"Here it comes!"

"Oh, oh!" I tensed up.

Those first few drops felt like ice, but within moments we were dancing in the dirt and getting soaked. We stripped ourselves down to as little clothing as was moral, and swung each other about, dancing and laughing like lunatics. He never once took his eyes off of me. He pulled me in closer and closer until we stopped twirling. He held me in his arms and stared at me those searing blue eyes, burning with desire. I began to laugh and broke free of his grip. He smiled as he watched me go. I knew he was tightening his noose about me and the feeling was both seductive and scary.

It proved to be a decent downpour. Not only did we top off our water barrel, but also on opposite sides of the wagon we were able to soap up and scrub down. When it came right down to feeling wanted or feeling clean, I couldn't say which I preferred the most, but standing naked on opposite sides of the wagon was probably the most arousing sexual experience of my life.

"Don't you be sneaking any peeks, ya hear!"

"What!"

"You heard me!"

"I beg your pardon!"

"Pardon accepted."

"Pardon accepted? Pardon—. You—you. Ohhh!"

That night, I sat at the fire and found myself watching him across the brim of my cup without break or pause as he lit up fresh cigar. I hoped he wouldn't notice the way in which I was filling my senses with the sight of him. I was plunging deep into the pool of his charm, drowning in my desire for him. He was showy on the surface, but below all the splash, there was a complex character. Much, much more than what met the eye. I was a good judge of personality and I knew this as well as I knew anything. What I didn't know was why he kept his real self so secretive. I wondered about who he really was and how he came to be out here.

"You're staring."

"How did you come to be out here, Luke? I can tell you are a learned man. What are you doing out here? What keeps you in this desert? It doesn't fit you."

"What makes you think anything *keeps* me in this desert?"

"I don't think it. I know it. You're the wrong kind of person to be wandering in this place. You're educated, polished."

"And you're not?"

"I'm out here for a reason."

"And what would that be, to find the man of your dreams?"

THE BLOOD OF LIFE

"Funny you should say that."

"Are you serious?"

"It's not what you think."

"Why don't you let me be the judge of that?"

"No, no, no. You are not going to change the subject on me. I want to know why you are riding around out there in the middle of those ten thousand godforsaken miles as you call it."

He looked at me with a complete lack of expression, as if his soul was suddenly yanked back into some other world. When he returned, he looked away toward the last streak of purple light that trimmed the horizon.

"I just like the wide open spaces. It makes me feel free. I think you know what I mean."

It wouldn't be forthcoming. I didn't pursue it, but also; I didn't know what he meant. I did know it was a struggle to survive out here, and nobody wandered around for years side-stepping snakes for the sake of spectacular sunrises and sunsets. It was obvious to me that Luke Laredo, or Lucky Luke, or whoever he might be, was running from something he was not about to reveal.

My question completely changed the mood of the evening. He had lost his sense of playfulness. He very nearly stopped talking to me. He sat somber, drinking his coffee and looking out across the plains, buried deep in his own thoughts. I so badly wanted to know what was going through his head.

The afternoon rain had brought a chilly wind and for this reason or maybe for an excuse, I asked Luke if he would like to sleep with me in the wagon. I made it perfectly clear I would not tolerate any advances on his behalf. I was offering him a place to sleep off the ground and out of the chill in trade for his word, which I was willing to accept as honorable.

He accepted my offer with gratitude. We never fully dressed after the shower, instead wrapping in blankets as our clothes dried before the fire. And so, we climbed into the wagon, covering under the same covers that wrapped us. Luke commented on the thickness and comfort of the furs that made up my bed, but spoke of little else. My offer might well have been a mistake, for I soon realized the difficulty I would have trying to sleep. The nearness of him kept my senses aroused and restless.

He lay there for the longest time and then spoke to me in a whisper.

"Are you awake, Elizabeth?"

"Yes."

"Do you remember when I said that the nice thing about not knowing you, is not knowing your secrets? Whatever those shortcomings are, those dark regrets that often lurk in your past?"

"Yes."

"I said I came out here for the wide open spaces and that was true enough. But, it wasn't to see anything, it was so I might get lost forever in its vastness. It was the only place that was so large, I knew it could swallow me whole and hide me from what I had done."

I lay still and silent. I was almost afraid to breathe. I knew I was about to hear something that I would wish desperately not to know. I knew as well, I must hear it, or I would go crazy wondering who was this man. It was black as pitch in the wagon and the air was empty of all but his voice.

"I haven't talked to a kind heart in so many years, I honestly came to believe earth was the dominion of the devil. The worst part of it is that amongst those demons I know; secrets are what relationships are built upon. If the truth were ever to be known, we lost souls would cease to be. We run to hide. Do you understand what I am saying?"

"Yes."

"It strikes me funny that when I should meet someone pure in heart such as yourself, instead of keeping those secrets, which is what I do best, I am compelled to divulge all my sins. I suppose it is like the need to go to your mother and reveal that you stole some cookies, just so you can have a clean conscience and know you are worthy of her love."

There was a long pause, after which there arose from the silence another voice. This one soft but tortured as if afraid to unlock the gate to his soul. The words came—slowly at first, troubled, as he released his secrets and allowed those locked memories of a tragedy to escape his hold.

"When I was twenty-seven years old, I was working as a book keeper in one of my fathers concerns. We were a wealthy family and due to my work, I was reasonably aware of my father's worth. My father was no longer involved in the running of the business because of failing health. He was lying intestate under my sister-in-law's care, she being married to my oldest brother. I had been summoned to my brother's house, for my father had taken a turn for the worse, and it was paramount he should make known his will and last wishes. Thus, the whole family had been called.

"I arrived with my fiancée, and the two of us sat alongside the rest as we listened to my father dictate how his numerous concerns would be divided amongst his heirs. It was a long and arduous task lasting most of the day. However, we worked our way through many thousands of dollars worth of assets amicably with no complications whatsoever. It was only afterwards, as conversation was being made regarding odds and ends, silly things really, like what would become of father's violin and things of the like that a discussion ensued between my older brother and myself.

"You see, years before, I had purchased a desk for my father; a splendid piece I felt might add some enjoyment to his work. The desk was imported, a one of a kind. It was irreplaceable and of a workmanship unparalleled. It was such an impeccable work that it was most difficult for me to part with, even in light of the fact I had purchased it with the sole intention of giving it to my father.

"As my father grew weaker and began to step back from doing the day-to-day tasks of managing the business, my eldest brother automatically assumed those duties now increasingly left unattended. He was spending more and more time at my father's house, at my father's desk, working late into the night. His wife Anna was none too happy about it. I might add also, she was well within her right to air such complaint, for my father gave us children precious little slack.

"Anyhow, after hearing of my sister-in-law's objections, my father felt some remorse and elected to send the desk along with the records cabinets to my brother's home, where he might work in the company of his wife and family. It was a practical matter. Simply move some furniture, and save disturbing the contents and order of concerns in which after all, my brother was over-seeing, he being the eldest son.

"The problem arose because of the amount of time passed, and the fact that my father never actually gave the desk to my brother. It would have been awkward for him to do so, as it was I who presented the desk to him as a gift, and it should have rightfully been returned to me. But, it had been loaned to my brother for convenience and remained in his possession for a number of years.

"Unfortunately, it was such an exquisite piece of furniture that my sister-in-law had taken it upon herself to make it the focal point of their study. I find no blame in what she had done, she believed it to be hers, and the desk itself was sufficient to be the centerpiece of any king's study, bar none."

Luke went silent. I opened my eyes to the dark and waited.

"Elizabeth?"

"Yes?"

"I was wondering if I had put you to sleep. I realize this is nothing of your concern."

"I wish to know, Luke. Please, go on. You have already told me much I've wanted to hear, and I feel better for having heard it."

"You say so now, Elizabeth. I hope you will feel as good when I am finished."

"As do I, now go on, I wish to hear the rest."

Luke took a breath.

"You must understand that the issue had nothing to do with money or worth. It was simply a matter whereby I was very partial to the desk and my desire for it was no less obvious than that of my sister-in-law. I felt strongly that I was entitled to it. It is true that my father is entitled to give away his possessions as he pleases, but I had paid for the desk in whole, and I had paid dearly. At first I reserved my opinions out of courtesy, wishing to enlighten my in-laws to my position in a polite and gentlemanly manner. Unfortunately, politeness soon gave way to a pointed discussion and finally a full-blown argument.

"The argument then became ugly as our tempers got the best of us. It was the two of them against me, and I could see that this desk to which I was so attached and expecting to retrieve was about to be lost. I could understand my sister-in-law being upset for she honestly believed the desk had been given to her and Claude. She was very fond of it and understandably reluctant to even consider giving up the piece.

"My complaint was not so much with her, but with my brother who was failing to enlighten his wife, and made matters worse by insinuating that my father may have indeed given him the desk rather than loan it for temporary use as I claimed. He argued that if I had given my father the desk as a gift, then it was his right to do with the desk as he pleased no matter how disappointed I might be. He offered to buy the desk from me, but made no mention of ever returning it.

"At this point the entire family was standing about embarrassed by the commotion before them, for our tongues were now getting the best of us. My brother's refusal to take the moral ground so infuriated me that I lashed out at him in sheer blind anger. You must understand that the word of my brother, he being the eldest, is taken as gospel, and therefore in an argument I am essentially moot.

"My father's mind was less than sound at times, especially if excited as it had now become. He was unable to settle the argument, uncertain as to the origin of the desk amid all the commotion that clouded his mind. My mother, God bless her soul, attempted to shed some truth on the matter, but my brother, now stubbornly passionate to allay his wife's concerns, would hear none of it.

"Without thought to cost or consequence, I struck my brother hard upon the jaw with my fist. I heard it crack. That was unforgivable, but it was nothing compared to what followed. I knocked the sense right out of the man, and he fell over backwards. As he plummeted toward the floor, he caught his head on the corner of the fireplace, which had a raised hearth. The fall crushed the back of his skull and immediately paralyzed him. I suspect he died shortly thereafter."

Luke's voice suddenly cracked with emotion. There was silence as he suppressed his sobs, but I could feel the heaving of his chest through our blanket. As much as I wanted to turn about and take him into my arms, I could not. I understood in the darkness of night as a grown man, he could shed his tears privately without witness, but the pain was evident and my heart bled for his misery and misfortune.

"I—I—don't think it is possible to—to explain what goes through one's mind during those few seconds after the storm has blown over. I looked at my brother lying there—in a pool of blood. It was running freely across the floor. I thought to myself, there lay a man whom I—."

Again the silence. I dared not move a muscle. My own tears swelled up within my eyes.

"The man whom I loved the whole of my life, a brother who had faults like my own, a brother who only moments before was laughing heartily with my family.

"Well, you can imagine the scene. The room went completely silent. Everyone froze in their places, stunned, stunned beyond words. My sister-in-law fainted right away. My fiancée who saw our relationship and her entire future vanish before her in the blink of an eye went senseless. She just stood there, suddenly an outsider thrust into the hell of a family destroyed.

"I couldn't bear to meet the eyes of all who looked upon me, so I turned to run. And as I left the house, I looked one last time to see the empty stare of my mother following me out the door." Luke took another breath and then had a change of heart.

"So you see, Elizabeth. We were called in to see to it that my father got off to heaven in a proper fashion, but it just goes to show you the absurdity of life, he stuck around long enough to see his youngest son kill his oldest. He was in good company though, for the whole family saw it with him—even my brother's children. Some uncle, wouldn't you say?"

Abruptly, Luke sat up and climbed out of the wagon. I sat up quietly as well to follow his shadow until it disappeared into the darkness of night.

NINETY-FIVE

I dozed in and out, moving from troubled sleep to bad dreams until I heard Luke return. The sound of him milling about outside the wagon brought me comfort and sound sleep for some hours until that time at which I awoke fully rested. I looked past the wagon doors and stared into a blackness where only stars distinguished sky from earth. It was long before sunup. I had no desire to tempt another nightmare, and so lay quietly in the warmth of Ho'neheveho's furs while recalling Luke's words.

He had passed on to me the remorse of a lifetime. It was a revelation that I was certain he would regret come light of day, for even I was uneasy about being a party to such intimate knowledge. In a way, I wished that he had never opened up—that he had kept his secret to himself, for the familiarity was oppressive and burdened my heart. As I lay with my thoughts, I sought peace in my understanding that Luke needed a compassionate soul to hear him out, to offer support, but most of all—to forgive.

The problem with forgiveness was how to find it when one drifted alone and felt prayers insufficient. Luke was searching for someone who might give him the benefit of the doubt, and apparently that someone was me. My only hope was that after doing so, after having listened to his story, he might not some-how become a changed person. It was a worrisome thought, and half of me feared to face him, while half begged to run to his side. To remain in the wagon was not an option, and so I dressed, for I had but the one choice.

I stuck my head outside and saw Luke sitting at the fire nursing a fresh brewed pot of coffee. The night air was still and saturated with its aroma.

"Brrrrr. It's cold out here." I startled him.

"Brrrrr, you should be sleeping."

"Brrrrr, you should be offering me a tin of hot coffee to keep me warm."

"That's one option."

"The only option."

He laughed as I climbed down from the wagon and walked over to the fire. He handed me my tin; and after taking a sip, I looked down at him.

"That was some story you told me last night, Luke."

"You liked that, huh?"

"No, I never said that. I said it was some story. I don't think it's anything I would want to tell my kids at bedtime, but I would tell you;—I believe with all my heart that you are an honest man. I believe you are a good man. Life isn't fair, Luke. I have discovered that myself, and it has been painful. Being a gambler, you should know best; it's just how the cards fall, how the deck gets split. But as for your story, better you than me." He looked at me quizzically, shook his head and chuckled.

"Here." He topped off my tin. I gathered up my blanket and sat down next to him to face the warmth of the fire.

"That wagon of yours is something else."

"What's the matter with my wagon? I like my wagon."

"I was thinking how last night I began to feel like I was in a confessional. You know; tight quarters, dark, just me, and a priest with an ear for sins. Not that you remind me of a priest or anything—well—a touch celibate maybe, nothing more. In case you can't tell, I was raised Catholic."

"A touch celibate. *A touch celibate?* I clearly am *most* like a priest in my ability to *forgive* you your transgressions. Lord knows with you, they come one right after another—and rapidly." Luke laughed heartily.

"Of course, how shortsighted of me to miss such benevolence, silly me, silly, silly me."

"You should be so benevolent. You should have stayed closer to the church."

"No thank-you. My church days were done when I watched a four day old infant freeze to death during gospel. *'Dying of Baptism'*, they called it. To me it looked just like murder. *'A newborn must be baptized the first Sunday after birth! That is the word of God!'* God's word lasted all day at that

913

congregation, sun-up to sunset and no food between. And no heat either, in spite of the fact it was the dead of winter. They lived in dread of the church burning down, so only footwarmers were allowed. If you were fat you were fine. If you were skinny, you sat and shivered in misery. I sat and shivered in misery while I watched a baby freeze to death. *'He went to heaven! He went to heaven!'* I hope they all went to hell. Church is a good thing. You are right, I should have stayed with it."

I looked at him for a moment somewhat baffled. "You sure have a way of killing my spirit. I don't want to hear anything more about dying babies. I only wanted to say that if I truly had priestly powers, I would have forgiven you of your sins. Clean slate. New soul. You could die with a clear conscience."

"That's what you think."

"What do you mean?"

"All the while I have been sitting here looking at you, my head has been filling with sinful thoughts anew—quite rapidly."

"Luke, I swear, you're the one headed straight for hell."

* * *

A morning that might have been most awkward turned out to be rewarding on many levels. We worked our way through the aftermath of his confession with a lightheartedness that put the matter to rest. His family was never mentioned further, but there seemed no need to do so. Instead, we discussed plans for travel and the one other issue. The one I had sidestepped earlier.

"So, now it's your turn."

"My turn for what?"

"Your turn to bare all."

914

"I have nothing to bare."

"You have plenty to bare.",

"I have nothing to bare." I clenched my teeth. Just as I felt that his play on words was becoming too direct to be respectful, and very nearly annoying, he escaped blame by reverting to seriousness. He could duck faster than a prairie chicken.

"Really? I disagree. I get the feeling we have a lot in common; difference being I am trying to lose a life, whereas you are trying to find one. Otherwise, why would an upper class Boston Harbor, New England type be wandering out here in the middle of ten thousand godforsaken miles of nothing? Secrets. I think you have secrets. Who is Christopher? And don't be bashful, I showed you mine, now you show me yours."

"I didn't ask to see yours." I conveyed both sides of the meaning clearly and the message got through. Luke quieted for a moment, having been put in his place.

"Point taken." He winced.

"I wonder sometimes."

"Trust me, it's merely the romp of a lonely heart. Now, tell me who is this Christopher fellow."

"For starters, he's not my husband and he's not my lover."

"I like him already."

"Stop it."

"Stop what."

"You know what."

"Oh, go on, Elizabeth. I'm just teasing. Go on, tell me who is this Christopher?"

"Who is Christopher?" I repeated. I thought about the question. I thought about all the ways in which he controlled my life, just as I had thought about it many, many times before.

"I don't know if this is simple or complicated, but let me say that this man I am looking for goes by the name of Christopher Claussen.

"In a word or less, I would describe him as an institution. He is wealthy beyond your wildest dreams. Yet, even though that is the first thing the average man would say about him, there is much, much, more to the man than money. I was raised by the Claussens, and when I think of Claus—that's what I call Mr. Claussen—I think first of generosity. He is the most giving person I have ever known, ever met for that matter. He has done more for the poor, especially the children, than anyone I know. He is a wonderful man, Luke, a wonderful man."

"So what is the world's wealthiest wonderful man doing out here in the middle of ten thousand godforsaken miles of dry dirt."

"It's a good question isn't it? He says he's looking for a pass through the Stony Mountains, but I think he's doing the same as you. He is running from his past, but unlike you, he's done it for so long that he no longer knows it. It's become his life."

"You mean he killed somebody in the world of finance?"

"No-o-o-o, I should say not. But that might have been easier. Actually, his wife died a gruesome death in a fire. I was about twelve when it happened. As a matter of fact, I was in her care that night, but escaped with my life. When she died, so did Claus. No one bothered to bury him, so he still walks around."

"Lord, with all his money, he never found someone new? Why didn't he remarry? A man that rich can have any woman he wants. He could have a different woman every night. I should be so lucky."

"You are starting to sound very shallow, Luke, and Claus is not like that. Besides which, you never knew Lady Rebecca. They were perfect together. She had proven to him time and again that she was blind to his wealth, and for that reason he was devoted. Don't get me wrong; I'm not saying that he's out here moping around in misery. I'm just saying this is how I believe he escapes the past—no different than you."

916

"Touché. But what does this have to do with you being out here all alone."

"I'm looking for him. You probably can't understand that, but Claus was the most influential force in my life, and when Lady Rebecca passed on, he fled all that was close to him including me. When he stepped out of my life, my world went upside down, turned inside out. I was muddled up for a good long time.

"Like him, like you, I went on with my life, picking up the pieces and moving forward, but even after all these years there is still something missing—something that has to be put to rest. I can't tell you what it is, but I am convinced that once I see him again, I'll find a certain peace in my life, a fulfillment that escapes me to this day. I guess that's about it. Like I said, maybe it's simple; maybe it's complicated. Any more questions?"

"No, but I know about that pass through the mountains."

"The Stony Pass!"

"Yes, ma'am. Been there. Goes right through them Rockies. Best way through as far as I know."

"I can't believe it. I can't believe this. What luck. That's where Claus is. I am positive of it. I know it in my heart. I know that's where he is."

"It won't take much to convince me. Somebody out there has some serious money because there is a lot of activity going on, buildings and such."

"Do you think you can show me the way? I would be ever so grateful. I will make it well worth your while, I promise."

"Now, exactly what do you mean by that? *Well worth my while.*"

"Not what you're thinking. I mean well worth your while financially. It would prove to be very profitable for you, and being that employment out here leaves a lot to be desired, I should think the offer attractive."

"It is. I could use the money, but I want you to know something first."

"What?"

"I would do it for free, if only to enjoy your company as long as I may. Money can't buy the likes of you."

"Now you know why Christopher Claussen never remarried."

NINETY-SIX

We picked up camp while still dark, hitched the team, and headed out at the first hint of morning's light. It was early even for me, and there was a certain thrill to being wrapped snug in my blanket, warding off the morning chill as I sat alongside Luke and watched a new day begin. The sun rose at our backs and so clipped the very tops of the granite peaks then slowly worked its light down into the shadows below.

It brought me back to my days as a child sitting at REBECCA's rail before sunrise. I remembered the warmth of my ship's blanket and watching the reflection of glistening harbor lights slide back and forth across the heavily dew-covered decks.

Besides old memories, the recent rain and morning dew combined to draw out even the most delicate desert scents. We faced a gentle westerly breeze, which swiped perfume from the petals of flowers yet unseen beneath the shadows at our feet. The smell of sage was especially rich and encouraged me to inhale deeply, taking slow fulfilling breaths.

No longer in the distance, mountains now dominated a landscape that had been showered, prettied up, and splashed with wildflower fragrances—I thought maybe for the sole benefit of

Luke and myself. It was a perfect start to the day and my spirits were soon bubbly and carefree. I was in a fabulous mood.

"How far is it to the pass?"

"Well, if I'm where I think I am, then I would guess no more than a couple of days, three at most. I couldn't have been too far from it when I stumbled into those Blackfeet."

"Three days? Three days. Isn't it odd? I have been traveling for months now, and suddenly three days sounds like eternity."

"It'll pass before you know it. Too fast for my liking; I could sit next to you for a year and even that would be too fast."

"You are such a sweet talking devil. Sing me a song. Here, give me the reins. Get your guitar. I want a song."

"Say pleeeeease."

"Pleeeeease."

"You're too easy. I should be charging you a fee for my entertainment. I think maybe…oh let's say, one kiss, one song. That's plenty cheap enough. Of course, you'll no doubt think it disrespectful."

"Not necessarily, the problem is you men never settle for just one kiss. You only start with just one kiss, and that is where we girls get into trouble."

"It's not my fault if you want me to sing twenty songs."

"Singing songs and stealing kisses are two entirely different things."

"Maybe so, but relationships have to begin someplace. What better way than a kiss?"

"Relationships! Huh! Since when do men want relationships? You men and your carnal cravings, sins of the flesh—that's what men want. I'm not a child, Luke, even I know that much."

"Oh, but you are a child, Elizabeth," he corrected me. I averted my eyes from his knowing stare and blushed from the truth of his words. I stammered, suddenly lost for words. I felt naked and looked the other way. Luke's arm slipped across my shoulder and pulled me in close to his chest. "It's what I like most about you, Elizabeth. There is a certain innocence in your nature that brings out the best in me. I can't remember the last time I enjoyed a truly good-hearted person." He then whispered into my ear. "You are my angel, and I am praying—."

My heart was racing. He turned my face toward him and leaned in to kiss me. I sat frozen in place until the very last second, while in the heat of his breath; I turned away, leaving his heart painfully exposed.

Why! Why! Why, did I do such a thing? Why was all of this so dreadfully difficult for me? Why didn't I just kiss him? I couldn't answer these questions. All I understood at that moment was an overwhelming need to breathe freely, to catch my breath, to regain my bearings.

By turning away, I knew I slammed a door shut. I was furious with myself. My childish fears were surpassed only by my stupidity. Only a stupid woman would reject Luke's advance, stupid, stupid, stupid! Dim-witted.

That sole refusal to allow him into my heart brought the best part of our relationship to a dead halt. He never attempted to kiss me again, and I lost all opportunity to savor its sweetness. I found him wonderfully attractive, and yet I managed to trample asunder everything joyful about him, everything gay about this budding union. The delicate dance of our hearts, the searching of our souls, the arousing flirtations, the secretive gazes, all seemed instantly erased. I tried not to let my mood show itself, but I was falling sick with depression.

"Well, I guess I didn't really deserve that kiss, being I didn't sing the song and all. I just thought a down payment might take a bit of the bite outta the bill."

"A bit of the bite outta the bill?"

"Something like that."

Luke was gentle, but I was now unbearably self-conscious in his presence, and there was nowhere in ten thousand godforsaken miles I could hide. I could see he was receptive enough to realize something of how I felt, and I prayed he didn't think I rejected him because of the confession about his brother.

His attentions that so filled me with pleasure were now reined in. It wasn't that Luke was being cruel. It wasn't anything he was doing. Ironically, it was everything he wasn't doing. He was trying hard to be sensitive, to be respectful. Maybe he was blaming himself, when it was I who could not sort out how to accept a simple kiss. Only I was to blame for my inability to enjoy a brief touch of ecstasy in a place where no one stood witness to pass judgment on my desires, my actions, or me.

We continued across the desert and while I only looked ahead at the mules, afraid to meet his eyes, he tried to make something good out of my botched state of affairs.

"Maybe, if I sang a love song about you, you would feel better about me. What do you think?" I glanced in his direction, just long enough to see the sparkle in his eyes.

"About me? I don't feel as though I deserve a love song. Luke, listen—I didn't mean—I didn't want—."

"Shhh. You worry too much. Look at me. Do I look worried? Of course not. I know in time you'll give me that kiss and I can wait. There will come a time when your heart will say *now*. You won't even think about it. It will just happen. Don't misunderstand me; I *am* praying it will be in this lifetime—." He gave me a wide grin. "You're a fine woman, Elizabeth, and that is rare enough in the middle of Manhattan, let alone out here. In my eyes, you are beautiful, and beauty is what men sing about—remember?"

921

"You're making me blush."

"Good, I guess I do have an affect on your heart."

He worked that grin again, and I swore to myself that if he were to give me a second chance, I would be his lover—however he might have me. I just needed a second chance. This was my secret, my need for a compassionate heart, my need for his support. It was obvious that I was a desperate old spinster who could ill afford to be this foolish so far from the strike of Cupid's arrow.

Luke was studying the fret board, searching for some special chord. It allowed me to look in his direction unnoticed. I was still too self-conscious to face him, to meet his eyes. He rambled on to make good of the situation, to ease my discomfort.

"Now let's see—a simple love song. First, I must select a perfect chord to open your heart, for music is never threatening except for possibly in Boston. Then, I must consider my feelings and translate them into a melody of words and harmonies that slip surreptitiously into that opened heart—this to soften its owner's persuasion. That part is very important. The softening part is very, very important." He strummed his guitar lightly and made up the words as he went.

Majestic mountains surround me,

To frame these endless skies.

Flawless blue and heavenly

A reflection of your eyes.

He opened my heart like the sun opens tulips. Bright red tulips, but I couldn't bring myself to look at him. Instead, as the mules plodded along, I laid my head upon his shoulder.

922

Inside that thick skull, I screamed for him to lift my face, to kiss me, to brush aside my fears. Oh, how I longed for him to kiss me, for any notion of a man singing love songs to me disappeared with the dinosaurs. I was actually being seduced.

I've seen this desert often glow

With a million blossom's light

Yet, such splendor fails to show

my heart's brighter—.

How my heart —.

Delight—To the light, hmm, hmm, hmm.

"Something's wrong here. Ummm. Let me see. Maybe you could give me a hand with this. How would you say your love affects my heart?"

"Oh, please!"

"What? You mean, you can't find a little something to add? A little anything? No direction, no guidance, no feeling. Have I the only heart here? Nothing at all?"

"No. You're embarrassing me."

"Fine. I'll do it myself." He strummed the opening chords again.

I've seen desert blossoms bright

Squashed to ugly brown

After Elizabeth Dennison Claussen's heart

Stomps 'em to the ground.

"Oh, you swine! That was romantic? You want a kiss for a song like that?"

"I wanted a kiss for the sake of a kiss. It's you who's making it nearly impossible to get one. I think I'm going hoarse."

I was crushed.

"Luke, I know what you must think, it's just that—."

Luke raised his hand to silence me. He squinted his eyes, staring ahead at a cloud of dust rising up beyond a ridge. In a matter of moments four silhouettes shimmied in the distant heat, all headed our way. Luke spoke to me, at first in slow drawn out words.

"Elizabeth…I don't think…I like the looks of this…four men riding hard, traveling light, middle of ten thousand—. Nah—don't like it." He looked at me. "I want you to climb in back and put fresh loads in the guns. Keep down low and be real quick about it. Remember what I showed you."

I wasted no time climbing over the seat into the back of the wagon. Luke kept a wary eye on the approaching riders while I loaded the guns. That fear, which is bred into all women began to well up inside. I was entering that dark place where women are stripped of hope, that place of abject loneliness where women confronted threatening men who moved toward them unchallenged. I remembered a warning—*here there are no witnesses to haunt the wicked.*

"What are they doing, Luke?"

I reached out from behind him to place his pistols on the bench.

"Riding hard. Now, get back. Get down and stay out of sight. If they're up to no good, I don't need them being tempted by the likes of you. Right now you're my ticket to trouble."

I held my gun at the ready. Instinctively, I chose not to argue the point, for I could hear the concern in his voice. He began to stress his points under his breath.

"Get down flat on the bed. If they stop and nose around I don't want them seeing you in there. Better yet, get under the furs."

I laid down flat on the wagon bed alongside Luke's long arm and the repeater. I pulled a hide up over my body. I looked over at the gun case for ol' Smokey and began counting the cartridges inside by memory. I stopped counting at the first sound of pounding hooves that reached my ear. Luke called out for the mules to halt. I saw his hand move near the gun. As I lay there looking at the back of him, I could feel his worry.

"Stay down. Stay down. Stay—*ah hell, Elizabeth*, I was afraid of this." He raised his gun.

What few pans I had still hanging overhead rang out sharply as wood splintered throughout the inside of the wagon. In the same instant I heard three loud blasts of gunfire. The sound hammered me, shredding me with terror and coating me with dampness. I feared for Luke and looked up through a cloud of dirt and debris.

The strangers stormed past the wagon on both sides and kept riding. A second later, as if from the wind of their passing horses and spent gunpowder, Luke toppled over backwards and fell upon me. He was bleeding terrible, not gushing, but changing color all over at once. I became frantic. I slid out from beneath him and moved about in order to help him. He wasn't moving. He was looking at me with a blameless stare.

"What's happened? Oh, god have mercy, what's happened, Luke. Luke! Luke! Say something, Luke. Please, Luke, say something. What should I do? What should I do?"

I rested his head upon my lap. His blood was everywhere. His face, his chest, his arms, my hands, my clothes, the inside of the wagon, everything was smeared with its color. I had heard three, maybe four blasts of gunfire and knew that he had taken the full force.

Then it came to me. I saw it in his eyes. I felt it in my heart. He was dying in my arms.

"No, no, no," I cried. "Don't leave me Luke, Oh god, don't leave me." I held him tight; I rocked him. I pleaded with him. I had no thought of fear or riders. My only thought was of him. His eyes never left mine. His face moved to smile in that gentle manner that so thrilled me only moments before.

I opened my eyes wider to see past my tears, and I watched with despair as his slowly closed.

"No, Luke, no. Please. Please don't die."

Without thought, I acted instinctively. I leaned over and kissed him. I hoped to make his heart race as he did mine. I wanted it to beat strong, to go on forever. I wanted to give him all the reason in the world to live. As our lips parted, his last breath crossed my breast. My tears broke free to flood across his bloodied face. I sobbed uncontrollably. I was filled with anguish and remorse.

"Oh, Luke. I so wanted your kiss."

NINETY-SEVEN

I was pulled away from my guilt, pulled away from Luke by the sound of returning horses. I quickly reached for the remaining pistol on the bench and dropped back into the shadows of the wagon. The outlaws were soon circling, looking over the collection of goods outside. They were carrying on, bellowing, and hollering with elation at having obtained a peddler's wagon.

I reached up quickly to lock the back doors of the wagon and then buried myself beneath the blankets with my feet toward the front and my head at the back. There was now only one way inside. I looked at Luke lying next to me, his clothes soaked in blood. I ran my fingers through his hair as words of advice filled my head. *'Never, never, never leave your gun behind'*.

"I'm keeping the guns close."

I spoke to him in whispers. I spoke to him intimately, never considering him not to be present. I drew all the guns near. I knew my fate would be predictable at the hands of these men, and as always, I made sure there was a round with my name on it. I tried to control my breathing, tried to relax. I raised my bloodstained hands and watched the way in which they trembled. I suppressed the shaking by picking up Luke's long arm. I opened the flash pan, checked the charge, pulled back the hammer and waited. I looked over at the pistols and ol' Smokey.

Within moments, I heard the men dismount and walk toward the wagon. They were laughing hysterically about the way Luke 'flopped over backwards' and the 'look on his face' when they started shooting. Luke's legs were still dangling outside, laid over the backrest of the bench.

"Died with his boots on!" One of the men bellowed.

"Life's short."

"Shorter for some than others." They howled.

"I gho look eenside. Mebee, I find more esome uwater."

"Mebee, you better watch yerself, Hernando. I don' wanna see nothing bulgin' outta them pockets or I'm gonna fill yer ass fulla shot, ya hear."

"Yah, I hear, boss. I know uwhat choo say. I thdo more tay work, you get more tay gold."

"Don't you be fergettin' it either. Now get yer ass up there an' see what we done stumbled upon. Hoooo-weeeeee!"

The wagon rocked as the Mexican climbed up and stuck his head inside. He was unshaven and brutish looking. He glanced

927

at Luke and was unmoved. He started fingering some of the drawers and then peered toward the back of the wagon to see what all it contained until his eyes came to meet mine. They opened wide. I lay on my back perfectly still and watched his expression as he soaked up the sight of me like a kid sucking candy.

"Ooooohhh laaaa laaaa."

I read his thoughts clearly and knew what was in store for me, but it wouldn't be by this man. From beneath a blanket, I raised Luke's long arm and the two of us looked down the barrel, but from different points of view. I squeezed the trigger. Click—the Mexican barely comprehended his fate in that split second before the powder ignited and the ball passed through his head.

A spot appeared upon his forehead, but behind the brute, I saw a red cloud of mist erupt into the sunlight. It was as though the gun smoke blew right through his skull. He slumped backward off the bench and fell out of sight from my window to the world. I heard him hit the ground. The rapport of the gun spooked the mules, and they started forward a short distance, pulling the front wheel over the Mexican's body.

A thick whitish cloud of gunsmoke rolled out slowly from inside the wagon. Outside, it went instantly silent. I knew I had crossed the point of no return.

"What in tar-na-shenn—?"

"Whoa! What's going on, boss?"

"Looks ta me like Hernando, jus got 'is blimey head blown off." There was a short pause for thought.

"Hey, bossh, Ya thenk schomebody'sh schtill in the wagon?"

"Geesh Jo-shee! I don't know. I was thinkin' may-beee it was a mouthful of water that blew up in his ugly ass Mexican head! Course there's someone in the wagon ya brickhead."

928

"Whadya wanna do, Charlie?"

"Well, Cal, ya could go have a look inside an' see jus' what we're dealin' with."

"Yeah, an' you can kiss my ass." There was some grumbling. "Get serious, Charlie. It's too damn hot to be playin' aroun', an I ain't talkin' bout just the sun."

"We got some time. I wouldn't be worryin'."

"I ain't sheen nobody followin' ush."

"Josie, you ain't gonna see anybody following you until it's too late. C'mon Charlie, let's get what we want an' get the hell outta here."

"Yeah, bosh. Bessht we get the schow on the road."

"Hey, Jo-shee. I give the orders around here, not you, got it?"

"Yesh, bosh—what choo lookin' at?"

"I'm lookin' at that wagon. I say we pump it full o' lead. Grab what goods we need and get." There was a sound of agreement among the men, and then I heard the boss yell out.

"Hey, mister! Ya better hope like hell ya got nine lives to lose cuz it's time to start countin'!"

My blood went cold with terror. Then as if outlaws could communicate by thought, the wagon began to splinter and shudder from the barrage of gunfire they let loose in unison. I could do little but cover my face and be grateful for my trunk and all the furs wrapped around me. It seemed that nothing could penetrate the hides stuffed into the wagon. Above me it was a different story as sunlight began to pour in through freshly made holes behind cabinet doors that were being blown open. It pained me to see the children's drawings being ripped apart. The air was crisscrossed with dozens of blazing swords that skewered the smoke filled shadows of my coffin.

The firing stopped momentarily. I took a gamble that the men were reloading and wondering to themselves if anything had lived through the barrage of gunfire. I reached for ol' Smokey. I arose slowly to my knees so as not to move the wagon, and then turned to face the rear door. I released the lock, then the latch and pushed gently on the postern, opening it but a few inches.

"Whaddya think, Charlie?"

There before me, no more than twenty feet was a sandy haired European sort with a large brimmed hat looking off to one of his comrades. He then looked down to reload his gun, which caused his wide brimmed hat to block me from his view. He answered the voice that belonged to Cal.

"I think I wouldn't want to be in that wagon, that's what I think. No sir."

I centered the barrel of my pistol in the opening of the door. Along the barrel, I watched the man pour a fresh charge into the pan. As I was about to pull the trigger, I gave thought to how I was committing cold-blooded murder. I thought regardless of what good or bad this person had done, I alone was about to take his life. I hesitated. I thought about my fate, and still I hesitated. Then, I thought of Luke.

My shot caught the unsuspecting man square in the chest. The force of the ball jarred him severely. He dropped his gun into the sand and clenched his shirt. He began to tear it open, but collapsed lifeless into the dirt before succeeding.

"Tar-na-schennn! Cal, the bosh'ish bin' shot."

"What?"

"The bosh'ish bin shot. I shaw him get it. Now itch jush you an' me, Cal."

"Charlie? Charlie? Charlie!" Cal hollered out. "Damn! What's going on here?" There was a moment of silence, then— "Hope you like lead, you bastard!"

I was met with a fresh round of gunfire and a great deal of swearing. The outlaws were livid, but they had no idea whom, or for that matter, how many were in the wagon. All they knew for sure was they were suddenly down two out of four comrades. I could hear them calling out to one another, but little else, until the one who went by Cal hollered out.

"Stop shootin,' Josie. Get over here."

"How we schplittin' up the gold, Cal?"

"Two for me, one for you. Now get over here."

"That ain't fair, Cal. That ain't—."

"Shuddup, Josie! Yer driving me nuts."

"Yer jush like the bosh, Cal. It ain…."

The voices drifted off into the distance. I realized that at least for the time being I had stood them off. What they were up to, I couldn't imagine. I peeked out the doors, but the men were staying clear for fear of being sniped at. During the next three hours, as we moved into the heat of late afternoon, nothing else took place.

I was at a complete loss as to what to do with myself and so did the only thing I could. I waited. I determined to reload the long arm and barely considered making up more cartridges when a jolt of adrenaline shot through my bode. My mouth went dry as dust.

In a panic, I looked over at the place where Luke had set the keg of black powder. In all the confusion it had completely escaped my thoughts. I understood now it was miraculously untouched. It had been stored in a corner formed by the water barrel and my trunk. I just stared at it in disbelief. I shoved one of the hides up against its exposed side. For whatever reason, the spirits had been with me. I clasped Shadow Hunter's amulet and held it to my chest.

"Thank you, Shadow Hunter; thank you, Luke; thank you, Dusty, and thank you too, Lady Rebecca."

I also gave thought to the water keg. It appeared as though it had been hit a couple of times, but the balls were spent after passing through the wagon sides and lacked the power to penetrate the stakes. I packed some additional protection around it for peace of mind.

During the lull in activity, I began to consider how much ball and powder the outlaws had used up pulverizing the wagon in order to kill me. I knew for a fact that nobody could afford such expenditure. If it had been me, I would have just stuck a shotgun around front and blasted the inside of the wagon. As soon as that thought formed in my head I went sick to my stomach. I hardly dared think the thought, lest the outlaws read my mind. I only had to look at Luke to see first hand the result of those blasts.

I was then entirely preoccupied with protecting myself from such an attack. I climbed beneath a second hide. They were very thick and would prove to be my best shield against a ball or blast. This was apparent by the amount of lead laying about me on the wagon bed. It seemed impossible to shoot anything though the tough leather.

Unfortunately for me, lying fully dressed between the furs was a most wretched ordeal. I was forced to suffer the unbearable temperatures inside the wagon as it sat baking in the midday sun. I propped the hides above me to circulate air, but I hardly dared expose myself. I worried that a gun could appear pointed at my head at any second, so I remained mostly concealed to cook in misery. Luckily, my long time companion, the desert wind was still with me. This time instead of chapping my lips or pelting me with sand, it sent a breeze through the opened doors to cool my sweat and bring me much needed relief.

Between the heat, the stress, a poor night's sleep, and an early morning rise, I found myself completely drained of energy and actually drifting off to sleep. I was amazed I could do anything

932

of the sort, knowing to fall asleep most certainly meant my death. I kept slapping myself, forcing my eyes to open wide, absorbing the painfully brilliant daylight that entered the front door and forcing it back into my sleepy head.

I was in that half-awake state, staring into the bright light outside, when a black rope like silhouette appeared instantly in the air. It came flying toward me too fast for me to make any sense of it until after it slammed hard into the hide spread across my chest. I snapped out of my stupor and let out a scream of sheer horror as I focused on an enormous rattlesnake that rolled off me in a writhing ball of pent up fury, squirming, hissing, rattling and ready to strike.

It was huge, all of five feet. Every muscle in my body locked up as it slithered across me in search of a place to hide. All the while I lay face to face with this serpent, gunfire splintered the wood in every direction. Ball and shot were blowing holes through the wagon sides and dropping on top of the snake and me like metal rain.

The reptile curled up alongside Luke and poised itself for a strike. Its rattles were vibrating fiercely and it held its head retracted, ready to lash out at me. I shuddered with every blast that rocked the wagon, but dared not move an inch. I looked about frantically for something to ward off the creature and spotted a couple of hatchets I had kept for myself.

I looked back and forth between the hatchets and the snake. The shotgun blasts were wreaking havoc on the wagon sides and the spray of splinters was keeping the serpent agitated. The gunfire was suddenly child's play compared to my fear of confronting the venomous fangs. I slowly slipped my hands beneath a blanket and positioned it for a throw.

I threw the blanket. At the same time, the snake struck out at me, but the fabric foiled its move. As it retreated, the blanket floated down, spreading out above it. I immediately reached for one of the hatchets and began swinging wildly at the shape as it twisted about under the blanket.

933

I threw caution to the wind and rose to my knees, risking the danger of gunshot in order to swing the hatchet forcefully with both hands. The steel head was sharp and sliced its way through everything, the blanket, the snake, and possibly Luke.

The deathblow couldn't have come any too soon for me. Which one it might have been I couldn't know, for like Luke, the bulge beneath the blanket continued to move even after it had been killed. A final gunshot blasted splinters into my face and returned me to sanity. I dropped back onto the furs.

The gunfire had come to a stop and I as I lay trying to settle my nerves; I listened to the outlaws laughing hysterically.

"A woman?"

"She musht be a real pishtol."

"I woman. I can't believe it." Cal laughed till he nearly split a gut. "Charlie would be turning over if he had a grave."

"We gonna bury 'im, Cal?"

"You wanna go get a shovel out of the wagon, Josie?"

"No."

"Then I reckon we won't be burying nobody, lessin' you plan on diggin' with your fingers."

I had no recollection of screaming or making any kind of noise, but the men outside were laughing hysterically upon discovering that I was a 'she' and not a 'he'. Picturing me in the wagon with the snake pleased them to no end.

What really annoyed me was how once the outlaws discovered I wasn't a man, it served to remove all fear from their minds. In fact, it turned the situation into a charade, a game of cat and mouse, which delighted them enormously. Even in light of my having killed two of their party, I was now nothing more than entertainment. They were emboldened at once and began to describe in graphic detail what lay in wait for me. It was a presentation of horrors that is reserved only for a woman's benefit.

From their point of view, there was no longer any need to hurry the affair. They made no attempt to confront or provoke me the remainder of the day. The sun waned and those glorious late evening hues poured into the wagon. I had watched Luke for hours and now found myself crying. I recalled how he had laid next to me the night before, filled with life, joking and also crying. I recalled how pleasant it was to feel secure for that short time. I wondered how all those emotions could simply cease to exist. I wondered where they went. I wondered if he was gone or still with me.

I fought sleep, fearing its consequences, but lost the battle nonetheless. When I next woke, it was the dead of night. For the better part of an hour, I listened to Josie and Cal snoring before I was confident that they were intent on sleeping on through. I fell back to sleep.

When next I opened my eyes, the air was cool and refreshing. The pale light of early morn was sneaking down into the mountain valleys. Towering above them, peaks were snatching the earliest rays of orange from the sky. I watched those peaks begin to glow, peeling away more and more of that morning light from the heavens and pushing it down the slopes to disappear into the mists. It was almost painful to see something so beautiful and peaceful belie the reality of my situation.

The morning came and went in all its glory as day moved toward noon, and never once did the outlaws harass me. I could occasionally make out voices if one or the other laughed, but nothing more. As I lay in the wagon suffering through the heat of afternoon, I was finally enlightened to their cruelty.

"Hey, lady! How you an' yer man gettin' 'long? He gettin' ripe yet?"

"Yeah, he must be schtartin' to schmell purty schweet."

They continued to laugh at my expense. I realized that they believed I was married to Luke. I gave thanks to the Lord that I didn't have to endure what surely would have been the most

935

unimaginable misery had I been a loving wife. It was bad enough, my feelings being passionate as they were, but to lie here next to your dead husband was inconceivable to me.

I had no choice but to stay still and that was exactly what I did for the next two days. Their plan was to drive me mad by keeping me confined in close quarters with Luke's corpse. The temperature during the heat of day hovered near a hundred, and Luke was transforming himself into a bloated mass that was no longer recognizable. He gave every sign of an impending explosion. His skin took on a milky green shade and then began to blister. I finally could no longer look at him and folded a blanket over his body to hide it from view.

Luke was as dead as dead could be, but he never stopped moving. To see such a thing was most unsettling. His arms and legs shifted positions, and he was filled with the noise of gas moving about his insides. I hadn't noticed the smell of him, but this was because at first it changed gradually. Not so with the flies that were now gathering in great number about the inside of the wagon, especially upon Luke's blanket. They led me to suspect what the outlaws already knew. In this heat, Luke immediately started to rot. He became so distended beneath the blanket that I suffered dreadful thoughts of him rupturing with unimaginable consequence.

During my imprisonment, I lay for hours on the wagon bed pressed to know what was happening outside. I focused on all the holes blasted into the sides of the wagon. They made tiny windows, each with a slightly different view. I invested my time carving out the wood that surrounded these little holes, picking away at the splinters and quietly enlarging the holes until I could watch nearly every move that Cal and Josie made.

I couldn't always hear their conversations, but I could keep a relatively good eye on their activities. I could also see that they were either becoming impatient with the standoff or simply bored because they were restless. I couldn't imagine why they would be so interested in the wagon, but for whatever reason, they stuck around. I watched as they paced back and forth and occasionally fired off another round into the wagon to keep me on edge.

I was starting to feel safe from gunfire because I learned that there were still enough items inside the wagon to keep a ball or shot from reaching me. So far, nothing had passed through the buffalo hides. The lead was pretty well spent after busting through the lower part of the wagon sides and had little if any power left to cause me harm.

However, I became quite concerned when after staring through a hole, I saw Cal raise a finger to his mouth in order to silence Josie. I watched intently after he left Josie behind and stooped low to sneak toward the wagon with a loaded gun at the ready. I went from hole to hole following his approach to the point where he crawled under the wagon. Josie was staring intently in our direction.

My mind raced, and I instantly determined that Cal was planning to shoot up through the wagon bed. I stood up both quickly and quietly atop the folds of the hides at the front of the wagon. At the same time, I was struck with the realization that this could be a game played by two, and I reached for ol' Smokey. I opened the flash pan, cocked the hammer and clenched my teeth in preparation for Cal's blast.

Boom!

It came just as expected. I saw Luke's body move, but paid little mind because I was racing for the rear edge of the furs. With my left hand, I yanked them back off the wagon bed, and with my right hand I pointed ol' Smokey at the wood and fired a round straight through the planks.

I doubted Cal had ever given a thought to me watching him approach the wagon through all those little holes he made, or given thought to the stupidity of lying flat on the ground in the worst possible position for a quick exit. It was probably just like him to believe he could just lie there on his back, reload at leisure and fire off a couple of rounds for the fun of it.

I was choking on the smoke, it was suffocating, but nevertheless an immense feeling of satisfaction filled my being as I heard his cry of pain then anger. Ever more confident, I grabbed one of Luke's poker game pistols and fired a second round through the bed. I then grabbed the matching piece and leaned out the front of the wagon to fire a round at Cal's backside as he scrambled out from under the wagon like a frightened jackrabbit, holding on to his arm and bounding for his life.

"Hope you like lead, you bastard!" I screamed out his earlier threat.

I didn't know how bad I hit him when he was lying under the wagon, but he was both swearing and howling like a banshee. Josie was crouched low in the field with guns in hand, raised high, and poised to fire. I dove for the hides. The crack of splintering wood followed immediately overhead, but only from the two rounds and nothing more.

I lay on the hides trying to catch my breath and found myself giggling at the thought of Cal hightailing it across the field. I was giddy with delight. Unfortunately, my laughter was short lived; for I was suddenly overtaken by the most putrid smell imaginable. Cal's round had plowed into Luke's bloated frame and essentially caused him to burst. There was a great deal of pressure that needed to be relieved and the stench emanating from beneath his blanket was absolutely revolting. I turned away to bury my face in a blanket, but between the oppressive heat, my anxiety, and a smell that was so utterly invasive it could be tasted; I vomited involuntarily.

Luke had to go. My heartfelt feelings for this man were quickly reduced to memory by his present condition. Being cooped up in the desert sun with a rotting corpse moved one to view mortal remains with a good deal less respect.

I looked through the holes and noted that Cal was occupied with wrapping a bandage around his upper arm. Josie was busy enjoying Cal's pain. I was free to move about, and so began wrapping Luke's body with the blanket. I then took a deep breath and put my every ounce of strength into lifting his torso up an over the bench seat backrest.

Even though he had stiffened, it was nearly an impossible feat for someone my size. I put new pain into old wounds, ribs that were being taxed to the limit. To make matters worse, as I moved underneath Luke, I found myself pressed up hard against him and sliding in the ooze of his innards as pressure forced them out through the hole made by Cal's gunshot. I was dripping with the mess, but too far engaged to back down. One last strenuous push and Luke toppled over the front of the seat to plow into the earth below.

I was breathing hard, but hardly dared open my mouth but for the thousands of flies swarming inside the wagon. I swatted the air in an attempt to drive out the pests, but I was too well soaked in Luke's discharges to evade their determination. I ended up stripping off my clothes, mopping up the wagon bed of Luke's remains and my vomit, and throwing all of it outside.

I smelled my hands. I turned my face as I gagged in preparation to wretch again. I held it in, but I immediately sacrificed some drinking water to wash. I reached for a cloth, which I dipped to dampen. I rubbed my hands across the bar of soap and then wiped them off. I sought out my lavender lotion and applied it to both my hands and neck. I rubbed some on my face and at last freed myself from the gut wrenching stench that permeated everything surrounding me.

I collapsed back upon the hides, in an effort to reclaim my sanity. I wondered how much more of this was I to endure. I was feeling sorry for myself until I focused my attention on the mules. They had been kept in their harness for days without food or water and appeared in terrible shape. The sight of them so filled me with distress, I lay upon the hides and wept. I was embarrassed to having been so full of self-pity.

As night approached, I gave thought to slipping out of the wagon under the cover of dark, but there was no place to go. To the last ray of light, I scanned the mountains for any hint of the south pass. Luke claimed it was only a couple days distant, but I had no idea of where. I was certain that without water to sustain me, I would never find it on foot.

No matter how much I might wish different, I was facing a choice of dying in the wagon or dying in the desert. I concluded it was better to die in the wagon. Death in the desert would be from the heat as I slowly baked. Death in the wagon would most likely come after taking a stand against my attackers and meeting my end quickly, but until that happened, I had plenty of water and food.

My gut instincts told me it was best to stay put and fight it out to the bitter end. It was in this frame of mind that my thoughts at last became incoherent. After hours spent listening for any suspicious movements by Josie and Cal, I allowed myself to drift nervously in and out of my dreams.

NINETY-EIGHT

The sound of gunfire awakened me early the next morning with a god-awful fright. I bolted upright, but for being half asleep and lacking sufficient sense to lay low. Wits returned, I ducked down and cleared my head. I realized right off that there was no wood splinters raining down own me, and determined no one was firing my way. Maybe they were hunting. I figured that they must have been low on food and water. I raised my head barely enough to peek outside before falling back upon my bed choked with despair.

Josie shot one of my mules.

It was a senseless act of brutality that shattered my spirit. Any thought of the act being done out of hunger or need was quickly put to rest after there came a second gunshot that prompted me to sit up and bear witness to the systematic killing of my team one by one. All the while Josie dropped the animals, Cal kept his shotgun aimed at the wagon. He screamed obscenities and dared me to show myself. He cursed me for shooting him and killing his partners. He swore I would soon die in a torturous fashion. He was an angry man and delighted in threatening me in a most descriptive and uncouth manner.

Terrified that he might discharge his weapon out of sheer meanness, I slid quietly beneath the thick buffalo hides for safety. I had suffered with each discharge of the pistol, knowing how the despicable act not only killed another mule, but also any hope I might have had for leaving this place.

So began in earnest my thoughts of escaping on foot and wondering how would I fare. Could I keep myself hid on an open plain, once they discovered I had slipped away? God help me if I were caught out there. I would need to bring my pistol. What if I did make it to the mountains and survived the searing heat of the sun? What then? How long would it take me to find water? What about bears and mountain lions? What all would I need to survive in the hills—a blanket, a pan, a cup, a knife, powder and shot, flint, a trap or two? It would never work, I thought to myself. I could never carry near the amount of supplies needed to survive even a few days.

I thought about all these things from every angle and always arrived at the same conclusion as the night before—my chances were slim if I left the wagon. I had little choice but to stay put and focus on the best ways to improve my situation. Even if I managed to kill both men, how long would my water last? Without the mules, I was good as dead. On the other hand, I thought to myself, there were horses. I only needed one, and there were five to pick from, counting Luke's. I only needed to figure out how to steal one. I needed a horse and a means of carrying water.

Subconsciously, I looked about the wagon for a suitable container. I wasn't like these outlaws who could go on forever without a drink, or the need to cry. I just wasn't like them. How ever did they manage on so little water?

This last thought puzzled me. These men sat outside and baked in the sun for hours on end. How could they do that on so little water? I hadn't given much thought to water because I had plenty of it, but Cal and his cronies were riding with few provisions and surely couldn't have that much water to drink. I remembered Luke's words:

...four men riding hard, traveling light, middle of ten thousand godforsaken miles....

This question plagued me. It nagged me. Something about the issue warranted my attention, and as I pondered it bit by bit an entirely different realization came to mind. It occurred to me that whatever impatience these desperados voiced might be due to something other than a desire to flee some unknown crime. Make no mistake, they were on the run; that much was obvious from things they said, and I was heartened to think that in order to be on the run, one had to be running from something. There had to be a camp or settlement or something nearby. Maybe I was closer to the south pass than I realized.

But this was a thought that at present needed to be put aside. Water was the immediate issue. What if the outlaws had been riding those few days before arriving at the wagon? What if they had intended on stealing whatever water the wagon carried? What if what they needed most was the water?

Luke had never seen a wagon out here. I supposed these men hadn't as well. They must have been overcome with excitement at the prospect of robbing a peddler's wagon. The wares would have been worth a fortune if traded for pelts. The temptation was too much to leave behind, but every hour they remained was another hour without water. First, their thoughts must have been of robbery, then most certainly rape, but now it surely had to be water above all else.

What if they couldn't wait me out as I had earlier thought they would? I was thinking the bandits had all the time in the world to their advantage, but what if they didn't have enough water? Maybe they passed the point of no return while waiting to rob and rape. It was plain enough to me that they were restless. Dying of thirst would be enough to make anybody restless. It was they who were sitting out there unprotected in the sun, not I, and I knew first hand that it didn't take much of that to get under one's skin.

Maybe they no longer had a choice but to leave. In that case, I could imagine them killing off the mules to make sure the wagon remained. They probably figured with a little luck, I would be gone or more likely dead by the time they returned. The wagon would go nowhere without its mules, I couldn't carry anything, so the spoils would sit and wait for them to return at a later date.

It was all starting to make perfect sense, and yet I had just been given my first ray of hope. As far as water went and this game of life and death, as long as we just sat here, I would surely win. Of course, I knew they weren't about to sit around and shrivel up for the lack of anything else to do. They had after all, already killed my mules. Mules had substantial value, and they elected to sacrifice their worth. They must be desperate. Yet, if they were on the run and couldn't return from where they came, where would they go for supplies? I knew of no place. Luke and I hadn't passed a waterhole. We had collected our water with rain tarps.

Water was the key, water and food, I was sure of it. I just had to figure out a way to use this to my advantage. All the while I struggled with my thoughts, the men grew increasingly more restless by the hour, much more so than the day before.

Cal was becoming very vocal, swearing profusely and periodically firing rounds into the wagon to suffer me continued anxiety.

He and Josie were clearly irritable. They were beginning to bicker with one another, and I knew that the standoff would soon be drawing to an end. As for me, the knife-edge terror of my situation had worn off substantially during the days passed. I took time to think out my options, and I no longer found myself afraid of these men, nor of the prospect of getting beaten and raped. Whether justified or not, the fact was I had killed. The fact was, I would kill again to save my life or keep my honor. I was no longer unlike Taa'sooma'hane. I understood.

I laid low and set free the smile that fought to cross my face. Those boys were baking. Those boys were breaking. There wasn't one single, solitary object available to use as shade from the merciless sun—nothing. I knew about the sun, and I watched with pleasure as it pressed down hard upon them.

I remembered how Luke had rode up to the wagon suffering of thirst. He struggled to keep his patience, to keep from busting past me for a drink. I remembered watching him drink with a vengeance to quench his parched insides. A might powerful thirst, he called it. Yes, indeed, I thought to myself, *a might powerful thirst.*

I lay there calmly staring out the holes, watching every move Cal and Josie made while my mind raced through one plan after another, one possibility after another. Mentally, I followed each and every idea through to its conclusion. I couldn't afford to let them leave; I couldn't afford to let them live.

Eventually, my thoughts condensed into a single scheme, an idea that would bring death to at least one of us, if not all. The plan was an all or nothing bet based on their need for water and my cunning. If it came to brains, there would be no match, but it was said that luck was wasted on the brainless, and in view of the amount of luck I needed, I doubted I could ever make myself that stupid.

I held the men off one more miserably hot day. I knew they would have to make a move very soon or seriously face the prospect of death. Their speech now sounded thick and dry. I had watched them poke around the wagon in search of spent lead after which they huddled about a fire to mold new balls. They had caught another large snake, but this time instead of throwing into the wagon, they ate it. They were in a foul state of mind, arguing a great deal, and perfectly primed for my needs. They would be apt to do stupid, thoughtless things.

There came a spell of real concern when Josie, dim-witted as he was, nearly did me in. He became so upset while sitting at the fire making lead balls that he picked up a piece of burning wood and threw it at the wagon in a fit of anger. It was as though he and Cal were simultaneously struck with the same bolt of inspiration as they joined forces to grab the flaming pieces of wood and toss them at the wagon in hopes of setting it ablaze or at least smoking me out.

The prospect of choosing between fire of wood or fire of gun filled me with panic. Fortunately for me, the desert wind never stopped blowing, and its breeze even when light served to ward off the flames and smoke. There was seldom enough wood to burn on the plains and so Cal and Josie quickly concluded that they could never collect the fuel needed to meet their needs. If they could have walked up to the wagon and concentrated a small fire in a crucial place they might have succeeded, but good sense prevailed and they didn't get their heads blown off trying.

Let it be said, their ambitions convinced me my time had come. I had thought out every detail of my plan and aimed to turn this situation around to my benefit. I looked about me and assured myself all was ready and in order. I looked at the water barrel. I looked at my guns, loaded and ready. I looked at the buffalo hides now folded against the back of the wagon bench to be used as a shield.

As quietly as possible, I dragged my trunk to my left side and the water barrel to my right. I pulled the powder keg in alongside me. I counted my inventory of percussion pins and charges. I fondled the pistols, taking aim and shooting at mental images of Cal and Josie until they died a thousand deaths. I was as ready as I would ever be.

I waited until the worst heat of late afternoon was upon us before putting my plan into action. When the sweat was streaming down my face, I looked out one of the holes. I picked up a hatchet and slammed the butt end of the head hard onto the now exposed wood of the wagon bed. Cal and Josie jumped with a start and nervously looked my way. They were motionless, undoubtedly wondering what I was up to, and whether or not they should duck for cover.

I then filled a tin with water, and after taking a drink, I flung the remaining water outside high into the air. I watched it unfold into a million glistening diamond-like prisms that reflected the brilliant desert sunlight before disappearing into the dry sand below. I refilled the cup took another drink and did exactly the same thing again. Again, and again, cup after cup, slowly, methodically, I threw the water out the open door.

I was positive that at this very moment Cal and Josie were either nearly out of water or completely out of their minds. On the last count, they proved me out, for they could barely conceal their anxiety as hushed tones erupted into loud grumbling, hollering, and swearing between themselves. I dared to say they had lost a gamble by staying too long at the wagon. All I needed to do was drive them crazy enough, and after tossing out ninth or tenth tin full of water, I achieved my goal. Cal was on his feet stomping about like a nervous bull.

"Hey! Hey! What in hell's name ya doin', lady?"

"My mules are dying! My mules are dying! Can't you see that?" I cried out. "I want to die! I going to die! I have nothing left to live for. You killed my husband. I have nothing—nothing." I let my voice fade away and feigned sobbing. I ranted in gibberish for a moment then cried out anew. "My mules are dying!. They're dying! We're all dying! There's not enough water left for anybody to live in this godforsaken place. You'll have your precious wagon soon enough. Just leave me alone. Leave my mules be! Ya hear me! Let 'em be!" I threw another tin full of water out across the dead mule carcasses. I moved quickly to watch through the holes, to see their reaction. I held my breath so I might hear their whispering. They were looking at each other mortified and mystified at the same time.

"The mules?" Josie asked in a whisper. "What's shee talkin' about, Cal? The mules ish dead."

"I donno. Maybe—maybe, she's gone plumb crazy."

"Think, sho?"

"Yeah, yeah. She must think the mules are still alive. Yeah. Her min's gone. Women's min's can't take it. I'm surprised she lasted this long after that snake an' all, after bein' cooped up in there a coupla days with a dead man."

"Her hushband."

"Yeah."

I tossed out another tin full of water.

"There shee go ish agin."

Cal rushed forward.

"Whoa! Lady, hang on now! There ain't no need for anybody t' be dyin' fer lack a water, ya hear me? Too many's died already, ain't no need. Listen to me, wastin' water ain't goin' t' do you or anybody else a bit o' good. Them mules is jus' fine. Now, how 'bout you settlin' down a bit, and we'll work somethin' out t'make ever'body happy. I know ya wanna go, an' so do we, so jus' settle down an' we'll work somethin' out. We don' need no wagon, but we could use some of that water. That's all, a little water and we'll leave ya be. Ya got my word."

Lying, murdering, thieves, I thought to myself, as I worked my plan for all it was worth. I readied the pistols. I searched the floorboards of the wagon for gunshot holes and cracks that had been opened up by the dry desert air. I then commenced to pouring water onto the bed and watching it leak through the boards, headed for the sands of death below. I knew this act would be excruciating to observe.

"Hey, Lady! What in tarn-ation are ya doin'!!" The exasperation was easy to hear in Cal's voice.

"I'm taking a bath." I said, nonchalantly.

"What! What! A bath!"

"Why shee takin' a bath?"

"Oh, fer god sakes. Shut yer pan, Josie, fer I kill ya muh self. How'd I know why she's takin' a bath. She's nuts! Crazy as a coot! Do I gotta 'xplain it to ya? She thinks the damn mules are alive. Or din' ya hear that part!"

"Jush ashkin, ya know, jush ashkin. No need getting' all fired up."

"Just shut up, will ya. Just shut up!"

"I'm tired of this dried up desert. I'm tired of the dirt and the dust. I tired of the filth. I'm tired of never being clean. A proper lady deserves a bath. A cool refreshing bath. I poured more water down through the floorboards. This all but devastated the two men."

"Lady! Lady! Damn it! Don't be wastin' no more o' that water. Ya can't be doin' that out here. Jus' tell us what ya want an' it's yours. We'll give ya whacha need an' git ya on yer way. I promise!"

I kept pouring ever so slowly, allowing the boards to continue an endless drip. I peeked out a bullet hole and watched as they stared at the liquid of life dissipate before their very eyes. The look on their faces was all I needed for encouragement. I played out the crazy woman tactic for all it was worth.

"How do I know you aren't lying to me?" The men stopped bickering and stood silent.

"We're a lotta things, lady, but we ain't liars!"

"I don't know." I responded lifeless. "We're all going to die."

I took a mouth full of water and gurgled as loudly as I was able. I spit it out the front of the wagon. I watched through the holes. There was another moment of silence, and then some hushed talk, and even some laughter. It was good they were growing confident. I wanted them to believe they held the upper hand.

"No, no, nobody's gonna die no how. Whadya think, lady? We gotta deal or what?" Cal asked.

"I don't have any supplies! I'm not a peddler! My husband and I were just using the wagon to reach a stake in the Stony Mountains, but we got lost. I got some picks and shovels. Some food and water and bedrolls and that's all.

"I'll throw out some food and water if you'll promise to ride off and leave me be. You've already killed my husband, isn't that enough?"

"We're sorry 'bout that. We din't mean to kill nobody. He drew his gun first. It was all a mistake. We don't need no picks and shovels, lady. Just a little o' that water, an we'll be on our way. Ya seem t' have plenty 'nough to spare. Why don't you jus' step outta that wagon an' be neighborly?"

"No, I'm afraid to. I gotta gun!" I tried to sound stupid.

"Yeah, we believe ya, lady. So whadya wanna do?"

"Here!"

I threw out a large chunk of pemmican. I watched as Josie moved cautiously toward it. He snatched the bundle and hurried back to safety. I watched to see how fast they took to eating the meat. Josie started right into it. Cal said something to him and he stopped dead in his tracks and looked at the wagon.

"Hey! How d'we know you ain't tryin' to poishun ush or shomethin'." I resisted the urge to be cocky with them. Instead I decided to come across as nervous.

"I...I...I don't know. How would I do that? I don't have anything but dried buffalo and water. I got picks and shovels and my gun. And I'll shoot if you get any ideas, so ya better watch out!"

"Oh yeah, we hear ya, lady. We know all 'bout that gun o' yers. We got two dead friends out here cookin'."

"Well, they started it." A nice touch, I thought to myself. It made me sound like a complete idiot.

"Yeah, well, I don't think ya even wanna be going there lady or I'm gonna lose my patience. Now, where's the water. That's part o' the deal. You said so yerself."

"I have to find something to put it into."

"Why don' ya jus' let us come an' get it?"

"You stick so much as I finger in this here wagon and I'll blow your head off." I heard them chuckling under their breath.

"All right, then. Just hurry up. I'm damn powerful thirsty."

A might powerful thirst, I thought to myself as I stooped over the keg of gunpowder. I poured water over it, soaking it good and letting the run off pass through the cracks in the wagon bed. I knew they could see it falling to the ground and would assume I was filling a container for them.

"Mother of Jesus, woman! Go easy. Ya look to be pourin' half of it on the ground. Ya don't wanna be wastin' no more o' that, ya hear!"

I didn't respond, but waited up a bit to prolong their agony and build anticipation.

"C'mon lady, what's the holdup. We gettin' some water or what?"

950

I watched them through the holes until I felt they were at the point of least control. "All right. Now you take this, an' leave me be. You promised to leave me be. I gave you food, an' I now I'm givin' ya water. Now you go! You leave me be!"

I stood up, and after summoning every ounce of my strength; I threw the dripping wet powder keg out the front of the wagon as far as I could manage. It didn't go nearly the distance I had hoped, but it had the right effect as it rolled along causing the sand to stick to its wet wooden staves.

I dropped onto to my knees behind the hides and grabbed Luke's long arm. I laid the very end of the barrel across the back of the bench, keeping it hid within the hides as best possible. I trained my sights squarely on the keg. Even if they saw me with the gun they would already be too close to the powder keg to live through the blast.

Cal moved cautiously toward the wet keg. I didn't want him to study it too closely and so I worked to distract him.

"Remember, you promised to leave me be. I gotta gun, ya know."

"Yeah, I know, lady. Don't worry, I keep my promises."

I kept Cal nervous enough to keep a wary eye on the wagon and me. He stepped closer to the keg. I had to keep his eyes off of it.

"Promise me I can go, or I'll shoot."

"Yeah, I promise. You jus' settle down now, lady. We don' want no one getting' hurt."

"I don't believe you. You're lying. I think you're lying!"

I wanted to make Cal as nervous as possible. I wanted him to think I might shoot at any second. He dared not take his eyes off me for a second.

Out of the corner of my eye, I caught motion. Cal had played his own game. He had been trying to hold my attention as well. Unfortunately for him, through the numerous gunshot holes, I saw Josie's shadow pass along the side of the wagon to take me by surprise. He was about an arm's length away when I was forced to swing the long arm around and blow a ball through the side of the wagon just where he stood. Josie let out a yell and cursed me to hell, but backed off as I ducked down into the hides. To my utter dismay, I didn't kill him, but he must have caught a face full of splinters. Cal, on the other hand, thinking I had expired my shot began to laugh.

"You stupid women can't hit the broadside of a barn."

Everything after that happened fast within a fragment of a second. Cal unloaded both his pistols in my direction in order to pin me down and provide cover for Josie who proceeded to mount a second attack. Cal ducked low to the ground merely a couple of yards from the keg.

"I'll show you stupid women!" I screamed.

I raised the repeater over the backrest and fired at the keg, which took both men by complete surprise, stopping them in their tracks. Josie dove back behind the wagon. Cal halted only briefly after suffering from the pain of sand flying into his eyes. Half blinded, he took his chances and charged the keg out of fear that I would bust it open with a round and cost him his water.

"Kill that wench, Josie!"

Joise raised both his pistols and I heard the discharge as wood and debris exploded throughout the wagon. I never flinched. For me time suddenly stood still. I stared down the barrel to focus on the keg now cradled in Cal's arms. I eased the trigger back a second time. It was just as Luke had promised. The look in Cal's face said it all as the round came his way so quickly on the heels of the first. I kept the repeater trained on his form as he disappeared within the smoke and fire that gave me power. I pulled it again, and then again, and again.

NINETY-NINE

How long I was unconscious, I could only guess. I sensed that I had lost three or four hours, maybe more, for I awoke to a late afternoon sun. Fighting to regain something of my wits, I found myself in terrible pain, nauseating pain. My head was pounding fiercely. I suffered between both excruciating pain and numbness that reached deep into my shoulders and arms.

I had been lashed to the spokes of a wagon wheel, and my wrists were rubbed raw from unconscious efforts to free myself from the bindings that held me exposed to the heat of the sun. I felt crucified.

The agony of merely raising my head was beyond words. It felt as though I had a large spike driven into the back of my neck with smaller nails embedded across my temples. The pain caused my stomach to turn and twist, keeping me on the very edge of vomiting myself inside out.

Ever so slowly, I forced my head up in order to look around. It hurt to open my eyes, to let in the light of day. I was unable to focus. My first sensible image was that of a parched desert ramping up to a background of mountains. I was no longer in my wagon. In fact, I now observed that my wagon surrounded me, wrecked beyond repair, and scattered as far as I could see. It appeared drawn out into a string of disconnected planks, pot and pans, hides, furs, foodstuffs, a total of everything I owned. Then came a memory of shooting at the powder keg.

I was sweltering in the heat, burning up. My lips were stiff with a coating of blood long since dried out. My nose and ears had bled down to my shoulders and across my blouse. I studied my blouse. I noticed it was unbuttoned, as was my skirt, which was twisted wrongly about my hips. I tried to make sense of why much of my undergarments were missing. It seemed improbable that they had been ripped away by the explosion.

Feelings of despair welled up inside once my conclusions gave rise to the fact I might well have been violated. I didn't feel any different, and I was sure I would have, had I been raped or something similar. It was hard for me to keep my thoughts coherent, but in light of the fact I was tied up, it seemed simple enough that I had been the object of someone's attention. Clearly, I wasn't the only one still alive.

In short time Josie came up behind me. He bent over me and placed his rough shaven, smelly face on my shoulder and kissed my neck freely. The stench of whiskey and rotted teeth engulfed me. I was in too much pain to complain, let alone resist or ridicule him, and maybe that was for the best.

He stood up and moved around to a place where he could be seen. He seated himself upon a cabinet alongside the water barrel, which appeared to have miraculously survived the explosion. It was still intact with a good share of its contents, and the thought of it washing across my parched lips was torture second to none, unless possibly the man before me.

Josie suddenly produced my whites, and waved my under-garments in front of him like a flag of victory. He then held them up to his face, took a deep breath and exhaled with a great toothless smile. It would have been so much easier had I just died—no more Josie, no more thirst, no more pain. What exactly was it God wished of me now?

"Mmmmm-mmmm, the shmell of a woman. Yeshirree. Nothin' like it anywhere. Coursh thesh ain't ash parfumy ash the one'sh the ladiesh I know wear. Shtill, thar'sh shumpin' shpeshial 'bout a pure lady. Shumpin' that jush getsh me all fired up. 'Xshpeshially when she done killsh off my three besht friendsh. But then, I guesh it ain't your fault if God didn't give them the brainsh he put into a chicken."

Even lost as I was, I knew that was quite a statement coming from Josie whose face popped in and out of sight as my eyes opened and closed, opened and closed. They were open for me to watch again as he inhaled deeply then rubbed my whites all about his scraggly face. I closed my eyes intentionally to shut out his ugliness, but even more to shut out a world that raised my pain to a level unbearable. I had to listen to his ravings, much of it going by me without comprehension. I was in a bad way.

"Coursh you know thaysh xshpectin' me to 'venge their deathsh. Xshpecially Cal, he washn't ash shtupid as Hernando. He dint go off shtickin' his head in a wagon and gettin' it blowed off."

Josie interrupted his own oratory in order to study the debris, whereupon he reached over and picked up one of my bottles of whiskey. He uncorked it and downed the brew in large gulps after which he tossed the bottle aside and continued to rave.

"Ain't nothin' left of ol' Cal sheptin' hish feet. Theysh schtill schtuck in hish bootsh. Ha! Thatsh funny, no? Cal died whit hish bootsh on, no head or body, but he kept hish bootsh. Aha, ha. I reckin' the devil won't be able t' find 'nough of 'im t' take t' hell. Whadda you think, darlin'? You shure got hish assh good. I can't help but t' laugh jusht sheein' 'im cradlin' that keg like a dern fool. Aha, ha, ha, ahhh, mershe me.

I think dat wush about the last thing I shaw for the shake of shand in my eyesh. Damn near went blind. I can't figure out how t' hell did you live through that blasht. I mean lookit thish messh." He looked around and shook his head. "Nobody can live through thish. You musht gotta heck of 'n angel, honey. Heck of 'n angel." He studied me a moment then glared. "And yer gonna be needin' 'im, darlin'. I promish ya that."

He rose to his feet and ambled off out of my sight. After a moment, he returned with another bottle of whiskey, one of Luke's cigars, and some of my dried beef, which he was slicing up with a large knife. He continued to drink heavily as he chewed on the beef and smoked. His ramblings soon turned his tooth-less slur of emotions into a worse slur of emotions, if that could even be possible. He was feeling his oats, and I was bracing myself for what was about to become my worst nightmare.

Finally working himself into a state of combined courage and semi-consciousness, he stood up and began wailing.

"You got Cal's ashh good, an now I'm gonna have yoursh. In the name o' Cal, an' Charlie, an' Hernando, you are about t' get yoursh, darlin'. You are about t' get yoursh!"

He began to remove his shirt and boots, and finally after numerous drunken falls back to his start point on the ground, he removed his pants. He arose to stand before me naked and fully aroused.

I had never seen a man this way before, and under any other circumstance I would have been utterly mortified or fully taken in by infallible curiosity. However, Josie had lost his appetite for dried beef and was now only swinging that large knife and terrifying me half to death by way of whatever small amount of sanity I still possessed.

I was reduced to something just short of a mumbling idiot from pain and fear. His words were now so badly slurred as he talked to himself that I could do little more than look up at this deranged maniac. It was the snap of sunlight across his blade that sliced through my semi-consciousness and fully riveted what there was of my attention.

Josie stood above me spread-eagled, screaming to Cal, saying that this was for him. His outstretched arms rose to heaven with one hand holding up the knife and the other a bottle and cigar. He looked supremely happy to take his revenge, and with head raised skyward, crowned in the glory of intoxication, he took a slug in the center of his chest.

It came as a dull thud, barely perceptible in my state of consciousness. It was followed by the rumbling boom of a gun, which seemed to blow him over backwards like a fallen snow angel upon the hot blowing sand. He lay as he stood, spread-eagled, arms outstretched still gripping the knife and bottle. He was not nearly so erect.

I was so mentally abused at this point that although I witnessed what happened, it hardly made an impression. I simply looked at him lying there with a small bead of blood on his chest as I listened to the approaching sound of galloping horses. Almost as once a group of riders rode up from behind me. They stopped where their shadows stretched out to touch Josie's feet.

I raised my head long enough to look into the sun and see the silhouettes of four men on horseback wearing wide brimmed hats. They dismounted and as they moved away from the brightness, I could see that three of them looked like western types; the fourth was slightly more polished in appearance.

He carried himself a little differently as he walked my way. He knelt down before me and gently raised my head. He brushed the hair away from my face and looked into my eyes.

"Ma'am—judging by the looks of things, I'd say ya had a time of it, but your gonna live. Don't you worry none. It's over. You'll be fine."

I felt him stoop over me and begin working the ropes that bound my wrists. He finally pulled a knife and cut me loose from the spokes. I was unable to raise myself, and seeing this, he attempted to lift me to my feet. I went limp in his arms. I cried out in agony, but for the shuddering pain that shot across my shoulders. I had no space left for strength of character.

"C'mon, ma'am. You gotta get on your feet. I can imagine how them arms and shoulders must hurt, but you gotta work out the stiffness. You gotta stand up now, c'mon."

It seemed as though there would be no end to my pain, but as my senses struggled to return, I soon gained back my balance and a measure of control. I was suddenly conscious of my being exposed and fumbled to cover myself proper; there had been no loss of the morals that ran as deep as my thirst. I looked into the face of this man who saw more than he should, but he gave no hint of the fact. My gratitude was offered in a feeble whisper.

"Thank-you."

"Your welcome, ma'am. It isn't often a man gets to prove his worth."

His words slipped past my ears as sounds that went unheard, for I was focused on the Josie's naked body lying dead in the dirt. I was assuring myself that he was truly dead. The stranger turned my head away from Josie.

"He's dead ma'am. He's dead as dead can be. It's over. Can you stand?"

Carefully, he released his grip and I stumbled over to the water barrel where I dropped back to my knees. I drank to quench my thirst. I soaked myself in the glistening liquid. I wanted to drown in its pleasurable flow. Its refreshing quality brought me tremendous relief. It helped revive me and return something of my awareness and a sense of order and under-standing. It was only then that I realized the stranger was still talking to me.

"...name, ma'am. Do you understand me? What is your name, ma'am? Are you strong enough to travel?" He asked. I looked up at him momentarily, working to untangle his words, trying to give them meaning. I turned back to the life-giving water and closed my eyes.

"Do you understand me, ma'am?"

"Yes. I can travel. My name is Elizabeth. Elizabeth Dennison Claussen." I gave the answers I thought expected of me. They seemed right.

The men suddenly went silent and looked at each other in surprise. All except for the one who cut me loose and was speaking.

"Elizabeth Claussen? Would you be related to Christopher Claussen?"

"Yes."

I never so much as opened my eyes. I dismissed his statement without thought, not appreciating what had just been asked. My head needed time to clear further, but this would probably take forever as it throbbed terrible. I raised my trembling hands to my temples and pressed hard.

I rose to my feet. I had all I could do just to stand there and observe the mess of my world spread across the field. It looked like vanishing art, a mosaic of my belongings, bits and pieces lying low alongside or beneath clumps of sage and scrub grass, slowly disappearing beneath the shifting sand, all except for the forms of my fallen mules. I saw Shadow Hunter's amulet and reached down to retrieve it.

"This is mine."

"Yes ma'am. Why don't you collect what you can."

I started sifting through wreckage when I found myself facing Luke's remains lying among the dead mules. I started to cry. It wasn't so much that I cried for Luke, as it was I cried for the whole of my situation. I fought to hold on to any semblance of sanity or decency in a world that I felt had raped me as much by its harshness as anything Josie might have considered.

"Was he with you?"

I nodded.

"We'll see he gets a decent burial." The stranger called out to the others. "Need a hand, boys. Got one to bury proper. I see a couple of shovels and a pick. Let's get it done."

I couldn't bear to look at Luke. It wasn't a memory I wanted. I wished only to look at the heavens and see them as a reflection of his eyes—endless blue skies, endless blue eyes.

The men understood, and were kind enough to save me the grief of witnessing Luke's remains being laid to rest. They left me to wander about the field looking for my belongings. It was from the safety of distance that I watched as the men shoveled out a shallow grave. They went about collecting stones, which they piled up respectfully upon Luke's corpse. With these tasks completed, we stood together and bowed our heads. I was too far-gone to further cry for Luke. One of the men said a short prayer. I simply wished him farewell.

ONE-HUNDRED

We stepped away from Luke's grave and two of the riders set out to round up the horses that belonged to the desperados. The explosion had badly frightened the animals, and they could be seen grazing off in the distance. They were led back to what was left of the wagon, and then saddled with the remains of the three dead men. Aside from Cal, who was blown to oblivion, and unlike Luke, who was now buried, the bodies of the other three were strapped across the horses for a return trip to Hell Hole. That was where we were headed.

The name humored me, for it sounded like the perfect spot to bury dead outlaws, not to mention that after all I had been through, it seemed like the kind of place where I would feel right at home. The outpost was said to be a close enough ride to warrant bringing back the bodies instead of leaving them to lie even though the men couldn't go directly into South Pass as they had hoped because of the number of Indians in the area. The riders had been discussing a reward posted for capture of the murderers, and I suspected little if anything topped dead bodies for living proof.

After retrieving the horses, the riders decided to go rabbit hunting, this because of the amount of busted up wood laying about from the wagon, which made for an easy fire. In no time, the skewered jackrabbits and a couple of snakes were roasting.

Grease dribbled onto the burning wood, and caused the flames to flash upward from the bright red letters that once spelled 'DUSTY PEDDLER'. The letters had been scrambled by the random tossing of planks into the fire, and now read: ST-U-PED. I stared at them and contemplated the message. Was it truth or a joke? With Luke it had always been hard to tell. I watched as the letters changed from brush strokes of bright red paint to boards of radiant red embers. Their heat touched my face like a warm and sorrowful kiss.

I was offered the first piece of meat, but the sight of the burning wood broke my heart and tears slipped quietly from my eyes. The strain of emotion only added to the physical pain, which refused to subside. It blocked any hope of having an appetite, and so I set aside my meat and left the men to their fire.

I returned once more to the water barrel to quench an insatiable thirst, and then set out to search for my bottle of laudanum. The throbbing in my head barely allowed me opening my eyes enough to look about. As I picked my way through the debris, I collected what I could and laid those things alongside my trunk to form a pile for later retrieval.

I never found the laudanum. Josie found the whiskey, but never lived long enough to locate the brandy. I picked up the bottle as though it were liquid gold. I wiped off the sand and uncorked it. I tipped it high and drank greedily. I looked over at the men, who were now all looking at me. I tipped it high again. I started to cry. I drank and I cried. I cried and I drank. The riders sat in silence and watched.

I was eventually separated from my bottle and assisted into the extra saddle to be escorted away. It was obvious that aside from his boots and horse, nothing of Cal would ever be found. The boots were tied to one of the corpses, both feet still inside. The riders were not inclined to remain for the night, instead preferring to travel during the evening or early morning hours when temperatures were cooler, this for the sake of men and animals alike.

I prayed this day to end, and I watched with weary eyes as chilly blue shadows crept up steep and barren granite faces of mountains that were topped with light dustings of snow.

The sky overhead remained a bright pale blue, as if hours away from sundown, but below, the base of the mountains became lost within the obscurity of deepening shadows—shadows that beckoned me.

I was suffering from depression and days of exhaustion. I was suffering from the scorch of sunburn. I was suffering from the pain of bruises black and blue, from red streaked lacerations that covered me head to toe. I was also utterly soused, drunk as a sailor. I wanted shadows, I wanted night; I wanted to sleep and to leave my misfortunes and discomfort behind. I wanted this miserable day to end.

Between my weariness and my drunkenness, sleep came almost at once. So, it stood to reason that after the third near fall from my horse, which startled me half out of my wits, and at the same time made the men especially wary, it was determined I was incapable of remaining safely in the saddle. Yet, the men had no intention of stopping in my behalf, so I was placed under the care of the rider with the strongest horse. I doubt I ever opened my eyes, but immediately collapsed upon his back with my arms pulled tightly around his sides and held firmly within his grip.

The night was cool, he was warm, and we rode together in this fashion for many hours. I dozed freely in and out of my dreams, knowing I could rock back and forth upon his horse without the fear of winding up flat on the ground with the wind knocked out of me.

At some point beyond my perception, the four men called it quits for the night and dismounted. I was released from the rider's hold, pulled down off the horse, and actually carried to a bedroll. There, I was carefully covered with a number of blankets. Dead men slept eternally, and for them, the cold meant nothing so there were blankets enough to spare.

In the security of my saviors, I slept hard without dreams until early morn when I awakened disoriented and deathly sick. I had no recollection of lying down to sleep, and little ambition to awake. I curled up tighter within the warmth of the blankets that had been wrapped about me with care and compassion.

I tried to prolong my escape from reality, tried to remain still, tried to keep my awareness dulled as long as possible in order to avoid resurrecting a world of aches, heartbreak and certain invitation to a morning of retching. I was stiff and sore as I might have expected, but suffering most from an overwhelming need to relieve myself.

As a rule, I was never one to sleep in late, no matter how cold or how tired I might be. It was a given that in spite of my efforts to the contrary, I would start this day out just as early as any other, for both my stomach and my bladder were burning with discomfort.

Buried beneath my blanket, I listened to snaps and popping sounds nearby that compelled me to emerge from my cocoon, pry open my eyes and have a look about. A sole rider was sitting over the heat of a rekindled fire now crackling with vigor. He was stirring breakfast with one hand and swirling a pot of coffee with the other. My movement caught his attention. He looked my way and nodded. The sound of snoring reached my ear, and I understood one or more of the others were yet fast asleep. He spoke to me in a low voice.

"Ah biled me up a lil' coffee. Would ye be a wantin'? Het's hot."

"Sir, if I don't find a place to relieve myself, I am going to explode." I lay there afraid to move. The man looked around in a full circle.

"Ah see yourn parblim. Bein' a woman'n all, reckon het'd be nice t'have a bush r sump'in now'n then, huh." He twisted his face in thought. "Ah feared thar hain't much aza single sol'tary tree here'bouts standin' dead'r'live. Ah'm liked t'hold a blainket b'hind me fer yourn privicy? Ah'm liked t' doin' het rat now while het's still dusky dark."

"Anything. Anything, but please hurry. Ooooh, I'm not going to make it."

"Hang on nah, jus' hang on—." The man leapt to his feet, and snagged one my blankets. "Cuh'mun, git a move'n foller me." He beckoned me to follow as he ran off a ways and passed the blanket behind him, draping it from his outstretched arms.

I was in too much agony to worry about being embarrassed and after stepping off his heels, I stooped behind the curtain. I was learning by experience that it was pointless to complain, and in fact becoming more and more admirable to accept these crude aspects of necessity. Once finished, I stood up behind the man, arranged my clothes, and placed my hands upon his shoulders.

"Thank-you. You are a gentleman."

"Don' make me no never mind, Miss Claussen. Mod'sty's a mite strange out here'n a wunder t' b'hold."

We made our way back to the campfire, and I sat down next to the man. He folded the blanket in half and placed it across my shoulders.

"How ye feelin' this heren mawnin'?

"How yuh feelun' this mawnun'?"

"Terrible. Look." I held up my hands so he might see how they trembled. "I'd love to sip some of that coffee."

"Well, let me jus' fetch ye a lil' ol' cup."

I opened my blanket like wings and collected the heat of the embers. The man retrieved an old tin cup and looked inside. He rapped it on his knee to dislodge the sand and then blew out the dust. He poured in the black liquid and offered it to me with care. I embraced the hot tin cup and sipped the grounds off the surface. I nibbled at them. The coffee did much to invigorate me.

"Tastes good. Thank-you."

"Mah plaisure." He rubbed his hands. "Het's a colt one this mawnin'. In a min'it here, Ah'll fix ye up wit' some corn dodger'n that'll warm you'n settle yourn stomach at the same tahm. Ah even got me some sugar outta yourn wagon b'fore we left. Ah hope ye don' min' none."

"That sounds wonderful." I had recognized his voice as the man that had watched over me. "Forgive my asking, but have we been introduced? I don't much remember...."

"Ah don't knows iffen het'd be fair t'call het a 'troduction. You'uz'n none too good a shape las' naght—tarred. You'uz raght tarred, jus' plain took. Name's Clettis. Clettis Culahan."

I studied the man for a moment. "I rode with you last night, didn't I. It was your horse, wasn't it? I appreciate you hanging on to me. I just could not stay awake. Actually, I don't think I wanted to stay awake."

"Never ye mind. Ah don't care to he'p ye . Wuz my pleasure. No 'fense 'tended, but women's rare'uz God's teachin's out here'n Ah just figgered Ah's pretty lucky t' hav'un in m'arms."

"Even if she's so drunk she can't sit up? I should of been better company."

"Oh no, ma'am. Best comp'ny Ah've had'na long tahm. Watchin' ye a sleepin' on muh shoulder—well—het brought back lots o' mem'ries, good mem'ries, good feelin's. Ah'll parb'ly r'gret 'mem'brin' so much, but Ah'll take me a chance."

"Sounds like you have been out here a long time."

"Three yars, give'r' take. Too long, thez fer shore."

"Where are your roots?"

"I'uz raised up K'tucky, Carolinny way."

"You miss it? You ever wish you were back?"

"Sometahms. Thar's good'n bad wherever ye go. Thar's days when Ah get to a-thinkin' 'bout barn raisin' an' apple

965

peelin', an bran hullin. Ah miss the singin' parties, ye know, singin' ol' timey songs."

"Oh, I love to hear people sing. I'd love to hear anything aside from wind and blowing sand."

"Yuh no what Ah miss most?"

I shook my head while carefully swallowing the hot coffee. "No idea, tell me."

"Ah miss muh mamaw's yard. Ah miss the hollyhocks an' larkspur. Ah miss the asters. Ah miss sourwood honey. Lordy, sometahms Ah get me a cravin' fer a jar o' her blessit honey. Ye hain't tasted noffin' lessin' ye put yourn tongue to mamaw's sourwood honey. Larrupun' good het'uz, larrupun' good. God Al'matty, I'z settin' m'mouf to a-waterin' jus' a-thinkin' on het."

"You're making me hungry."

"Mmm, here, this'll do ya." He handed me a couple of hot cormeal cakes and then the sugar. He then stretched and looked out into the desert twilight. "Thing is, thems gums'n'bees is all gone. So's mamaw. Passed on long 'fore Ah ever came out this-a-ways. Ah guess, Ah miss mamaw most. Crazy fer a grown man, eh?"

"I don't think it's crazy at all. I think it's wonderful. I never really had a mother or grandmother in that sense." I arched my back. "Oooh, my shoulders still hurt."

"Hol' yerself still a min'it." He reached over to me. "Ye gotchcha a smudge o' dried blood o'sump'n' in yourn heeair jus' thar." He reached toward my hair.

"It's no wonder. Lord knows I need a hot bath and a good scrubbing. I don't know if I even remember what a hot bath feels like." I reached up and met his fingers in the stringy mess atop my head. He pulled away as if burned. I paid it no mind, and instead looked around for my belongings.

"I'll be right back." I set down my corn dodgers and went off toward my bed roll. I searched through my bag and after a moment returned to the fire. Mr. Calahan raised his nose to the air and looked at me with amusement.

"Is that thar par-fume?"

"Yes, it is. Do you like it?"

"Ah'll be switched. What smell that bein'?"

"Lavender."

"Shore 'nough. Matty plaisant, yes'm, matty plaisant indeed."

"It's my favorite. I may be forced to live with stringy hair, filthy nails, and wretched appearances, but at least I can still smell good."

"Amen!" He laughed. "Lucky fer us all. Sweeten the place up a bit. Speakin' o' luck, yer lucky t' be alive. Me'n the boys'uz a-talkin' 'bout that s'plosion fer some tahm b'fore we went off a-sleepin. Someone's a-watchin' o'er you, most cert'in. Ye got a lucky star'r'sump'n'."

"Funny, that's what Josie said just before you shot him. I guess I figure it depends on how you look at it. If you mean lucky because I am alive, then I guess it's true, otherwise I could easily argue that I have to be the unluckiest person I know. You wouldn't believe half of what I've been through."

"No, Ah parb'ly wou'n't, but Ah still say you're matty lucky. Ah cain't figger ner understand het, but ye got the Lord on yourn side, hain't nobody here gonna tell het differ'nt." He nodded his head, affirming my good fortune. "Tell me sump'n', jus' cuz we'uz a'talkin' las' naght an' a-wund'rin'. How far off ye reckon wuz that thar keg o' powder when ye done shot het?"

"I don't know." I looked around. "I was in the wagon. About where the horses are, I guess, couple of rods I imagine. It was heavy, and I had all I could do to throw it that far."

"Ho, Mammy! Ah'd be hog-tied, tarred'n feathered b'fore Ah'd know how ye done lived through that. Yer sayin' twenty, thirty feet iffin any. God Al'matty! What fer made ye do that-a-way. Have ye no fear? Weren't ye a'feerd o' what mat o' happen'd when het blowed?"

I looked up him and thought about his question for a moment as I sipped at the coffee.

"You know that man we buried yesterday—Luke?"

"Yes'm."

"He once called me dim-witted." I snickered. "He wasn't serious, but maybe he was more right than wrong because, honestly—I never gave shooting that keg much thought. I was only looking to kill his murderers. I thought a lot about how they killed off my team, and that my only way out alive was going to be on one of their horses. That was the main thing on my mind, getting on one of those horses. I had plenty of food and water in the wagon, but without a horse, I was good as dead." I began to reflect on the episode. "I guess it was probably the hides or my trunk that saved me."

"Say 'gin?"

"All those robes and furs, all those buffalo hides; I had a wagon full. Well, I don't have to tell you, you gentlemen dragged them out of the wagon, not me. Coming across, I met up with some Cheyenne, and they gave me that pile after I left them with most all of the wares originally in the wagon. They wanted to say thank-you and show me their gratitude, so they loaded the wagon with hides, food and water.

"I didn't ask for the hides. I had no use for them, or so I thought, but they insisted. They knew that traders always wanted hides and such, and I imagine they thought I would want them as well. I couldn't really refuse, it would have been rude, and I'm glad I didn't because when my wagon was being shot to pieces, the hides did as good a job of stopping lead as did my trunk.

"Looks like they saved me from the worst of the explosion as well. I was right down in them when shooting at Cal and that keg. Frankly, if I had any prior notion of what it's like shooting a keg of powder, this story would have ended differently. Ignorance is bliss, and luckily I didn't die, but then either did Josie. So, when I came to, I was tied to the spokes and facing that maniacal lunatic."

"Sometahms seems them devils don't never die nohow. Ye mat be rat though, thems that know best say het's hard t' bring down buffalo wit' a gun, hides too thick, arrow works best, less'n yer Elb. Ah promise ye this; the boys'll wanna hear the whole story, start t' finish. Het'll be good jawin' fer ahr ride home."

"Speaking of home, I remember hearing talk about Hell Hole. Where is that?"

"Souf side o' the Pass."

"The pass?"

"Ye know yourn way roun' here at all?" He studied me.

"No."

"A moment ago, ye said *'that man'* we buried yesterday. Ah take het he wasn't yourn husband."

"No. He was someone I met while traveling. I only knew enough of him to know that he was a good man. A decent man who shouldn't have died the way he did."

"Amen. Are ye sayin' then that yer trav'lin' out here by yerself?"

"Well, yes and no. I've been working my way west, looking for some sort of pass, sounds a lot like the one you're talking about. I'd say half of the time I'm traveling in company. When I was traveling with Luke, he seemed to think I was looking for the South Pass. I heard him call it that. I'm actually looking for a man who goes by the name Christopher Claussen."

"Ah heerd ye say yer kin t'Mr. Claussun." Clettis reflected.

"Do you know him?"

"Yes,'m. We all do. Ah 'spect er'body 'roun' the Pass knows o' Mr. Claussun."

"Oh, tell me it's so! I *can't* believe it! You can't imagine what I've been through trying to find that man. Is it possible for you to take me to him?" My eagerness was blatantly apparent.

"Well, Ah dunno liked to that. Ah mean, Ah really don' know where he is *'xactly.*"

"I do."

I turned away from Mr. Calahan to look up at the man who just spoke. He leaned over and offered his hand. I accepted it. He was the man who had untied me from the wheel.

"Martin Angers, at your service."

"Elizabeth Dennison Claussen."

"Yeah, I know. It's a pleasure to meet ya at last."

"Do you know me?"

"I do in a way."

"Are you acquainted with Claus?"

"Who?"

"Christopher Claussen."

"Yes, ma'am, I am indeed. Been working directly for Mr. Claussen."

"Is that a fact?"

"Yes, ma'am."

"Here." Mr. Calahan poured fresh coffee into my tin.

"Thank-you, Clettis." I turned back to Mr. Angers.

970

"What is it you do for Mr. Claussen, if I may ask?"

"People like him hire me to scout, find people, things like that."

"Is that so?"

"Yes, ma'am."

"Are you currently in his employ?"

"As we speak."

"I can hardly believe it. That is the best news ever. Honestly, that is the best news ever. Maybe, I can finally say I've reached my destination. This is wonderful. Can you take me to him?"

"Yeah." He nodded. "I'm sure we can."

"That is so good to know. I just can't believe it." I let out a breath and savored the moment. My miseries were suddenly diminished. "So tell me, who are you looking for now?"

"Ha! Who do you think?"

I looked at the man quizzically.

"You." Mr. Angers was chuckling along with Clettis and the others, who were also now awake and picking up their bedrolls. I watched them for a moment, while I gave thought to what he said.

"Oh. Well—I often wondered if word of my travel ever reached him. Lord knows I asked many a soul of his where-abouts. Knowing Claus, I guess I shouldn't be surprised."

"No, ma'am."

"How did you find me? Is that what brought all of you out here?"

"No ma'am, not exactly. I hired on with Clettis here, to give him a hand trackin' the bandits."

I looked at Clettis, who nodded toward the corpses.

"They'uz killers. Ah'z gettin' paid t' bring 'um t'justice. They done gunned down three placer miners inna small pannin' an' trappin' camp up in them thar hills 'bove Hell Hole. Made off wit' quite a haul. Figgered het was worf twenty percent if we could get 'em back the gold an' a hun'erd dollar a haid daid'r'live. We'z a'closin' in on 'em rat smart when ahr luck changed fer the worse'n we rode drect'ly into a band o' them thar Blackfeet a-comin' norf. Yee day, they'uz bad'uns. Hateful."

"Thanks to Elb, we shot 'em up pretty good," said Mr. Angers, "But even with that, they kept us pinned down in the hills for all of a day and a half until we managed to slip out after dark. The killers gained a lotta ground in that time. It took some ridin' before we picked up their trail again."

"When you set off that keg o' powder, I think everybody clear to the West Coast heard it, includin' us. We figured the explosion was too much a coincidence and started out in that direction going careful and expectin' trouble. We weren't disappointed."

"Elb learned hisself good how t'shoot thet long rifle o' his," said Clettis "Ah swear he can pick off a flat snake layin' low, half-mile out. We'uz a-keepin' low'n the scrub ahrselves, easin' in an a-watchin' up. Elb, he'uz a-lookin' through his glass'n sees ye tied up'n a-lookin' to be in'a fiercesome 'mount o' trouble. Ye can like t' 'magine how we'uz a-cussin' an' carryin' on an' a-wantin' t' hurry in'n rescue ye . We figgered you'uz ter'ble skaired. But ol' Elb, he says t'shut up yourn moufs an' stay put. He's jus' a-sittin' calm's can be, a-watchin' o'er ye an' a-waitin', a-sattin' his rifle an' a-feelin' the breeze, ye know, jus' a-sortin' things out. Fine-lee, he up'n sez thar's only one o' the vermin t' be seen, hain't no other'n an' kaBOOM! Tha'uz the end of that."

Clettis spit into my bowl, picked at some dried food and then went on to wipe it out. While he was busying himself, the other two members of the group approached us. The first one yelled out.

"Blared!"

Clettis looked up and grinned. "Yes, sir! Blared! Blared, he'uz! Daider'n'daid'n eyes wad open. Yes, sir." The two men laughed.

Their attention turned to me.

"Mornen' ma'am, name's Farish Creek. You're looken' a meght healthier this mornen'." He offered his hand and a warm smile.

"Elizabeth." I answered, then glanced at the other man.

"Elb Nichols."

"Mr. Nichols. A fine shot." The man grinned knowingly as I shook his hand. "I don't take to killing, and yet, I can't possibly show you gentlemen my appreciation for all you've done. This might well have become my worst morning ever. Yesterday, I honestly thought I was *'gonna get mine'*. That's how it was put to me."

"Don't you thenk on et twice, Messus Claussen," said Farrish. "Elb had hem dead long before he eveh knew et."

"Amen!" cried the others as they accepted my gratitude in unison.

"So are all of you from around here?" I asked.

"Me, Elb'n Farish spend most ahr tahm in'n ' liked to these here parts. Martin comes this-a-way now'n'then. He comes a-ridin' from east-ways."

"Albany," said Martin.

"Albany!"

"Yes ma'am"

"That's interesting. I recently spent a few months in Albany. In spite of some sorrowful things, I rather enjoyed Albany— busy place."

973

"Yes, ma'am. I was hired out of Albany to start lookin' for you."

"In Albany?"

"Yes, ma'am. Mr. Claussen heard from some of his concerns along the canal that you were travelin' westward in search of him. He was *mighty* concerned for your well being. When he called upon my services, he was anxious, to say the least. Claimed you could attract more trouble than ten foot o' lightin' rod swingin' in a storm. His exact words were *'only a lunatic and Elizabeth Dennison would be of a mind to go west of St. Louis alone'*. And I must say that I'm entirely inclined to agree with him after trying to follow ya for the last couple of months.

"Had no problem pickin' up your trail in Albany an' over to Buffalo, because ya made quite an impression there, especially with that school boat and them old ladies you saved in that coach. They couldn't say enough good about ya, and put themselves directly at my service, no expense spared. They brought me to your friend Dorrie—."

"Dorrie! You spoke with Dorrie? I can't believe it. Is she all right? Is she getting along? How are the boys?"

"She was doin' fine, family's doin' fine, lotta kids. She looked good, sounded happy, misses you a great deal. She made that plain. Said if I was ever to catch up with ya to give you her warmest regards."

"Oh, I miss that girl. I so enjoyed her company. We became best of friends while in Albany, but I guess right now that's neither here nor there. Please continue, you were saying...."

"Only that I gathered from my conversation with Dorrie, you might have gone visiting a friend in the Michigan Territories, and that ya planned to head out west, maybe up the Missouri. I made the mistake of going for Michigan an' hunting for ya over in that wilderness.

"You boarded one of the last ships sailing west on Lake Erie, an' the weather closed in soon after. I had no choice but to take the south shore trail along Erie on horse. Finally made it up to Detroit. The weather slowed me way down, and maybe because of it, I met up with some folks that recalled an attractive blonde woman traveling in the company of an Indian and a couple o' slaves. Said ya spent a few days in town. I eventually learned you had gone to Chicago. I know them trails in and out o' Chicago an' down along the Illinois River and was makin' good time.

"I was gaining on ya by the time I reached Beardstown, and hot on your heels come St. Louis. Almost caught up with you there. Talked a fair amount to Rachel and Caleb—."

"Oh—."

"Yup, their doin' fine as well. Lots o' kids. Everyone knew about ya. Then you boarded the WAVERLY and damn!. Everything went against me. You were only a day or two ahead of me before I had to wait for another boat goin' upriver. To make matters worse, that boat caught a snag which stove in our hull just north of Franklin and forced us to ground a few miles north of the landing. I lost nearly two weeks because nothin' else was headin' upriver an' the lot of us had to wait out repairs on the river.

"Anyhows, in due time, I reached Rapid Run, heard all about your mishap and near drowning, an' how ya were laid up there a couple of weeks. If we hadn't wrecked, you and I would o' met there an' then. Crocker told me 'bout how ya purchased the peddler's wagon an' lit out lookin' for the pass. And try as I might, that was where I lost ya.

"Started out with a perfect trail from Rapid Run to the horizon, then came one hell'uva storm that wiped the earth clean. I worked the ground for a week straight, but it was just too much space and too little left to go on. Besides, I was seeing too many Cheyenne, too many for comfort. I backed off and headed south. I knew if the Indians didn't get ya, you'd have no choice but to head south along the Rockies.

"I figured you were well on your way to South Pass and with a little luck, and providing you didn't get yourself killed, somewhere along the line I'd catch sight of ya, but it never happened. You did good though. If we hadn't been ridin' out on the chase an' run into ya, you'd a found Claussen on your own. I'll give ya that. South Pass is only a coupla days ride o' here."

Suddenly, I felt as though I had been traveling with a long lost cousin. A vast land was suddenly small. It was an odd sensation discovering this total stranger had been shadowing me for weeks. We had no connection save one, but we had a relationship.

"So there is a South Pass."

"Sayin' ye hain't never heeard tell of that thar?" asked Clettis.

"Just rumors."

"Sayin' ye been a-ridin' rat along not knowin' not noffin' thar?"

"I never really thought of it that way. Something inside said it was there. I just had to find it."

"Yee day! Aren't ye sump'in 'pecial."

"Well, you can trust your instincts; there most positively is a pass," said Mr. Angers.

"Tell me about Christopher. Do you know him well? How is he? Is he in good spirits? Is his health good?"

"Only met him two or three times, but not a man to forget. Spoke to him 'bout business, 'bout you. Yeah, I'd say he's fine. Looked fit as a horse to me—big as a horse anyways."

"Now—does he *live* in Hell Hole?"

"Oh, lord, no, ma'am," spouted Elb. "Hell Hole esn't the kend of place for someone the leks o' Claussen. Hell Hole es lettle more then a tavern and traden' post, couple o' cabens an' thet's about et, rowdy place. Nothen' but trouble there."

"Claussen keeps a place opposite side of the pass," said Mr. Angers. "I've been there, but his main stake, at least according to what I'm told, is north, way up the range—settlement known as North Pole. They say it's a couple a hundred miles up along the Rockies, this side of Powder River."

"North pole?"

"Yes, ma'am. Never been there myself, but I hear there's a large pole driven in the ground with a flag attached to the very top. I hear he's got four of these enormous poles standin' upright and markin' the ends of a couple of trails. One to the north, east, south, and west.

"Word has it he plans to take a steam engine, something like them he puts into his riverboats, and fit it onto a wheeled cart that rides along steel rails nailed down to timbers that lie upon the ground. I heard 'em called railroads, railways, tracks and things similar. Got some on the east coast, I hear. Matter of fact, while in Albany I heard talk 'bout one coming in from Boston. He's planning on building one out here. As I hear it, one of them tracks is being laid to run east and west through the pass, and another north and south along the east side of the Stoney mountains. The poles are already up to mark the end of the runs."

"Some biggity brigity talkin'," said Clettis. "Must be he 'spects lots o' sump'in 'sides bars an' c'yotes to take up out this-a-way. Het don' figger. Cain't nobody live down there nohow. Hain't no place for waterin.'"

"Don't get me wrong," continued Mr. Angers. "The man's sharp. He's all o' that. I'll be the first to tell you that water or no water, settlements are sproutin' up fast around those places he gets to surveying. He's supplying most of the folk movin' up and down along the mountains from the Upper Missouri down to the pass, and even farther down, maybe all the way down to Santa Fe. There's a lot of business to be had down that a way as I hear it."

"Do you think Claus is in South Pass now?"

977

"He was a week or so ago when I was there last. I spoke to him in person to tell him what I knew 'bout you bein' in the area best I could tell. He travels between North Pole and South Pass Junction quite a bit, surveying I reckon. It don't much matter, both places have trading posts, rooms to let, liveries and most all the basics. Ain't nothin' like Hell Hole. I don't reckon Hell Hole will be around much longer. People are already moving to the north side of the pass, over to the junction.

"You'll see it soon enough. I think your skin is thick enough that we can put you up there to rest a bit with Farish and Elb, give you a chance to take that hot bath you were mentioning. Clettis says he'll ride north with me across the pass and look to find Mr. Claussen.

"Who knows you might even get bored, though I doubt it. I know riding up to Claussen's place sounds good, but is probably pointless because he is never to be found home. The man lives on his horse best I can tell, and Clettis and I travel faster if we go it alone."

"Iffen I had me a stake the likes of hisn, I would shut muh door fer good. I'ud find me a dang rat smart woman. I'ud kick muh feet up on the hearth, an' watch the world git on past from my winder glass," said Clettis.

"You and me both, Clettis, but Claussen prefers to survey; sure don't seem the kind to settle down." Mr. Angers laughed.

"Is that not the truth of it." I couldn't have agreed more and joined in the laughter.

"You set your mind to resting up in Hell Hole and nothing more," said Mr. Angers. "Meanwhile, we'll start asking about and following leads. He's lookin' for you so I have no doubt we'll be getting the two of you together soon enough one way or another. You can pretty much bet on it."

* * *

We five slept out in the open three nights in total and always woke up hungry. Nobody ever asked me to cook up breakfast, but I could see they figured even if it was the 'same-ol'-same-ol'', if it was slid off a skillet and onto a plate by a woman's hand, it just had to have a better taste. It was the same ingredients, but they all swore up and down that it was the best breakfast they ever had.

I finally had to tell them to hush-up, for I had never been married, never had children, had no family, and hardly knew how to cook. I told them that they were all plumb out of their minds and too lazy to make their own breakfast. I spoke God's truth on every count except for the cooking. They just laughed aloud and insisted on seconds.

All in all, we traveled either side of day's heat for four days, being forced even farther south by Indian sightings before circling back up to the southern side of South Pass. There, we headed up into the foothills until at last we reached our destination—this place they called Hell Hole.

ONE-HUNDRED-ONE

"Welcome t' Hell Hole, Mrs. Claussun," said Clettis.

The path stopped at a small pond sunk at one end of a handful of run-down structures. We halted our horses to gaze down at the thin glass-like pool of water. Mr. Calahan nodded toward it.

"Hell Hole gits half hets name from this lil' ol'pothole, or pisshole as we gener'ly hear of het."

I observed what amounted to little more than a trickle of water leaking down from somewhere up in the pine-shrouded rocks. The flow had barely enough depth to cover the bed of gravel that lined the creek bottom and most of the countryside.

The stream smoothed out as it entered the pothole bordered by broken and craggy banks.

"Ye should wanna see het inna spring. Gets a-flowin' matty forceful affer them thar snows starts a-meltin' an' t'washun' down. Whoosh, rips rat smart through here'n haids on down that-a-way t'ward the pass. 'Bout then ye 'd think het's a waterfall. Pond's deep then. Don't take but no tahm 'fore het settles down 'n by summer's end het's all but done drahd up."

"True 'nough," Clettis chuckled. "Been drah all over, but thar het tis, still wet'n like to be th'only water 'at makes het down this close to the pass. Ye can ride further up the slopes'n fin' good water, but het's a rough ride up that-a-way fer a drink, not that het hain't done reg'arly come fall.

"'Sides which, folks come by this way knowin' when they fill up theirn jugs, they's usually sump'in' goin' on. They's usually some good company t' rest up an' take in the views acrosst the pass, t' the norf, east'n that-a-ways west." Mr. Calahan raised his arm to sweep the horizon. The view was superb. "Thems yonder hills—at's Souf Pass Junction. At's whar ye go if'n yer a-lookin' t'sleep. Here'uz whar ye go if'n yer a-lookin' t'raise tarnation."

I strained to dissect details on the horizon, hoping I might possess some special ability to see buildings that far away, or spot Claus, which of course I didn't. I looked hard, but resigned myself to relying on my imagination.

"Course then, lets a times the compeny en't so good. These boys are a good exemple o' thet'n thet 'counts for the other half o' the name," said Farish as he nodded toward the bodies draped across the horses behind us.

"Amen," said Mr. Culahan. "Ye can parb'ly 'magine when more'n three, fahr men gets t'sitting 'roun' the waterhole, how fun gits t'startin.

"Ye gotcher trappers'n'panners'n, yer English'n'French, now'n then some Spanish. Ye gotcher Injuns wit' squaws fer a-tradin'; an' ye stir 'em all up wit' a coupla o' bottles o' whiskey'n next thing ye knows, all tarnation breaks loose—usually o'er th'squaws or bad dealin'.

"Thar be no shortage o' hard drinkin' or fattin 'n some tahms even a killin'r two. Most o' that's 'tween whats 'n Injuns, or 'tween Injuns'n Injuns. Not too oft'n 'tween jus' whats. But the killin' always starts wit' the drinkin', 'spesh'ly wit' thems thar Injuns. They is bad'uns." He stopped a moment as if to take in another thought. "Yeah, this place'uz called Hell Hole long 'fore any o' these buildin's uz up."

"Is it still like that around here?"

"Shoot, no. No ma'am, not lek et used t' be," said Farrish. "Them days pretty much been en' gone—get a few rowdies, but most folks gone over t' the Junction nowedays—better food."

By my count, Hell Hole stood all of eight badly abused buildings divided by the path, the oldest structures being made out of logs. The saloon and the boarding house faced each other and were built at a later date. They were made from planks.

Planks were peculiar because they were used over and over again. As towns died off, disappeared and reappeared a couple of miles upriver so to speak, the planks often became humorously scrambled. They made for interesting structures that seemed in need of shedding false histories.

For example, the east wall of the boardinghouse was sided with planks that had clearly legible remnants of a livery and stagecoach billboard painted on them. As were the letters 'loon' out of the word 'saloon', which ran along the planks just over the front door of the structure in old weathered and faded peeling blue paint. Somebody had added a fresh 'y' appropriately enough with dark blue stain.

The saloon on the other hand, which might have made some use of 'loony', had instead a dozen planks from a grainary, and of all things, planks from a prayer revival stage once located in a place called Cannonsburg, Virginia.

Mr. Calahan started pointing out a couple of the run down structures. "Used t' be a blacksmiff'n a gunsmiff put up in 'em two cabins full tahm, 'long wit' a carpenter'n a cobbler in thems o're thar. When they wadn't trappin' or pannin' they'd take t'fixin' ye up. Used t' be a tanner lived in that'un, kept hides in that thar lean-to 'longside the cabin o'er there. Now, they's all'n Souf Pass. They come by now 'n 'gin t'see what needs a-fixun' cuz the tradin' post keeps busy 'nough anymore to make 'em a profit."

"I'm thinken' et's getten' busier," said Elb.

"Seems thet way don't et. Hey, ya neveh know. Shoot, might be we're getten' more people out this way en' we'll be needen' t' fix up this side o' the pass for 'comma-da-shens'," said Farish.

"I doubt it," said Mr. Angers.

As for me, out here, I expected anything was possible, but for now, based on what I saw before me, the structures were empty and good for little more than protection from wolves and bears at night. The cabins were long since left to the ravages of weather, the weeds, and the snakes.

"I wouldn't count on takers anytime too soon." I remarked. "I'm seeing clean through that cabin side to side."

Farish Creek looked at me with amusement. "Shoot, Messus. Claussen, thet's the best o' the lot. Wenna know why?"

"Farish, when it looks like that, I don't think I want to know why."

"Oh, no, thes es funny, ma'am. Them bears all jus' love thet caben, cuz they ken smell us sleepen' enside. They start clawen' et the logs en' tryen' to pry 'em apart to get a good sneff o' Elb. Them bears, they jus' love Elb. Soon as they steck thet snout as far en between them logs as they ken get for a wheff, he stecks thet gun barrel o' hez up agen' their nose from enside en' blows their heads clean off. I en't thet crazy 'bout eaten' bear meat, but then;—shoot, we en't neveh had to chase one to get us a dinneh."

"What happens if he knocks on the door and you open it?" I asked.

Farish just looked at me for a moment, at which point the others began to laugh at his expense. I was distracted by movement beyond his shoulder, and noticed three men heading in our direction. They had walked out of the saloon, and by their calls, I understood them to be interested in the dead desperados. Mr. Angers passed a few words on to Mr. Calahan and then both men turned their horses about. He looked at me.

"Mrs. Claussen, I reckon Clettis and I will be on our way— the sooner gone, the sooner back. You'll do fine here long as you keep an eye on these two. Don't let them get to wandering off or drinking too hard. We'll be back in no time, so you just sit tight, all right?"

"That'll be fine, Mr. Angers. I'll busy myself until then."

"We'll see ya boys later. Give us a little time to look into Claussen's whereabouts. I don't know if he's in South Pass or not. Either way, don't be drinking up my cut. I'll be back in a week or so to collect my share."

"Sounds good. See ya then," answered Elb.

"Ah'll see ya in tahm, Miss Claussen."

"Good bye, Clettis."

With that, the two men were off. I couldn't blame Mr. Calahan and Mr. Angers for staying in the saddle and saying good bye to Hell Hole; I was sorely tempted to do the same. Instead, as Elb and Farish took up conversation with the strangers, I stayed put in the saddle and watched Clettis and Marty follow the path down the slope of the foothills, making their way north to cross the pass.

At the conclusion of business, Elb headed off in one direction with horses and dead men in tow. Farish walked toward me.

"C'mon, Messus. Claussen. I'll tek ya to the boarden'house."

He reached up to assist me off the horse, and then walked me toward a small shamble of a one-room building. The closer we approached, the poorer repair the building proved to be. It looked a great deal worse close up. I started to laugh as I thought of Van Mereden's boardinghouse in Albany.

"Somethen' funny, Messus Claussen?"

"I was thinking about what we learn to live with out here. This building might have made an admirable outhouse some-where in the world, but boardinghouse? I don't know."

"Shoot, it's gotta roof. Don't get much better'en thet."

"Yes, Farish, well—I will give you that."

Surprisingly, the building had been fitted with a small but honest to goodness raised plank porch. Even more to my liking, it possessed a raised plank floor on the inside instead of swept dirt. Undoubtedly, it gained such luxury through the demise of some other building, for a hint of color remained to reveal that billboard lettering once covered the floor. It had long since been worn away by the action of sand grinding across its surface beneath years of shuffling boots.

It also boasted a tub and a stone fireplace. I wasted no time getting to thoughts of putting both amenities to good use.

"I know what yer sayen', Messus Claussen. Et en't much, but et'll keep out the bears'n cats en once we get some water for thet tub, I recken you'll get thet beth ya wanted."

"It's fine Farish. Doesn't anybody stay here?"

"Duren' the night the men'll come around t'sleep enside. You know, t'get off the ground."

"I see. Well, I'm going to sweep the place out and settle myself in. I'll be fine."

"I'll be jest across the road et the saloon. Elb's there waiten' for me. Jes' gev a holler when you're needen' water er anythen'."

Farish left to meet Elb, and I set about making a broom, cleaning, and eventually collecting firewood, which I used to stoke the fireplace for heating stones. I chose not to call upon Elb and Farish and instead fetched water from the pond myself with an old coffee pot. The tub filled woefully slow. It took all of a hundred trips back and forth between tub and pond, but the drudgery saved me the added misery of waiting for the stones to heat.

I watched the stones sizzle in boiling fury, and even crack in half on occasion, each time I lowered them into the tub of cold creek water. It had taken me hours to prepare the bath, but between the anticipation of the pleasure to be had and the look of my dirty dried out toes, the wait would surely be worth the while. I had nothing now but time on my hands, the makings for a grand soak, and one last unsolved issue.

Privacy proved to be a problem. My parading back and forth to the pond stirred up a lot of interest, I being the only female among a collection of mountain men and drifters. To make matters worse, inside the boardinghouse there were no walls, and when all manner of strangers were not drifting in and out to have a look at me, and *possibly* contemplate the meaning of a bath, they were certain to be caught peeking through the wall-boards from outside.

Most were merely curious and left embarrassed after a sound scolding, but two men in particular were not so easily dissuaded. They stood outside the back wall, opposite the street where they were not so apt to be seen.

"Hey, lady. What'cheh doin' en thehr?"

"Preparing a bath. What are you doing out there?"

"We're watchen' you."

"That's rather rude don't you think?"

"I thenk et's rude yer're maken' us wait so long to see yeh take thet bath." The men laughed.

"I'm not making you wait at all. I prefer you leave."

"We prefer yeh tek a bath."

"Rest assured, I'll hardly be taking a bath while you're about."

"Fraid we'll git a lil' peek are yeh?"

I didn't bother to respond.

"I think yeh oughta let me soap up them breasts."

Instinctively, I looked for my bag, where I kept the repeater.

"C'mon lady. How 'bout given' us a lettle look 'n see, a lettle kess 'n feel."

The men laughed aloud. They had been drinking. They succeeded in making me uneasy and so, while waiting for the water to reach temperature, I simply ignored them and went about suspending a couple of blankets from the ceiling. As soon as the curtain went up, the two men blurted out a slew of obscenities but thereafter departed.

Until that point, I had been promoting the pleasures and prospects of a hot bath to my visitors in trade for privacy, but selling snake oil to a swindler would have been easier than obtaining any working arrangement from the last two brutes. Just knowing they were about was worrisome. I studied my newly erected curtain and deemed it now an inadequate guarantee of privacy and peace of mind. With fresh memories of the coarse comments spoken by the two foul-mouthed outsiders, I was compelled to walk across the path in search of Elb and Farish.

"Whazza nehms?"

"Elb and Farish." I told the unknown patron. He disappeared into the saloon and a moment later my heroes came running out.

"What'sa matteh, Messus Claussen? You alreght." The two men were looking up and down the street for signs of trouble.

"I'm fine. Everything's fine, but I need some help with my bath."

"Shoot! I'd be honored t' scrub yer back, Messus Claussen."

I looked at Farish with apathy. He was grinning ear to ear.

"What whiskey does to a boy. I'll pretend I never heard that. You're young enough to be my son."

"Ouch!" said Elb. "E'm sorry, Farish, sounds lek et's an older man she'll be needen'." He started laughing.

"The only thing I'll be needing is for one of you to park your butt on that front porch, and the other to watch out back while I take my bath—and see to it that no one decides to join me. Do you understand?" I looked directly at Farish. "Can I trust you?" My voice carried a hint of annoyance.

"As a son trusts hez mother." He responded with assurance.

"Good boy." I leaned over and kissed him daringly on the cheek. I immediately started back to the boardinghouse with both men close behind.

"Hey, how kem the good guy doesn' t get the kess?"

"Don't worry. In return for the favor, I promise to keep the water hot and fresh for the two of you to enjoy a bath after I'm finished."

"A bath?"

"A bath, Farish. It'll do you good. You boys can wash out your mouths." I closed the boardinghouse door behind me.

After a sound scolding and a demand that Elb and Farish stop peeking through the planks and face the path, I slipped behind

987

the curtains and stripped. I eased myself down into the hot water and moaned myself into utter ecstasy. I peeked about momentarily searching for any overlooked split in the curtain and when feeling confident of my privacy, I closed my eyes to the world. The only measure of time was a wait for my last brick-hard bar of soap to dissolve.

Curious bypassers were on the rise and came by to ask about me. In short time they were told that I was soaking in a tub. This caused quite a stir and soon enough five or six men had collected on the front porch to converse. Along with Elb and Farish, they took up guard of the door in my behalf. Although Elb and Farrish were in no rush to take a bath, there were a number of others not nearly so opposed to a good wash. It was one of them that disrupted my peace as I dozed in and out of near sleep.

"Miss Claussen! Miss Claussen! Ken yeh hear me?"

"What!" I barked out with annoyance in a raspy voice.

"Sorry to bother yeh, Miss Claussen. My name es Jake Dempsey en' Farish here wez jest tellen' me how he's not much o' one fer taken' a bath, en' I was wonderen' if I might go en his place."

"Sure—so long as you're not opposed to fetching firewood and water?"

"No ma'am, not et all."

"Fine—start collecting."

"Yes, ma'am."

"Miss Claussen?"

"Miss Claussen?" came a second voice.

"What now?"

"My name es Timothy Lawson end I wez wonderen' if I could soak after Jake. Act'shlee they'z a few of us thet would lek t' soap up. Ef'n yeh don' mind."

Rest and relaxation was over. I rubbed the sleep out of my eyes.

"You tell whoever wants to take a bath to help Jake fetch firewood and water, and get in line. Now hush and let me bathe in peace."

"Yes ma'am!"

When it came time for the men's baths, I found it quite humorous to see how incredibly uncomfortable they were to remove even a stitch of clothing while I was present. All my years suffering the horrors of sexual inadequacies and embarrassments, and suddenly I discovered men to be far more timid than I. Turning my back was totally unacceptable; I couldn't even be in the building, curtain or no curtain. I shook my head in wonder while standing out on the porch until each man was safely submerged beneath suds.

When allowed back inside, I made it perfectly clear I was not about to get all sweated up attending to the needs of the men. I supervised the heating of rocks and boiling of fresh water, but kept clear of the heat until the day cooled. Instead, I went about the business of folding blankets that were given to me and placing them on the floor to make up as accommodating a bed as possible. While busy at my task, a man in the tub spoke up from behind the curtain.

"Madam"

"Yes." I listened to voice of a soft-spoken Frenchman who when in line stood all of six feet and nearly that across the shoulders.

"I weeshed you to know eet ese goo' t'ave a woman 'ere. Eet shanges everyteen' about za place."

"Thank-you."

"You watsh fair snakes an' spidairs beneas' zee floorboarts. Zey lyeek za cool dirt down zere."

"Thank-you for the warning." I gulped. From that moment on I stared deep into the cracks between the planks upon which lay my bed. With a wary eye, I bemoaned the loss of my wagon with its security, privacy, and comfortable furs.

The baths continued and the heat of day and fire was fully replaced by the chill of night. The room had become warm and the baths much enjoyed. Nine men in all ended up soaking their hides. The baths drew out so many of saloon's patrons in order to keep fresh water and firewood coming as needed, that the saloon owner locked his doors and brought a few bottles of drink to serve the crowd at the inn.

A few fresh kills of meat appeared skewered across the fire alongside the boiling water and permeated the air with a tantalizing aroma that blended with the smell of cigar smoke wafting in from the front porch where was heard a chorus of laughter and good conversation. The unplanned event had given me good opportunity to meet most of the men currently visiting Hell Hole.

ONE-HUNDRED-TWO

All had enjoyed a grand time that evening. I more than anyone, but for endless attention, compliments, and flattery paid my way. Nonetheless, such merriment faded fast into memory as I sat alone on the front porch sunup to sunset the next day and each following day thereafter while awaiting word from Mr. Angers and Mr. Calahan.

I understood now the meaning behind the phrase *boarding* house, for by the hour, I gave fresh testimony to the term. I was *bored* indeed, thoroughly bored, impatiently bored—bored to tears—*bored to death*. It was a thrill just to chew my nails or spit at passing ants when no one was looking my way. I had absolutely nothing worthwhile to do, save sit and wait for Claus's arrival, or at the very least, word of his whereabouts.

I took it upon myself to bundle up some grasses and pine boughs for fashioning a new broom. In no way did I feel it my duty to clean up after men because I was a woman and it might have been expected of me. Rather, I swept because I had too much time on my hands, and if I was going to continue pacing the floor, I might just as well hold on to a broom and make the best of wasted footsteps.

I began with my stall and worked my way across the floor in both directions from wall to wall. I was certain that this was something that had probably never been accomplished in Hell Hole before my time. I swept the same dirt over and over again in pointless effort as I battled boots and blowing sand. I stirred up shadows beneath the wooden planks with each sweep of dirt atop the cracks. I was positive that there were indeed snakes and spiders down there, and my skin crawled every bit as much as did the shadows.

A couple of the men who shared sleeping quarters in the boardinghouse took note of my efforts, and one even asked if I wished him to remove his boots before entering. It was an absurd request, but it amused me, as it showed a trace of civility from somewhere in the man's past. It was something I noted in many and as with most of the others, I wondered from where he came. I wondered from where he brought his manners.

As I swept, my mind wandered, and I kept thinking about what Mr. Angers had said in so many words; *'knowing where Mr. Claussen lives and finding him at home are two entirely different matters'*. I had no idea how long I would have to wait. He promised that if no sign of Claus turned up within a week or so, they would bring me north to wait at South Pass Junction. It had been all of a week and more.

My remaining two saviors, Elb, the rifleman, and Farish Creek, did their best to wait it out with me, but they were clearly going crazy with boredom as well. I watched as they became increasingly restless, and this only served to make me all the more uncomfortable. I felt responsible for their situation. I would have much rather faced the wayward souls milling about Hell Hole, knowing I brought those folks no complaint or belief that I was the anchor about their necks.

I sat idly by, as Elb and Farish took turns drinking at the saloon and keeping me company on the front porch. Attempts at conversation were becoming a strain after so many days and so little in common. Unlike back east, here, even the weather refused to change enough to warrant mentioning. It was easier just to sit back side by side, and stare into the open door of the saloon.

I would prompt Elb to tell me about panning for gold and trapping beaver just to keep him occupied until he was finally relieved by Farish, who I would then prompt to tell me about panning for gold and trapping beaver to keep *him* occupied. I suffered the most, but at least they were never in the saloon at the same time long enough to realize our conversations were identical almost word for word. The three of us were driving each other politely insane.

There had been little need to prove how badly Elb and Farish were itching to go up into the hills and pass some time panning and trapping. I took hold of this desire and worked it for all it was worth until after hours of discussion, I convinced the two of them that I was wholly capable of looking out after myself and that the boardinghouse was a safe and comfortable place full of folks that I already knew.

I smiled warmly at the passersby, and pointed out how the strangers were friendly and helpful as though I had made many friends during the night of the baths. Of course, I hadn't met nor talked to anyone since, but Elb had assumed that while he was sitting in the saloon I was improving relations with the locals passing by the porch under Farish's watchful eye and with Farish it was vice versa.

Both men commented on how, since my arrival, a good many more men were showing up in camp. I was the talk of the saloon. I was the talk of the mountain for that matter. In spite of this becoming a potential problem, and after much urging on my part, I finally persuaded the two men to go up into the hills and 'trap'n'pan' the creeks for a couple of days.

They were plenty reluctant to leave, but I was becoming adamant to the point of being pushy and rude. My winning argument was in pointing out how they would be able to spot Clettis and Martin crossing the pass much quicker from the higher elevations of the mountain. I could no longer deny that I was in great need of ridding myself of their blank stares and routine exhalations, and if not for my own sanity, then for the sake of us all.

The following day, I was sitting on the front porch in a much-improved mood when I observed four young people walking along the path in my direction with two horses in tow. The only time I had seen children since leaving St. Louis was in the Indian camp. I kept my eyes on the four, as did they on me. I was unsure as to why they should watch me with such interest and began looking around to make sure I wasn't mistaken about what held their attention.

As they approached, I observed a boy about thirteen years of age, a second about seven or so, and two girls, one about eleven and the other about four or five. The four approached me without pause.

"Are you Mrs. Claus?" asked the oldest boy.

"Mrs. Claus?" How odd to be addressed in that manner, I thought to myself, it being a nickname for Christopher. "I don't believe I've ever been called that before. I go by Elizabeth. Who are you?"

"D'ya know Mr. Claus?"

"Do you mean, Mr. Claussen?" The children all looked at one another and fell into a short discussion.

"That's him, Paulie. Mr. Claussen's what folks in South Pass call'im, 'member?"

"Yeah," said the boy thoughtfully.

The boy looked at me. "Are ya Mrs. Claussen, then?"

I didn't expect this conversation to go very far, and so for the sake of saving time and the complication of explanations, I answered quickly.

"In a manner of speaking, I guess you could say that."

The two oldest children looked at each other in astonishment. The girl then turned to me with a wide-eyed expression.

"We din' know he's married. We never knowed."

"Wait—." Instant regret. I began to correct her, but was interrupted by the boy.

"Maybe not, but so what. It's none o' our business what Mr. Claus is or ain't."

"True." The girl responded.

The two looked at me, as if searching for a sign. I smiled and suddenly their faces broke into broad smiles as well. They closed in about me with a feeling of affection as if I were their mother of years. They overwhelmed me with a flurry of chatter and giggling. The youngest two children moved right to my side and devoured my every word and gesture. I focused on the oldest girl, whose name was Pratty.

Following her accounts, I was told how Claus had come to their aid after their mother had died in labor and their father had disappeared while hunting. Mr. Claus had fed and housed them near the North Pole.

"We's passin' nearby, an' a couple o' trappers we knowed were tellin' us 'bout how we'd be needin' a mother fer the young-uns. They'uz sayin' there's a woman in one o' these cabins, an' sumpthin' 'bout ya bein' kin t' Mr. Claus." The boy then spoke up.

"We adda come see fer r'selves. We jes wanted t'say that if there's anythin' we ken do, anythin' ya need, we'll do it. Mr. Claus's been real good t'us an' we owe 'im in return. So f'ya need some food'r'somethun', we'll git it. 'F'yuh need somethun' washed'r' fixed, we'll scrub it, or somethun' made up, jes you ask."

They quieted, waiting and watching me as if starved for a command. I was hard pressed to think of anything.

"Well, uh, I don't know—. Let me see—."

"Anythun', Mrs. Claus. Just say it," encouraged Pratty.

"Well, let me think—uhhh—. Oh, I know! How do you kids get about?"

"The horses," said Paulie. "Mr. Claus gave us these two. I ride with Ginger, an' Pratty takes Stevie with her."

"Just the four of you rode across the pass, by yourselves?"

"Yup, wasn't no big thing. Act'chlee, we don' half' t' worry s' much 'bout the wolves down there as when coming down from the Pole. We go all over."

"Is that right?"

"Yes ma'am." Paulie expressed his confidence.

"Is the Pole where you live?"

"Manner of speakun' ma'am," said the eldest boy.

"Is it a big place?"

"No ma'am, not really. It's a nice place. Mr. Claus has a nice place there an' a tradun' post."

"We like it cuz there's lottsa kids live at the Pole," said Pratty.

"Is there anyone living with Mr. Claus?" I tried to conceal my concerns about Christopher having a lover, a wife, or family. The children looked at each other and frowned in confusion.

"No ma'am, don' think so."

I was quick to change the subject. "Well, you truly are a brave lot. I don't think I could ever be so brave. I'll tell you what. About three days east of here lay the scattered pieces of a wagon. In the middle of that mess you'll find a trunk and a number of things that belong to me. If you think you can return the trunk to me, you may have whatever else lies about for yourselves, and there is plenty enough to please you, I promise. There are a number of nice robes and hides, and a lot of tools. You'll like what you find. It's only a matter of whether you can find the wagon."

"Oh! We ken find it fer sure!" said the boy, boastfully. Their eyes were big as saucers. "Them tracks stays ferever."

"In that case, I have a horse around back. You can take him along to carry the load, and I would try and find one more at least. All I ask in return is this; if I'm not here when you return, you just keep my trunk and see it gets to Mr. Claus or me when-ever you are able. Can you do that?"

"Yes, ma'am!"

"Well, then, get on with it, and I wish you the best of luck. Be careful."

The two youngest were excited, but they followed Paulie and Pratty's lead and made no move without them. Meanwhile, Paulie and Pratty stood somewhat hesitant, as if to get one last look at me. Pratty spoke up.

"Mrs. Claus—I mean, Mrs. Claussen, would'ja tell Mr. Claus that Paulie'n'me, an' the kids are gettin' on fine. I know he cares 'bout us an' I know he'll be worryin' a plenty. He always does. He's kinda like a father."

"He's kinda like a father t' a lot o' kids," said Paulie. "I don't think he ever got any o' his own." Suddenly, he looked at me as though he were the fool. "I mean t' say that I jus thought the two of you —."

"Jus' never you mind, Paulie!" Pratty glared as she elbowed him.

"I'll be sure to tell him. I promise. He'll be happy to hear it, I have no doubt."

The kids went around to the yard in back of the boarding house and returned with Cal's horse. Their faces had gone serious and better showed the difficult lives that haunted them. They gave short good-byes and headed for the wood from where they came. I watched them go, when suddenly Pratty turned around. She was smiling brilliantly.

"Mrs. Claus, *Claussen*—I ken jus' tell that you're the perfect wife for Mr. Claus! I hope you have lottsa kids! Bye!"

She waved, as did the other three. I raised my hand to return the wave, while at the same time; I glanced around to see if anybody had heard the remark, for I felt more than a little embarrassed. Fortunately, no one did, and I was free to laugh about the assumptions without worry or regret.

ONE-HUNDRED-THREE

I settled back upon my bench, and followed the steps of the four youngsters until they disappeared into the trees. Our meeting had lasted little more than an hour, yet I found it a refreshing change that forced a surge of relief into the grueling monotony of my wait. The encounter emphasized the extent of my social intercourse in Hell Hole, which at best was a nod of recognition as a man tipped his hat or stared my way while passing to or from the tavern.

Meeting the children served to underscore how deprived I felt of friends and companionship. It accentuated a lifetime of restraints that were expected of women, and which now prevented me from crossing the threshold of the tavern doorway. I was uninvited because of an unwritten law, and therefore isolated from the most prominent activity that a person might enjoy in *ten thousand godforsaken miles.*

It was a man's world that surrounded me—a man's world that dictated how I should behave. I found it a selfish and often cruel world that was probably originated by a disgruntled Adam to punish Eve eternally for not sleeping with him after the apple incident. Poor losers.

I wondered if those men who walked by and tipped their hats expected me to sit on the bench for however many days, months, or years it might take before the riders returned. It would have been easier to pour salt into an open wound, as let me sit alone to watch the world pass freely in and out of the saloon that stood barely a hundred feet away beckoning all to enter, save one.

My eyes followed the backside of every individual that passed through the perpetually swinging door. I found myself obsessed by a need to know, a need to make sense of the shadowy movements inside the doorway where men were drinking, singing songs, and raising dust off the floor. I knew a man named Jake played the fiddle, another played the guitar and banjo, and a third played the flute.

It always sounded like fun, and I was left baffled as to how so many men could acknowledge me, offer every courtesy, yet, never once think to invite me into their festivities. At first, I wondered if all men could be that callous, but as time went on, I began to realize that they wished me no displeasure or suffering. It was apparent that they had no idea how depressing it was to endure my confinement behind invisible bars day after day as I listened to the jollity and camaraderie they enjoyed just across the street.

These men simply assumed that I would never consider going into a tavern filled with drinking men for fear of losing their respect or even worse, tarnishing the good name of Claussen. Nothing could have been farther from the truth. The Claussen name would have to deal with whomever or whatever I was, and as for respect; if ever a woman could stand in a den of whores and maintain her virtue—*that person had to be me.*

I doubt if it ever occurred to these men that a woman in these parts needing something more for entertainment than staring at a sky to form faces out of clouds. I imagined they felt I would be content to busy myself by sweeping the boardinghouse floor one more time or giving them all another round of baths and a piece of pumpkin pie. I wondered if they entirely lacked the compassion to consider how degrading it was to be entirely shut out of their world except for those times when they demanded that women sleep in their beds.

I let loose a long exasperated breath. Maybe, I was just too hard on men plain and simple. I was a spinster and my opinions were probably as jaded as one might expect. Truth be known, I had watched the roughest troupe of men God ever created pass through the door of that saloon. Back east, a woman would have fled in fear of these near barbarians. I wouldn't say that in Hell Hole I didn't have to exercise a measure of caution. After all, I had been watching these men for the past week, and they were all watching me back and making a great to do about there being a lady in town. Yet, whatever their motives, whatever their hopes or fantasies, these men had been for the most part respectful, talkative, hat-tipping folk, flashing smiles and acting neighborly.

Reflecting upon the fact I had never been accosted, and considering how miserable I felt being confined to the porch like a caged canary, I finally reached the limits of my frustration and spread my wings all but ready to fly. It was time for a change. I had my gut full of sitting around listening to all the song and merriment, all the laughter and carrying on, all the signs of the good life that were remarkably absent on my side of the path.

And so, in a fit of belligerence I sprang from my bench, grabbed my bag, barreled off the boardinghouse porch and headed directly toward the saloon fully determined to put straight this social injustice. I sized up the situation before me, and without a moment's hesitation or a second thought, I walked straight through the front door.

ONE-HUNDRED-FOUR

The hustle and bustle inside came to an abrupt halt as though these men had been sitting about for years preparing for this one violation. The place went dead still. If I had been perfectly naked I would have drawn only half of the attention now paid me. In fact many of these men probably saw me as perfectly naked, for their eyes were riveted to my frame as they forcefully twisted their heads about to follow my passing.

I sat down on a bench close by a trio of men who had been playing instruments and leading the place in song. No one moved to stop me. No one stirred. The musicians never plucked another note. They only stared at me in speechless surprise, as did all those in the room who were now waiting and wondering what would come next as the bartender stepped up nervously to the table.

"Beggin' yer pardon, Mrs. Claussen, es there somethen' yer needen'?"

"Yes, something to drink please, but not whiskey; I find it too strong. Possibly some lemonade or plain water with lemon— I'd die for a glass of cold sweet cider—*oh well*. Cooled tea, that sounds good, have you a glass of cooled tea?" I was feeling a little testy and looked squarely into the man's eyes, daring him to object. The man looked around at his patrons and then once more at me.

"I'm sorry ma'am, I got no lemons, an' the closest thing here t' cider would be applejeck an' that's mighty powerful drink fer a lady."

"Are you saying you don't have a drop to offer the timid drinker? I know better."

"Ma'am, this here es what I'd be a sayen'. Thes es no place fitten' fer a lady cepten' those doing a service ef yeh git my meanen'. I'd be fearen' fer yer honor an' countenance, but fer the words bein' aired, raw as they is." The man looked stressed, he was wringing and twisting a towel between his hands.

"I understand your meaning and am grateful for your concern. I can assure you I am no lady of service—."

"Oh, no! Mrs. Claussen, I wasn't meanen' t' say—."

"As for the ambiance of your establishment, you might discover that entertaining a lady for an afternoon could bring a fresh change of air and soften some of those distasteful outbursts. But, if you can't find me something to drink then I'll just sit and abide my time listening to the music. It sounds good from the porch, and I suspect it must be ever the more satisfying when enjoyed up close." I was determined to remain put.

The Frenchman, who looked like a grizzly bear in trousers, walked up to the table and dropped to his knee. Even as he knelt, he looked like a small building. He was the soft-spoken man, who warned me about the spiders and snakes. He was one of the many faces I recognized from the night of the baths. He placed his folded hands upon the table as if to be praying and spoke to me with a strong French accent.

"Madam, I am Pierre La Chappell at your sair-veece. I weesh on-leh you shoot know, I 'ave nawt 'ad zee plea-shure ov dis beauty as you possess, to see een s'ree or four 'ears. Eef you woot do me zis honor to stay, I woot feast my eyes an' feel my 'eart wis' your face, an' dis I woot carry wis me across dese mountains, qui? I ask you pleace, yes? Stay. Do not listen to dis man, he ese blind or crez-zee, no? I beg you stay an' honor us. We want dis, yes?" He offered a broad smile. The bartender rolled his eyes in despair.

"Thank-you Pierre, you are very kind. I would love to stay, will you join me?"

"Oui, madam, I woot." He gushed with gratitude. Then there appeared another, soon followed by more, all sliding down the bench toward me, or crowding around the table to introduce themselves.

A lanky arm with a glass attached to its end, penetrated our inner circle; a voice trailing it from behind sounded out.

"Move 'side, step 'side. Sas'fras fer theh lady, I have sas'fras fer theh lady." A young man leaned in to show his face. "Ma'am, I hope this'll be more t'yer lekin'. It's chelled sas'fras tea thet's been bottled an' kept en the cool wateh o' the creek, jes' as yeh were askin'. It's a splended brew if I'uz t'say so meself."

"Oh, I am grateful. I agree, it sounds the perfect drink."

From out of nowhere, the men broke into a tongue-twisting chorus that must have been part of a song they all knew.

Make it whiskey for me, a whiskey for me,
but take tea to my lady, tea to my lady.
Make it whiskey for me, a whiskey for me
But take tea to my lady, take my lady a tea.

The men pounded out the words with their mugs and glasses on the table and almost at once a whole pitcher of tea appeared at my table. I raised my glass and toasted to the men's good health, which they appreciated most sincerely. After seeing all this, the musicians relaxed and began to play the first bars of 'The Shepherdess Forlorn', when I suddenly stood up in an obvious state of annoyance and objected.

"Wait! Now hold on just one moment, please!"

My outburst brought the room to a second bout of complete silence, and all heads turned up to hear me out.

"I have been listening to you play day in and day out for the last week, and I have never one time heard you play 'The Shepherdess Forlorn'. I don't want 'The Shepherdess Forlorn' or 'The Cottager's Daughter' or anything that sounds like a Puritan prayer! I want you to play the same outrageous songs I have listened to for the last eight days. I want to hear 'Charlotte the Harlot' or 'Violate me in the Violet Time' or 'Lilly Anne', yes, 'Lilly Anne'. I want to hear 'Lilly Anne the Lover'."

I stood glaring at the musicians whose eyelids were folded back into their heads leaving their eyes bulging out of their sockets with shock and just short of popping to the floor. Looking to be rescued, those collected eyeballs rolled around nervously scanning the room until a single patron suddenly exploded into a roar of applause that expressed wholehearted approval for my selection. The others immediately joined him.

"Wha dya waiten' fer, Jake! Ya heerd the lady. Play it!"

The musicians looked at each other in resignation, shrugged their shoulders, and set off in a wild rollicking rendition of the first true bawdy western camp song I ever heard up close. It was a dilly.

Oh! Lilly Anne licked 'em all as a lover
She had mastered her art like no other
She would lift up her dress
And offer them her best
Features to fondle under cover.

Its been said she once was a darlin' daughter
Of a mean and ornery mountain logger
She perfected her trade
Watchin' logs gettin' laid
In ravines runnin' fast with western water.

Lilly Anne wasn't much of a drinker
But we knew she sure could be a stinker
You might never see her pissed
But get bumped once off her list
An' she'll drop your little friend like a sinker.

Oh! Lilly Anne licked 'em all as a lover
She'd make you beg an' crawl like no other
She wore satin underpants
And she'd give you one free glance
Then make ya pay through the nose for another.

She could tell when a man's heart was breakin'
An' take his mind off the hurt an' the achin'
With a stroke of her hand
He'd return a gay man
With a smile no soul could be fakin'

When they're shy she'd start slow that's for certain
Til she'd eased 'em behind her velvet curtain
Then it's brawlin' bears in heat
While we're laughin' in our seat
Cuz we know she ain't in there just a flirtin'

Oh! Lilly Anne licked 'em all as a lover
She could lay big or small like no other
But the boys in our camp
Never called her a tramp
They referred to her fondly as—'their mother'.

It's been told, gold is cold, an' I agree, sir
'Less in the hands o' Lilly Anne 'before' your liesure
For unsociable she ain't
Been no customer complaint
An' we pay her all she wants just to please her.

Oh! Lilly Anne licked 'em all as a lover
She'd get deep in your pants like no other
She had a figure of her own
Make it cash or a loan
Or trade her somethin' special if you'd ruther

I was red faced and laughing as hard as ever with embarrassment. But it was all right; I was having a good time. Of course,
the sight of me blushing drove the men wild. They jumped up
from their seats and started twirling about arm in arm, downing
their whiskey, howling like fools, and sliding right into the
follow up song.

Amblin', ramblin', Dandy Dan
was a well-known western gamblin' man,
Whose stoic poker face—deadpan,
belied the cards he held in hand

He cashed in copper, sold off silver, gave up all his gold
Traded his possessions if they couldn't be quickly sold

He would bust a bank wide open to get himself a stake
A seat at Friday's poker game and another chance to make

An impression on the lady of the local town saloon
Lilly Anne the Lover, bathed in the best of French Parfume

Dandy plied his trade all day and played his game all night
He'd shuffle and he'd deal them cards 'til morning's early light

Amblin', ramblin', Dandy Dan
was a well-known western gamblin' man
Whose stoic poker face—deadpan,
belied the cards he held in hand

"Mark my words, gentleman!" Dandy always said
"I'll deal these cards faithfully until the day I'm dead."

But the lovely Lilly Anne sang to a different tune
Said, "I think I'm gettin' tired of my work in this saloon."

"Dandy, take your gold from this table of your dares
And spend it on me sensibly in my bedroom up the stairs."

Well Dandy Dan went crazy, clearly out of mind
When Lilly Anne said, "Be my man, we're two cards of a kind."

Amblin', ramblin', Dandy Dan
was a well-known western gamblin' man
Whose stoic poker face—deadpan,
belied the cards he held in hand

Torn between his poker chips and lust for Lilly's puckered lips
Dandy Dan chewed and spit the nails clean off his fingertips

His poker pals said plainly that his mind was all but lost
Their reason being mainly, he could have her at no cost

He was looked on even lower than the lowly deuce of spades
By Lilly Anne's acquaintances and all the bar room maids

He even raised some eyebrows in the friendly Friday club
His chair turned up missing as though he were being snubbed

Then a scholarly old gentleman stepped out in front and said
"Just deal her out a diamond Dan, and play poker in your bed."

Amblin', ramblin', Dandy Dan
was a well-known western gamblin' man
Whose stoic poker face—deadpan,
belied the cards he held in hand

He gave a sigh of such relief, his fears now being diminished
He merely played a different stake; the game was never finished

Oh, Dandy Dan, the gamblin' man lost his stake to Lilly Anne
With such relief, his fears diminished
Knowing the game was never finished

Oh, Dandy Dan
Oh, Dandy Dan
Oh, Dandy Dan

ONE-HUNDRED-FIVE

From the first line of 'Lillie Anne' and on through the next three hours, I was treated with all the respect given a proper lady in any city back east. Pierre, Jake and the rest were stumbling all over themselves, spoiling me with attention, courtesy, and muted expressions of desire. With exuberance and gaiety, they competed with one another to teach me their favorite reels, kicks and twirls.

I collapsed onto my bench both winded and amazed at the freedoms and fun loving nature this wild county bred into its inhabitants. Nobody faulted me for my presence or for enjoying myself, and I pressed on having the time of my life. It was so outrageous, this relaxed morality.

My upstanding, moral, and all too often hypocritical circle of hometown Bostonians would have never stood for this unrestrained backroom hullabaloo. Not the free association, not the feverish dance, and especially not the bawdy songs, which fascinated me and fed a mind so starved to understand anything about the nature of men. Thank god, those missionaries bent on penetrating the desert to preach scripture to the savages, somehow failed to mind their own flock.

On the other hand—it was far too easy to overindulge in these free associations, and I found myself losing sight of the protections afforded by those same Bostonian restraints I so despised. Have no doubt, after so many days sitting alone on the porch, I was all too carried away with the flirting and attention being paid me. I overlooked more than one of those sensible New England reservations.

It was just such foolish behavior that left me parading before the attention of one man in particular, a man I had never seen walking the path in Hell Hole. He entered the saloon with a friend, and as he crossed the floor toward me, he hollered out his demand for the bartender to fetch him a bottle of whiskey in a manner both loud and boisterous. I recognized the voice at once.

Like most women, I was given those specific instincts that offered me protection, yet served men to no advantage. And so I was at once attuned to this man's presence and warned from within to be on guard. I understood by some primitive awareness that he was a predator who would forcefully maul me for his own pleasure.

An equally large man such as Pierre might fight this stranger to the death without fear, but for me this was not an option. The stranger frightened me to the core at first sight and prompted me to search the room for an exit and a makeshift staff. Mentally, I reviewed my lessons from Dorrie.

The contrast between Pierre and myself was apparent by his marked indifference to the stranger as opposed to my immediate alarm. Pierre was enjoying himself immensely, whereas I was being subconsciously compelled to flee the saloon in spite of my reasoning that argued such fears to be irrational within the company of so many friends.

The man hadn't yet paid me full attention, and so I stepped at once into the shadow of Pierre and the others in hopes of becoming invisible. Fortunately, those I had befriended tended to smother me, keeping close, and although I made no mention of my concerns aloud, this offered me the protection that my instincts deemed necessary. From that point on, I reined in my carefree ways and kept much more to myself.

I kept close account of this man's moves and mannerisms as best I could by means of furtive glances in his direction, while being careful not to meet his eyes. To my alarm, once he discovered my presence, his eyes never left me. I could see that he was taken by the sight of me, only being distracted briefly when addressed by his companion or when feeling the need for another swig of whiskey. The situation had all the makings for 'a bad time a comin'.

For the benefit of my friends, I maintained a mask of laughter and joviality, while inside, my stomach was binding up into one of its contorted knots. I continued to dance and joke, but below the surface I was fully on guard and cautiously assessing my companions, wondering which of them I might count on for help if things got out of hand. I trusted Pierre from the very start and moved closer to his side in hopes of giving the impression that I belonged to him, thereby warding off any unwanted advances.

With each toss of whiskey, the stranger became louder and bolder. He was now beginning to compete with the others for my attention. He was beginning to assert his position. His voice rose above the rest as he leveled ever more disrespectful and abusive language in my direction, much like the night of the baths. He and his friend were making a nuisance of themselves, getting drunker by the minute, becoming obnoxious and ever more noticed by our group.

Although, I was given assurances by the others and did my best to ignore the stranger, discounting the man only served to goad him further. He and his friend forced a couple of the others to remove themselves from our table so that he might sit closer to where I was dancing. While those about me might have shown some concern, they were not women, and could not be expected to comprehend how I was already in complete dread of the situation.

The stranger was attempting to meet one of my furtive glances, which he did at last. He held my attention long enough to say with his eyes that he had taken possession of me. He then sneered and threw his head back to pour down more whiskey as if a patient man, yet acting impatient to reach that state of drunkenness that gave him the needed excuse for acting out his incivilities.

It wasn't even how much he drank, as it was the manner in which he drank, upturning his bottle in the crudest of fashion. I knew men often asked for their drink by the bottle and dispensed with the glass, but on this day, my newfound friends refrained from such practice for my benefit. They joked about putting on airs, about pretending to be in a *'Boston Harbor'* saloon back east. They laughed about using glasses and tins, and swirled their spirits daintily like upper-crust gentlemen. Some were even substituting whiskey for sassafras to impress me the more.

Wishing to distance myself from the stranger, I directed Pierre away from that end of the table. Preferring to keep my company, Pierre was quick to follow my lead, but what I hadn't expected was his sudden request to be momentarily excused in order to step outside and relieve himself. I protested gently, pretending I was having too much fun, while trying at the same time not to be so forward as to give him the impression I wished for something more. Needless to say, nature's call was the louder.

I never saw the stranger rise from the bench, for my back was toward him as he made his move, but he wasted no time. Pierre's shadow had barely left the doorway, when the stranger's two large hands gripped my waist and swept me cleanly off the floor. I was in deep trouble.

Badly frightened, I was carried to the back wall, whereafter he spun me around and pressed my back hard against the boards. With his weight and a brutish kiss to my neck, he kept me pinned in place. I resisted his assault as best I could, and complained that I was not a whore in service, but my words fell upon deaf ears.

I swallowed hard. My mouth went dry at the realization that no one was rushing to my aid. The situation was made all the worse by the way in which the room quieted noticeably. Maybe, the others were confused. Maybe they thought I knew this person. Maybe, they were mortified in my behalf, knowing not one among them had the courage to stand up to this monster of a man. I felt not only abandoned, but sensed a creeping concern that the others might actually turn on me and partake in his attack. To my relief, they did not. Instead, they began to object strenuously.

Not a moment too soon, I saw Pierre come walking back through the door. At first he looked at me with a confused expression, but once he heard the outrage of the others, he understood what had taken place and leapt forward to my defense.

"Hey! What ese dees!"

Pound for pound, Pierre was every bit the size of the stranger and more. He might have settled the score that very second, had it not been for the stranger's cohort who immediately drew a pistol and leveled it at Pierre's head. In drunken shouts, the man fully dared Pierre to take another step closer. It seemed my only hope had been dashed.

The man chastised Pierre for interfering with a bit of harmless bar room fun. He then forced him to sit down and shut up, or suffer the consequences. Pierre hesitated. He looked at me and he looked at the gun. The man grew instantly furious that Pierre should think twice on the matter, and began to scream obscenities at him. Like my attacker, the scoundrel was also accustomed to getting his way, and I watched as the man's face grew deep red with anger giving rise to the veins on his neck. He cocked his pistol and swung it about threateningly. The situation became extremely dangerous for Pierre for there was only one law in this land—*survival.*

I knew Pierre felt responsible for my staying in the saloon, and that he had no choice but to back down. The risk was very real that he could lose his life over a woman he didn't know, would never sleep with and very likely would never see again. Not to mention, that in Hell Hole, it would be considered absurd to risk one's life for honor that would hardly be remembered the following day. Pierre sat down, eyes lowered and defeated.

It was at that point that the entire room came to a standstill. Those fun-loving patrons now shrank away to stand motionless at the edge of my worst fear. I observed the men standing together at that thin line between right and wrong where males could be held spellbound by their natural desires, and find themselves apt to watch every detail of a rape with fascination and longing, wrong as that might be.

For the whole of the afternoon, I experienced how my flirting could be so utterly arousing, not only for these men, but me as well with all the dancing, playful teasing, talk, and

1012

innuendos. I saw the dreamy look in their eyes. Behind a semi-transparent veil of respect, I could see how badly they craved me. I felt their desire.

I even dared to encourage them because I was drunk with the thrill of having such power over their emotions, of commanding such attention. I had them eating blindly out of my hands like little puppies, and the sensation was as morally corrupting as any other form of power. I received all the attention I beckoned, but now I was held hostage to that same attention by pups turned wolves.

I had raised the level of sexual awareness in the saloon to the point that my attacker now offered these men something so tempting that no one man could easily resist its call or feel he was directly responsible for its outcome. After all, had it not been my decision to enter this man's world? Had I not been asked to leave? Would any rabbit enter a den of wolves? Had I not been warned; *'they had no lemons'*.

And so, I watched their eyes as they watched the brute's hands reach for my breasts. He rubbed hard against me while he gnawed at my neck, starved for the feel of a woman. My eyes welled up with tears of humiliation. The embarrassment of being assaulted in front of all these men whom I had come to know and enjoy was absolutely unspeakable.

In one short moment, the lie of a lifetime was revealed. Instantly shattered was the belief that my body was sacred and given to me by Almighty God to protect and care for as his temple. How could a body so easily defiled, be a fortress for a soul? How could this stranger merely walk up and strip my soul of its most sacred shelter. How could anyone be capable of that?

I concentrated solely on that one question, for more than anything else, I needed to be angry. It was how I protected myself. I absorbed the feel of this man and assessed him for what he was, a scoundrel, a pig, and nothing more. He was a ruffian; he was reviling, but he wasn't invincible and I swore my revenge.

My tears began to change from those of humiliation, to those of frustration for being unable to physically overcome this person. I strained against his strength, but it was to no avail. The brute was a mountain man in every way and as strong as a bull. My inferior strength only served to increase his sense of power and pleasure.

I pleaded with him to leave me be, but he would have none of it and so my anger was to be my only ally. I could feel it blending with my blood to protect me emotionally now, as it had the whole of my life. As it coursed through me, it brought forth invisible tears, dry tears that helped to mop up the wet of my eyes. I accepted my situation and searched for a way out. I understood that I was alone in this matter.

I turned my head just enough to see through the man's mess of greasy straggly hair and gage my distance from the door. I only needed one chance to run, one slip of his attention. Unfortunately, I knew his attention was hardly about to slip anytime soon. What tears remained, blurred the faces of all whom were standing or seated at the table before me, but I could feel them staring, witnessing my despair.

A few looked away, embarrassed for their lack of courage, guilt ridden by their inability to stand up to the man even if they were to be beaten in their attempt. It was a matter of honor and they had to face the fact they possessed none. They cowered behind the excuse that making one rash move might cost Pierre or someone else their head. I heard the brute's cohort laughing hard after someone cautioned both he and Pierre to tread with care. Apparently, my assailant was known by some of the patrons, and was considered to be a person avoided at all cost.

Again, the brute lifted me off the ground and pinned me back against the wall to kiss my neck from the other side. As my feet dangled in air, my toes barely scraping the floor, I looked at the musicians who had stopped playing to stare at me with that same dull look of uncertainty they possessed earlier when I first requested 'Lillie Anne'.

I studied the obstacles between the door and me while searching for a route of escape. I determined it best to go over the tabletop instead of around because the brute's friend sat there with his gun still pointed toward Pierre. The man was bound to block my pass should I near him. I also wanted my bag, which was sitting centered upon the table.

I studied the expressions of those I could see seated near my bag. I looked beyond them, across the room at other faces. I wondered who would step back to usher me out, or who would step forward to block my way. From the corner of my eye, I saw the bright light of the entrance. I watched as shapes of men crowded into the light, their number blocking the entrance. If they wished to keep me prisoner inside the saloon, then I was lost, for I could never pass by them without their permission.

I closed my eyes and wondered whether or not they would let me pass. Would they be friend or foe? Did they know the brute? Were they enjoying the spectacle? This monster was mauling me without restraint. I prayed the men would move quickly away from the door should I escape his grip. I blinked hard to wring out the last of my tears. I needed clear vision to run. I needed to see my way through.

Then, as if answering my prayer, the men stepped inside the saloon, leaving the door wide open, unobstructed as if beckoning me to enter its light. I felt my chance was now at hand. I would bite. I would bite hard and make my break. I struggled to see past the brute's head. My eyes darted about back and forth searching, focusing, watching for an opening in the crowd, studying faces—.

Christopher.

Christopher.

Could it be? I squeezed my eyes dry and pushed violently against the brute, allowing myself a moment of clarity in which to look straight into the man's face. He was different, older, not the same Claus; more weathered, but my heart knew what my eyes still questioned. It was he. It was indeed, and I reeled from the shock.

Instantly, everything in my life was insignificant. The brute, the attack, my situation, all of it was now nothing more than an irritation, a distraction. From my earliest days as a child, I knew Christopher righted every wrong. He helped the helpless. He fed the hungry. He swayed the seas. My eyes flooded with tears of relief. Then came the calm.

In this hellish predicament, my heart absorbed peace from Christopher in the way children absorbed sunshine through cracks in a storm-clouded sky. Serenity washed through me like warm tea on a cool desert night. I closed my eyes and let the troubles of life fall quietly away. I smiled, for he had returned with the riders—five solid men to save me, *four having done it once before.*

I began to smile in spite of the moisture in my eyes that kept the details of Christopher's face broken into kaleidoscope abstractions. I knew his frame as if it were my own. He appeared older and heavier, twice the size of any man in this place except for Pierre and the brute, but he was Christopher through and through. It was a fact one felt with certainty when in his presence.

My fear abated. A rush of elation shot through me, followed immediately by a surge of anger, for my temper was now boiling hot. I was determined not to shed another tear or do anything stupid that might force Christopher into an uncompromising position. I had every confidence in him. I knew the table had just been turned. It was easy now. I let the fool grope me; let him remain distracted to mumble away in his state of temporary stupefied bliss.

I resisted him just enough to keep him preoccupied, to keep firm his grip upon me as he had his way. My eyes locked onto Christopher. He walked confidently toward me. He moved past the table of the drunkard's friend, who drew a second pistol, which he pointed at the back of Christopher's head.

"Hey!"

This time he was met with the guns of the riders, Clettis, Elb, Martin and Farish, all of whom had followed Christopher inside. The Frenchman took the man's weapons and cuffed him hard. Through his cohort's cries, complaints, and the commotion that followed, my assailant remained buried in my neck, reeking of whiskey and expressing his torrid desires. The fool was indifferent to his surroundings. He was stupid and careless, but still armed and dangerous.

Christopher walked up to stand directly behind the man. He was close enough to kiss me himself. I could see the concern in his eyes as he looked deep into mine. He was calm. He was confident and in control. He studied the situation and smiled, putting me at ease. He winked at me and then leaned in close to my tormentor's ear and began to speak in his low and authoritative voice. Its sound resonated deep into the brute's awareness, deep enough for him to remove his hands from my breasts. He barely pulled his lips off me in order to listen up. He never turned around to look at Christopher. His breath remained hot on my neck. Christopher went on to advise him.

"Sir, I can see by your actions that you are either very brave or a complete fool. You might wish to know that in the space of a week, four others not so unlike yourself approached this lady without invitation as you do now.

"She put a round between the eyes of the first man, a round in the heart of the second, the third one she blew up leaving nothing more than his feet in his boots. The last one died with his whiskey in hand, his pants around his ankles, and a bullet in his chest not six feet from where she sat. You must believe for whatever reason, she is watched over, guarded like no other.

"When they found the last unfortunate fool, he was as drunk as you are now, naked as a plucked chicken, and still clutching his knife. A smart man would do well to ask if she wants to be kissed before taking any liberties. In your case it may already be too late. I can't say."

Christopher watched as the drunkard twisted my hair about his fingers and quite painfully forced me to my knees at his side. He drew out his pistol and gave Christopher an evil look of defiance then spit at his feet. He pointed the gun at Christopher's head.

"Tell yer men t' drop them guns'r I'm gonna blow yer haid off."

"We all die sometime. I'm plenty ready. The question is are you?"

"I don't think ya haird me clear. I said, I'm 'bout t' blow yer brains out. Now back off! Yeh got t' the count o' three to tell 'em t'drop them guns'r—."

"Or what?"

The man now pulled me up by the hair and moved his pistol away from Christopher. He jabbed the barrel hard under my jaw, driving my head back. It drove a stab of pain right through me. My eyes watered, but I uttered not a sound.

"Er, I'll blow her haid off, being yer so brave an' willen' to die." he grinned. Christopher never flinched.

"Either way, you're still a dead man. You get one shot. The choice is yours."

"Tell me, is she yer whore? Zat it? Well, yer a lucky may-an cuz she tastes good, she feels good—nice body an' all." He laughed menacingly. "Betcha can 'ave her back. She hain't nearly worth the trouble. No woman is."

With that, he thrust my head viciously into Christopher's chest. Christopher took me into his embrace. He kissed me affectionately on the top of my head as I tried to rub out the pain beneath my jaw. He comforted me with his strength, but I was too angry to accept consolation alone.

The man stepped around Christopher, and walked boastfully back to the table. I looked past Christopher's shoulder and watched the man climb over the bench. He sat down smugly pleased with himself. He was daring the riders. He believed because he had let the girl go, no one could justify causing him harm. They would say he was seated at the table and considered too drunk to be aware of his precarious position. He holstered his gun and swung his bottle up to gulp more whiskey. He laughed harder and his friend laughed with him. They were never the ones to pay the price.

I was incensed. Their laughter blinded me with rage. I had been made into a pathetic fool by this man and humiliated beyond my ability to convey. And now, after causing me such pain, he was simply to walk away feeling good about himself for having taken what he wanted without repercussion. Over my dead body! I swore I would savor the sweet taste of revenge, however right or wrong that might be.

I stepped free of Christopher's embrace and went to the table, where I grabbed my bag. I was seething. Reckless with anger, I slid it along the table until it was in front of the two ruffians, where I sat down upon the bench to face my molester.

To the surprise of everyone, I looked squarely into the brute's smug face as I reached into my bag and pulled out Luke's repeater. I held it firmly in both my hands and rested the heel of the grip on the table.

"What are you drinking?" I glared at the animal.

"Mmmhhpphh." He pulled the bottle away from his mouth and gave me that nasty sneer. I pulled back the hammer with my thumb and immediately got the look I wanted. I knew he wasn't afraid of the gun, he was afraid of the crazy dishonored woman behind the gun, and I was about to give him good reason. It was one thing I could do, for men feared crazy women. They believed women had no common sense and were capable of doing anything least expected when upset. In fact, for once I felt men were right.

"It's the devil is it not? I have no feel for a gun, but I know killing your kind feels great. I am always told one should squeeze the trigger slowly instead of jerking it the way I do. I really don't care because I discovered that if you are close enough to smell the whiskey on a bastard's breath, it doesn't make much difference if you squeeze or jerk. He dies either way. Now, I'm going to ask you one more time, what do you drink?"

"Whiskey." He responded, this time a lot less obstinate.

"Bartender! See this man gets another whiskey. This one's on me."

The bartender arrived nervously and placed a glass of whiskey upon the table next to his bottle. Christopher and the riders were watching the patrons and me closely.

"Down it," I ordered him.

"Wha'dya aim t'do, missy?"

"Are you afraid?"

"O'what?"

"Of me."

"Ha!"

KaBAMMMMMMM!

"AAAAAaaaaaaahhh!"

The brute and his friend lurched in opposite directions as I unloaded a round between their two heads. Everyone watching from behind the two men hit the floor, scattering like rats in sunlight. The two men jumped up from the bench.

"Sit down! Sit down!" I screamed in a rage.

The riders all kept guns trained on the two and suggested they do as I bid. I eased the chamber around, ready to fire the second round. Christopher watched me, but never moved to interfere. He said not a word. The riders looked at one another. No doubt, they were wondering about me, but they still felt in control of the situation.

"Now listen, up." I spoke to the brute.

"Listen up! Hail, I ken't hair nothen'. Ya blew out my bloody ear!" He held his hand to the side of his head, running his fingers through his scraggly hair.

"You can hear plenty good enough with your other ear, for what I have to say. Now drink up." This time the man picked up the glass and downed it in a gulp. I was so full of anger, I felt as though I were in another place. I felt distant. I felt numb.

"You've had your drink and you've had your fun. It's a good life and a fine way to end it. Right now the only thing between you and that end is a hair's distance of travel in this trigger." I arose from the bench and slowly crawled over the table to settle alongside him. I pressed the barrel of my gun hard and without mercy under his jaw, forcing his head back in the chair as painfully as I could. I wanted him to have a taste of his own medicine.

"Just a hair's distance." I whispered in his ear. "Now I'll kiss you my way." I twisted his scraggly locks tightly about my fingers and did my best to pull it out of his skull with my left hand while keeping the gun barrel rammed hard below his jaw with my right.

Having his head clamped thus, I leaned over him and placed my mouth upon his. He was breathing hard and nervous. I then slowly ground my teeth through his bottom lip. He shuddered from the pain, but knew he was just one blink of an eye from the gates of Hell.

The flow of his blood filled both our mouths. I raised my head and watched with great satisfaction as the blood streamed down his chin and cheeks from the half-severed lip. I looked into his frightened eyes, and spit his blood back at him.

"Why—why shouldn't I just kill you." I stood up and backed away. "You've had your kiss and feel. Remember, it was you who asked for it at the boardinghouse."

I lowered my gun and looked at the men about me. They stood silent, wide eyed, and astonished. Only Christopher held a look of concern, or maybe it was bewilderment, or even uncertainty. Maybe, it was a look of disapproval, but I didn't care.

I briefly turned toward Pierre.

"I know you would have helped me, Pierre. I wanted to say thank-you and tell you how much I enjoyed our dance."

"Merci." He smiled and patted his chest, indicating he would carry me in his heart as he had said.

I wished he not feel remorseful, as would the rest who now either looked away or stood staring in apologetic silence. I wiped my mouth clean of the brute's blood and kissed Pierre gently on the lips. After that, I swung my pistol across the crowd, which frightened many of them into dropping to the floor a second time. In an atmosphere of silence and wonder, I lifted my head high and walked out of the saloon.

Once in the street, I found the real me trembling terribly. I understood it was a reaction to the stress of fear and anger, and there was nothing I could do but wait for it to pass. I was a sight to see with fresh blood smeared across my clothes, my hands, and my face, which was still marked by the explosion of a week before. I felt dirty and disoriented. I willed myself to settle down and allow the afternoon breeze to carry off my fury so I might be refreshed. I stood facing it with eyes closed, when my shoulders were gripped firmly by Christopher's enormous hands. I instantly thought of Luke.

"Are you finished with your business today, Elizabeth?"

"I certainly hope so. I am tired."

"You've changed somewhat since last we met. I've seen a side of you heretofore unknown."

"Christopher, for you, most of my life as been heretofore unknown."

"Mmm. I guess I have that coming."

"I mean no offense. I'm upset. But, I do have a temper."

"Not that I noticed." He made me smile. He continued.

"The important thing is you appear unhurt, shaken, but unhurt. Do you feel up to traveling?"

"More than you can imagine. I have seen both halves of Hell Hole, the hell and the hole."

"In that case, let us get your things, and we'll leave at once. I don't wish to invite another encounter."

"Are you worried they will come after us?"

"Lord, no! I'm worried of what you might do. The sooner we leave the better, lest you kill someone yet."

"Don't say that, Claus. You still know me better than many, and longer than any. I'm not like that and you know it."

"I'll give you the benefit of the doubt, but I am concerned that you may have picked up some bad habits over the years. It would be difficult for me to know."

"You would know. You always know. You know before I know."

"Mmm."

I walked back to the boarding house with Christopher and the riders at my side. I collected what few things I possessed and expressed my eagerness to head for South Pass as Farish came into the room.

"Where's your horse, Elizabeth?" he asked.

"I gave it to some kids."

"Some kids?" He looked at me clearly confused, but elected not to ask. "Here, take mine, I'll fetch another."

As Farrish walked away, I turned to Christopher. "Paulie, Ginger, Stevie and Pratty all asked me to tell you that they are fine and thinking of you." He nodded his head in thought.

"Good children, each and everyone. Thank you for telling me."

"You're welcome."

"I have a place in South Pass, Elizabeth, and every confidence you will find it comfortable. I'd say, we'll be a day and a half riding to get there, but I'm certain you'll find it worth the trip. I promise you a hot bath, a hot dinner, and more pampering than you can possibly stand for the duration of your stay."

"You best be careful or I may never leave."

Christopher smiled. He lifted me effortlessly onto my saddle. He patted me on the leg and offered a warning.

"Trust me, I aim to spoil you rotten, for not only haven't I had a guest in my home for ages, but to have an attractive young lady travel two thousand miles to see how I fare—well, now—that calls for something very special in return."

'An attractive *young lady*.' It was hard to believe I could still be someone's little girl. How wonderful to see him again.

"Are you still there for me, Christopher? I wondered many times. I confess, I no longer know."

"Always, Elizabeth, as the sun rises, as the sun sets, always."

"You remain my hero then."

"I see you still insist on being a girl that makes me out to be something more than I am."

"So you say, but what girl would go through life without her knight in shining armor? Don't ruin a good thing."

"I dare say; you need no knight. I can't imagine what enemy might stop you on your crusade though life. If not safe by your own hand, have no fear, Providence surely watches over you. I've known it from the first time I set eyes on you."

"I've been told that, and I must admit it has brought me to you safe and sound."

"Mmmm. Well, on that one account, there may have been some divine mistake. But, mistake or not, you'll soon be safe and sound and sleeping in South Pass."

ONE-HUNDRED-SIX

We struck out from Hell Hole late that afternoon, descending through the foothills and then northward across the arid flats toward this junction called South Pass. Martin and Farish caught up with us toward evening and the six of us rode together for hours into the night. We slept briefly, arose early, and rode all of the next day.

I felt compelled to keep to myself while in the company of the riders. I found doing so unbearable, a trying ordeal, for my heart was suffering to set free years of pent up emotions. Behind my smile, I was irritable and annoyed by my situation. I was impatient to ask Christopher the million questions that needed answering. He was so close—an arm's length away. I wanted to reach out to him. I wanted to see his response. I wanted him to come to me. I had waited too many years for him to replenish what was lost in my life.

I prayed the others would disappear, just vanish into thin air and leave the world to us. I felt overcrowded in a lifeless land. I despised myself for being so ungrateful. These were but wishful fantasies, and in fact, the men may have saved me from the worst sort of embarrassment. Lord knows what I might have said in privacy during a careless rush of emotion. Truth be known, Christopher and I were different, the place was different, the time was different. I was no longer a child and my approach had to be different as well.

I resigned myself to entertaining the men with courteous conversation. For once, I wished I was anything but the center of attention. I craved silence. Unfortunately, when no one talked, my thoughts raced. I often returned to the sordid episode in the saloon. In my mind, I could still smell the whiskey on the brute's breath. I could feel his lips on my neck; his hands pressing hard against my chest. I delved into my feelings of helplessness against the man's strength. Over and over, I recalled the fear, the repulsion, and worst of all, now that is was over and I was far from harms way, *the enthrallment.*

Hour after hour, I physically plodded forward across the desert floor while mentally I remained behind reliving the ordeal. It was almost an obsession, for much to my complete and utter disgust, in a safe place the sickening memories entirely aroused me. I prayed for forgiveness and a return of my sanity.

To make matters worse, I found myself staring endlessly at Christopher. He generally rode a few feet ahead of me, as if ready to grab the reins of my horse, as if to watch over me second to second. I studied every detail of his body. I did this without shame. I did this with deep yearning. My mouth felt wet with a gnawing insatiable hunger. I watched his reflexes as he rode—his balance. He was unusually fluid for a man of his size. I absorbed the resonance of his voice. I felt the peace that came with its sound. I felt the joy that came when his words were for me.

I wondered if Christopher truly was a mere mortal. Was he indeed something less than a giant among men. I wondered if I had wasted my life dreaming about a man who couldn't possibly exist. Did I make too much out of him as he always claimed? My eyes refused to take leave of him, and if I had to make my decision based on the hours of watching him in the saddle, I would definitely have said he was all of a giant and more. Maybe, I was delusional. Maybe, I was the fool, but to my heart he was everything. He was a god, and I was flush with happiness and contentment when in his presence.

We arrived at South Pass Junction late in the night on horses that were completely run out and yet somehow managed to get us to Christopher's lodge. Martin, Clettis, and the others bid Christopher and me a good night, and then made their way to the bunkhouse. Christopher was met by a stablehand who welcomed him home, took our horses, and left us be.

"Come." Christopher held out his hand.

Just as I accepted, the ground flickered with a bright light. Instinctively, we both looked up to the sky and I for one was taken aback by a sudden show of shooting stars. It was at first a fearful experience that held me captive and wary. I had seen many a shooting star at night upon the desert, but nothing remotely comparable. The flares streaked brilliantly across the sky without end.

"Unsettling, is it not?" I moved in closer to Christopher.

"Unsettling! My word, Elizabeth, how can anything so rare and spectacular be *unsettling*. I say it is an omen. I believe we witness heaven's tears of joy falling across the blessed earth that brought you to me."

I started laughing. "Christopher Claussen, leave it to you to say something like that. I think heaven is having a hard cry."

"I think this cold air is drawing the warmth from your heart. I better get you inside before it is too late." I continued to laugh as he led me onto the raised porch and spoke to me in a low voice.

"I have a servant, Helena. She doesn't know I am here, and so is sleeping sound. I prefer not to wake her otherwise she will be most distressed at being caught asleep upon my return."

"Very well." I giggled.

"Ssssh."

We stepped quietly toward the door. I was suddenly over-whelmed by the fact that I was actually standing alone with Christopher upon his porch two thousand miles distant from my home—two decades distant from my heart. He reached around from behind me to open the door, and the closeness of him stopped my giggling short. I felt a rush of anxiety. I was suddenly wrapped in memories of our dancing together—of him lying in my bed, of a kiss at my kitchen table, of my swimming in his arms as a child. These memories and many more tumbled toward me all at once in a charge of emotion.

Instead of stepping inside straight away, I hesitated. I looked cautiously through the doorway and into the private domain of this mysterious man. I could sense the essence of his being in the murky details of the darkened room before me, intimate or otherwise, that made this cabin his home. I wondered if I could ever dissolve enough to blend into his world.

"Are you all right, Elizabeth?"

"Yes, yes, of course. It's just now that I am here, I think back and ask myself how is this possible. How could I have found you?"

Quietly, I stepped across the threshold and turned to wait. I watched Christopher gently close the door behind us then secure the latch to shut out the cold mountain air and fears of night. He turned to step in my direction, only to be tripped by my closeness. He stumbled into me. Clumsily, we reached to hold on to one another and found ourselves face to face.

"Forgive me. I thought you had gone in," he whispered.

"Haven't I always waited for you," I whispered back. He chuckled.

His massive hands crowned my shoulders, steadying my frame as we stood momentarily in awkward stillness, the two of us—adults, both unsure of our place, both unsure of each other. Yet, without a word spoken, I felt my heart move to his. I felt my tribulations drain through his fingers like those many miles of desert sand.

In blackness barely parted by candle's light, and silence broken by the slightest breath, I forced him to stand still so I might make something of this apparition. He was in darkness, as he was in life—more felt than seen; my conscience, my guardian, my ghost. I carried questions the whole of my life, but for now I remained quiet, peaceful, preferring only to realize his presence. Later, I would ask many things. I would ask why I was here.

NAKED I STAND BY YOUR DEMAND
MY FLESH AND SOUL DISPLAYED
WILLING I DO GIVE YOU MY HAND
THIS CHOICE BUT ONCE BE MADE
AND KNOW MY GLOW OF CHILDISH GRACE
IN SPITE OF HOW IT BEAMS
DOES NOT DISPEL THE FEARS I FACE
ABOUT TOMORROW'S DREAMS

THE VIRGIN

Where Credit is due...

As with Volume One, the richness of this second work must be credited in part to the direction and opinions offered me by the following good natured friends. Mary Van Heck, Donna Hunter, and Jon Hunter. A very special thank-you to Nancy Smith

To my wife, Nancy, who has accepted my obsessive daydreaming in dark corners while our house continues to crumble.

To Maria E. denBoer, my editor, whose limitless support remains but a phone call away.

A special thanks to Frederick Biller, whose bloodline, background, and willingness to assist, made perfect my German characters. Thank-you, Fred.

Not to be outdone, a special thanks to Anthony Van Berkum, whose bloodline, background, and willingness to assist, made perfect my Dutch characters. Thank-you, Tony.

Again, to Martha Hart, whose generosity, advice, and encouragement made this 'MH' edition possible.

Finally, to my daughters, Britany Michelle and Tawnie Allison, who taught me how make-believe is properly presented with conviction.

I thank you all.

C. John Coombes